Never Forget

Books by Jody Hedlund

The Beacons of Hope Series

Out of the Storm: A Novella

Love Unexpected

Hearts Made Whole

Undaunted Hope

Forever Safe

Never Forget

The Heart of Faith Collection

The Preacher's Bride

The Doctor's Lady

Rebellious Heart

The Michigan Brides Collection

Unending Devotion

A Noble Groom

Captured by Love

Historical

Luther and Katharina

Newton and Polly

Young Adult

The Vow: Prequel Novella

An Uncertain Choice

A Daring Sacrifice

Beacons of Hope — Book Five

Never Forget

JODY HEDLUND

NORTHERN LIGHTS PRESS

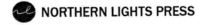

Never Forget
Northern Lights Press

Print Edition

www.jodyhedlund.com

ISBN: 978-0-692-77087-0

Library of Congress Control Number: 2016918190

Scripture quotations are taken from the King James Version of the Bible.

Cover Design by Lynnette Bonner of Indie Cover Design
www.indiecoverdesign.com

Cover Photograph by Sarah Davis Photography
www.sarahdavisphotography.com

To my assistant, Rel Mollet

Thank you for helping lighten the load.
Not only have you been a Godsend,
you've also been a true friend.

Chapter 1

ROSE ISLAND LIGHTHOUSE, RHODE ISLAND
JUNE 1880

"I'm warning you, girl," Zeke Crawford called from his dory. "You and your crazy grandpa can leave the island nice-like. Or I'll run you off."

Abbie Watson shielded her eyes against the bright morning sun and glared at Zeke across the glittering water. "We're not leaving. I told you last time you came out here that Gramps has no intention of retiring from his position. Not now. Not anytime soon."

"He ain't fit to be a keeper no more, and you know it!" Zeke's voice bellowed over the gentle lapping of the low tide. He was a man as big and gruff as his voice, causing his boat to sink lower under his weight. As if his size weren't enough, his black beard and dark bushy eyebrows made him look even meaner and surlier.

His two boys sat at the oars, their faces as sunburned and red as the lobsters they trapped.

Abbie figured they weren't older than ten years, but they rowed with an expertise that said they'd been born and bred in these waters—just like she'd been.

"We're taking care of the light just fine," she called, with a glance toward the thirty-five-foot octagonal tower that rose from the side of the keeper's dwelling. Set on the surviving bastion of old Fort Hamilton, the light was actually forty-eight feet above the water. A mile from Jamestown to the west and Newport to the east, Rose Island Lighthouse was in a strategic location to guide passenger steamers, fishing boats, and freighters through the east passage of the bay, especially through the dangerous shoals to the north.

"It's my turn to take over," Zeke said. "Hosea's been there long enough."

"Gramps loves this place. It would kill him to leave." Gramps had been the keeper at Rose Island Lighthouse since it was built over ten years ago. "Besides, you're doing fine where you're at. So leave us be!"

Zeke was the keeper over at Goat Island Lighthouse. At the entrance to Newport Harbor, it was an easy assignment compared to some of the more isolated lighthouses like Rose Island. Zeke didn't have nearly as many rescues or receive the battering from storms.

Sure, Zeke Crawford was known for moving. He'd been keeper at more lighthouses around Narragansett Bay than a crab had legs. Even so, Abbie couldn't understand why he was so determined to take over the Rose Island light. Surely, there were other lighthouses he could choose.

She leaned against her clam rake, the long claw-like tines

sinking into the sand. Due to the rising tide, the water was tickling her ankles and burying her toes with sand, the sign that her clamming for the day was over. Her bucket was almost full anyway, enough to warrant a trip to Newport. She'd keep a few clams for clam dumpling soup—Gramps' favorite—but sell the rest.

"Hosea's lost his mind," Zeke hollered. "And it's only a matter of time before he burns the light to the ground."

"We keep our eye on him." Her voice rang with a confidence that belied the unsettled waver in her gut. Zeke was awakening the nightmares she wasn't ready to face, visions of Gramps harming not only the light but himself.

"We?" Zeke chortled. "You mean you and that no-good husband of yours that hasn't shown his face in months?"

"He'll be back soon." She'd lost count of the times she'd used that line. The truth was, Nate was dead. Even though no one had been able to identify the decomposed body the fishermen had found on the shore down by Brenton Point after the spring thaw, she'd heard enough to know it was Nate. How many other men had a pocket watch with the words *To Crabby* engraved on the back? Nate's brother Ross had given him the pocket watch, and he'd treasured it dearly, especially after Ross died. When she'd heard about the watch on the dead man, she'd known without a doubt, the body was Nate's.

But she hadn't told anyone. If the local lighthouse superintendent—or Zeke—realized Nate wasn't returning, she'd lose all her leverage for staying on the island. With Gramps' increasing senility, Nate had been appointed as acting keeper. Without her husband's status, she had no official title or claim to the lighthouse.

The Office of the Lighthouse Board didn't care that she'd

been living on Rose Island over half her life and that she knew how to run the light better than anyone else. They didn't care that Nate hadn't done a lick of the lighthouse work, that she'd shouldered it all anyway. The board gave out positions based on politics, not expertise. And without a husband to legitimize the acting keeper position, she had no doubt that if Zeke Crawford pushed hard enough, he'd be able to shove her and Gramps right off the island.

"Nate's coming home any day now," she called again.

"Good," Zeke replied. "Having that drunkard back will give me all the more reason to ask for your removal."

"He promised to quit his drinking."

"I'll believe it when I see it."

"Go on, now. Stop bothering us. We're here to stay, and you can't scare us away." She twisted her skirts higher, tucking the hem in her waistband before sloshing out to the wire basket, where her clams were soaking in deeper water and expelling the excess sand from their shells. She lifted the basket, shook it to dislodge water and sand, and then with the clam basket in one hand and her rake in the other, she trudged back to the shore.

"Like I said," Zeke called after her, "I'll make you leave. You just wait and see."

She shook her head and refused to engage him in any further discussion. Right now, all she had was her bravado and bluster to protect her. If Zeke sensed a crack in her shell, he'd pry it open. She had to appear strong and self-assured, even if her insides were quavering like raw oyster meat.

The slamming of the keeper cottage door told her Gramps was awake and making his morning visit to the outhouse. After he finished, he'd head back to the house, sit down at the kitchen table, and have a cup of coffee while he waited for her to fry him two eggs.

After breakfast, he'd begin his daily chore of whitewashing. It didn't matter that he'd whitewashed yesterday and every day since the weather had turned warm. Today, he'd do it all over again. On her last trip to Newport, she'd purchased enough lime to keep him busy for a few more weeks. At least she hoped so.

She couldn't complain about his work. Everything always looked fresh and clean. The house, tower, oil shed, the rounded bastion base beneath the lighthouse—Gramps kept them in perfect condition.

As she ascended the sandy bank, a chorus of clucking greeted her.

"Good morning to you too," she called out to the half dozen hens roaming in the open grassy area between the lighthouse and the remains of Fort Hamilton barracks. The brick structure was long and low, with the roof torn away or collapsing in many spots. Originally started in 1798, the building had been constructed to accommodate three hundred men. The four-feet-thick walls formed nine bombproof chambers. But the government had never completed the project, and now it sat in its permanently dilapidated state. She supposed it served as a reminder of the wars the country had fought in times past and the role Rhode Island played in so many of them.

Gramps had speculated that someone with money had persuaded the military to build the fort on the mainland, closer to Newport in order to protect its citizens better. Whatever the case, another defensive fortification, Fort Adams, had been started in 1799 on the tip of Newport Harbor. Now it stood like a sentinel, guarding the waters and town. Gramps used to listen for the sundown gun, the cannon blast from Fort Adams, before he'd go to the tower to fire up the light for the evening. He didn't listen for the blast anymore. But Abbie still did. It was a familiar habit she'd clung to amidst all the changes in recent years.

"Well, hello, Rosie." She set down the clamming basket and flexed her arm, sore from the weight of the clams. She clucked her tongue and held out her hand toward the speckled hen scuttling toward her. "How are you?"

The hen chattered at her, as though carrying on a conversation. Abbie smiled and scratched the beautiful black-and-white spotted feathers, earning a warbling song from the sweet little creature.

"Yes, I think we're in for some storms today," Abbie replied, with a glance to the west. Even though the skies were clear now, red had tinged the clouds earlier in the morning when she'd turned off the light. "My garden can use the rain. And so can the cistern. The water level is getting low."

Another speckled hen approached. "There's my dear Daisy. How are you my sweetie?" She scratched the second hen's side before the others drew closer and vied for her attention. One by one, she made conversation with each chicken before hoisting her clam basket and resuming her trek up the incline to the house.

From the rise of the old bastion, the bay spread out before her. On a clear day, sometimes she could see all the way to Rhode Island Sound. Zeke Crawford's dory was halfway to Goat Island. The small boat bounced up and down against the waves, taking Zeke away and giving her and Gramps one more day on the island. Unfortunately, his threats still lingered and rose to taunt her.

Zeke had started pestering her in the spring and had grown more persistent in recent weeks. She wasn't sure how much longer she could keep him—and others—from reaching the conclusion that the dead body had been Nate's. As long as they believed her husband was still alive and coming back, she had hope of staying, at least until she could figure out a new plan for her and Gramps.

Gramps stepped down from the outhouse and let the door bang behind him. His silvery hair was thin, leaving the top of his head almost bald. Brown age spots were sprinkled across his scalp and over his face. Although his shoulders were stooped and his steps slow, overall, he still managed to get around. If only his rheumatism hadn't worsened over the winter.

She stopped at the edge of the yard, unable to halt the sadness that stole over her at the realization that he was continuing to decline both mentally and physically.

"Good morning," she called, holding her breath and hoping this would be one of his lucid moments, one of those rare times when he'd recognize her and she'd have her grandfather back—even if only for a few minutes. She'd greedily take just a few seconds.

At the sight of her, he squinted, his brown-green eyes, so much like hers, flickering with recognition. He gave her a wide smile that was hardly visible beneath his overgrown mustache and beard. "Good morning, Bella."

Her lungs deflated at the mention of the assistant keeper's wife he often mistook her for, but she forced a return smile.

"How's Steele this morning?" he asked. "I haven't seen him around yet. I hope he didn't have too much trouble last night with the light."

"Everything is just fine," she reassured him, as she usually did, acting as though Gramps' assistant keeper from forty years ago—and her supposed husband—was still alive. "Steele rowed into town for the day to get supplies." Nowadays, the lies slid off her tongue as smooth as melted lard. She didn't feel guilty any more for keeping up pretenses with Gramps.

When his memory had first started fading a couple of years ago, she'd learned that he was much calmer when she went along with him and pretended she was living with him four decades in the past when he'd been keeper at Beavertail Lighthouse. If she tried to correct him, he only became agitated.

"Did we need supplies?" Gramps asked, his brow furrowing with worry.

"You know Steele." She tried to infuse her voice with cheerfulness. "He's always looking out for us. He hates to see us run low on anything."

The furrow eased. "That's right. Steele's a good man. I couldn't get by without his help."

"Well, today, the two of us will get along great."

At her statement, which she meant to be reassuring, he threw out his arms and swirled about in sudden distress. "Where's Ruth?"

Abbie wanted to palm her forehead. Instead, she dropped the clamming basket and jogged toward Gramps to keep him from becoming too disconcerted, as he'd done last time he'd remembered his late wife. He'd spent an entire day pacing the length of the parlor, waiting for her return. "Ruth's visiting her family over in Newport. Don't you remember that she's gone for the week?"

Gran had died five years ago, but Abbie wouldn't tell him that. Not ever again. Last time she'd tried to explain that Gran was now in heaven with their only child, Elijah, Gramps had nearly killed himself with his anger and grief.

He stopped and stared east, across the distance of the bay to the faint outline of the town. "Did she take Elijah with her?"

"Yes," Abbie lied. "Elijah went too."

"Oh." He stared at the town, and she prayed he wouldn't get it in his mind to try rowing there today. After a long moment, he shrugged. "Good. I'm glad they have the chance to visit with family while the weather's nice."

With that, he resumed his halting shuffle toward the keeper's cottage, leaving Abbie behind. When he entered and let the door slap shut, she expelled a breath. Another disaster averted.

Some days, she felt as though her main job was keeping Gramps out of trouble. Thankfully, the eighteen-acre island was fairly safe. Due to its lack of a natural water source, wild animals couldn't survive. Her chickens and cats roamed freely, without the threat of an attack from foxes, raccoons, or skunks. Even her big garden was safe from the usual rabbits and deer that liked to help themselves to fresh produce.

Because of the security and isolation, the island had become the nesting habitat for dozens of species of migratory birds, including blue heron, snowy egrets, and the glossy ibis. She loved rowing around to the northeast side of the island, where she waded ashore and watched the birds.

A short, strident meow and the bump against her sandy calf drew her attention to a tortoise-colored cat. "Good morning, Martha. How's my lovely girl today?" Abbie bent and scratched the cat, much the same way she had the chickens, and was rewarded with a rumbling purr.

"I'm glad to hear that you're doing well. How are all of your darling children?" The kittens were at least six weeks old. Abbie had taken time each day to entice them out from underneath the oil shed to tame them and turn them into friendly cats. They'd be old enough to leave their mama in a couple of weeks, and Abbie would need to take them to Newport and find homes for the adorable creatures.

Knowing the kittens would end up with loving families didn't console Abbie. She was too much of a softy when it came to her pets. And saying good-bye had never been easy.

"You're waiting for your breakfast, aren't you?" Abbie gave the cat one last pat before scratching the head of one of the tomcats that had appeared—ready for his meal too. Straightening, she stifled a yawn and combed away the strands of her brown hair that had come loose from the braid that flopped down her back.

Although many keepers stayed up all night to watch over their lights, Abbie had never been able to do it. Instead she woke up and ascended the tower at regular intervals throughout the night to check on the lantern. It wasn't ideal, and she never got quite enough sleep. But the system allowed her to complete all the other responsibilities she had during the day—mainly watching over Gramps.

The breeze coming off the bay carried the familiar scents of eelgrass and the sea. She closed her eyes and let the wind blow against her. She relished the cool dampness on her cheeks and forehead.

Gramps couldn't leave Rose Island. That was true. The one and only time she'd taken him to stay with her sister, Debbie, in Newport last year had been a disaster. He'd grown so agitated that he'd snuck out of Debbie's house in the middle of the night and had started rowing back to the island. When Abbie had gone up to the tower at midnight to check on the light, she'd noticed a skiff with a lone stooped-shouldered figure at the oars, attempting to battle the tossing waves.

She'd rowed out and towed him in. Even though she'd agreed with Gramps' declaration that he could have crossed the last distance home just fine by himself, she'd only been able to think about all the things that could have gone wrong.

Ever since that night, she'd vowed never to take him away from the island again. Two months later, she'd married Nate Watson, who'd been sweet on her. Smooth-talking, he had said all the right words, made all the right promises.

The marriage had been a desperate act on her part. A gamble. Which she'd lost.

With a deep breath, she retreated toward the clamming basket she'd deserted.

She wouldn't lose again. Nobody, including Zeke Crawford, could make them leave Rose Island. She'd do anything so that Gramps could live out the rest of his days in the only place that brought him peace. Anything.

After all, she'd already done the worst by marrying Nate Watson. Whatever else she had to do to keep Gramps on the island would be easy in comparison. Wouldn't it?

Chapter 2

Nathaniel Winthrop III gripped the helm. His fingers were numb and his knuckles white.

"Reef the mainsail," he shouted.

A crack of thunder drowned his instructions. The rain was finally beginning in earnest and was pelting his face and head with stinging ferocity. The spray of the waves had already dampened his garments, and he'd tossed aside his suit coat to keep from being waterlogged.

Because they'd been sailing downwind, the boat hadn't been heeling, so he'd failed to notice the increasing wind. At least that's what he'd been telling himself. His lack of attention to the storm had nothing to do with the fact he'd been busy with the tall brunette who'd sidled up next to him. Yes, she'd been a pleasant distraction, and so had the bottle of brandy. But he could sail his yacht in his sleep.

He'd already steered the boat toward the wind and eased the mainsheet to reduce pressure on the sail. But they had to reef. Now. The wind was over twenty knots. And every good sailor knew that waiting too long to drop the sail in a storm was dangerous.

"Charles, my good man," he called louder, while maintaining a steady hand on the helm. "Help me, will you?"

His friend and sailing companion still had an arm tucked intimately around a woman whose name slipped Nathaniel's memory. The couple laughed as another spray of water splashed overboard and drenched them.

Nathaniel was sober enough to realize that the storm bearing down on them was no laughing matter. One big gust could capsize them.

"Charles," Nathaniel shouted again, wishing he hadn't been so quick to dismiss his crew earlier in the day when he'd decided to take the yacht out.

"Lend me a hand, Samuel!" he yelled at his cousin in the bow with his lady friend, only to have the wind carry his voice away.

Through the slashing rain, Nathaniel tried to judge how far they were from the shore. If he maneuvered the yacht toward the harbor, he didn't want to risk the wind driving them into the shoals, which would be even more dangerous. It would be better to lower the sails and stay out in open sea until the storm passed.

Considering that most of his companions were too inebriated to be of much assistance, he'd have to do the reefing himself. He released the helm and stumbled toward the mast.

Charles cut in front of him. "We need to reef the mainsail!" his friend called, as though he'd awoken from a stupor and realized that a summer storm had blown upon them. Charles ducked under the boom and snagged the halyard line.

The vessel swayed so that the starboard side dipped dangerously low in the water. Nathaniel lurched and reached for a buoy ring. He'd outfitted the yacht with several flotation devices, but he couldn't remember where he'd stowed the remainder of them. Were they in the cabin?

"Samuel," he shouted to his cousin. "Find the life rings for the ladies, just in case we capsize!"

Samuel was too busy fawning over and clinging to his newest fling to pay attention to him, clearly using the opportunity to his advantage. At least Charles was helping now. Together, the two of them could bring the yacht under control.

Maybe.

Nathaniel watched Charles for a moment, waiting to see if his friend could manage the rigging. Charles was one of the best yachters in Newport, almost as good as Nathaniel. They made a great team, along with the rest of their crew when they raced. But the empty rum and brandy bottles rolling around and clinking together in the hull told Nathaniel that his friend had imbibed too freely for so early in the evening.

Not that Nathaniel could condemn Charles. Over the past couple of years, Nathaniel had led a much wilder life than Charles had. That's why he'd been dubbed "Bad Boy of Newport" this social season and last.

His reputation had worsened two days ago when Kitty Martin sent him word she was pregnant with his child. The news had devastated his mother. Sobbing, she'd begged him to do the honorable thing and go over to the Martins and get married to Kitty before anyone got word of the scandal, before Kitty's life was ruined forever.

Nicholas had said nothing. But his brother's eyes radiated

with accusations, telling Nathaniel he'd taken their father's place in causing Mother grief.

Even with guilt swirling in his gut like bilge water, Nathaniel hadn't been able to ride over to the Martins. Hadn't been able to face Kitty. Least of all, he hadn't wanted to face the possibility he'd be a father. That fact alone was enough to make him want to run away.

When his mother, in tears, pleaded with him again that morning to visit Kitty, he'd told her he would—after his sailing excursion. All afternoon and evening, he'd delayed, staying out on the water much longer than he should have.

Nathaniel glanced back at the brunette waiting for him. He realized full well that women flocked to him because of his wealth and because he was from one of New York's most prestigious families. He wasn't under any illusion that the women cared about him as a person. They were using him. That knowledge didn't justify him using them in return. In fact, it only made him more loathsome.

There were days when he couldn't remember what his life had been like before he'd gained his current reputation. But that was the point, wasn't it? He didn't want to remember those days. The days when he'd been a godly young man worthy of a woman as sweet and kind as Victoria Cole. Luckily, she hadn't married him. Luckily, she'd been kidnapped on the way to their wedding and whisked away into hiding until her perpetrator was found. Luckily, she'd wed her courageous bodyguard instead of him.

He hadn't deserved her. Maybe at the time he'd thought he was worthy of her. He'd kept himself busy with wholesome activities—like traveling and overseeing his family finances and helping his mother host parties. He'd treated Victoria respectfully, giving her lavish gifts and showering her with his love and attention. He'd cherished her purity and had only kissed her chastely once or twice.

But now he realized he would have cracked eventually. His true self would have shown up and made Victoria miserable. He would have subjected her to the same disgrace his father had cast upon their family.

He didn't know why he'd ever thought he'd be different from his father. The old adage was true in his case: *Like father, like son*. It was inevitable. And he'd stopped fighting it.

It didn't matter that since his father's death he was now the heir to the Winthrop fortune. It didn't matter that his mother begged him to stop being so rash and undisciplined. It didn't matter that his wild living was sullying his family's prestigious name even further.

If he was destined to end up like his father, then what difference did it make how he lived or how good he tried to be?

"I think we should furl the jib too!" Charles called, as he grabbed the winch. "And backwind it."

"Go slowly! We're tilting again." Nathaniel hung the buoy over his shoulder and tucked it under his arm. Then he grabbed onto the port side and made his way back to the helm. He locked the controls into position so the boat would move along without turning broadside to the waves. As long as the jib partly furled and backwinded, they would hopefully prevent a wave from rolling or breaking over the vessel.

He brushed raindrops out of his eyes and squinted through the growing downpour toward the mast, where Charles attempted to loosen the line. He was fumbling, his efforts uncoordinated.

Nathaniel edged his way to the mainmast, determined to help Charles before anything happened. Under normal circumstances, they were both proficient sailors. They'd honed their skills and had weathered many a summer storm together. But today, neither of them was in his best condition.

"Get her reefed!" he yelled at Charles. "Let's go!"

Suddenly, the rigging broke free of the winch. The pressure of the wind in the sails caused the loose line to rip away from its cleat. The sail flapped hard, snapping Charles in the face. He cried out, covered his cheek with his hands, and staggered against the mast. Getting whipped by the edge of a heavy canvas in gusts like this would sting like a blow from a cat-o'-nine-tails.

Nathaniel cringed at the sight of blood oozing between Charles's fingers. Before he could offer a word of comfort to his friend, he caught a movement out of the corner of his eye. The boom was swinging directly toward him.

Charles had apparently knocked the horizontal beam at the foot of the mainsail loose. Normally used to change directions, the boom careened out of control. The speed at which the long hard metal beam was moving gave Nathaniel no time to duck. It slammed into his head. The force lifted him from his feet and sent him flying backward over the port side. He was vaguely conscious of splashing into the water and gulping in a lungful of the sea.

As the cold waves crashed over him, his skull seared and his head felt like it would explode. His last thought before blackness enveloped him was that as much as he loathed himself, he wasn't ready to die. At least not yet.

Chapter 3

Abbie picked up the binoculars from the tall table in the tower where she kept the logbook and exited through the half door onto the gallery. After a stormy evening and night, she'd expected at least one rescue. But the traffic around the bay had been minimal. She suspected most seafarers had used caution and stayed off the turbulent waters.

She pressed the cold rings of metal to her eyes before studying the choppy water. During the night, she'd scrutinized the bay and coastline several times. Now at daybreak, she'd do a final search before climbing down and starting her morning chores.

Due to the island's central location, all kinds of things washed up on the shore. The debris was mostly cargo thrown overboard by captains hoping to lighten their loads—lobster cages, fishing gear, and crates of supplies. Usually, the owners came to recover their belongings after a few days.

One time, she'd found a crate of chickens. They'd been

half-drowned, half-dead. She'd nurtured them for days, and several had lived. When no one came to claim the creatures, she'd named them and had eventually purchased a rooster.

To the east, the sky was hazy, the early morning light creeping through the fog. It would burn away in a couple of hours, and they would have a clear day, thankfully. Rainy weather was always the hardest with Gramps. Being cooped up made him restless and more confused. Once or twice on wet days in recent months, he'd even grown feisty and called her his jailor because she'd told him to stay inside.

At those times, she missed the old Gramps the most. She hated when he became short- and mean-tempered in a way he'd never been while she was growing up. She'd watch him and wonder what had happened to the patient, loving man who'd been the only father figure she'd ever known. It was almost as if a different person had taken up residence in Gramps' body.

Fortunately, he kept busy during the day with the whitewashing. Today, while he was occupied, she'd row out into the eelgrass beds and do some more crabbing. Every bit of extra income helped. Light keeper salaries were notoriously low—enough to get by on, but certainly not enough for extras or emergencies. And now with Gramps' worsening rheumatism, she had to have extra money to purchase the costly medicine for his aching joints.

The binoculars grew sticky with the humidity that had rolled in with the rain. Beads of perspiration trickled down Abbie's back between her shoulder blades. But she ignored them as she swept her gaze over the bay from Goat Island in the southeast to Fort Adams. The billow of smoke from a distant steamer rose into a black puff against the gray mist.

She turned the binoculars to the eastern beach of Rose Island, scanning it carefully. For a moment, she saw nothing but the usual sandy shore that lined the southern end, but then she touched upon a dark form lying half in the water and half out.

Leaning over the catwalk, she twisted the ring in the middle of the binoculars to bring the image into better focus. Was a seal stranded upon the beach? Although rare, she had, on occasion, helped a sick or floundering seal return to the sea. Most harbor seals, however, came in to the bay from late October through early April. During the summer, they moved on, and she hadn't seen any in the area in weeks.

It was likely just a piece of flotsam. Nevertheless, she needed to check on it to put her mind at rest.

With a last scan up and down the shoreline, she ducked into the lantern room. She'd already cleaned the glass prisms and lens of the sixth order Fresnel light, which were the smallest size of all lighthouse lanterns and didn't take long to wipe down. She still needed to polish the bronze frame, wash the tower windows, and sweep the floor, but those duties would have to wait.

As she climbed through the hatch and closed it behind her, she promised herself she'd return later in the morning to finish. She'd never been particularly fond of cleaning. She much preferred to be outside gardening or clamming or crabbing or fishing.

No one could fault Gran for trying to turn her into a proper young lady. The dear woman had taught her how to sew, do laundry, cook, and preserve food for the winter months. But Gran had more luck with Abbie's sister, Debbie, who'd been a willing and eager learner. The outdoors had always beckoned Abbie—and still did.

In the five years Gran had been gone, Abbie had spent even less time inside. She only gave the house a thorough cleaning when Debbie came over to the island and helped her. She needed to clean more often to keep the place pristine for any surprise visits from the lighthouse superintendent. But as much as she tried, the housework always fell to the bottom of her chore list.

The tower stairs were damp beneath her bare feet, likely from another leak. Thankfully, Gramps still had enough of his mind to make repairs when necessary. She'd have to cajole him upstairs later and help him find the leak. Once they found it, he'd patch it up in no time.

Careful not to wake him now, she skipped the stairs that squeaked and tiptoed through the house and out the backdoor. She retrieved a coil of rope from the oil house before making her way down the bastion to the beach. She headed east in the direction where she'd seen the flotsam, figuring she'd have to drag the storm's deposit further up on shore, where high tide wouldn't be able to reach it. If the object was heavy, the rope might come in handy.

The sand was cool and wet against her feet, making walking easier. At the sight of the single trail of footprints behind her, she released a short laugh in remembrance of her girlhood dream of strolling hand in hand along the beach with the man she loved, leaving two sets of footprints instead of one.

How naïve she'd been. She'd expected to grow up and have a marriage like Gramps' and Gran's, one that brimmed with laughter and love. After all, Gran had said the best marriages were fueled by laughter.

Although Abbie hadn't loved Nate when they'd gotten married, she thought they would have plenty of laughs together. Whenever he'd come to the island to visit or when she'd seen him in town, he always had a twinkle in his eyes and a funny story to tell. For the most part, she'd enjoyed his company.

He'd been so persistent in pursuing her. He'd seemed to want to be with her. Even though he admitted to spending evenings at the tavern after a long day of lobstering, he'd argued that he only went there because he had no family in the area to go home to. He'd promised that once they got married, he would be with her.

Abbie laughed again, bitterly. She should have known he wouldn't stay. No one in her life ever did. Not her father. Most certainly not her mother. Gran had died and left her for heaven. Debbie had gone off and gotten married to Menard. Even Gramps lived forty years in the past as a young lighthouse keeper, leaving her stranded alone in 1880.

When Nate showed up half drunk at the chapel on their wedding day, she should have cancelled the ceremony. If he'd needed to be inebriated to follow through with marrying her, that should have been a huge warning.

But the fact was, she'd been too desperate and had ignored the early signs of problems.

Her desperation had started last autumn when Gramps' stay with Debbie had ended so disastrously. It had awakened Abbie to the realization that moving Gramps from the island would turn out to be the death of him. Then when the local lighthouse superintendent, Mr. Davis, came out and discovered just how bad Gramps' memory had gotten, he'd mentioned the possibility of giving the position to Zeke

Crawford, who'd been inquiring about the job.

She'd asked the superintendent about appointing her as acting keeper in Gramps' place. But he'd told her that, at eighteen, she was too young and that because Zeke was more experienced, he deserved a shot at the job first. Mr. Davis hadn't come right out and told her he had to give precedence to a man, but she understood well enough that her gender didn't give her the necessary clout.

When Nate had proposed to her last November, she'd concluded that marriage might be the answer she was looking for, especially when the superintendent agreed to assign Nate as acting keeper in Gramps' stead. Even if Nate didn't have any experience, she'd promised to train him and, of course, be there to help him.

After the December wedding, she thought she'd secured Gramps' future on Rose Island. But Nate had lived on the island for a total of sixty days. Even then, he spent most nights over at the tavern, rowing back to the island in the wee hours of the morning. By the time she finished the keeper duties, he'd been sprawled out in bed, snoring. He'd slept all day before getting up in the late afternoon and repeating the process.

One cold morning in February, he hadn't returned. He'd been gone ever since. Some of his lobstering companions claimed that Nate had talked about running off with another woman.

But ever since that dead body had been found down by Brenton's Point containing Nate's pocket watch, Abbie had realized she was a widow, even if no one else did. Of course she'd been horrified to think about Nate's death and how he may have suffered. No, their marriage hadn't been good, but she hadn't wanted him to die—especially like that.

Nevertheless, she wasn't planning on saying anything, at least until she figured out the next step for keeping Gramps on the island. As long as the superintendent believed Nate was coming back, she could buy herself more time.

A ray of sunshine broke through the mist and bathed her in its warmth. It blinded her for a few moments, but since she knew the shore so well, she could dodge the indentations where Gramps dug every evening.

His nightly digging, like his whitewashing, was another one of his routines that kept him calm. It didn't harm the beach because he always filled his holes at dusk before calling an end to his treasure hunting.

While growing up, Gramps had regaled her and Debbie with stories of the pirates who once found refuge in Rhode Island, in the days before the Revolutionary War, when Newport had been a pirate haven. Gramps claimed pirates had buried treasure all around Narragansett Bay.

The biggest legend was that Captain Kidd had buried gold across the bay in Jamestown. But rumors also abounded that a pirate named Thomas Paine had bought a farm on Conanicut Island to the north with his fortune and that his friend Captain Kidd had buried treasure there too.

Whatever the case, treasure seekers were always speculating and searching for hidden loot. Gramps, whose family had lived in Narragansett Bay back to the time of the pirates, seemed to have treasure hunting in his blood. Abbie hadn't known a time when he wasn't looking for one fabled treasure or another.

Most nights, he dug in the same spot. Or at least in the same area. Though Abbie had agreed with Gran that the treasure hunting was only a wild goose chase, she never made any effort to keep Gramps from his hobby. Since it kept him happy and occupied, she didn't have the heart to stop him.

Grasping her rope, she rounded the slight bend on the southern shore and caught sight of the black, seal-shape she'd seen from the tower. She shielded her eyes with her hands to get a better view, but the angle of the sun made closer examination impossible.

The waves ebbed and flowed with the melodic rhythm she'd been listening to all her life. Today's heavy crashing contained the remains of the storm's fury. The sea had moods just like people did, and things always went more smoothly if one could gauge the mood.

"And what have we here?" she asked, as she came upon the debris. For a moment, she stared at the unmoving form, trying to make sense of what she saw.

Then with a gasp, she dropped to her knees. It was a body. A human body.

A man wearing black trousers and a vest over a white shirt lay face down in the sand. His hands were outstretched, as though he'd crawled from the bay and collapsed in exhaustion. A white cork life ring lay in the sand beside him. He wore no shoes or socks or hat.

Was he dead?

Abbie reached for his wrist and felt for his pulse. After a few seconds, she found a sluggish beat. He was alive. But she couldn't be certain for how much longer.

Working rapidly, she rolled him over. He wasn't an overly large man but was clearly no weakling either. He had a muscular build, with a slim waist and long legs. His hair was wet and plastered with sand as was his face. In spite of the sand, his features were striking and distinguished.

She held her fingers against his mouth. A feathery exhale told her he was breathing.

How long had he been lying on the beach? Since the storm last night?

She glanced around for signs of a boat or anything else that might give her a clue where he'd come from.

He coughed hoarsely. She immediately turned his head so that any remaining water he'd swallowed would drain and keep from choking him. As she moved his head, her fingers grazed a slick spot in his scalp. She pulled back her hand to the sight of dark blood.

She probed at his scalp, pushing away his hair until she discovered the source of the blood. A gash several inches in length. It wasn't deep or bleeding profusely and probably wouldn't need stitches. But it needed tending.

She wasn't sure if he was unconscious from his drenching in the sea or from the blow he'd taken to his head. If she had to guess, she'd pick the latter. Yet, if he'd been unconscious, how had he made it to the shores of Rose Island without drowning? Perhaps the life ring had kept him afloat. Or perhaps his boat had wrecked close by and he'd been tossed ashore here.

Whatever the case, she needed to take him to the cottage, clean him up, bandage his wound, and keep a watchful eye on him, particularly if he'd sustained a concussion. When he awoke, she'd be able to discover more about what happened, who he was, and where he was from. Surely, he'd have friends and family who would be worried about him if he didn't return. She glanced at his hand and noted that his fingers were free of a marriage band. If her guess was right, he wouldn't have a wife wondering what had become of him.

She searched the beach area for something flat she could use as a makeshift stretcher. Her mind raced over the various spots she'd thrown driftwood that had washed ashore. Was there a piece big enough in one of her piles?

After walking further down the beach and dragging back a plank she estimated could carry her patient, she rolled him onto it, secured him to the wood with her rope, and used the leftover length to slide the plank through the sand like a sled.

By the time she reached the bastion, her muscles screamed from the exertion of pulling the man's weight. Sweat trailed down her face and her breath came in gasps. She didn't have enough energy to greet Daisy, Rosie, and the other chickens that strutted toward her, expecting their usual attention. It was all she could do to haul the man up the hill. She stopped every few minutes to rest and allow air into her burning lungs.

When she finally crested the top, she caught sight of Gramps exiting the outhouse. She froze, not sure what to do next. Any disruption in his day, unusual happenings, or visits by strangers confused him and made his agitation worse. Bringing a wounded, unconscious, sand-covered man into the keeper's cottage was likely to cause problems.

"Bella?" he asked cautiously.

"Good morning, Hosea," she said.

He squinted and frowned at her. "I hardly recognize you this morning."

"It's me. Bella. I'm a little disheveled. That's all." Most days she played the part of his past assistant keeper's wife well—or at least tried to.

He stared at her a moment longer, as if still uncertain of her identity, before shifting his gaze to the plank behind her. "What's wrong?"

She hesitated. Did she tell Gramps the truth about the person on the stretcher, or did she make something up? The dilemma was familiar—and all too often she chose lying, so that now the lies slid off her tongue all too easily.

How could she preserve her integrity and sanity at the same time? To tell Gramps the truth was to unleash a maelstrom. Lying, on the other, maintained the eggshell of peace that surrounded them.

"Don't tell me that's Steele." Gramps' voice rose.

"Yes," she lied. "He's been hurt."

Gramps' face crumpled with anxiety, and he shuffled across the grassy yard toward her. "Well, heaven's sake. Don't just stand there," he shouted. "Let's get him inside."

"That's what I've been trying to do," she explained as she hefted the rope, aware of the rope burns that ran across her palms and shoulder.

"Let me help," he called.

"No, Hosea. I'll manage." She didn't want him getting too close to the stranger and chance realizing he wasn't the assistant light keeper from all those years ago.

Gramps muttered and shook his head. "You're letting me help you carry him. Steele weighs more than a finback whale."

Abbie tried to pick up her pace, but she decided Gramps was right. Her patient did weigh more than a whale. At least, it felt that way after having dragged him so far. Before she could think of another way to avert disaster, Gramps intercepted her. He rounded the plank and stared at the man.

She braced herself for the outpouring of his wrath. Gramps would accuse her of lying and deceit and sabotage and whatever else came to his mind. And she'd be helpless to respond. She'd stand silently, wishing she could admit to her lies, wishing she could explain the truth without confusing him, and wishing, more than anything, she could have her old Gramps back.

"He sure looks different without his beard and mustache, doesn't he?" Gramps finally said.

She nodded tentatively. She had no idea what Steele or Bella looked like. And she could only pray that after so many years Gramps' recollection had faded.

"He's battered himself up good this time, hasn't he?"

"He's got a nasty head wound."

Gramps bent down and reached for the pallet. "Well, no sense standing around here yakking. You take the front and I'll carry the rear."

She did as he instructed, hoping Gramps wouldn't strain himself by lifting so much weight. He'd likely pay for the exertion later and need extra pain medicine. She was surprised when they made it up the slab step and inside the kitchen without any trouble. With the fuel-burning stove in one corner and a cupboard taking up most of another wall, the space was cramped.

"Let's put him in the back bedroom," Gramps instructed, as he maneuvered past the round table that sat four. "It'll be too hard to carry him upstairs."

She'd wanted Gramps to move to the downstairs bedroom so he didn't have to navigate the steps. But he'd insisted on staying in his room to remain close to the tower. Even though he rarely performed any of the lantern duties now, she knew the younger version of Gramps would have been insulted not to be near the light, in case of an emergency.

Most of the time, they kept the spare room downstairs closed off unless Debbie came for an overnight visit, which was rare in recent weeks since she was pregnant with her second child and nearing her due date.

Somehow, Abbie and Gramps carried the injured man to the bedroom and slid him onto the bed. She wasn't sure how she would have done it without Gramps' help and whispered a grateful prayer that he was in a cooperative mood even if he'd be surly later due to his aching bones.

As she began the process of nursing the stranger, Gramps hovered in the kitchen, helping to warm water, cut bandages, and bring her towels.

"How's Steele doing?" Gramps asked every time he came into the square room that couldn't fit much more than the twin bed and chest of drawers.

"He's still unconscious," she said every time in response.

With some wrestling, she pulled off her patient's wet trousers, vest, and shirt. From the quality and tailoring of his garments, she assessed that he was well-to-do, probably from one of the rich families that came to Newport every summer. His hands were without calluses, his fingernails clean, and his body toned to perfection—likely from spending his days playing tennis, yachting, or engaging in another one of the leisure activities of the wealthy class.

When he was down to his drawers and undershirt, she didn't blink an eye. She wasn't a blushing bride anymore. Her scant visits from Nate may have been in the dark, revealing little. But even if the intimate moments of her short-lived marriage had been undercover, the fact was, she didn't care that her patient was of the male species. He was a person in need. And she'd never been able to turn down a rescue attempt, either on sea or land.

After cleaning and bandaging his head wound, she began

the process of bathing him. She started by washing his face. As she scrubbed away the sand, which revealed his features more clearly, she realized he was even more handsome than she'd first thought.

Nate had been attractive in a rounded, roughened way, with the deeply tanned complexion of most fishermen.

Although this man was sun bronzed, his skin wasn't weathered. Instead, he had a smooth suaveness to him that, again, spoke of his class. His face was thinner than Nate's, his jaw was sharply defined, and his nose was long and straight—unlike Nate's, which had been broken several times.

A slight layer of stubble shaded the stranger's cheeks and chin, but she guessed that he was usually clean-shaven. Now that his hair was drying, it had turned a light shade of blond, the color of dry beach sand.

She dipped the washcloth into the fresh basin of warm water Gramps had brought her, rinsed the rag, and pressed it to the man's neck. She wiped at the sand coating his throat and under his ears before deciding to take off the silver chain he wore. Tugging it loose from his undershirt, she slipped it over his head.

Once she cradled the chain in her hand, she realized it had a ring attached to it—a gold signet shield band with the initials NRW engraved in elegant lettering. She removed the ring from the chain and studied it, turning it over, noting the fancy details on both sides. Some parts were smooth and faded, a sign that the ring had been worn a lot over the years. Why wasn't he wearing the ring around his finger anymore?

She turned it back to the shield and traced the cursive NRW. Were those his initials? If she could figure out his name, she would have an easier time searching for his family in

Newport when she went ashore later.

She checked the open door of the bedroom. At the clank of the stove opening and closing, she guessed Gramps was busy heating more water. She glanced from the ring to the stranger's hand. Then she let curiosity get the better of her. She fumbled for his hand and slipped the band down his long finger. It was slightly loose, but overall, it fit well.

NRW.

She didn't know of too many *N* names besides Nate.

Noah? Nick? Norbert?

She shook her head. None of those seemed to fit this striking young man.

He gave a low moan and jerked his hand out of hers.

"I'm so sorry," she said, jumping away. She expected his eyes to fly open and for him to frown at her forwardness with the ring. He rolled his head back and forth on the pillow and moaned again. But his eyes remained closed.

Was he regaining consciousness? If so, she needed to remove the ring and return it to the chain. Otherwise, he'd realize that she'd been meddling.

With her gaze on his face to gauge his wakefulness, she reached for his hand. At that moment, the kitchen door scraped open, and a voice called out in greeting. "Good to see you, Hosea. How are you today?"

"Do I know you?" Gramps replied.

"Mr. Davis, the local lighthouse superintendent," the person replied hesitantly. "Don't you remember me?"

Abbie's heart crashed against her chest and came to an abrupt halt. "Oh, no!" she whispered. After her encounter with Zeke Crawford yesterday, she should have prepared herself for the superintendent's visit. She'd expected Zeke to file another complaint. She just hadn't expected Mr. Davis to follow up so soon.

The man on the bed released another groan, this one louder than before. Her attention shifted to his bare legs and his drawers.

What would the superintendent think when he discovered a half-naked man in the house? Even if the stranger was injured, Mr. Davis was sure to question why she was alone in a bedroom with a man who wasn't her husband.

Abbie's pulse careened forward until it was racing at twice the speed. She surveyed the small bedroom. Could she hide her patient? Maybe under the bed? No. The narrow area was stuffed with extra blankets and afghans that Gran had made over the years. Besides, it was too tight of a space for a large man.

She'd have to find an excuse for keeping Mr. Davis out of the bedroom.

Even though the room was hot with humidity, Abbie grabbed the bedcover from the floor and draped it over the stranger. She wadded his garments into balls, opened the bottom dresser drawer, and threw them inside. She dumped his silver chain into the drawer too.

"What happened to Mr. Trout?" Gramps asked referring to the superintendent from his past.

Abbie shoved at the overflowing drawer. She had to get out into the kitchen and avert the disaster that was brewing between Gramps and Mr. Davis. She couldn't expect the superintendent to lie to Gramps the way she did.

The patient thrashed again, kicking the blanket off his legs.

Her nerves tightened at what this man would say when he regained his wits in a strange room in his undergarments and wearing his ring on his finger.

She glanced at the bottom drawer. Maybe she'd been too quick to act.

With a shake of her head, she started for the kitchen. Right now, she had to keep both Gramps and the superintendent calm. While doing so, she'd pray that her patient would remain unconscious. Because she had no doubt when he awoke, he'd be blazing mad.

Chapter 4

Someone was pounding his head and wouldn't stop. With a moan, Nathaniel rolled and pressed his hand to his temples to make the pounding go away. But as his fingers connected with his head, burning pain radiated from his scalp down to his stomach, making him suddenly nauseous.

For a moment, all he could do was gulp in air to try to keep himself from retching.

As the burning subsided and the pounding resumed, he touched his head again, this time more warily. His fingers grazed strips of linen that wrapped around his head, lapping over his forehead and covering an injury on the left side of his scalp.

What had happened?

He fingered the bandage, waiting for a memory to return, waiting for something to come back to him. But strangely, his mind was empty of any awareness of what had caused his injury.

He dropped his hand, and as it made contact with a mattress, he realized he was in a bed. Was he in a hospital?

His eyes shot open, and he found himself staring up at a whitewashed ceiling streaked with cracks. His gaze fell to the foot of the bed to an arched metal bedpost. Above him, a high rectangular window covered by a thin faded strip of calico didn't do much to contain the sunlight streaming into the room. He shifted his sights to the opposite direction, finding a tall dresser against the wall next to the door. A braided rug and a bedside table were the only other furnishings.

This couldn't be a hospital, could it?

He glanced over himself, searching for other injuries, and saw that his blanket was askew, revealing his underclothes and bare feet. If he was undressed, then he must be home or in a hospital. Since this tiny room didn't appear to be in a hospital, then he must be home.

But where was home?

Again, he waited for memories to flood back. For the picture of this room or any other room in the house to slip into his consciousness.

Only black nothingness greeted him.

He closed his eyes. "All you need to do is wake up. Let's go." He popped open his eyes and tried again to remember something about where he was. Surely, he'd seen the dresser before or the window or the hallway outside the door that led to the…

Where did it lead?

His heart fluttered with anxiety.

Maybe this wasn't his home. Maybe he'd been injured and someone had brought him here. But if so, then where was *his* home? "Come on. Think." But even as he attempted to scour the dark corners of his mind for details, he couldn't find one single thing.

His body tightened, and his pulse spurted with a burst of panic so overwhelming that sweat broke out on his forehead. Not only did he have no memory of his home, but he realized he had no memory of his family.

Who were his parents? Did he have any siblings? Who was *he*?

In spite of the throbbing in his head, he forced himself to rise to his elbows. His whole body was trembling now—from pain or fright, he didn't know. What was wrong with him? Why couldn't he remember who he was? Had the blow to his head wiped out his memories?

If only he could visualize what he was doing before he'd been knocked unconscious. Even if he could picture yesterday or last week or last month or last year…

"Come on, now," he urged himself in a desperate whisper. "Remember something."

"We're getting along just fine," came a young woman's voice from down the hallway.

"Of course we are," another voice followed quickly, an older one. "Now that my assistant is back, we have nothing to worry about."

Assistant is back. Was that him? Was he the assistant? If so, what kind of assistant was he?

"I'm glad to hear it," said a third, equally unfamiliar, voice. "To be honest, I hadn't expected your husband to return."

"Heaven's sake," the older man cut in. "Why wouldn't her husband return? He's a good man, as good as they get."

"It's all right, Hosea," the woman said in a soothing tone.

Was the woman his wife? He shook his head. He had

absolutely no recollection of ever getting married. None.

He lifted his hand and realized he was wearing a ring. Was this his wedding band? He squinted at it and had a vague sense of having seen it before.

NRW. They were likely his initials. But what did NRW stand for?

His mind scrambled to find the answer. Surely he hadn't forgotten his own name.

"I'm sure you're eager to return to your whitewashing, Hosea," the woman in the other room said. "Don't let us hold you back. I'll finish up with the superintendent."

The older man grumbled something, and then a few seconds later the door opened and closed heavily behind him.

After a pause, the other man spoke again. "I hate seeing your grandpa this way."

"He still loves this place, you know."

Another moment of silence settled, and Nathaniel felt only slightly guilty for eavesdropping. He was too desperate to glean information to fill the void of his life. He hoped something in their conversation would jar his memory.

"I know," the man said with a sad resignation in his tone. "I don't want to make him leave the island or the lighthouse."

"Then don't."

"But his memory is gone. I've tried overlooking it because I like Hosea. But Zeke raised some good points, especially about the safety of the lighthouse with Hosea here."

"Mr. Davis, you and I both realize that I can handle this place better than any man out there, including Zeke Crawford."

Nathaniel liked her spunk and determination. He liked the sound of her voice. The confidence and the fight.

Was her grandpa the light keeper? If so, did that make him the assistant keeper? That made sense. But what didn't make sense was that he had no memory of how to run a lighthouse or any cognizance of ever being in one. If he was an assistant, wouldn't he remember something, even a little?

"I know you can handle things," Mr. Davis said. "But what about Nate?"

Nate. Nathaniel.

He dropped back to the pillow and expelled a huge breath. His name was Nathaniel. The *N* in the initials stood for Nathaniel. He knew that with certainty.

For a moment, he basked in the security of being able to recall one small thing. If he'd remembered his name, it was only a matter of time before other things would come back to him.

"Does Nate really matter?" The woman's tone turned defensive.

"I'm afraid he does."

"Why?" This time her question came out almost angry, and Nathaniel got the feeling she didn't like him.

He sat up on his elbows again. Why wouldn't his wife like him? Surely, he was a likable fellow, wasn't he?

"Zeke threatened to go to the Lighthouse Board regarding Hosea's senility. If Nate isn't here acting as keeper in Hosea's stead, my hands will be tied."

So he was acting as keeper? What did that mean?

"You know I've already done all I can to make this work, Abbie. But I may have little choice but to give the position to Zeke."

Abbie. His wife's name was Abbie.

"Because he's a man and I'm a woman," she responded.

"He's older and has been doing this longer."

"But if Nate is here helping, then we can stay?"

Why wouldn't he stay and help? The pounding in Nathaniel's head forced him back to his pillow. This time there was a decided ache in his chest as well as his head. Maybe he hadn't been a good person. What had he done to his wife to make her dislike him? On the other hand, did he really want to know? Maybe oblivion was better.

Mr. Davis heaved a loud sigh. "*If* Nate stays—we both know that's a big *if*—and *if* he stops all the drinking, then I'll have more leverage for allowing you to remain here. Zeke's case against you won't be as strong."

Nathaniel was suddenly all too aware of the bitterness of alcohol at the back of his tongue. Apparently, he had a drinking problem. The pounding in his head probably had more to do with a hangover than from his injury.

So not only was he a lousy husband, but he was also a lousy drunk? He closed his eyes as the weight of the truth pressed on him.

"I don't understand why Zeke won't leave us alone," Abbie said.

"I'm sorry, Abbie. Really, I am."

She didn't reply.

Nathaniel tried to picture her. What did his wife look like? He wouldn't forget that, would he?

"What if I give you two more weeks to see how things go?" Mr. Davis suggested.

"Only two? Why not three?"

"All right. Three. But remember. Nate has to stay on the island this time. He has to remain sober. And he has to make an effort to learn the keeper duties. If he doesn't follow through on those things, then I won't have a choice but to give Hosea's keeper position to Zeke."

"I understand," she said with a thread of defeat in her voice, a defeat that said she didn't expect him to follow through with any of the superintendent's stipulations.

Nathaniel swallowed hard, tasting the bitterness of his rancid alcoholic breath once again.

"Maybe it would help if I talk to your husband," Mr. Davis said.

"No," she cut in quickly. "He's unconscious. I'm not exactly sure what happened, except that he has a gash on his head."

"Abbie," Mr. Davis said in a tone that made clear he realized she was excusing and shielding her drunken husband.

Shame washed over Nathaniel.

"I know you married him so you could stay here at Rose Island," Mr. Davis continued. "But you deserved a lot better than him."

The superintendent's words pierced Nathaniel's heart as swiftly and sharply as a bayonet. What kind of terrible person was he that he was unworthy of the woman he'd married? As much as he wanted Mr. Davis to be wrong, somehow the words rang true. Somewhere in his lost memories, a part of him recognized the validity of the words. She deserved better than him.

"What's done is done," she said matter-of-factly, even though he caught a slight tremor in her tone. "If I made a mistake, then it's one I have to live with."

Melancholy drifted over Nathaniel and made him sink further into the sagging mattress. His wife thought she'd made a mistake by marrying him.

"I hope you'll be able to turn things around." From the changing inflection of Mr. Davis's voice, Nathaniel could tell he was walking toward the door and ready to depart.

Abbie didn't respond, which told Nathaniel much more than words could—that she didn't think they would be able to turn things around.

The door scraped open. "Good-bye, Abbie. I'll see you again in three weeks."

"Good-bye, Mr. Davis."

After the door closed, several long minutes of silence followed. Nathaniel started to think that perhaps Abbie had gone out too. But then soft footsteps made their way toward the bedroom.

A bubble of panic swelled in his gut. What should he do? Close his eyes and pretend to be unconscious and buy himself a little more time to figure out how to handle this strange situation? Or should he face her like a man and admit he'd heard every word of her conversation with Mr. Davis?

If only his memories would come back. He scrunched his face in concentration, held his breath, and tried to make his mind work. But no matter how hard he focused, nothing was there. His mind was blank.

Her footsteps padded down the hallway, drawing steadily nearer.

His heart raced faster, and he did the cowardly thing—he closed his eyes. He told himself he needed more time. He needed to regain his memories first before facing her. Deep down, though, he knew the reality. He was embarrassed and guilt-ridden.

According to the discussion he'd just overheard, he'd caused Abbie's problems. If he didn't change over the next three weeks, they'd have to move from the lighthouse.

She halted in the doorway.

He tried to calm his erratic pulse and still his labored breathing.

When she crossed the room toward him, he held himself motionless. She stopped at the edge of the bed. He felt her presence above him and sensed that she was watching his face. He guessed that her expression contained the disgust and dislike that had filled her voice when she'd been speaking with Mr. Davis.

Could he find some way to change her opinion of him? He didn't remember anything he'd done, but a deep shame inside told him he'd been awful, that he deserved her disdain.

Self-loathing rose to choke him. Had he sunk so low he was beyond reform? Or was it possible he could be a better man, a better husband?

A gentle graze against his hand almost made him jerk. Her fingers brushed his and moved to his ring. When she tugged the band upward, swift protest swelled inside. He didn't remember much about anything, but he did remember the ring belonged to him. It was his only link with who he was, and he didn't want to part with it.

With a quick reflex that surprised him, he captured her hand in his.

She gasped.

His eyes flew open to see her startled face above his. A startled but beautiful face. Wide brown eyes flecked with green stared down at him. Long strands of wavy brown hair had come loose from a braid and fluttered about her flushed cheeks. She had a delicate nose and mouth and a dainty chin.

His breath caught in his chest. She was the prettiest

woman he'd ever laid eyes on. Something in his gut told him so.

And she was his wife?

She didn't move. Not even to breathe. She appeared to be studying him as much as he studied her.

He shifted his gaze to her body hovering above him. She was petite but exuded a strength and determination that matched what he'd heard in her voice. Her blouse and skirt weren't fancy, but they outlined a decidedly womanly form that again made him marvel she was his. His wife.

How could this be possible? Why would this beautiful woman ever consider marrying him?

For several seconds, the doubts rolled in and told him this was a horrible mistake, that he'd taken someone else's place, that this wasn't his life.

But then her conversation with the superintendent came rushing back. She'd been desperate enough to stay at the lighthouse that she'd wedded him even though he wasn't worthy. She'd placed all her hope in him. And he'd let her down.

He sought her gaze again. Her wide brown-green eyes met his. For a moment, they opened like windows to her soul, giving him a glimpse of her hurt, desperation, and fear.

God in heaven, but suddenly he wanted nothing more than to take all that away and to replace it with the love and joy she deserved. Maybe he'd been a fool in the past. But that didn't mean he had to remain a fool, did it?

Since the past seemed to have disappeared from his mind, perhaps this was his chance to start over, put his mistakes behind him, and forge a new life. He could be a better person, be the husband Abbie deserved.

It was worth a try, wasn't it?

Chapter 5

Abbie jerked her hand free of his. "I'm sorry," she said, backing away. His gaze was too intense, too probing, and she shifted her attention to the end of the bed to his feet poking out from the bedcovers. He had clean, groomed feet, so unlike her own, which were sand-gritted and calloused. Just one more sign he belonged to a different world than hers.

How long had he been awake? How much of the discussion with the superintendent had he overhead?

"Abbie?" he said hesitantly.

Apparently long enough to learn her name. She squirmed and fumbled at her rolled-up sleeve that revealed her sun browned and freckled arm. If he'd learned her name, then he'd also witnessed her deception.

When Gramps had insisted to Mr. Davis that her husband had returned, she hadn't contradicted him. She hadn't wanted to confuse or agitate Gramps any more than he already was at seeing Mr. Davis.

However, after Gramps left the house, she should have cleared up the misunderstanding with the superintendent right away and explained that the man in the bedroom wasn't her husband, but was instead someone who'd washed up on the shore during the previous night.

Things had gone from bad to worse when the superintendent had given her the ultimatum of having three weeks left to turn things around. She hadn't been able to tell him that Nate wasn't really back—that he was dead and would never return. Somehow, the truth had stuck in her throat. She'd pictured packing Gramps into the skiff and rowing over to Newport, with him growing angrier and more confused with every stroke she made away from the island.

She'd told herself after Mr. Davis left that she'd figure out something, that she'd gained herself three weeks to come up with a solution. She couldn't blame the superintendent or be mad at him for finally giving her a deadline—even if it had been at Zeke's prompting. Mr. Davis had already gone out of his way to ignore Nate's neglect of his duties over the winter and hadn't made an issue when Nate had disappeared. But Mr. Davis couldn't let things go on without Nate indefinitely. She should have known he'd have to ask her to leave at some point.

She just hadn't anticipated that the injured stranger in the bed would overhear their conversation, including the part where she hadn't corrected the confusion regarding his identity.

Stupid. She'd been stupid. So stupid. "So," she said, "I guess you heard everything?"

"Yes." The one word was strangely laced with sadness. She'd expected anger or surprise or even indignation.

Not remorse.

She twisted her big toe into the braided rug. "I'm sorry—"

"Don't apologize," he interrupted. "If anyone should be sorry, it should be me."

Her gaze jerked up to his again, to eyes as green as the explosion of vegetation on the island in the summer. What did this stranger have to be sorry about?

"I have to admit," he said slowly, as though sensing her question. "I don't remember anything. The blow to my head must have caused me to lose my memories."

"Lose your memories? I don't understand."

He closed his eyes, and the muscles in his well-defined jaw rippled with movement. He seemed to be fighting to clear his mind. But when he opened his eyes, they slanted with frustration. "I don't remember what I was doing to get this head wound or where I was."

"It looks like something knocked you pretty hard."

He nodded. "But that's not all." He paused and sucked in a shaky breath. "I don't remember anything about my life. Everything is gone."

"Everything?" she asked, trying to make sense of what he was saying.

"My mind is blank. And no matter how hard I've been attempting to recollect things, my mind feels like an empty closet with only a few cobwebs left." When he met her gaze again, his eyes were stricken, and she knew he was telling her the truth.

She didn't understand how such a thing could happen, but after living with Gramps' deteriorating memory for the past couple of years, she'd learned that the brain was capable of doing funny things when it wanted to. "There's got to be something you can recall."

"Only my name. Nathaniel."

Her breath hitched, and she glanced to the ring with the NRW. So that's what the *N* stood for.

"But apparently I've shortened it to Nate?"

Did he think he was her husband, Nate? She shook her head. She hadn't spoken up and clarified matters with Mr. Davis, but she wasn't about to make that same mistake twice. She needed to set this man straight immediately.

"Bella?" The door slammed and Gramps' call came from the kitchen.

She hesitated. She wasn't ready to face Gramps right now.

"Bella?" His tone grew insistent.

She sighed. "In here, Hosea."

"Bella?" Nathaniel's brow rose. "I thought your name was Abbie."

"It is," she whispered. "But Gramps is senile. He calls me Bella."

The confusion on Nathaniel's features remained.

"Please just go along with him," she softly pleaded. "Please."

He nodded, but before he could ask any further questions, Gramps was standing in the door.

"How's your husband?" Gramps' face crinkled with anxiety, and he rubbed at his bushy beard nervously.

"I'm fine, Hosea," Nathaniel said. "My head's a little sore, but otherwise, there's nothing to worry about."

Gramps removed his hat and smoothed down the smattering of silvery strands. "Are you sure?"

Nathaniel smiled at Gramps. "I'm positive."

Gramps returned the smile. "I always knew you were

made of tough stuff."

"Plus, I have a beautiful wife looking after me." Nathaniel gave her a quick, questioning glance that seemed to ask if he was doing all right.

She nodded. He was doing more than all right.

Gramps' shoulders visibly relaxed. "Well, since you seem to be in good hands, I'll be heading back out to finish up my work."

"I'm in very good hands."

Something about Nathaniel's tone made Abbie believe he really meant it. Either that, or he was an expert at pretending.

Gramps turned to leave but then stopped. "Don't worry about trying to resume your duties. I'll take over until you're back on your feet."

"Thanks, Hosea."

Gramps gave a brief nod and shuffled away. When the kitchen door opened and then closed, Abbie released a breath of relief.

"I like Hosea," Nathaniel said.

"Thanks for going along with him."

"It's the least I can do." Again, sorrow edged Nathaniel's voice that she didn't quite understand. Whatever the case, she needed to clear up the misunderstanding. She might make a habit of dishonesty with Gramps, and she'd let the deception pass unchecked with the superintendent. But she had no intention of lying to this poor helpless man and letting him go on believing he was her husband.

"Listen, Nathaniel," she said.

"No. Don't say anything," he interrupted. He crossed his hands over his chest and stared at his ring, as if that somehow could unlock the mystery to his life. "I may not remember anything right now. But I do know that what Mr. Davis said is true—you deserve a lot better than me."

"No," she rushed to clarify. "You misunderstood—"

"Abbie, let me finish," he said with a thread of desperation to his voice. "Please."

"But I need to explain first."

He shook his head and continued before she could speak. "I might not remember any specific incidents, but I sense in my soul I've been the worst kind of man. And I haven't been worthy of you."

His confession was so sincere and sweet that she couldn't find a response. She could only stare at him open-mouthed.

"I know I don't deserve your forgiveness and have probably hurt you more times than I can count. But I'd like to make it up to you. I promise I'll stay on the island and remain sober for the next three weeks so we don't have to move."

The sincerity in his summery green eyes was too hard to resist. It reached out and caressed her, almost as if he'd touched her with his hand. Her heart quavered as the early months of her marriage with all of its uncertainty and frustration and loneliness came swelling back into her chest like the rising tide.

She couldn't deny that this was exactly what she'd wanted from Nate—for him to admit his mistakes and promise to make things work. She'd wanted it so desperately that she'd buried the longing deep in her soul, where she wouldn't have to think about it, so it wouldn't hurt. After his death, she'd thought the frustrations would go away.

But now, all it took was this man, this stranger without a memory, coming into her home. In one instant, he'd dredged up everything, all the agony, all the disappointments, all the sorrow from her failed marriage and reminded her of what she'd missed and now would never have.

A sob tightened her throat. She pressed a fist against her mouth to keep it back. Nate wasn't worth crying over, she told herself angrily. Not anymore.

"Please," Nathaniel whispered hoarsely, his sincere eyes beseeching her. "Give me three weeks to prove to you that I can change, that I can do better, and that maybe eventually I can be the kind of man you deserve."

Why couldn't this man be the real Nate? Why?

Tears stung her eyes. The sob swelled, trying to work its way free. She attempted to swallow it, but it only managed to creep higher. She needed to get away before she broke down and wept.

Without answering him, she spun and fled down the hallway, through the kitchen, and out of the house. With unshed tears blurring her vision, she ran down to the beach and her boat. She shoved it into the water, jumped in, and started rowing.

Nathaniel tried to sit up, but the pounding in his head turned into a gong any time he moved too quickly. Whatever had happened to cause his memory loss had also likely given him a concussion. Even if the pounding came from that and not a hangover this time, the rancidness of his mouth wouldn't let him forget his problems.

He wanted to get up and go after Abbie. He wasn't sure what he'd said to hurt her. He'd only wanted to assure her that he'd try to be a better man. At least that's what he hoped.

He released a frustrated sigh. The longer his memory was

gone, the more he was beginning to wonder if the knock against his head was a second chance for him. Was God wiping his slate clean and giving him the opportunity to fix his mistakes and do things right this time?

God?

Once again, a gut feeling informed him he hadn't necessarily been on speaking terms with God in recent years. But he must have been at one time, otherwise why would thoughts of the Almighty enter his conscience?

Whether or not he'd ever been a man of faith, it wasn't too late to start. "God," he whispered to the cracked ceiling, "I don't know anything right now except that apparently I've lived a selfish life and hurt people in the process. Please help me to do better, be stronger, and live like You want me to."

He probably ought to pray that God would help restore his memories too. Most normal men would want their memories back, wouldn't they? Even so, something inside him resisted. He'd already learned enough about his past in the short conversation he'd overheard between Abbie and the superintendent. He wasn't sure he wanted to hear anything else—especially if it was more like that.

Sure, he wished he remembered his family. He couldn't picture his mother or father. He didn't know if he had any siblings. He had no inkling where he'd grown up or what his childhood had been like. But what kind of ghosts might he unearth if he remembered his family? His intuition told him he was better not knowing.

He ran his fingers over the quilt that covered him. He had no idea how long he'd been an acting keeper. How long he'd lived at the lighthouse. Or even where the lighthouse was.

How long had he been married? Did he and Abbie have

any children?

At the thought of kids, he jerked upward. A wave of dizziness made him so nauseous that he rapidly lowered himself.

"God," he prayed again, "please, no children. Please." If he'd been a lousy husband, he could only imagine what a terrible father he'd been too.

Abbie seemed too young to have children, and he hadn't noticed any young voices since he'd awoken. Surely, if they had any little ones, he would have heard them by now.

And he was young too, wasn't he? He browsed through the empty corridors of his mind, searching once again. But he could find no dates, no numbers, nothing to indicate his age. Maybe if he saw himself in a mirror, he'd be able to tell how old he was.

At the opening and closing of a nearby door, he peered down the hallway, praying Abbie was returning so he'd have the chance to talk to her again. He supposed that all the talking in the world wouldn't make things right, that he'd have to prove to her with his actions that he meant what he said. Nevertheless, he wanted to apologize again.

Hosea appeared in the hallway, and his shuffling footsteps drew nearer. He stopped in the doorway, his old brow wrinkled, not only with age but also with worry. "How are you doing?"

"I'm doing fine, Hosea." Not much had changed in the past five minutes since Hosea had been in the house and asked him the same question. But Nathaniel supposed the older man didn't remember that he'd just come in and checked on him. At least, Hosea seemed to genuinely care.

"You're sure you're fine?" He'd taken off his hat again and

twisted the brim in his paint-splattered hands.

"I'm positive."

"Good. I always knew you were made of tough stuff."

The conversation was a repeat of before, but Nathaniel didn't mind. He couldn't be impatient toward a man with memory losses when he was struggling with the same thing. "I'm sure if I rest today, I'll be as good as new tomorrow."

Hosea entered the room, took hold of the wooden chair next to the dresser, dragged it across the rug, and positioned it next to the bed. He angled it and then sat down facing Nathaniel. "I'm done with my whitewashing for the day. I'll sit with you a spell."

From the way sunlight streamed through the window, Nathaniel guessed that it couldn't be past midmorning. He doubted Hosea had finished his work. But who was he to argue? If Hosea wanted to spend time with him, he wouldn't turn him away. In fact, talking with the older man might be the most profitable use of his time. If he got Hosea to discuss the lighthouse and its operation, perhaps he'd be able to return to his duties without making an utter fool of himself.

And maybe, just maybe, he'd be able to learn a little more about Abbie too. He was curious about this woman he'd married and wanted to know more. He could see why he'd been drawn to her on a physical level. She was very attractive.

But, surely, he'd married her more than for her looks, hadn't he? "Abbie—I mean Bella is certainly a beautiful woman, isn't she?"

Hosea grinned and shoved Nathaniel in the arm. "So is Ruth. We both ended up with the prettiest girls on this side of the Atlantic."

Nathaniel guessed that Ruth was Hosea's wife.

"God's blessed us, and we can't forget it," Hosea added.

Nathaniel settled back against his pillow and folded his arms across his chest. He may have forgotten everything else, but Hosea's admonition struck something in him. God had blessed him, and yet he'd apparently taken those blessings for granted. Maybe that was one more reason he'd been knocked over the head—to remind him to stop focusing on all the negatives in his life and to start counting his blessings instead.

Chapter 6

Abbie hefted her bucket of crabs to the backdoor into the shade of the house before she stooped and pulled out two near the top. She held them from behind at the bases of their swimming fins so they wouldn't be able to pinch her.

In spite of being distracted, she'd had a successful catch. After the storms of last night, the crabs had been hiding in the eelgrass. She'd caught several that had just molted their shells. They'd been too weak to swim away, and she'd been able to capture them without any bait.

She'd stayed out crabbing longer than she usually did. Now that the sun was overhead, it was past time for the noon meal. She'd have to boil a couple of the crabs and toss together a salad of kale and lettuce from her garden. Gramps wouldn't be happy with the simple fare since he expected the women to prepare a filling dinner.

What he didn't realize was that Ruth and Bella were no longer living. Maybe all those years ago his wife and his assistant's wife found time to cook big meals every day. But Abbie didn't have time, not when she shouldered all the keeper duties as well as the task of earning extra income from clamming, crabbing, and fishing. Not only did she have equipment to clean and maintain, but she had to make frequent trips into town to sell her fresh catch. In the summer, she also had her vegetable garden to keep her busy, including all the preserving of the produce for winter.

But it didn't matter that most days she operated on a few hours of broken sleep. Gramps would never be able to understand how hard she worked or the sacrifices she made for him. She didn't expect him to. Not anymore.

On the most difficult of days, she tried to remember all the ways he'd sacrificed for her and Debbie over the years, especially after their mom had run off and left them. Abbie had been only six and Debbie eight the summer she'd gone.

In the days following her disappearance, Abbie had heard Gran and Gramps whisper about how Mom had never gotten over losing her husband in the War Between the States. Of course, Gran and Gramps had been devastated, too, to lose their only child, Elijah. But for some reason, Mom hadn't been able to move on with her life. Or maybe she'd wanted a new life away from the reminders of the man she'd lost. Whatever the case, she'd left Abbie and Debbie.

With both parents gone, Gran and Gramps had raised them. Gramps hadn't made much with his keeper salary, but he'd done his best to give her and Debbie everything they'd needed. He'd even rowed them over to Newport every day for school until Abbie turned ten, and he admitted she was a better rower than he was and allowed them to go on their own.

Abbie gingerly opened the backdoor, careful to keep her

grip on the crabs away from their pinchers. She expected Gramps to be sitting at the table waiting, and she readied an apology. So when she stepped inside and found his spot empty, she started with surprise.

Had something happened to him while she'd been gone? Normally he stayed at his whitewashing all morning. After the dinner meal, he slept most of the afternoon. Then once he ate supper, he spent a couple of hours digging on the beach. His routine rarely varied.

Her heart sputtered with an unease that had been growing with each passing day. Every time she left him by himself, she was taking a chance. Anything could happen to him. He could fall from the ladder he often used for whitewashing or wander off somewhere on the island or decide to make a meal for himself and burn the house down. She'd thought of every scenario and realized it wouldn't be long before Gramps would need more supervision than she alone could give him.

Was it finally time to leave the island? The question had plagued her during the crabbing. What difference would three weeks make? When Mr. Davis returned, he'd realize the truth, that Nate wasn't really there and that she was in the same predicament as before. Why prolong the inevitable? Especially since Nate was dead and was never coming back.

She dropped the crabs into a pot of water and brushed her hands on her skirt. She was about to head outside and search for Gramps when voices in the bedroom stopped her.

Was he visiting with their guest?

She tiptoed to the hallway. The distinct thud of dice hitting wood echoed loudly.

"Double fours," Gramps said in a triumphant voice. "I've got you beat!"

Nathaniel gave what appeared to be a good-natured groan.

Gramps counted off his moves and chortled. "Three games to your two. Are you finally going to admit that I'm the backgammon champion?"

Nathaniel and Gramps were playing backgammon?

"One more game," Nathaniel said. "Just one more."

Gramps bellowed a hearty laugh in reply.

He hadn't laughed like that in years, and the sound of it brought swift tears to her eyes. For the second time in one day, she'd almost been reduced to tears. What was wrong with her?

She'd spent the morning trying to erase her conversation with Nathaniel. She'd told herself his plea for forgiveness didn't mean anything. How could it, when it was the confession of a confused stranger?

Even so, the sincerity and the sweetness of it had wrenched her heart and made her keenly aware of how empty her marriage had been.

"My stomach is gurgling for dinner," Gramps said. "I'm surprised the womenfolk don't have something ready for us yet."

"Maybe she's busy with other things today," Nathaniel said slowly, as though uncertain how to answer.

"She's a hard worker, that's for sure," Gramps replied. "Too bad her sister isn't here anymore to help."

"Sister?"

"Debbie's a good girl too."

Was Gramps having one of his coherent moments? Abbie strode down the hallway. Whenever his mind cleared, it was like having a long-lost friend come home for a visit, and she didn't want to miss a single moment of his return.

When she halted in the doorway, the men shifted to look

at her. Nathaniel reclined in the bed against several more pillows that apparently Gramps had brought from the other bedrooms. The backgammon board rested on the bed, and Gramps had pulled up a chair.

Nathaniel's face was pale and dark circles had formed under his eyes, showing him to be tired and likely in need of rest. He was probably in a great deal of pain as well. But there he was, playing backgammon with Gramps anyway. He offered her a tentative smile. "Hosea taught me how to play backgammon."

"You mean I've been beating you in backgammon," Gramps interjected.

"That too."

"You'll have to play Abbie sometime," Gramps said. "She's almost as good as me."

Abbie laughed with delight that Gramps remembered her name. "I'd better be good since I learned everything from you."

Gramps chuckled. He reached for her hand and patted it, much like he'd done when she'd been young.

Abbie relished the calloused texture of his craggy fingers, a touch she rarely experienced any more.

"I like your new husband, Abbie," he said smiling up at her.

"New?" Nathaniel echoed, his brows arching in surprise.

Abbie's heart dropped to the bottom of her chest like an anchor hitting the ocean floor. She had no idea what to say. Gramps was still confused. Yes, he'd seen Nate on occasion, but apparently not enough for him to remember how Nate looked. She was surprised Gramps even remembered that she'd gotten married.

How could she explain to Gramps that this man he'd

played and laughed with was just a stranger who'd washed up on Rose Island last night? Confusion and frustration would roll in to replace the rare laughter and joy she'd just witnessed. Maybe he'd even get angry. Or revert to the past, where he lived most days. She wasn't ready to lose him again so soon.

"We're newlyweds?" Nathaniel asked.

"Not exactly," Abbie replied, scrambling to think of something to say that wouldn't send Gramps back to the past.

"I thought you got married in December? Or was it January?" Gramps tightened his hold on her hand, as if he, too, realized that their time together was always so brief. "Whenever it was, I remember it was cold."

"It was December," she said. Gramps probably remembered how cold it had been because they'd waited so long inside the unheated chapel for Nate's arrival.

"What month is it now?" Nathaniel asked.

"June." She couldn't meet his gaze, lest he see the deception in her eyes. She'd tell him the truth later. For now, she didn't know what else to do except go along with Gramps.

"So that means we've been married for six months?" Nathaniel asked.

She hesitated but finally nodded. "Yes." Once the word was out, shame crashed through her. Nathaniel thought she was trustworthy. He was looking to her for all the answers to memories he'd lost. And here she was, lying to him about everything.

"I've been married to Ruth for forty-five years," Gramps said, patting Abbie's hand again. "So in my book, six months counts as new."

"I suppose it does," she said, trying to infuse cheer into her voice. She wanted to make the most of this moment with

Gramps and not waste it with guilt.

"Speaking of Ruth," he said, standing up and releasing Abbie's hand. "Do you think she's done getting dinner ready? My stomach is telling me it's time to fill it." He didn't wait for her to answer but shuffled across the room to begin his search for Ruth. Even in his most lucid moments, the confusion plagued him.

"I'm planning to boil a couple of the crabs I caught this morning," she called after him as he made his way out of the room and down the hallway.

"Thank you, honey," he replied. "That sounds wonderful."

She stared at his retreating form with longing, wanting to call him back, wanting to hold on to the rare occasions they had together. But as he reached the kitchen and called for Ruth and Bella, she knew her moment with Gramps was gone.

With a sigh, she turned to Nathaniel.

He'd shut his eyes, and his face contained a pinched quality.

"Are you in pain?" she asked, as she began to gather the pieces of the backgammon game.

"The wound on my head is tolerable." He opened his eyes, revealing a dark shadowy green. "What pains me most is realizing how much I've hurt you."

"You haven't—" The sudden grip of his hand around her wrist stopped both her words and her efforts to pick up the game.

"I could see it in your eyes and hear it in your voice," he said in a low tone. "You might be able to keep it from Hosea, but you can't keep it from me."

She glanced to his fingers circling her wrist. They were long and lean and impeccably clean. She should just tell him now they weren't married and that he felt guilty for something he hadn't done. She forced the words out. "I have to be honest with you, Nathaniel. Yes, the past six months have been difficult, much more than I imagined they'd be, but you're not to blame."

He shook his head, and before she realized what he was doing, he'd lifted her hand to his mouth and pressed a kiss into her palm. The touch was gentle and took her by surprise.

She ought to jerk her hand away from him. He wasn't her husband. He had no right to touch her in such an intimate way. And she had no right to let him.

But for an infinite moment, as his gaze locked with hers, she couldn't make herself move. The tenderness in his eyes was framed by remorse and a silent plea—a plea not to push him away as she'd done earlier.

"Nathaniel." She needed to tell him everything. Now.

He touched his lips to her palm again, and this time she was entirely conscious of the fact that his lips were soft and warm and that his breath was tickling her skin. "Will you give me three weeks to prove to you that I'm a changed man?"

She had to say no. She had to put an end to the misunderstanding. But at the sound of Gramps' muttering in the kitchen and his growing agitation, her despair swelled. She desperately needed the three weeks to come up with a new plan.

"Please?" he said again. Something in his tone told her that perhaps he needed this chance to prove himself more than either of them realized.

"Okay." The word slipped out before she could stop it.

"Thank you." His lips curved into a smile.

What in heaven's name was she getting herself into?

At the clatter of a lid hitting the kitchen floor, Abbie tugged her hand free and took a step back. "I'd better start dinner before Gramps decides to do it himself."

Nathaniel nodded.

"Why don't you rest?" she suggested. "And maybe when you wake up, your memories will be restored." At least she hoped so. Then she'd be spared trying to explain the truth to him later.

The remainder of the day, Abbie tried to stay away from Nathaniel, hoping that by avoiding him she could avoid telling any more lies. Thankfully, he slept most of the time, and when he wasn't sleeping, Gramps kept him company.

At dusk, as she headed up to light the lantern, she paused in the hallway, surprised to hear Nathaniel reading the Bible to Gramps. She suspected Gramps had initiated it because the passage was his favorite. Nathaniel's reading voice was smooth and articulate, a clear sign he was well-educated. When Gramps asked him to read the passage again and Nathaniel obliged him, it became clear that he was patient as well.

Abbie took her time in the lantern room. After lighting the Fresnel lens, she tidied up—sweeping the floor, dusting the interior wall, and polishing the oil can. She knew she was desperate to avoid Nathaniel when she polished the lighthouse-issued handheld lantern too.

Finally, when she'd cleaned all she could, she sat on the gallery with her feet dangling over the edge and stared south at the dark bay lit by the moonlight and the red rotating beam that came from Rose Island Lighthouse.

Three weeks. Mr. Davis told her he'd give her three more weeks to live there. But after that where would she go? And what would she do?

Her life was the light and the sea. Every once in a while, she'd heard tales of a woman being appointed as a keeper after her husband died. However, she highly doubted that Mr. Davis would appoint her to a different lighthouse, not without a legitimate connection—namely a spouse.

Debbie would invite her and Gramps to move in her home until Abbie found a job. But living with her sister wasn't a permanent solution either. Debbie and her husband, Menard, lived in a tiny house and had a small income. Although Debbie would never turn them away, Abbie didn't want to add any more burden to her sister's life.

Abbie peered unseeingly at the waves rolling onto the shore, crashing against the sand, and then pulling back out, only to do it all over again. Over and over and over.

Routine. Gramps thrived on routine. It was the thin thread that kept all the tattered and jagged pieces of what remained of his memory from falling completely apart. She had to do whatever she could to preserve his routine.

What if she let Nathaniel stay for the three weeks? What if she didn't correct the mistake and allowed him to believe he was her husband?

As soon as the thought came, she shoved it aside. She couldn't do that. It would be cruel to continue letting him think for even one more day that he was someone he wasn't. Maybe it wouldn't hurt her or Gramps, but it would hurt Nathaniel.

Yet, wouldn't he need time to recuperate from his head wound? He could stay until then, couldn't he? That would give her longer to make arrangements for her and Gramps' future. She would go to Newport and inquire about work. Sometimes wealthy families were looking for additional maids during the summer months.

Abbie shuddered. The mere thought of being inside all day cleaning someone else's home repelled her. If she couldn't stand cleaning her own home, she'd be miserable doing it for someone else. But the fact was, she'd do anything for Gramps. She'd scrub toilets in outhouses if that's what it took to provide for him.

She released a tense breath and stood to her feet. "Just a few more days," she whispered. Then she'd row Nathaniel ashore and try to figure out who he really was. In the meantime, she'd pray for a miracle.

Chapter 7

At the sound of Abbie's footsteps in the kitchen, Nathaniel feigned sleep.

Yesterday, he'd only seen her a few brief times from a distance or when she'd brought him a meal. During those encounters, Hosea had been visiting with him. While he enjoyed Hosea's companionship and had learned a great deal about the man during their visits, he hadn't been able to glean much about Abbie because most of the time Hosea was reliving the past during an era before Abbie had been born.

At first, Nathaniel had assumed Abbie was just busy. But he'd soon realized she came to check his wound, bring him fresh water, or tuck his blankets back over him primarily when he was sleeping—or thought he was. He'd finally come to the conclusion she was avoiding him.

Since they hadn't been married long, he guessed he hadn't known her well anyway. Now, with his memory loss, he knew nothing.

Time to remedy that. With each passing hour, her absence had made him more determined to be with her. Whenever he glimpsed her, he'd grown more curious about this beautiful woman who worked hard, loved her grandpa, and loved the lighthouse.

Why didn't she love him too? What had their relationship been like? Had there ever been a point when they'd enjoyed each other's company? Or had he been such a scoundrel that she'd always avoided him?

Her footsteps drew closer and stopped at the doorway. After several more seconds, she entered the room and crossed to the bed. He sensed her standing above him. The moment her fingers grazed his bandage, he snagged her hand.

"Good morning, beautiful." He opened his eyes and peered up at her, giving her what he hoped was his most charming smile.

She was indeed beautiful, with her bright eyes, flushed cheeks, and long, loose hair. She attempted to tug free, but he wasn't about to release her now that he had her within his grip.

"You've been avoiding me, haven't you?" he asked.

"I've been busy." She met his gaze for only an instant before looking at the dishes piled on the bedside table. But it was long enough for him to see he was right.

"Let me do something to help you."

"You can't. You need to rest." She tried to move, but he held her fast. He was almost tempted to pull her down so she'd have no choice but to sit on the bed next to him. But he wasn't sure what the nature of their physical relationship had been like before his accident. With no memories to guide him, he had to be cautious, or he might frighten her away for good.

Besides, he reminded himself, the lack of memories meant he could do things over, and maybe this time he could do it right, be a better husband, and make her feel special and cherished and adored. He was confident he could woo her with a little patience and perseverance.

But he wouldn't be able to make any progress if he wasn't able to spend time with her.

"I'm feeling stronger today," he said, although he'd already tried once to get out of bed and had nearly passed out from the effort. "I'd like to move to the kitchen."

Her eyes crinkled in doubt.

"Please?" he said, surprised at how smooth and convincing his voice sounded, even to himself. He added a lopsided smile, having the gut feeling that his smile had worked to allure plenty of women in the past into doing exactly as he wanted.

Was that what he'd done wrong? Had he been unfaithful to her? The thought sobered him. "If I ever compromised our marriage by having liaisons with other women, I'll let you drag me outside, tie me to the tower, and whip me with a switch."

At his bold words, she shook her head adamantly and avoided his gaze, clearly embarrassed. "No. Nothing like that. At least I don't think so."

"I don't see why I'd want anyone else," he said softly. "Not when I have someone like you." The words rolled off his tongue easily enough, telling him that he'd been a smooth talker and could lay the charm on as thick as oyster soup. "I mean it, Abbie." Even though he didn't remember anything about her, he liked what he'd already learned.

The tension in her hand eased. He was softening her. He could tell.

"Please, let me spend some time with you," he pleaded

gently. "We can at least learn to be friends, can't we?"

She narrowed her eyes. "I see right through what you're doing."

"What am I doing?" he replied innocently.

"You're being nice and trying to get me to do what you want."

He smiled again. "Is it working?"

"A little."

He chuckled and was pleased when he noticed that her lips twitched into a tiny smile. "Then you'll help me up?"

She expelled an exasperated sigh, but her lips curved higher. "Okay. For a little while."

He pushed himself to his elbows. Then she linked her arm into his and assisted him to a sitting position. He blinked back several waves of dizziness before swinging his legs over the edge of the bed. The covers fell away to reveal his undergarments.

"You need to get dressed first." She shifted her attention from him, a slight pink coloring her cheeks.

"Do I?" He couldn't keep from teasing her. "I'm sure you've seen me in my drawers before."

She didn't respond, except to focus on her bare toes poking out from under the damp, sandy hem of her skirt. Her feet were slender and delicate but gritted with sand. She twisted her big toe against the braided rug and didn't look at him.

Had he been one of those barbaric husbands who reached for his wife in the dark, sated himself, and rolled away from her when he was done? He prayed he'd been more affectionate than that. He pictured himself as the kind of man who'd want to please his wife as much as himself. But what did he know?

As though sensing his confusion, she started to the door.

"I'll go find some clean trousers for you."

She hastened away, and after a moment, he heard her footsteps in the bedroom overhead. Was it the bedroom they'd shared? He clearly had a long way to go in reclaiming her love. Perhaps his task would be harder than he'd first imagined. Even so, the more he learned about his past, the more he was determined to make it right.

She took so long he began to wonder if she'd decided not to come back. But when she returned with a shirt and trousers, he released the tight anxiety that had been building in his shoulders.

Wordlessly, she handed him the clothes and retreated again. From the banging of pots and pans in the kitchen, he realized she was giving him privacy to get dressed. His efforts at putting on the garments were slow and painful, and when he finally had them on, he saw that they were definitely not tailored. Apparently, they could only afford to buy ill-fitting factory made clothing. The waist was large, and the trouser legs short. Nevertheless, the suspenders helped to hold them in place.

He tried to push himself up from the bed, but the pounding in his head swelled, making him sway with dizziness. He plopped down on the bed.

"Are you ready?" she asked from the hallway.

"More than ready." Ready to get out of the confining room. Ready to discover more about his life on the island. Ready to dive into that life and do his part.

As she stepped into the room and took in his appearance, something flashed across her face. Was it embarrassment? He glanced down at his apparel, at the coarse brown trousers and simple red-checkered shirt. He certainly didn't feel at home in the clothing. In fact, he felt rather awkward. He supposed without having groomed himself for the past two days, he looked even worse than he felt. No wonder she was avoiding him.

She gripped his arm, assisted him to his feet, and helped steady him. For the first few moments, he was so lightheaded that he couldn't think or see clearly.

Standing side-by-side, he was conscious again of how petite she was, not more than five feet three inches, several inches shorter than him.

"You should stay in bed for another day or two," she said.

"I'm stronger than I look."

She took a step forward, and he shuffled along next to her, trying not to lean on her too heavily. By the time they reached the kitchen table, he'd given up on maintaining his dignity, and she all but carried him.

"I'm sorry," he apologized, as he dropped into a chair she'd scooted out with her foot. He was breathing hard and his head ached as though someone had taken a sledgehammer to it. He wanted to fall into bed and go back to sleep. But now that he was in the kitchen, he'd have to make the most of the situation. "Maybe you were right about my staying in bed."

"Maybe?" She moved to the stove and pulled an iron skillet to the front burner.

"You were definitely right. Women usually are."

When she glanced at him over her shoulder, the surprise in her eyes made him grin. "I'm well aware of the severe limitations of my species. I may have forgotten everything else, but who could ever forget that women are superior in their reasoning abilities?"

His self-effacing statement earned him one of her rare

smiles. "Would you like me to carry you back to bed?"

"I have no doubt you could carry me if you chose to," he responded. "But I'll spare myself more humiliation."

At his words, her tinkling laughter spilled over and brightened the room more than the sunshine sneaking in the window. He reclined in his chair, feeling suddenly as if he'd won his first major battle.

He wanted to use the opportunity to delve into their past, to discover how they'd met, how long they'd courted, and where they'd taken their wedding trip. But he suspected any questions about their relationship would send her scuttling back into her shell like a hermit crab.

For now, he needed to focus on topics that were safe. So, as she finished preparing breakfast, he asked her about the island, the lighthouse, how long she'd lived there with Hosea.

"Who are Steele and Bella?" he asked, referring to the names that Hosea called the two of them. "Hosea's son- and daughter-in-law?"

She set a plate of eggs and bacon in front of him. "Steele was his assistant at one of the lighthouses he worked in when he was a young man first starting out. And Bella was Steele's wife."

"So even though I'm the acting keeper, Hosea thinks I'm his assistant?"

"Yes, most of the time."

"And what exactly is the difference between an *acting keeper* and an *assistant keeper*?"

"An acting keeper doesn't have an official position and fills in for a head keeper. But an assistant is usually an additional job at lighthouses that have fog bells which require extra work to keep going."

She returned to the stove, retrieved the coffeepot, filled a mug, and brought it to him. Her expression was serious. After placing the mug on the table near his plate, she finally met his gaze. "I appreciate your efforts to go along with Gramps. It's not easy to pretend or answer the same questions over and over. And it gets draining listening to him repeat the same stories. But I've found that contradicting him and trying to set him straight only angers him."

"He's a good man," Nathaniel said, fingering the rim of his coffee mug. "That still shines through loud and clear."

She nodded, visibly swallowed hard, then gave him a tremulous smile. "Thank you."

He took a bite of the eggs and was surprised at the lump in his own throat. He took a swig of coffee to wash down the egg. "He mentions Ruth and Elijah almost as much. I'm guessing they're family?"

"Ruth was his wife and Elijah his son."

"So Ruth was your grandmother and Elijah your father?"

"That's correct." She retraced her steps to the stove and began scooping eggs onto another dish. "Gran passed away five years ago after a battle with consumption. And my dad. Well, I never knew him. I was only a baby when he left to fight in the War Between the States. He didn't come back."

"I'm sorry."

She shrugged. "Gramps and Gran always spoke highly of him. My mom loved him. But I don't remember anything about him."

Nathaniel chewed his breakfast slowly. "What about your mom? Did you lose her too?"

"You could say that." Abbie's voice took on a decided edge of bitterness. "I was six, and Gramps was keeper over on

Prudence Island at the time..."

She paused, spoon in one hand and plate in the other. Her back was stiff and her shoulders straight. She apparently didn't have happy memories of that time in her life.

"You don't have to tell me more—"

"My mom ran off. Decided she didn't want to live at the lighthouse any longer, decided she was done being our mom and that she wanted to make a new life for herself somewhere else."

Nathaniel lowered his fork, his appetite suddenly diminished.

"Gramps and Gran raised me and my sister." She resumed filling the plate. When she turned, the anger was gone from her posture, and resignation had taken its place. She plunked the dish on the table across from him and then poured another mug of coffee.

Nathaniel expected her to sit at the spot and join him for the meal. But after she put the coffee next to the plate, she crossed to the stove and began to scrape the grease out of the pan into a jar. "I hope you understand now why it's important for me to do everything I can for Gramps."

"I completely understand." He made an effort to eat another forkful of eggs.

She paused and leveled him a hard look. "I'll do anything," she said in a low and serious tone, "to keep him on Rose Island."

He sensed that she was sending him some kind of unspoken message, maybe even an apology. But as far as he was concerned, she didn't have to be sorry for a single thing. "I'll do anything too," he offered.

"Will you?" Her brows rose, revealing the doubt in

her eyes.

"Anything." He didn't know exactly what she was asking of him, but he had the feeling he'd eventually find out. In the meantime, he'd go along with whatever plan she had in mind to make sure Hosea could stay.

"It would kill him to leave the island." Her statement was loaded with emotion, especially love, for the man who'd been everything to her. "He won't adjust to living anywhere new. I've already tried—

Footsteps descending the stairway cut off her words, and she busied herself again with scraping the pan.

"Good morning, Hosea," she said, as the gray-haired man shuffled into the room. "Your breakfast is ready."

"Thank you, Bella. I'll be back just as soon as I make a trip to the outhouse—" Hosea stopped in surprise at the sight of Nathaniel sitting at the table. "Well, good morning, Steele. I didn't expect to see you at this early hour. You've already turned off the light?"

Nathaniel glanced at Abbie, who gave a quick nod. "Yes, as a matter of fact, I did."

"Isn't it a tad early to turn it off?" Hosea's thick gray brows furrowed into one straight line across his forehead.

"The summer solstice is next week, Hosea," Abbie offered. "Since the days are getting longer, Steele's trying to conserve oil. That's all."

Hosea's attention shifted to the kitchen window and the bright sunshine coming in past the curtains. "Well, look at that. Guess it's later than I realized." He resumed his shuffle to the door. "No time to waste, not with all the whitewashing that needs to be done today."

When Hosea was gone, Abbie's shoulders slumped—in relief or defeat, Nathaniel couldn't be sure. "Thank you," she said. "I hate having to lie—"

"We're playacting. For him. There's no shame in that."

She studied his face. "You're sure you don't mind?"

"I'm positive."

Her eyes widened, revealing her vulnerability. She might appear strong and confident on the outside, but deep down, he caught a glimpse of her fear and pain.

As if realizing she'd opened herself up to him, she spun away and wiped her hands on her skirt. "I'm heading out to weed my garden before the day gets too hot." Before he could say anything else, she disappeared, shutting the door behind her.

He wanted to push away from the table and follow her and was frustrated that he could hardly make the chair move back a few inches, much less stand and walk after her.

"Patience," he whispered. He sensed that one of his strengths was patience. Now, more than ever, he needed to be patient. He'd made a few strides this morning with regaining some of his physical strength and his wife's trust. With perseverance, he was determined to reclaim them both completely.

Somehow, he recognized that chasing after her would only drive her further away. He wasn't sure how he'd accumulated such knowledge. But he realized he had to give her space and let her watch him from a distance before she'd learn he was trustworthy. He'd let her curiosity grow and her interest peak.

If he didn't reciprocate the interest—at first—that would help too. Maybe eventually, she'd even seek him out because she wanted to, and not because she had to.

Yes, he was a patient man. And he'd wait for her. As long as it took.

Chapter 8

Abbie coiled the rope slowly, letting the evening breeze sweep off the bay and add to her pleasure. She was taking a long time putting away her crabbing equipment in the oil house after drying it all day in the sun, but she was close enough to Gramps and Nathaniel that she could hear their conversation without them realizing she was listening.

Nathaniel was gaining strength each day. The first morning she'd helped him out of bed, he hadn't lasted long before needing to rest again. But after four days, he was finally strong enough to leave the spare bedroom on his own. In fact, after supper, at Gramps's request she'd carried two kitchen chairs outside, and Nathaniel had joined Gramps on the lawn, his first time out since his accident had landed him on Rose Island.

Now the two were playing backgammon on an upside-down crate Gramps had positioned between them. If they followed the same pattern of the past evenings, they'd play several games. Then Gramps would head into the parlor and ask Nathaniel to read to him from one of his Charles Dickens' books. Gramps had chosen a different book each evening, first *Oliver Twist*, then *The Tale of Two Cities*, and last night *David Copperfield*.

Abbie wished Gramps would stick to one novel from start to completion because she missed hearing the stories he used to read to her and Debbie. Since she wasn't much of a reader herself, she'd listened with rapt attention to Nathaniel from the stairs outside the parlor after she'd turned on the lantern. She could admit, Nathaniel was a good reader—maybe even an excellent one. He had a natural way of bringing the stories to life that drew her in, and she could have listened to him for hours.

When Gramps yawned loudly, Nathaniel would stop, put the book down, and let Gramps hand him the thick family Bible. Every night, Gramps would instruct Nathaniel to read from 2 Corinthians, chapter 5: "Therefore, if any man be in Christ, he is a new creation; old things are passed away; behold, all things are become new." And every night, Nathaniel read the same passage to Gramps without a single word of complaint.

Abbie was beginning to believe Nathaniel was a saint. Not only was he sweet with Gramps, but he was attempting to be kind and considerate to her too. He'd cleaned up breakfast the past two mornings. She'd come in from her morning chores to find he'd washed the dishes, wiped the table, and swept the floor.

Today, she'd made a short trip over to Newport. When she'd sold her crabs and clams to the fresh fish market, she'd asked whether there were reports of any missing people. She'd tried to remain vague, but at the same time wanted to discover if Nathaniel had family or friends who might be searching for him.

To her relief, there had been no recent reports or searches, which made her conclude that Nathaniel wasn't from the area after all. Perhaps he'd only been visiting.

While in Newport, she'd also inquired into a couple open maid positions. She'd been discouraged to discover how low the pay was. She wouldn't make enough to provide for her and Gramps, especially for the expensive pain medicine he needed for his rheumatism.

She hadn't been gone but a couple of hours at most, but when she returned, she'd found Nathaniel in the kitchen frying several fish and steaming the beans she'd picked earlier in the morning. To say his efforts in the kitchen had surprised her was an understatement. Even Gramps had been shocked to find Nathaniel doing what he called "women's work."

But Nathaniel had only laughed off Gramps' teasing and had winked at her. "I've been watching Abbie cook the past few days," he'd said. "And I've been taking mental notes."

What had been even more astonishing was how the meal had turned out. Even though he'd over-charred one side of the fish, he'd done no worse than she usually did.

"Furthermore," he'd explained once they finished dinner, "you both are working hard. This is the least I can do until I'm back to full strength."

Abbie wrapped the final portion of rope around her elbow and peeked sideways at Gramps in front of the backgammon game, once again amazed to hear his laughter. Not only was he laughing and smiling more, he'd had another lucid moment last night at supper where he'd recognized her and called her Abbie. That made two incidents in one week.

Of course, during those brief coherent times, he referred to Nathaniel as Nate—assuming that Nathaniel was the one she'd married in December instead of Nate. But no matter Gramps' confusion or moods, Nathaniel remained flexible and respectful and light-hearted with him.

It was almost as if Nathaniel's presence had a calming effect upon Gramps. The dear older man enjoyed having the male companionship, and perhaps even thrived on it.

Whatever the case, Abbie had been putting off telling Nathaniel the truth about his identity. That day when she'd helped him out of bed, he'd all but given her permission to continue the playacting. She'd gotten the impression the real Nathaniel, the one who had washed up on the shore, would help her anyway, whether he'd lost his memories or not. Besides, now that she knew no one—at least in the area—was looking for him, she felt slightly less guilty. But only slightly.

Every time guilt attacked her over her deception, she told herself that she'd tell him soon.

"Well, I'll be tickled pinker than a lobster belly," bellowed a voice across the water. The dark burly form of Zeke Crawford bobbed up and down in the middle of his low-lying boat.

Abbie dropped the rope and stared at the dory that was coming all too close to Rose Island. From the cylindrical baskets piled high in the hull, she could tell that Zeke and his two boys were returning from picking up their lobster traps. He was probably swinging by because he'd heard from Mr. Davis that her husband had returned.

Even though Nathaniel wore a hat that shadowed his face, all Zeke would need was one glimpse to realize Nathaniel wasn't Nate. While Nathaniel had several days' worth of facial hair covering his jaw and cheeks, her husband had sported a beard and mustache. Her husband had also been shorter and stockier. If Zeke suspected anything, he wouldn't hesitate to come ashore.

"What do you want, Zeke?" she shouted, fisting her hands on her hips and glaring at him. She had to make him move on.

"Just coming to see for myself if Mr. Davis was right about that no-good husband of yours finally crawling back home."

Gramps and Nathaniel had stopped playing backgammon, and Nathaniel was attempting to push himself out of his chair.

"You can see that he's here," she called as she strode toward Nathaniel. "Now go away. And leave us alone."

She had to keep Nathaniel within the shadows of the house, where hopefully his true identity would remain hidden. Nathaniel wobbled as he stood, and the chair almost fell over behind him. He grabbed onto the back and steadied himself.

"Are you all right?" she asked, coming up to him.

But Nathaniel was staring hard at Zeke Crawford. The muscles in his face pulled taut, and his mouth pursed into a grim line. He took a step forward, releasing the chair, but he faltered.

She latched on to his arm to hold him up.

"I see he's still drunk as a skunk," Zeke shouted.

"I'm not drunk," Nathaniel replied.

"You sure fooled me," Zeke called.

Abbie prayed the distance would mask the difference in Nathaniel's voice.

"I haven't had a drink since I've been back," Nathaniel said. "And I don't plan on it ever again."

"Once a stinkin' drunk, always a stinkin' drunk." Zeke's laughter rolled over the water with the waves.

Nathaniel's arm stiffened.

"Give him a break, Zeke," she yelled. "He's recovering from a head wound."

"We all know what caused that so-called head wound," Zeke started.

Gramps cut him off. "Nate's as dry as the cistern in a drought."

"What do you know, you crazy old man?"

Gramps peered out at Zeke and confusion rippled across his face. "Who is this character?"

"Zeke Crawford's the keeper over at Goat Island," she started to explain.

"That rascal Zeke Crawford? Why didn't you say so?" Gramps stood and raised a fist in the air. "I know why you want this island, Zeke Crawford. And I won't let you have it!"

Abbie stared at Gramps with an open mouth. Apparently, Gramps' declaration was enough to silence Zeke too. He barked orders to his boys, who began rowing away from the island.

As the dory headed east, Gramps lowered himself into his chair and returned his attention to the backgammon board, studying it as if he hadn't a care in the world.

Nathaniel, on the other hand, was staring after the boat with a frown marring his handsome features. He swayed again, and Abbie slipped an arm around his waist to steady him. She'd grown accustomed to touching him over the past week as she'd helped him in and out of bed and chairs. However, all the touching had been confined to his arms or hands. This was the first time she'd taken the liberty of putting her arm around him.

He didn't push her away but leaned into her as if drawing

from her strength. The long length of his body dwarfed hers, but as she'd proven, she could be strong enough for both of them. If only her husband had realized that...maybe he would have turned to her and confided in her instead of pushing her away. Maybe if she'd been more supportive after her husband had learned about his brother's death...

She tightened her hold around Nathaniel's waist. She didn't have to make the same mistake twice. Even if her marriage to Nathaniel wasn't real, she could offer him some words of comfort, couldn't she?

"Don't listen to Zeke," she said softly. "He's nothing more than a big bully."

Nathaniel slid his arm around her middle and drew her to his side. He didn't say anything, but she sensed Zeke's accusations had bothered him deeply, perhaps dredged up memories or at least feelings regarding his own problems and past.

"Whatever you were before," she said, "I can tell you're trying to be different."

He stared at the sea a moment longer before turning his storm-tossed eyes upon her. The raw pain there stirred her compassion. "I can't remember anything specific, but Zeke is right. I have no doubt that I was a lousy drunk."

"But you're not anymore," she assured him. "And that's what counts."

"Once a drunk, always a drunk," he mumbled.

She broke away from him and faced him head-on. She wasn't sure why she wanted to convince him that Zeke's words were a lie, but the need to do so was swift and strong. "That's not true. If we're walking down the wrong path, it's never too late to make a detour and start running down the right one."

"Heaven's sake," Gramps said from his chair. "You gonna stand there yakking all night, or are you gonna let me beat you again?"

Nathaniel studied her face as though searching for clues to his past there. She wished she could help him, truly help him find peace with whatever mistakes he'd made. But she didn't know anything about his life.

"Three more moves, and I'll have you beat," Gramps said.

Nathaniel tossed Gramps a smile. "We'll see about that." He nodded at her gratefully before lowering himself into the chair across from Gramps and focusing on the game, almost as if she no longer existed.

For a minute, she watched them, realizing she hadn't been ready for their time together to end. She hadn't wanted Nathaniel to go back to the board game with Gramps. She'd wanted to talk to him a little longer.

All week, she'd done her best to stay out of his way, never dawdling in his presence, keeping their interactions brief. In return, he hadn't been pushy or demanding. In fact, he'd seemed content spending time with Gramps and allowing her to watch from a distance, as she usually did.

But watching him from a distance had only stirred her curiosity and her desire to understand him more. And now with the warmth from his arm lingering at her waist, and the sadness in his eyes tugging at her heart, she was all the more interested in talking to him.

She'd witnessed what a fine, godly man he was over the past few days. Although she should leave well enough alone, surely it wouldn't hurt to talk to him more often. Would it?

His pointer finger tapped against his black checker as he

studied the board and Gramps' latest move. Then he scooped up the dice, tossed them in the cup, and shook it. As though realizing she was still there, he stopped mid-shake and glanced at her. His brow quirked with an unspoken question: *Are you watching me?*

The slight lift of his lips told her he already knew the answer.

She took a rapid step back, embarrassed by her interest.

"What do you think, Hosea?" Nathaniel shifted his attention to Gramps. "Will the presence of my beautiful wife help me win or make me lose my focus?"

It wasn't the first time he'd called her his *beautiful wife*, but for some reason, this time the compliment made her feel shy.

Gramps grinned like a young schoolboy. "I wouldn't be able to concentrate one lick on this game if Ruth were here, that's for sure."

Nathaniel emptied the dice from the cup, crossed his arms over his chest, and then looked up at her again. There was something in his eyes that caused her stomach to flutter, something she didn't understand, but that made her more keenly aware of the fact he was a very handsome man.

She tilted her head and tried to make herself appear as nonchalant as he was. "Thank goodness that women are stronger and don't fall prey so easily to a pretty face."

His eyebrows rose in surprise at her witty comeback. She spun away from him before he could witness her satisfaction. Sensing his gaze trailing her, she started back to the oil house, holding herself erect.

"We'll have to put your theory to the test," he said.

Her heartbeat stumbled, which somehow made her feet do the same.

"Soon," he added. The thread of humor in his voice told her she hadn't fooled him with her grand exit, that he was well aware of his effect upon her and liked it.

Abbie picked up the binoculars from the table and studied the northern part of the island. She thought she'd seen a flicker of light. But as she scrutinized the darkness with her usual methodical and thorough scan, she saw nothing but blackness.

At the shuffle of footsteps on the stairway below the hatch, Abbie spun in time to see Nathaniel poke his head into the lantern room.

"Hi," he said breathlessly.

She was too surprised at seeing him to respond.

He didn't wait for her permission to ascend the rest of the way, but instead he finished climbing—albeit slowly. As he attempted to push himself up, she debated whether to rush over and help him, but after the strangely charged interaction earlier in the evening, she wasn't sure how to act with him.

When he was standing, he glanced around with curiosity. "It feels like the first time I've ever been up here."

For all she knew, it was his first time, but she ignored the voice inside that told her to tell him the truth, that this was the perfect opportunity. She was getting good at ignoring the voice of reason. Since coming up to the tower and lighting up, she'd done little else but think about the way Gramps was responding to Nathaniel's presence. It was almost as if Nathaniel was the exact kind of medicine Gramps' troubled mind needed. Somehow, Nathaniel had become the key to unlocking Gramps' present memories.

After debating with herself for the past hour, she'd decided she couldn't say anything to Nathaniel. Not until after the three weeks passed.

If he was having such a positive effect on Gramps after just a few days, what would Gramps be like in a few weeks? Maybe his memory would return to normal. If his mind didn't become completely normal, then hopefully it would be good enough to continue to run the lighthouse. When Mr. Davis came back, he wouldn't care whether Nate was there or not because Gramps would be able to manage the lighthouse for himself.

Since Gramps had recognized Zeke Crawford tonight, then surely he'd recognize Mr. Davis and be able to have a regular conversation with him, which would prove to the superintendent that Gramps was capable of staying at Rose Island Lighthouse.

It was the perfect solution. Except for the tiny fact that she was using Nathaniel. She'd tried to console herself that three weeks wasn't very long in the scope of his life. Three weeks of helping Gramps. How could he object to that?

Nathaniel circled the Fresnel lens at the center of the room, angling his head and studying it, even though the rotating red beam blinded him. "I guess you'll have to re-educate me. Because I honestly don't recall anything about how this lens works."

"You didn't come up often." Her husband had only been up in the tower twice. He'd listened to her instruction well enough, and if he hadn't been drinking so heavily, he might have eventually developed into a proficient light keeper.

Nathaniel met her gaze and must have read the truth there because the muscles in his jaw clenched. "I was too busy getting drunk?"

"That was in the past."

His forehead furrowed, and he stared out the window. "I don't need any memories to know I wasn't living a good life. I can feel it in the depths of my being, and I loathe the person I used to be."

The discouragement in his tone wrenched at her sympathy, as it had earlier in the evening. "You don't have to be that person anymore."

Hesitation flashed in his eyes, almost as if he didn't believe her. Then he nodded. "You're right. I keep telling myself that this accident is my second chance, that this time I get to do better."

"And you *are* doing better." If he'd been Nate, he definitely would be doing better. In fact, if he really had been Nate, she would have been astonished at the transformation. And pleased. Not just for herself and their marriage, but because maybe then he wouldn't have suffered so much. Maybe he wouldn't have left and died such an awful death.

Nathaniel's gaze upon her intensified, and she had the feeling he would say something about them. So she ducked her head and busied herself opening the bronze door underneath the lantern. She might have convinced herself that it was okay to continue the charade for Gramps' sake, but she had to set boundaries with the playacting somewhere. And she wouldn't lead Nathaniel to believe there was any hope for them, when none existed.

She began to explain the inner workings of the lantern and pointed out the various mechanisms. He joined her in front of the lens, listening to her instructions carefully and asking intelligent questions. At one point, when his arm brushed against hers, the contact startled her, making her all too aware of his nearness. A strange feeling fluttered in the pit of her stomach similar to before.

When she paused and glanced at him sideways, however, he was examining the gears, seemingly oblivious to her. She guessed their nearness affected her more than it did him.

As a man of some wealth, she guessed he'd had interactions with plenty of women.

She, on the other hand, hadn't had many opportunities to socialize with young men her age while living on Rose Island. She'd met Nate for the first time last summer when she'd been taking her crabs to the market. The evening visit had been unusual for her since she almost always rowed over in the morning. But she'd been busy helping clean up after a coal barge wreck on the western side of the island and had gone to town much later than normal, at the hour when the fishermen were returning with their catches. Nate had been one of them, cleaning his dory after a long week of lobstering, and had noticed her coming ashore.

After their first meeting, she'd been flattered whenever Nate would stop by Rose Island to visit. She'd also been flattered when he'd called her the prettiest girl in all of Rhode Island. It hadn't taken him long to tell her he loved her and wanted to marry her.

She assumed his love and desire for her would be enough to hold them together. But she should have known it wouldn't be. A marriage was stronger with the love of two people gluing them together instead of one. It shouldn't have been a surprise that at the first storm, they broke apart into a thousand tiny pieces.

Unfortunately, she hadn't known the storm had hit. Nate hadn't told her until after the wedding that he'd gotten a letter earlier in the month from his sister-in-law informing him of his older brother's death. But Abbie should have seen the signs—his trips to the tavern, his showing up at their wedding half drunk, and the weeks afterward of morbidity and grief.

If she'd been a better wife, perhaps he wouldn't have felt the need to drown himself in his drinking. Perhaps if she'd been more loving, he would have found comfort with her instead of with the bottle. But she hadn't reached out to him, had been too busy taking care of Gramps and the light to pay attention.

By the time she'd tried talking to him about his dead brother, she'd been too late. Nate hadn't wanted to speak of it, had shut her out of his emotions completely. Eventually, he'd shut her out of his life as well.

Even so, she hadn't expected him to leave. Some days, she'd wondered if he'd grown so despondent that he'd decided to take his own life. She'd heard rumors that the body discovered near Brenton Point had no visible wounds to indicate murder. If no one else had killed Nate and tossed his body in the water, how else would he have ended up in the bay except that he'd drowned himself?

"Thanks for my first lesson," Nathaniel said, once she'd finished explaining how the vent worked. "Will you let me light the lantern tomorrow night?"

"Maybe."

"Just maybe?"

"You probably need to watch me do it a couple of times before you're ready."

"I'm a quick learner."

She couldn't disagree. He was bright, intelligent, and altogether too charming.

He gave her a slow but knowing smile, as though he'd read

her mind. There was something about his lopsided smile that made her feel out of kilter. Was it because he was growing more attractive every day, now that his face had lost its pallor and had a week's worth of sandy scruff? Or was it the teasing—almost flirtatious—way that he sometimes had about him?

Whatever it was, she found herself admiring him again, even though she knew she shouldn't.

"Go on now. You should get to bed." She turned away from him, irritated at herself for the direction of her thoughts.

"Okay," he said easily. "But I thought you might like me to read more of this."

She spun around to the sight of a thick book in his hand.

"But since you think I ought to go to bed..."

"Is it *Great Expectations*?" Her tone rang with embarrassed excitement. He'd been reading *Great Expectations* to Gramps when the boom of Fort Adams' cannon blast had sounded the time for lighting up.

"If I say yes, will you still tell me I need my sleep?" His voice filled with mirth.

She crossed her arms. He'd backed her into a corner, and he knew it. "You're still recovering," she offered lamely.

"Just admit it," he said. "You're pushing me away as often and as much as you can."

His candor took her by surprise. "Don't worry. It doesn't have to do with you." It had everything to do with *her* and the fact that she was lying to him and had no business spending time with him.

"I'm not worried," he said. "I'll wait. You won't push me away forever."

Something in his tone seeped into her belly, turning it into mush. "My, my. Aren't you prideful?"

"I like to think of it as confidence." The lilt of his voice and the directness of his gaze stirred the mush inside her, making her suddenly warm all over.

She stared out the window lest he glimpse her reaction, which was surely evident in her face.

"So, do you want me to stay and read, or shall I go to bed?"

He was baiting her. And she was tempted to tell him she didn't care, that he could do whatever he wanted. But she longed to hear the story too much to send him away. She reached for the handheld oil lantern on the tall table adjacent to the door. "Let's sit on the gallery."

She didn't wait to see his self-satisfied expression. Instead, she ducked through the half door to the gallery walkway. She rounded the lantern room to the place that gave the best view of the southern bay. Then she situated herself in her usual spot, with her feet dangling over the edge, and placed the oil light beside her.

A moment later, out of the corner of her eye she saw him lowering himself. The lantern sat between them. Even though she was allowing herself to spend time with him and wanted to listen to him read, the heated globe would keep them from getting too close.

As he opened the book and began to read, she let herself relax and lose herself in the story. She told herself that she was doing nothing wrong listening to him and silenced the protests that whispered in the back of her mind.

She wasn't sure how much time had elapsed when Nathaniel gave a yawn that was louder and longer than his last. He finally closed the book. "I'm sorry, Abbie. I guess my inability to contain any more yawns is the sign that I really must go to bed."

Sitting forward, she realized that somehow they'd ended up reclining against the tower and that the lantern was not between them anymore, that it was on the other side of Nathaniel. It had begun to flicker, the oil almost gone. She scanned the sky for the position of the moon and realized that hours had passed. She gasped and jumped to her feet. "I'm the one who should apologize, Nathaniel. I should have been paying better attention to the time."

He rose to his feet and winced as he stretched. "Once or twice, I thought you'd fallen asleep, but whenever I stopped reading, you always asked me to keep going."

"Next time, you need to stop sooner, regardless of my wishes."

"Next time?" His voice was sleepy but most decidedly flirtatious.

Without answering, she ducked into the lantern room and crossed to the hatch. She headed down the steps, making herself go slowly so she could brace Nathaniel if he showed any signs of weakness.

When they were in the second-floor hallway, she paused at her door and let him pass by. She half-expected him to stop with her and tell her good night or make a remark about what a lovely time he'd had with her.

But he continued on without a word. Through the darkness, she watched him descend, unable to prevent the strange longing that cascaded into her limbs.

As if he'd sensed her attention upon him, he halted, his hand on the railing. Though the oil light was dying, it cast enough of a glow for her to see his smile. "Until next time?"

She fumbled for her doorknob, managed to get it open, and stumbled into her room, closing the door too loudly behind her. She leaned against it and pressed her hands over her overly warm cheeks.

What was it about Nathaniel that caused her to react so strangely?

She shook her head to dislodge the thoughts and images of him. But even as she fell across her bed into a restless sleep, his playful smile was the last thing she saw.

Chapter 9

Nathaniel cracked another egg into the frying pan. As the egg hit the melted lard, he relished the sparks and sizzle that followed.

Abbie had overslept. By at least an hour. He'd heard her jump out of bed thirty minutes ago and rush to the tower to extinguish the lantern. He'd considered going up himself and turning off the light, especially because she'd given him such thorough instructions the past few evenings. Since he knew now how to turn it on, he could probably figure out how to turn it off. But he'd also figured that his heavy footsteps outside her bedroom would awaken her. And he hadn't wanted to take the chance.

After how hard she labored every day, he decided her sleep was more important than saving lantern oil. And he'd decided this morning to make her and Gramps breakfast. Each morning, his strength was returning, even if his memory was not. In fact, today after breakfast, he'd ask Abbie to give him something more to do besides snapping beans or shucking peas from her garden.

Not that he didn't want to help her with those tasks. But today it was time to take another baby step with her. He'd already made some strides. His plan to read to her had worked better than he'd hoped. Once they finished with the lantern, they sat on the gallery, and he entertained her with page after page from *Great Expectations*.

That was all fine and good, but he had to start enticing her a little more if he had any hope of winning her affection by the end of the three weeks.

He hoped to have longer than three weeks with her, that the superintendent would let them stay at Rose Island Lighthouse together forever. But if things didn't work out to remain, if circumstances conspired against them, he wanted their relationship to be solid. At least, he prayed it would be so.

The mackerel in the pan opposite the eggs sizzled too. He hadn't found any bacon and had decided to fry fish instead. With the long-handled spatula, he flipped the pieces, adding a pinch of salt and pepper as he did so.

Had he liked to cook before the accident? He didn't think so. Both Hosea and Abbie had acted surprised to see him in the kitchen the first time he'd made a meal. He suspected Gramps was right about the kitchen being the place for the womenfolk.

Nevertheless, he couldn't deny he enjoyed the experience of preparing the meals. Since cooking seemed to be one of Abbie's least priorities, he didn't mind taking over so she could focus on other activities she preferred. He glanced into the front parlor, where dishes and shoes and papers were scattered about in disarray. Cleaning seemed to be at the bottom of her priorities too.

Maybe he'd tidy up today. He suspected that he'd never cleaned in his life either. But how hard could it be?

At Abbie's light slapping footsteps on the stairs, he forced himself to concentrate on the pans. After she'd entered the kitchen, he made himself slowly count to five before casting a brief glance at her over his shoulder. "Good morning."

He focused on flipping the eggs with the spatula, even though he had the urge to turn around and stare at her. In that one glimpse, she'd stunned him with her beauty, as she usually did. She hadn't pulled her hair back yet, and long waves cascaded over her shoulders. The sunlight streaking through the curtains turned the brown a rich shade. Like a thick luxurious mink coat.

Mink coat? For a moment, the image of a woman wearing one flashed through his head. An older but elegant woman.

"You know you don't have to cook breakfast," she said.

"I wanted to." He tossed her another—hopefully nonchalant glance—although, once again, he wanted to turn around and look at her to his heart's content.

Patience, he cautioned himself. He had to let her come to him. Even then, he had to remain indifferent.

That premonition he'd had before came back, the one that told him he was well experienced with women, perhaps too much. Whatever the case, he planned to use that experience to his advantage with Abbie.

Her footsteps drew nearer, until she peeked around him to see how he was doing.

"What do you think?" he asked, flipping the fish almost perfectly. "Does it look edible?"

"Surprisingly, yes."

"Surprisingly?" Time to flirt. He widened his eyes in mock

hurt and spun to face her. "Your lack of confidence in my abilities wounds me deeply, my lady."

Her eyes were luminous, the green more visible today than the brown. He found the shifting color fascinating and was learning it helped reveal her mood. The brown was prominent when she was serious. The color lightened to brown-green when she was more playful, like now.

"You're full of surprises," she said, studying his face with open admiration. Did she like what she saw?

He combed his fingers through his hair, tossing the strands back in a way that felt natural and flirtatious at the same time. She followed his movements before returning to examine his face. He winked before shifting his attention to the sizzling eggs and fish, sliding the pans off the high heat before he burned everything.

She didn't move. He could almost feel her presence behind him, as much as he could feel the heat rising from the stove. He was tempted to push aside all caution, turn around again, and stare at her the way she'd stared at him.

Thankfully, the backdoor opened, and she skittered away, preventing him from coming on too strong.

"Another beautiful day," Hosea said as he entered. He shuffled to his spot at the table and sat down.

"I think I'd better head out to do my crabbing," Abbie said.

Nathaniel sensed her slipping out of reach again. He had to act quickly, before she distanced herself too far. "I'll go with you." He grabbed the pans of eggs and fish, placed them both at the center of the table, and scooped a portion of each onto Hosea's dish.

When Abbie didn't immediately reject his offer and paused with her hand on the door, he took hope. He scraped a piece of fish onto her plate and pointed at it with the spatula. "You're scared to try my cooking, aren't you?"

She was scared to try him too. But he refrained from saying so. He just waved his spatula again at the dish and dared her with his eyes to walk away without eating. She finally gave him a hint of a smile and returned to the table.

As with most meals they ate together, Hosea dominated the conversation, sharing stories about his adventures in the past. Although Nathaniel was sure by now he'd heard everything that had ever happened to Hosea, the man continued to relay different adventures, always entertaining them.

When the meal was over, Abbie helped Nathaniel clear off the dirty dishes. She dumped water in the pans but apparently had no intention of washing anything. He would have taken the time to scrub them, except he didn't want her to leave him behind.

Although she hadn't agreed to allow him to accompany her crabbing, she also hadn't outright objected. So he followed her down the rounded precipice, upon which the lighthouse was built, to the dock, where her skiff bobbed in the waves. He only hoped her lack of refusal meant she was beginning to want to be with him.

A handful of chickens ran out of the tall grass near the shore. As they approached, she tossed her baskets and buckets into the boat. He expected her to shoo the chickens away and was surprised when she knelt next to them and scratched their backs.

"Good morning to you, too, Daisy," she murmured.

"Daisy?" he repeated.

She avoided looking at him and reached for the next

speckled chicken vying for her affection. "Hello, dear little Rosie. How are you today, sweet one?"

"Rosie? Sweet one?" He couldn't contain the humor in his voice.

She frowned at him before turning her attention back to the chickens. "Don't mind him," she said loudly, obviously for his benefit. "He's one of those crazy people who thinks chickens are good only for one thing. Your eggs."

"Actually, they're good for two things. Eggs and eating."

The chickens squawked. "Hush now," she admonished. "You're hurting their feelings." At the flash of mirth in her eyes, he was relieved that she saw the humor in the situation.

The lightness accompanied them as they situated themselves in the boat. He offered to row, but she insisted. Once again, she surprised him, this time with her skill and strength.

Her knowledge of crabs and how to bait and catch them thoroughly impressed him. As with her instruction on how to run the lighthouse, she patiently taught him everything he needed to know about crabs: where to look for them, how to lure them into the trap, and which kind were the best to eat and which ones to let go.

"Let me row back," he said when they'd filled two buckets and were ready to return to the lighthouse.

"You're still recovering." She hefted the crab trap onto the tangle of other equipment she'd already piled in the middle. She reached for an oar, but he grabbed it first so that her hand clasped around his.

At the contact, her eyes widened, and she sucked in a quick breath. She stared at their touching hands. Although he reveled at the brush of her skin against his, he sank against the stern and tried to appear unruffled, the same way he did every other time they touched.

He liked watching her reactions and took secret pleasure in knowing he affected her with the merest brush of his hand or arm. His persistent efforts were slowly wooing her. But she was still skittish, and he couldn't rush anything, or he'd be back to where he was on the day after the accident.

He attempted to make his body relax, and he waited for her to release him. She stared a moment longer at his hand before lifting her gaze to his. Her eyes were a strange mix of wonder and warmth. If he didn't know better, he'd almost assume that she was an innocent unmarried girl who'd never experienced a man's touch.

As much as he wanted to pretend that her hand surrounding his didn't affect him, the longer she touched him, the less he could hide his true feelings. She hovered above him, and suddenly all he could think about was pulling her down on top of him, unwinding her hair, and sinking his fingers into the long thick strands.

Embarrassment flashed across her face, and he had no doubt she'd seen his stark desire. Her lashes dropped, and she jerked her hand away from the oar and fumbled for the closest item she could find—a rope.

She scrambled to her bench, plopped onto it, and started winding the twine into a coil, looking everywhere but at him. He clutched the other oar, sat forward, and dug both paddles deep into the water, needing to release the tension that was shooting through his muscles.

The plunge of the oars in and out of the sea, the rolling of his arms, the strain in his chest—it was all a welcome sensation—a homecoming of sorts. As with other things, he was certain that in his past he'd had plenty of experience rowing. He was good at it, almost as good as Abbie.

By the time he rounded the island, fatigue began to settle in.

"Looks like we have a visitor," she said, her forehead crinkling in worry.

He followed her sights to the dock and realized she was right. Another skiff was tied there.

"Who is it?" he asked, praying it wasn't Mr. Davis. Not yet.

"My sister."

Abbie raced up the beach as fast as her bare feet would carry her. She didn't care that she was leaving Nathaniel behind with the supplies and the heavy buckets filled with crabs. She didn't care that she'd rushed off without a single word of explanation. All she knew was that she had to reach Debbie first and warn her about Nathaniel.

As she sprinted up the last stretch of the bastion, she had visions of Debbie meeting Nathaniel and demanding to know who he was and why he was on the island. If Debbie did so, Nathaniel would realize she was lying about his identity. Then her plan to save Gramps would be for naught.

Panting hard from the effort of running uphill through sand, Abbie glanced over her shoulder, relieved to see that Nathaniel was still unloading the boat. She prayed that she'd have enough time to convince Debbie to play along with her. And that Debbie would be in an accommodating mood. Sometimes her sister was stubborn, though. Abbie prayed this wasn't one of those times.

"There you are," Debbie called as she came out of the

house, holding the hand of a little girl who was the picture image of Debbie's husband, Menard. Pollyanna was blonde-haired, blue-eyed, and fair-skinned compared to Debbie, who had the same tanned complexion and brown hair as Abbie. Although they looked alike in many ways, her sister was bigger boned, not petite like Abbie. Now, with her hugely pregnant stomach, Debbie appeared to be double the size.

"I heard you came to town. But when you didn't visit me this week, I thought maybe you'd drowned," Debbie said sarcastically as she waddled toward Abbie, a fist pressed into her lower back.

Debbie knew as well as Abbie that to drown her someone would have to purposefully tie her up, attach her to an anchor, and drop her to the bottom of the bay. Even then, there was the excellent possibility that Abbie could save herself since her swimming skills rivaled her rowing.

"I've been busy," Abbie said, trying to catch her breath.

"That's no excuse for not stopping by. You forced me to row out here in my condition."

"I'm sorry."

"At the very least, you should have sent me word that your husband was back." Debbie's voice was laced with accusation, and she glanced around angrily, no doubt looking for her husband so she could walk up to him and punch him in the face. "Instead, I have to hear it at the fish market this morning."

Abbie peered back the way she'd come again, praying Nathaniel would walk up the hill slowly. Really slowly. "I need to talk to you about all that." She smiled down at Debbie's daughter, who was watching them both with wide eyes.

Abbie bent low and gave her niece a hug. "Hi, sweetie.

Would you like to play with the new kitties?"

Pollyanna wasn't quite two years old and likely wouldn't remember her Uncle Nate from the few times she'd seen him. But Abbie didn't want to involve her niece in this situation. As Pollyanna toddled away toward the oil house and the kittens frolicking in the grass, Abbie tried to think of how to persuade Debbie to lie for her.

"Where has that lowlife been all this time?" Debbie asked as she watched Pollyanna kneel and pet the gray and white kitten.

Abbie swallowed her reservations. The longer she stalled, the more precious time she was losing. "He's not Nate."

Debbie's attention jerked to Abbie. She started to speak, but Abbie cut her off. "I don't know who the man is. He washed up on shore a week ago with a severe head wound and no memories of his previous life."

Debbie's mouth froze around her response.

"After hearing me talking with the superintendent, the man thinks he's my husband."

"So a wounded man believes he's married to you?" Debbie's voice rose a notch.

"And I haven't corrected him. Yet."

Debbie's eyes filled with horror. "You've allowed a complete stranger to live in your home as your husband?"

Abbie cringed. Coming out of Debbie's mouth, her predicament sounded not only scandalous but dangerous. "He's a very nice man—"

"Nice or not, you're crazy to do such a thing, and I insist you put a stop to it at once."

"But I've realized this might be the solution I was looking for to save Gramps."

Debbie shook her head vigorously. "I realize you married Nate because you were desperate to save Gramps. But now you've gone beyond desperate to insane."

Again, Abbie tossed a glance over her shoulder. Nathaniel still wasn't in sight. "Listen to me—"

"No. You listen to me." Debbie grabbed her arm and squeezed it. "I should have gone with my instincts the first time and stopped you from marrying Nate. I won't stand by again while you do something even more foolish."

"It's just for two more weeks," Abbie rushed to explain. "I'll tell him the truth in two weeks, but in the meantime, I need you to go along with me and pretend he's my husband."

"I'll do absolutely no such thing." Debbie's fingers dug into Abbie's arm. "You will tell that poor man, whoever he is, the truth today. Then I'll row him back to the mainland. It's not fair to him. And it's not safe for you. There's no telling what he might do to you."

"He's not like that," Abbie said. "He's kind and gentle and considerate."

Debbie's hand dropped away, and she narrowed her eyes. "I can tell you like him."

Blood rushed to Abbie's cheeks. "No, of course not."

"You've kissed him."

"No!" Abbie cried out in frustration, more at herself for her attraction toward Nathaniel than anger at her sister. Abbie wanted to deny that she felt anything at all for him, but she liked him more than she should. "I'm trying hard to keep my distance from him while he's here—"

"You better," Debbie said. "You're still a married woman. You're not free to like someone else. As much as I despise that husband of yours, I won't stand back and let you dabble in adultery."

Abbie debated for only an instant before realizing she finally had to tell Debbie the truth about her husband. "Nate's dead."

Debbie's scowling reprimand faded into confusion. "What? How do you know? When?"

"The body found down by Brenton Point last month. It was Nate's."

"They said it was unrecognizable, too far gone to identify."

"The pocket watch they found on the corpse was Nate's. It had 'To Crabby' engraved on the back, which was exactly what was on Nate's."

Debbie studied Abbie's face and then sighed. "Why didn't you tell me sooner?"

"I thought if everyone was still expecting Nate to return, then Gramps and I would be able to stay here."

Debbie shook her head in disbelief. "You're really something, Abbie."

"Well, my plan didn't work because after Zeke Crawford's meddling, the superintendent came to throw us off the island anyway."

"And so now you think you'll replace one foolish plan with another."

"Please go along with me for today."

"No." Debbie's lips pursed with the stubbornness Abbie had seen there over the years, especially during those times when Debbie had stepped in and acted like a mother. "I won't go along with your nonsense. Not at all—"

"Well, Debbie dear," Gramps called as he walked around the house, carrying a pail and paintbrush. His face was alight with an enormous smile. "When did you arrive? Abbie, why didn't you tell me your sister was here for a visit?"

At Gramps questions, Debbie's mouth fell open, and she glanced at Abbie with eyes full of questions—like how was it possible that Gramps remembered her name now, when he hadn't recognized Debbie at all during the past year?

"It's because of Nathaniel," Abbie explained in a hushed voice.

"Who's Nathaniel?"

"The stranger who washed up on the shore," Abbie whispered. "He's amazing with Gramps. Ever since Nathaniel arrived, Gramps has been more himself than I've seen in years."

Gramps shuffled over, set his paint bucket and brush down, and pulled Debbie into a hug. "You're as pretty as always, dear." He patted her cheek lovingly, apparently not noticing the tears that streaked them. And apparently not noticing how pregnant she was either.

"You look good, too, Gramps." Debbie managed a smile through her tears.

"It's all the sunshine," he said, picking up the bucket. "And of course, I'm glad Abbie's husband is back. He's such a good boy."

Debbie exchanged a glance with Abbie.

Abbie nodded. *Yes, Gramps thought Nathaniel was her husband.*

Reading her unspoken message, Debbie's eyebrow rose.

"I hope you'll stay for dinner," Gramps said as he started across the yard. "Nate is becoming quite the cook."

Once Gramps disappeared into the oil house, Debbie wiped at her cheeks. Yet the tears continued to flow. She tried to say something, but a squeaky sob escaped, and she cupped her hand over her mouth.

"That's why we need to pretend," Abbie said, emotion clogging her own throat. "Nathaniel's presence is working a miracle on Gramps. Maybe in two more weeks, Gramps' memory will return enough that Mr. Davis won't have any reason to make us leave."

Something caught Debbie's attention behind Abbie, and her eyes widened.

Abbie turned to see that Nathaniel was finally coming up the bastion, a bucket of crabs swinging in each hand and the crabbing traps draped across both shoulders. He trudged slowly but steadily. At the sight of them, he angled in their direction.

"Please, Debbie," Abbie pleaded under her breath. "Please don't say anything to Nathaniel."

Debbie wiped her tears, her attention fixed upon Nathaniel.

Abbie tried to swallow the anxious lump that wedged in her throat as Nathaniel stopped in front of them and lowered the buckets to the ground. He tipped up his hat to reveal his handsome face. Her husband had been good-looking in his own way. However, Nathaniel took the meaning of handsome to a new level, with his clean-cut features, even white teeth, and strong jaw.

From the way Debbie stiffened her shoulders and examined him with increasing agitation, Abbie realized that Nathaniel's attractiveness would only make her sister worry all the more.

"Hi, Debbie," he said reservedly, as if he half-expected her to lash out at him.

A frown creased Debbie's brow, and she looked as if she

wanted to punch Nathaniel in the nose and send him packing.

Abbie grabbed her arm and pinched her. Debbie jerked free.

"Go ahead and hit me," Nathaniel said, pointing to his chin. "I deserve it for how I've treated Abbie."

"No," Abbie said. "Please don't do anything, Debbie."

"You're leaving the island with me," Debbie said sharply. But before she could speak further, the sound of laughter caught her attention, and she pivoted to see Gramps laughing, holding Pollyanna, and kissing her cheek. The sight was so tender and sweet that once again tears began to flow down Debbie's cheeks.

For a minute, Debbie silently and tearfully watched the interaction between Gramps and Pollyanna. All the while, Abbie held herself rigid and braced for the end. Nathaniel focused on Gramps and Pollyanna, too, the muscles in his jaw flexing.

When Debbie turned her sights back on Nathaniel, the animosity was gone. Through teary eyes, she studied Nathaniel's face before nodding. "Okay. Two more weeks."

The tension eased from Abbie's shoulders at the same time that Nathaniel released a breath.

"I promise, you won't regret it—"

"If you hurt Abbie," Debbie said, cutting him off, "I'll track you down, cut you up, and turn you into fish bait." With that she stalked toward Pollyanna and Gramps.

Nathaniel wouldn't hurt her. Debbie had nothing to worry about. No, it would more likely work the other way—Abbie would hurt him once she revealed the truth. And the more she got to know and like him, the more she dreaded having to hurt him.

"I can tell your sister loves you," Nathaniel said.

"I'm sorry about her," Abbie said. "She's always tried to be a mom, ever since ours left, even when I don't need one anymore."

"I guess I was a lousy husband. Worse than I realized."

"I'm not sure that any man could live up to Debbie's standards for me."

"I'm sure planning to try." His words were quiet, but they reverberated through her heart and pulsed through her blood. Even though she had to separate reality from this charade, she couldn't keep from wishing his words were true.

For an instant, she wondered what would happen if she never told him the truth. What if she allowed him to live with her indefinitely as her husband? What harm would come of it?

Just as quickly as the thought came, she tossed it overboard and let it sink from sight. Maybe Debbie was right. Maybe she was crazy. Only a crazy person would think like that.

Even so, something inside her wished she had longer than two weeks left with Nathaniel. Suddenly, two weeks seemed far too short.

Chapter 10

Abbie pulled her skiff alongside the dock and felt a twinge of unease. After Debbie's visit yesterday, Nathaniel had been quieter and more reserved. Earlier this morning when they'd gone crabbing again, he'd been more solemn as well.

"What's wrong?" she'd asked him.

His eyes had been as deep and unfathomable as the sea. "Debbie hates me. Tell me why. I need to know exactly what I did to you."

Yes, Debbie had hated her husband. But she didn't hate Nathaniel, and Abbie wished she could tell him that. She'd been so consumed by her guilt over the deception that she'd given in and told Nathaniel how she and her husband had met, what the first couple months of their marriage had been like with his constant drinking binges, and then how he'd disappeared for the winter and spring. She hadn't resisted telling Nathaniel the truth, even though afterward she hated that she'd taken the dishonesty to a new level by allowing him to believe he was the one who'd done all those things.

"Where did I go?" he'd asked almost bitterly.

"I don't know." She hadn't been able to face him the rest of the morning and had given herself some space from him by going over to Newport for supplies.

Now she scanned the beach, noting that everything was too silent. Even the chickens were resting in the shade near old Fort Hamilton.

Something wasn't right. Where was Gramps? And where was Nathaniel?

Her mind spun with a hundred possibilities, none of them good. What if friends had stopped by the island and recognized that Nathaniel wasn't her husband and told him so? Or maybe Nathaniel's memories had returned, and he'd realized she was using him. Maybe he'd hailed a passing boat to take him away. Maybe he'd been so angry that he'd left without saying good-bye.

She unloaded the skiff as fast as she could. Then she hefted a bag over each shoulder and started up the hill to the keeper's cottage. With each step, a familiar fear began to grip her chest until she could hardly breathe past the tightness.

Too many people in her life had left without a good-bye. She had no doubt it would happen again at some point. Because, for a reason she couldn't explain, she seemed to have a knack for driving people away, eventually.

Had she already driven Nathaniel off?

By the time she reached the house, her throat ached, and her eyes burned from holding back tears. She dumped the sacks on the stoop and shoved the door open.

"Surprise!" came Gramps' voice.

She stepped inside and froze. Gramps wore his Sunday best

and sat at a table that had been set with Gran's loveliest tablecloth, fine china, and even linen napkins. A huge bouquet of island roses decorated the middle of the table, with a lit candle on either side.

Nathaniel's footsteps came rushing down the hallway from his back bedroom. When he entered the kitchen, she was surprised to see he, too, was attired in a suit, which apparently he'd scavenged from among Nate's clothes in the closet upstairs. The suit coat was short in the arms and trousers baggy at the waist, but he looked sharp anyway. He'd combed his hair neatly and had taken the time to shave, giving him a clean, gentlemanly appearance.

"Surprise," he said with a half grin. "I thought I had another minute, but you must have run up the hill."

She released her pent-up breath and wiped at the perspiration on her forehead. She didn't want to admit she'd been worried that he'd left her. Instead, she glanced behind him to the stove, where several pots were bubbling.

"It looks and smells wonderful." She smiled in return. "What's the occasion?"

Nathaniel's grin only widened, and he crossed the room to the sideboard. He opened the cupboard and pulled out what appeared to be a cake.

As he turned, she realized it *was* a cake. A lovely round cake that looked very similar to the pound cake that Gran used to make.

"Did you bake this?" she asked, her mouth dropping open in amazement.

He chuckled. "Yes, believe it or not, I made it this afternoon."

"How did you manage that?"

"I used one of Ruth's recipes."

"I didn't know she had recipes."

"In the drawer there." He pointed to the sideboard. "There was a box of them."

The cake was slightly lopsided, but otherwise it was perfectly golden. And he'd garnished it with the fresh raspberries she'd picked earlier in the day.

"It looks beautiful," she said.

His face lit up at her praise. "Let's hope it tastes as good as it looks."

"I'm sure it will be just fine," Gramps said squirming in his chair. "If we ever get around to eating it."

"You still haven't told me the occasion that deserves so much trouble." She glanced around the kitchen again and noted how orderly it was. Had he cleaned the house?

Nathaniel lowered the cake to the table and then stood back. "It's your birthday."

The clamoring in her head and the pounding of her heart ceased. She stared at him, at the hopefulness that rounded his eyes, at the clear desire to please her and make her happy.

No one had ever been so sweet. The thought of all the work he'd done decorating and preparing and even getting himself cleaned up brought a tender ache to her throat. "How did you know it was my birthday?"

"The back of Hosea's Bible contains a list of all the births, deaths, and marriages."

When she'd awoken that morning, the thought that she was turning nineteen had crossed her mind only briefly. She hadn't celebrated her birthday since before Gran had died. Even then, birthdays had been simple, nothing more than a special breakfast.

"Happy birthday," Nathaniel said.

Once again, her eyes pricked with unshed tears. "Thank you," she whispered, afraid she'd break down and cry in front of him.

"Why don't you take a few minutes to change your clothes," he suggested. "While you're doing that, I'll put supper on the table."

She did as he bade, although changing into her Sunday dress felt strange for a midweek meal. She supposed that if Nathaniel was from a wealthy circle, he was accustomed to wearing different attire to his varied activities throughout the day. Debbie's husband, Menard, worked as a liveryman for the Coles, one of the wealthiest families in Newport, and he often told them about how the rich lived.

Abbie's dress wasn't anything fancy. It was a striped maroon gown with a few ruffles. As she slipped on her stockings and shoes, the confines hemmed her in as much as the gown. She could admit she'd rather tuck up her skirt and run barefoot—like she'd done all her life.

Nevertheless, she brushed the tangles out of her hair, pinned part of it up, and left the rest down. As she examined herself in the mirror above the chest of drawers, she frowned at her reflection and wiped the streak of sand off her forehead. She drew her hair over her shoulders, pinched her cheeks, and then practiced a smile before frowning again.

Would Nathaniel think she looked pretty?

Although it shouldn't matter, suddenly it did. Very much.

With a final critical glance in the mirror, she left her bedroom and descended into the kitchen. When she entered, Nathaniel rose from his spot at the table where he'd been talking with Gramps.

"There's our birthday girl," Gramps said with a smile.

Nathaniel approached her, taking in her appearance from her head down to her covered toes. She was relieved that his face seemed to light with appreciation. "Although I shall miss seeing your toes for the evening, I cannot deny that I like this version of you too."

"Then I don't look ridiculous?"

He stopped in front of her and offered her his arm. The green in his eyes darkened to the color of lush foliage. "I may not remember much, but I do know without a doubt you're the most beautiful woman I've ever laid eyes on."

At the sincerity in his tone, her insides quivered like custard. She hesitantly took his arm, unsure of the custom but guessing in his world, handsome gentlemen escorted their dinner guests to their seats. The moment she tucked her hand into the crook of his arm, she was aware of his solidness and his nearness.

He walked to her spot, pulled out her chair, and after she was situated, helped to push her in. Once he sat down across from her, he smiled at her tenderly. "Happy birthday, darling."

Darling? The word rolled off his tongue and sounded completely natural for him, but was not the kind of word that a brawny lobsterman like Nate would ever use. Even if Nate had been at his best, she couldn't imagine him baking her a cake or planning a special birthday dinner with roses and candlelight and fancy chinaware.

As they ate, she couldn't calm the lapping waves in her stomach. She was much too conscious of Nathaniel, of the way he'd combed and slicked his hair back, of the smoothness of his cheeks, and the suaveness of his smile.

She was also keenly aware that his attention kept shifting

to her. The admiration in his gaze was frank and made her feel more beautiful than she ought. She ignored the warning that buzzed in the far recess of her mind, reminding her that the evening wasn't real. Surely there was nothing wrong in pretending for one evening, on her birthday, that she really was a beautiful woman.

After they'd lingered over coffee and cake, Nathaniel stood and held out a hand to her. "Now for your birthday present, my lady."

"A present?" She sat back in surprise. Sure, Gran and Gramps had always somehow managed to give her and Debbie something at Christmas. But the gifts in Abbie's life had been about as rare as the compliments.

She glanced at Nathaniel's hand to his long fingers. She couldn't accept a present from him, no matter what it was.

As though sensing her hesitancy, he reached out further. His eyes beckoned her, the invitation there too hard to resist. "Come on."

She slipped her fingers into his. As the warmth and pressure of his hold encircled her hand, shivers of pleasure raced up her arm. If the brief brush of hands yesterday in her boat had elicited a reaction, she should have known that holding his hand would affect her even more.

Mutely, she stood and waited for him to direct her, unable to think about anything else but the feel of his fingers surrounding hers. Thankfully, he didn't seem to be paying attention to her swooning. Instead, he was speaking with Gramps. "I promise I'll read to you in a little while."

Gramps waved a hand at Nathaniel. "Take your time, son. You and that beautiful bride of yours go have a good time."

A flush rose into Abbie's face, and she prayed that

Nathaniel wouldn't notice it.

Without releasing her hand, he tugged her up the stairs. For a moment, her heart stopped working. He wasn't thinking about taking her to the bedroom, was he? Once or twice in recent nights, when they'd come down from the tower after their reading times, she'd wondered what she'd do if he halted at her bedroom door. After all, he thought he was her husband. And as her husband, sooner or later he'd decide to retake his place in her bed. Wouldn't he? That was only natural.

Besides the fact that she was still repulsed by the idea of repeating the intimacies she'd shared with Nate, she couldn't let her relationship with Nathaniel go that far. It was one thing to hold his hand. It was another thing to share a bed.

She was more than a little relieved when he passed by her bedroom without slowing down. In fact, as he directed her to the tower steps, she felt silly for even thinking he wanted to go to the bedroom. She had to remember how naïve she was when it came to relationships. She'd never touched a man before marrying Nate.

Clearly, Nathaniel was more accomplished at being with the opposite sex than she was. He was probably used to women hanging on him. After all, he oozed with a charm that would attract women like flies to honey.

When he opened the hatch and assisted her up inside the lantern room, she stopped short at the sight that met her. He'd strewn rose petals on the floor, petals of all colors and shapes.

"I think I figured out why the island was named Rose Island," he said with a grin.

"Some say it's because of the shape of the island," she replied. "But I've always liked to think the wild roses gave someone the inspiration."

He was still holding her hand, and she couldn't stop thinking of how warm his fingers felt against hers. When he tugged her toward the door that led to the gallery, she followed and prayed he was blind to her reaction to him.

He'd spread rose petals over the catwalk too. At the end of the trail on the west side, a medium-sized package was wrapped in brown paper and propped against the tower.

"I've wanted to watch the sunset from the tower with you. I thought tonight we could before we have to light the lantern?" When he faced her, his eyes were soft and almost shy.

She smiled shyly in return. "I'd like that."

Finally letting go of her hand, he helped her to situate herself, with her legs dangling off the gallery like she usually did, only this time it felt strange having her shoes on. She was half-tempted to take them off and toss them aside, but after the thought and effort Nathaniel had put into the evening, she decided to remain properly attired for him.

"This isn't much," he said, taking his spot next to her and handing her the package. "But it was the only thing I could think to give you."

"You didn't have to give me anything," she said.

"A birthday without presents?" he responded lightly. "Who's ever heard of such a thing?"

Maybe there were always presents and parties in his world, but not in hers. Instead of contradicting him, she took the gift and unwrapped it. As she folded back the paper, she uncovered a wooden cross formed out of two pieces of driftwood.

"I crafted it over the past couple of days."

"You made it?" She fingered the grainy beams that had

been sanded and shaped into different lengths and then somehow screwed together.

"Of course, Hosea helped me."

"You did an amazing job."

He beamed at her praise. "I'm not sure how I got the idea, but I thought it could be a reminder to make God the center of our marriage as we move forward."

She turned the cross over in her hands and tried to ward off the guilt. How could they make God the center of their marriage when they didn't have a real marriage to begin with? Besides, even if her marriage to him had been real, Abbie wasn't so sure God wanted to have anything to do with her. If she couldn't keep loved ones from leaving her, how could she possibly keep God's affection?

"I obviously didn't have enough strength on my own to be the husband you needed and deserved," he said solemnly. "I've been thinking that maybe I lost track of the real source of strength."

His voice was so sincere and so full of hope she couldn't say anything. Not now. Not after he'd worked so hard to make the evening special.

"It's okay if you're not there yet," he said. "I understand. I've put you through a lot—"

"Nathaniel." Guilt made her voice tight. "Let's not talk about the past anymore. Let's put it behind us and not speak of it again."

He hesitated.

She fingered the cross again. "You said this could be a reminder as we move forward."

He didn't speak for a minute. From the base of the bastion, the sound of the crashing waves filled the silence.

Finally, his fingers folded around hers so that both of their hands were on the cross together. His touch, once again, was welcome. She wanted him to hold her hand like he had before and this time not let go. But he patted her and then crossed his arms over his chest.

When he smiled at her, his eyes had that teasing, almost knowing, look in them that told her he realized his effect upon her and enjoyed it thoroughly.

It's for the best, she reminded herself. Keeping some distance was good, and she'd do well not to forget it.

Chapter 11

"Pudding made from seaweed?" Nathaniel's voice rose above the crashing surf.

"Yes, it's called sea moss pudding," Abbie replied over her shoulder.

"Sounds disgusting."

She laughed and lifted her face to let the gentle mist cool her. The low gray clouds and the dampness were a welcome change from the past few days of high temperatures.

"Only a desperate person would eat anything made from seaweed," Nathaniel added.

"Gran used to make it every summer." Abbie bent down and scooped up a handful of the seaweed that had washed up on the shore. She tossed it into the bottom of the bucket she'd brought for the clams.

The second week of Nathaniel's stay had gone by much too quickly. With each passing day, she'd grown more comfortable having him there. After the special birthday dinner and evening, she couldn't deny that she liked him a great deal. No man had ever treated her so sweetly. There were moments when she watched him with Gramps or when she listened to him read that her heart fairly burst with her growing affection. And there were times when he looked at her with a smoldering in his eyes that sent strange sparks into her blood.

But mostly, their time together was companionable and even fun. After he finished his nightly routine of reading Dickens and the same passage from 2 Corinthians to Gramps, he always came up to the lantern room and read to her for a couple of hours. Then in the morning, he'd taken over extinguishing the lantern, allowing her to sleep later. Not only that, but he prepared breakfast every morning too, so that she awoke to the scent of fried eggs and bacon or fish.

He'd continued to go crabbing or clamming with her. And in the afternoons, he kept busy with projects—like cleaning the cast-iron stove in the kitchen, repairing her chicken coop, and fixing several leaky windows. He hadn't known what he was doing, but that hadn't stopped him from trying and learning.

She liked that about him, that he wasn't afraid to try new things and that he kept going until he'd figured them out. Of course, Gramps had always been handy and would stop his whitewashing to help Nathaniel in whatever project he was attempting.

She also liked that Nathaniel was kind to Gramps no matter where Gramps' memory took him. Nathaniel easily adjusted to being Nate or Steele, depending on Gramps' frame of mind. And he was patient whenever Gramps was grouchy from his aching joints.

The truth was, she enjoyed her time with Nathaniel much

more than she should. She'd all but silenced the voice inside that told her she should be honest with him about their situation.

"If you're good this morning," she said, "maybe I'll make you sea moss pudding later."

"You leave me no choice," he said. "I'll have to be really naughty." At his words, an enormous splash hit her back. She gasped at the cold water that soaked through her clothes and ran like a river down her spine.

She pivoted to find him scooping his empty bucket into a wave. Before she could duck or move out of the way, he flung more water, drenching her front as much as her back.

She gasped again, tasting the saltiness of the sea and shivering from the cold.

He stood with his bare feet apart, his trousers rolled past his ankles, and his bucket dangling from his hand. With his hat pulled low, his face was shadowed, but the grin that tugged at his lips told her all she needed to know. He'd splashed her on purpose.

"Was that naughty enough to spare me the seaweed pudding?" he asked.

She advanced on him several paces. "No. It wasn't naughty enough. I'll still make it for you." Then before he could move, she dipped her pail into an oncoming wave and threw the water at him. She'd forgotten about the seaweed already at the bottom of her bucket and was mortified when both the seaweed and water splattered over him, including on his face.

He stood unmoving for a full five seconds, letting the water and the seaweed ooze down his body in a slow trail.

Uncertain what to say or do, her insides quavered at the thought that she'd made him angry.

Slowly, he removed his hat, let it fall to the sand, and then swiped at the globs of slime that remained on his face. "I suppose you're attempting to give me a taste of what awaits later today?" His voice was calm as he scraped the seaweed from his shirt.

"Yes," she replied, "as a matter of fact, that's exactly what I was doing."

With his hands full of the stringy moss, he advanced upon her, his eyes gleaming and his lips quirked into a half grin. "Maybe you should have a taste of it too."

Her heart raced. "No, that's okay. I'll wait until later."

His smile inched higher. "There's plenty here for both of us."

Before he reached her, she lunged away from him and began to run. She considered herself to be as fast and nimble in the sand as she was in the water, so she was unprepared for Nathaniel's equal sure-footedness. He easily caught up to her, grabbed her arm, and spun her around. Before she could protest, he smeared the seaweed into her face.

She squealed and attempted to break free, but her efforts only caused them both to stumble backward into the rolling waves.

"How did that taste?" he asked with a laugh.

She swiped the slippery strands from her face and rubbed it into his. The surprise that lit his eyes made her laugh in return.

As he started to once again scrape seaweed from his body and fling it toward her, she tried to break free of his hold. But his grip around her arm was firm, and she only managed to pull them both down so that the waves crashed over and around them.

Spluttering and laughing, she splashed him. With his

laughter ringing in the air, too, he sent a spray of water back, until they were engaged in an all-out splashing battle. Unable to match his strength, she broke for the shore.

Breathless and weighed down by the water drenching her clothes, she couldn't move fast enough. He caught her and dragged her down once again. This time they landed in the sand, the waves crashing over their feet and legs. She expected him to splatter her with more seaweed or spray her with water, but instead, he sprawled out next to her, his back against the sand, his chest rising and falling with his own breathlessness and short bursts of laughter.

She rolled to her back next to him, totally soaked, her skirt twisted in her legs, sand and seaweed covering her. Her hair was plastered to her neck and cheeks, along with remnants of the slimy moss. She was a mess, but she'd never felt happier.

They rested side by side, catching their breath while the sea lapped at their feet. Finally, she felt him move and wished that their playful moment didn't have to end just yet.

"Was I naughty enough?" he asked.

She shifted to find him lying on his side, propped up on one elbow and looking down at her with a smile—a crooked, devastating smile that sent strange flutters through her stomach.

She couldn't keep from smiling up at him. "Exactly what depths of naughtiness are you planning to stoop to in order to avoid eating my sea moss pudding?"

He lifted his fingers to her face, and at the gentle touch, she sucked in a breath. He peeled away a strand of hair on her cheek. She waited for him to drop his hand, to fall back into the sand, to make another joke.

But his fingers moved to her other cheek, to another strand

of hair. He gently wiped it back, making her breath stick in her lungs, especially as his smile faded and his green eyes took on a strange murkiness that made her insides flutter faster.

"I have a feeling I can stoop very low to get what I want," he said in a tone that rumbled with something she didn't understand but that warmed her all the way through.

He trailed a finger from her cheek to her neck. Languidly, he combed away more hair, and in the process, his fingertips seemed to burn her neck. She didn't realize she was breathing faster and harder until his gaze dropped to her chest that was rapidly rising and falling.

Her blouse stuck to her body, revealing the curved outline of her womanly form. Embarrassment coursed through her, and she lifted her arms to cover herself, until she saw the stark desire and appreciation that radiated from his eyes.

Her breath caught again, and she waited for him to do something—although she wasn't sure what. When he tore his attention away and forced his gaze upward to her neck, she realized she was breathing even harder.

She was unprepared when, instead of his fingers grazing her neck again, he dipped his head down and his lips connected with her wildly beating pulse. At the heat of his breath and the tender pressure of his mouth, she gave a gasp that echoed above the waves. She arched upward and was met by his palm against her belly.

His fingers splayed through the thin linen of her blouse, burning her skin. His leg tangled against hers as he leaned into her. And his lips moved against her neck, leaving a trail downward to her collar bone.

She was suddenly almost frantic with the need to feel his mouth against hers. She wanted to lift her hands to his face, to his hair, and dig her fingers into the wet strands, so she could guide him and let him know how much she wanted his kiss.

But how could she kiss this man? Not when their relationship was based on deception.

Her body froze.

At her sudden stiff unresponsiveness, Nathaniel scrambled away, putting a safe distance between them. His face was taut as he raked his fingers through his wet hair, combing it off his forehead.

She sat up, drew her knees to her chest, and wrapped her arms about them. She didn't understand the waterfall of sensations rushing through her—especially the desire. It was unlike anything she'd experienced with Nate. In fact, she couldn't remember ever kissing Nate, except the foul-smelling, smothering kiss he'd given her after their wedding.

And now, here she was on the beach with a man she'd known for only two weeks, and she wanted to kiss him.

"I'm sorry, Abbie." He pushed himself to his knees and stared out at the waves. "I got carried away."

They both had.

"I vowed to myself that I'd take things slowly with you." His voice was low and angry.

His bold words flustered her, and she stared down at her toes, wishing she could dig her head into the sand as easily as she could her toes.

"I can tell that in the past I wasn't very affectionate with you," he said. "You didn't like my touch, did you?"

Mortification rushed into her cheeks and face, and she couldn't answer him.

"That's what I figured." He'd taken her silence as confirmation. But truthfully, she liked his touch a great deal more than she'd ever liked Nate's.

He was quiet, and the crashing of the waves surrounded them. Finally, she sensed that he'd moved to sit beside her. His long legs stretched out next to hers, reminding her of the heavy pressure when he'd draped them over hers. But this time he was careful not to touch her or brush against her.

"Abbie?" His voice was gentle near her ear. "I promise I won't touch you again until you ask me to."

She had the strange urge to protest. She'd never be bold enough to ask him to touch her. And he was a man of honor who would follow through with his promise, even if it pained him to do so. If she accepted his vow, then she'd be agreeing to remain platonic. That's exactly what she needed to do so that it would be easier to cut things off between them when it was time.

Why, then, did the thought of never experiencing another one of his touches disappoint her?

"Abbie, please. Talk to me." His plea was so near her ear that the warmth of his breath caressed her. All she had to do was shift slightly, and her lips would be next to his. She could brush them against his and give him the permission he wanted.

It was clear something was happening between them. But where would it lead? If she allowed herself to become involved with him now, she'd hurt him even more later. And she didn't want that. She almost groaned with frustration. Why had she ever let their relationship develop in the first place? She should have kept her distance from him.

It was clearly too late for that, and now she'd have to figure out a way to tell him the truth without driving him away. Maybe if they became better friends first… "You're right about everything," she said. "Let's go slowly."

He released a breath, and his body seemed to relax. "I can do slow. In fact, I'll show you I'm an expert at slow."

As they stood and retrieved their buckets and clamming rakes, she silently berated herself for allowing even the tiniest amount of hope that a relationship could work out with Nathaniel. Such an idea was ludicrous. Friends or not, he wouldn't want to have anything to do with her once he discovered how much she'd deceived him.

With a grim set of her shoulders, she reminded herself that she had only one week left before the superintendent returned. One week to figure out how to tell Nathaniel the truth. And one week to come up with a new plan for her and Gramps. She needed to stop wasting time watching sunsets and walking on the beach with Nathaniel and instead focus on what really needed to be done—and that was finding a way to take care of Gramps and keep him as happy as possible.

Nathaniel wanted to bash his head with his rake for being so stupid. Why had he allowed himself to kiss Abbie?

He plodded behind her, his wet clothes sticking to his flesh and chafing his skin.

He'd been doing so well all week. He'd teased and flirted and yet had always pulled back just in time. Why hadn't he done so today?

Stupid, stupid, stupid, he chastised himself. They'd been having fun, and he'd had to ruin it by deciding to get physical with her. Now, after working so hard to earn her trust and affection, he'd taken a giant step backward.

She glanced at him past the tangles of her long hair and gave him a tentative smile. He forced his frustration at himself aside and returned her smile. At least she wasn't too angry about his forwardness on the beach. In fact, for a few minutes, she'd seemed to take as much pleasure in lying together as he had.

What had happened?

He shook his head. It didn't matter. What mattered now was making sure he carried through on his promise to go slowly. He wasn't sure if he'd loved her before the accident had taken his memory. If he had loved her, he clearly hadn't shown it well enough for her to reciprocate. He suspected he'd been attracted to her physically, because she was a beautiful woman in every sense of the word.

Over the past two weeks of getting to know her again, he'd realized she was as beautiful on the inside as she was on the outside. She was loyal to her family, giving to the extreme, forgiving, patient, and persevering. Although she was somewhat shy, she'd begun to open up to him, and they'd had many enjoyable moments—including the seaweed-water fight he'd ruined with his overexuberance.

She stopped so suddenly that he almost bumped into her.

"What's wrong?" he asked.

She knelt down and brushed her hand along the sand. "Someone's been here recently."

He crouched next to her and examined the beach. All he saw was a strange indentation, nothing that seemed out of the ordinary.

She walked a pace and inspected another indentation. "Someone's been digging around."

"Maybe Hosea's done some of his treasure hunting over here." After dinner, without fail, Hosea took a pail and shovel out to the beach and dug in the sand for a while. Abbie had explained that he searched for hidden treasures he believed pirates had buried long ago on the island. Nathaniel had agreed with her, that if such digging made Hosea happy, he wouldn't interfere. Hosea always came back after about an hour, ready to play backgammon.

"Gramps hasn't dug on this side of the island in years." Abbie straightened and scanned the beach.

"Could it be an animal?"

She shook her head. "A couple of times from the tower, I thought I saw a light out here."

"So you think someone's coming ashore in the dark?"

"Maybe."

Somewhere in the memories he'd lost, he had the vague sense he wasn't originally from Newport, that he hadn't been born and raised in the area the same way that Abbie and Hosea had been. Even so, the stories that Abbie and Gramps shared about the pirates who'd made the bay their home were familiar, which told him he'd lived in Rhode Island long enough to hear the local lore.

As one week had passed into two without his memory returning, he wondered that he wasn't more anxious or curious about his past. Or about his family. He glanced at the signet ring on his finger. He guessed a family member, maybe his father, had given him the ring. But again, as in those first days, he had the feeling that the more he left buried in his past, the better. Perhaps he was a coward, but so be it. He was content starting over and building new memories, better ones this time.

There had been a few days, especially when he'd still been bedridden, when he'd craved a strong drink. The need for alcohol had parched his mouth and made his head pound. He'd been glad he'd been too weak to do anything about it and had prayed that his craving would diminish as time wore on.

He'd kept himself busy enough the past week not to think about drinking. Now, the thirst for it was almost gone. Just to make sure he wouldn't fail in his attempt to avoid the stuff, he'd decided he wouldn't row over to Newport with Abbie when she went to sell their catch of crabs and clams. He'd been tempted once or twice that week to go with her because he was curious if seeing Newport would jog his memory any further and because he genuinely enjoyed spending time with his wife.

But fear had held him back. Not only had he wanted to avoid the temptation to visit the tavern, but he'd wanted to stay away from any old friends or fishing companions who might cajole him into any revelry. As far as he was concerned, the more isolated he kept himself, the better the chance he'd have of setting a new course for his life.

He'd meant what he said to Abbie that night of her birthday when they'd watched the sunset from the tower. He wanted God to be his strength and hope. Left to his own resources, he suspected he'd fail again.

Apparently, he would need an extra dose of God's strength to help him keep his hands off Abbie. He swallowed hard again just thinking about how lovely she'd looked lying in the sand next to him, her wet clothes leaving very little to the imagination.

At a distant call from down the beach, Abbie stood and peered through the mist, her forehead furrowing in anxiety. Dropping her clamming gear, she started toward the figure heading their way. After a few seconds, she began running.

"It's Menard," she shouted at Nathaniel. "Debbie's

husband."

Nathaniel gathered the buckets and rakes and followed after her. His footsteps dragged with dread at meeting another person from Abbie's family. If Debbie had hated him, he guessed Menard would too.

By the time Nathaniel reached the top of the bastion, he was surprised to see Abbie exiting the house with a carpetbag over her shoulder. Her eyes were frantic with worry. "Debbie's having her baby," she explained breathlessly, still wearing her wet garments. "She's having a difficult labor and sent Menard to get me."

Nathaniel glanced at Menard, a thin, somewhat gangly man, who was studying him curiously. Nathaniel gave his brother-in-law a nod. But Menard didn't respond, except that his eyes widened behind his spectacles.

"I don't know when I'll be back." Abbie stopped in front of Nathaniel and peered up at him with her beautiful brown-green eyes. Though worry still creased her forehead, trust radiated from her eyes—trust in him. "Will you be all right taking care of the lighthouse until I return?"

The thought that she trusted him again after all he'd done filled him with such gratefulness that he wanted to reach down and kiss her full on the lips. He fought the urge and instead gave her what he hoped was a slow and even smile. "Of course, I'll be fine. You've taught me all there is to know. And if I have any questions, Hosea can help."

"Are you sure?" Her gaze dropped for a moment to his mouth, and something flickered in her eyes. Was she remembering his lips against her neck, because he was definitely remembering how delectable her neck had felt and tasted.

"I'll be fine, Abbie," he said. "I promise I'll take good care of the light and Hosea."

"Thank you." She glanced at Menard and waved to him. "If you want to go ahead to the boat, I'll be right there."

Menard nodded and turned to leave, but not before giving Nathaniel one last puzzled look. Nathaniel was relieved that Abbie was in too much of a hurry to make introductions to the man.

Once he disappeared, Abbie returned her attention to Nathaniel. She opened her mouth as though she wanted to say something, but then she quickly pressed her pretty lips together.

He waited.

When her sights shifted to his mouth again, heat speared his gut and spread across his middle. Was she thinking of asking him for a good-bye kiss? They were only a foot apart, but he decided he'd make this easier on her by moving in more. After all, he'd told her he wouldn't touch her again until she asked him to. In fact, he'd promised it.

He leaned closer. His promise didn't hold sway with kisses, did it? He'd only said he wouldn't touch her. He'd said nothing about kissing.

But even as he bent in so that they were only inches apart, he forced himself to stop. She tilted her head up, the anticipation in her expression growing.

Ask me for a kiss, he tried to silently communicate.

Her lashes dropped shielding her eyes, but not before he glimpsed embarrassment.

His gut cinched with need. But he held himself in check. Over the past days, he'd hidden behind nonchalance and indifference. But today on the beach, his passion for her had blazed to life for all to see. Now she knew how he felt about her, and it would be all too easy for him to show her again how much he cared about her.

No, if she wanted him, she would have to say so. His next move was by her invitation only. Once more, his patience would have to hold him in good stead.

"Good-bye, Abbie," he whispered near her lips but without touching them. Then, before he lost his resolve, he stepped back.

Her lashes lifted, revealing startled eyes. And dare he say disappointment?

He forced back a smile. It wouldn't be long before she came to him. When she did, he'd show her what she'd been missing and make sure she never hesitated again.

Chapter 12

Abbie lifted Pollyanna into her crib and brushed the wispy blonde curls off her niece's forehead. She stood back and waited. When the little girl's eyelashes remained firmly in place without so much as a single twitch, Abbie released a breath.

She tiptoed out of the closet-like room and into the adjoining bedroom. The curtains were pulled and the windows shut. In the late June heat, the air had grown stifling. Debbie reclined against several pillows in the freshly made bed. Next to the white of the sheets, her face was so pale it was almost blue. Her eyes were closed, but at Abbie's approach, they flew open. For a moment Debbie's face contracted with panic. But as she glanced down to the swaddled bundle that was secure in the crook of her arm, relief soothed her features, and a tender smile cracked her dry lips.

Abbie reached for the glass of water on the bedside table. She helped Debbie sit up and take several sips, and then her sister fell into the pillows, weak and exhausted. The bundle at her side gave a small grunt.

Debbie's arm tightened around her new baby. "He's all right?" she whispered.

"He's perfect." Abbie smiled at her sister and pressed a cool cloth against her forehead.

"Thank God," Debbie whispered.

"Yes, God saved you both." After two days of intense labor under the ministrations of the local midwife, Abbie had thought she'd lose both Debbie and the new baby. But in the early hours of the morning, Menard had been distressed enough to put aside his pride. He'd gone to his employer, the Coles, and begged them to send their doctor to help his wife. Once the physician had arrived and made an incision, the baby had been born a short while later.

"Go to sleep now," Abbie said. "You need to rest and regain your strength for your son."

Debbie's eyelids fluttered closed but then opened just as quickly. She grasped at Abbie's hand. "Thank you, Abigail."

Abbie caressed her sister's cheek but couldn't say anything more past the tight ache in her throat. She'd almost lost Debbie. The doctor had said if Debbie had bled another hour, she likely would have died.

Abbie didn't know how she'd bear losing one more person she loved. She bent and pressed a kiss against Debbie's forehead and offered a silent prayer of gratefulness.

"You need to sleep too," Debbie whispered thickly.

Abbie hadn't slept in the two days that she'd been in Newport, except for a few minutes here and there when Menard had been home. But now that Pollyanna was down for a nap and Debbie was resting peacefully, perhaps Abbie could shut her eyes too.

Even though she had an overwhelming urge to row to the lighthouse and see how Nathaniel and Gramps were surviving without her, she couldn't muster the energy. Maybe if she slept for a couple of hours, she'd row out later.

She stumbled into the front room of the tiny home. The house was in disorder, every room a mess. Debbie would want her to straighten the disarray and do a little cleaning. But Abbie couldn't make herself care as she tripped over Pollyanna's wooden blocks scattered on the rug.

At a soft rap on the door, Abbie attempted to pull her long, loose strands of hair into some semblance of order. She opened the door to reveal the next-door neighbor smiling at her sympathetically and holding out a covered dish.

"Hi, Mrs. Pinkie."

"I've brought Debbie and Menard dinner," Mrs. Pinkie said, as she pushed her way past Abbie into the house, heading in the direction of the kitchen. Her portly frame waddled as delicately as possible through the obstacle course of shoes and toys.

"You're too kind." Embarrassed at the clutter, Abbie grabbed a lone shoe, placed it on a kitchen chair, and then swiped at a few crumbs on the table letting them fall to the floor.

Mrs. Pinkie's nose wrinkled as she took in the condition of the kitchen, the dirty dishes on the sideboard, the stale bread on the table, the crusted pans on the stove. The older woman opened her mouth as though she might rebuke Abbie, but at that moment Abbie released an enormous yawn. She tried to capture it behind her hand but was too late.

Mrs. Pinkie's rounded face gentled with sympathy. "Now

dear, you need to get some sleep, or you're not going to be of use to your sister or those dear children."

"I'll rest now," Abbie agreed, eyeing the sofa in the parlor. It was piled with clothes and blankets and toys, but it was more appealing than having to climb the stairs to the low-beamed dormer room upstairs, where she'd stowed her bag.

"I'll come over for the afternoon and help around the house," Mrs. Pinkie said. "Then you can get a good long rest."

"That sounds heavenly." Abbie yawned again.

"It's the least I can do for Menard and Debbie after all they've done for me." The older woman stacked several dirty plates and made space for her covered dish on the table. The waft of crab told Abbie that Mrs. Pinkie had brought over her famed crab cakes. The recently widowed woman made a scant living from baking and selling her cakes, along with several other fish delicacies. It wasn't a secure income, and Abbie had no doubt that Debbie and Menard shared the little they had with their neighbor.

Mrs. Pinkie headed for the front door. "I need to return home and retrieve a few things." She glanced around the room, as if making a mental list of all the cleaning supplies she'd need. "I'll be back shortly. In the meantime, you just go ahead and get some sleep."

"Thank you, Mrs. Pinkie. You're a true saint."

The older woman smiled with pleasure as she let herself out of the house.

Abbie released the knot of hair she hadn't known she was holding in place. She let her hair fall over her shoulders and stared with glassy eyes at the steep stairs that would take her to a bed. For a long minute, she couldn't make her feet move to begin the climb. Instead she leaned back against the railing and rested.

At a soft knock again, she sighed and made her feet move to the door. "Why, Mrs. Pinkie," she said, swinging the door open. "That was fast."

Mrs. Pinkie wasn't on the front step. Instead, a man stood there, hands deep in his pockets, bowler tipped low. At the sound of her voice, he lifted his head and pushed up the brim of his hat to reveal a handsome face.

"Nathaniel!" At the sight of him, her heartbeat sprang forward in giant leaps.

He smiled tentatively, as though he wasn't sure he was welcome. "You didn't come home. So I was worried."

"How did you get here?"

"I rowed."

"But how did you know where Debbie lived?"

"I pried the directions from Hosea during one of his good moments."

"Then Gramps is fine?"

"He's busy whitewashing."

"Has he been taking his pain medicine regularly?"

"I've been reminding him and helping him with the dosage."

She sagged with relief—the relief of knowing that Gramps had continued his daily routine without her there. Nathaniel's calming presence was apparently enough. She didn't know how she would have managed without him watching over the light and Gramps. In fact, without his help, she wouldn't have been able to be here for Debbie.

"How's Debbie?" He glanced behind him nervously, as though he didn't want anyone to see him. Debbie's house was several blocks from the waterfront. Other than a few young children playing down the street, the neighborhood was quiet.

Abbie swung the door wider and stepped aside, making room for him to duck in. "It's been a rough couple of days," Abbie whispered, with a nod toward the open bedroom door. "But by the grace of God, she and the baby survived."

Abbie gave him the abbreviated version of Debbie's unending labor—first the hours of slow and irregular contractions, then the realization that the baby was breech, the midwife's unsuccessful attempts to turn the baby, and finally the doctor's arrival, just in time.

When she finished, Nathaniel's expression was grave. "I figured something must have happened to keep you away for so long."

She nodded, unable to stop herself from studying the smooth lines of his cheeks that tapered into his strong jaw. She remembered the way she'd left him, almost begging him to kiss her. Embarrassed heat streaked through her at the thought, and she prayed he'd forgotten about it.

"I noticed you were able to get the lantern lit each night," she said, fumbling for something to say that would cover her nervousness. She'd made a point of walking to the shore after sunset to check for the red rotating beam.

"I had a good teacher." His smile was slow, as though he knew very well the effect he had on her and was enjoying it.

"So, you haven't had any trouble?"

"Not in the least."

"Then it sounds like you're getting along fine without me."

He crossed his arms and leaned against the wall casually. "No, we're not fine."

"You're not?"

"I missed you."

Her stomach rippled with tiny waves of delight. Even though she'd been preoccupied with Debbie for the past forty-eight hours, her thoughts had returned to Nathaniel much too frequently.

"Did you miss me too?" His voice was light, but it also contained a thread of something she didn't understand but that made her stomach quiver again.

She finally lifted her lashes and met his gaze. "Yes."

At her admission, he smiled again. She loved his smile. She loved the way it teased her, the way it encompassed her, the way it made his face even more handsome—if that was possible.

She attempted to return the smile, but a yawn slipped out instead.

His brows furrowed into a frown. "You're tired."

"Mrs. Pinkie, the neighbor, is coming over to help so that I can sleep."

"Then I'll go." He waved at the door. "Now that I know you, Debbie, and the baby are fine, I'll be able to rest easier tonight."

She didn't want him to leave yet. "Stay." The one-word plea came out before she could stop it.

His eyes widened, but he didn't say anything.

Mortification rushed through her. Why had she asked him to stay? Certainly not because she wanted to be with him. "I mean, *I'm* planning to *stay* for a day or two more. I hope you don't mind. That is, I hope you're willing to take care of Gramps and the lantern..."

"Don't worry about anything," he replied. "I'll handle everything for as long as you need me to."

"Thank you," she whispered, staring down at her bare

toes. "I don't know what I'd do without you."

"Abbie," he said softly. "I'm not running away again."

Her heart jumped into her throat.

"I promise."

Had he seen inside to her insecurities and fears?

"I still have a long way to go before I regain your trust, but I hope I can prove to you this week that I'm reliable and that you can depend on me."

She nodded.

He was silent for a moment. "Since Hosea is busy whitewashing, maybe I don't have to rush back..."

"Then maybe I don't have to rush off to bed..."

He glanced to the sofa and the wingback chair.

Out the front window, Abbie caught sight of Mrs. Pinkie exiting her house, a bucket filled with cleaning supplies in one hand and a broom and mop in the other.

Abbie pulled back with a spurt of anxiety. Even though Mrs. Pinkie had never met her late husband and wouldn't question Nathaniel's identity, the fewer the people who saw Nathaniel, the better. She'd already deceived enough people and couldn't bear the thought of perpetuating the lies with anyone else.

Besides, she didn't want to spend time with Nathaniel under Mrs. Pinkie's watchful eye. They wouldn't have much time together as it was, and she most certainly didn't want to share his attention with Mrs. Pinkie. Because, of course, Nathaniel would be too polite to exclude the dear grandmotherly lady from their conversation.

Without thinking, Abbie started up the steps. "The neighbor's returning. Hurry. Let's hide."

Nathaniel didn't protest but instead raced after her. They'd barely climbed into the slanted dormer room when the front door opened.

The triangular attic ceiling was high enough in the middle for standing. But even there, Nathaniel had to duck his head. A single bed in a rusty frame stood against one of the flat walls. Above the bed was a high circular window that allowed in some light. On the opposite wall was a cedar chest where she'd deposited her bag. Her garments and other toiletries lay scattered on the chest and floor.

Nathaniel surveyed the room. "This is your—"

She cut him off with a curt shake and a finger to her lips. She cocked her head to the stairs, hoping he'd read her warning not to let Mrs. Pinkie hear them.

With a silent tread that would have put the most daring of spies to shame, Nathaniel crossed to the door and closed it. Then for a long moment, they both held themselves motionless. As the clanking and thumps of Mrs. Pinkie's cleaning efforts rose, Abbie turned to Nathaniel with a smile. "We're safe."

"Well that's a relief," he whispered. "If I didn't know better, I'd assume she's a fire-breathing dragon who'd like nothing better than to catch us and roast us for her dinner."

Abbie laughed softly.

"Or more likely, I used to be an ogre and now Mrs. Pinkie can't stand me?" The hint of frustration in his tone rapidly wiped away her mirth. Did he think she was ashamed of him?

"It's not like that," she whispered, lowering herself to the bed. Was it finally time to tell him the truth? She couldn't let him continue burdening himself with Nate's mistakes. With a heavy heart, she patted the bed. "Come on. Sit down."

He hesitated. The shadows of the room and his hat hid

his expression.

She scooted up onto the bed so that her back rested against the headboard. She left plenty of space for him to sit next to her and stretch out his legs. The thought flitted through her mind that maybe a bed wasn't the best place to have this conversation, but she pushed it aside and attempted to bolster herself with determination for what she had to do.

"Please, Nathaniel."

He soundlessly crossed the room and lowered himself until he was barely perched on the edge of the bed, holding himself rigidly.

"Let's talk."

Still, he didn't move.

She stared at his back, at the blond waves curling over his collar. She was half-tempted to toss off his hat and comb those strands with her fingers. But she wasn't bold enough. Besides she needed to reserve her courage for the task ahead.

He held himself unbending for an interminable moment so that she almost began to think he was going to get up and leave. Finally, cautiously, he scooted back until he was sitting just as stiffly against the headboard. Even though the narrow bed didn't afford them much room, he was careful to keep his arms and legs from brushing hers.

"Nathaniel," she started, trying to squelch the fears that suddenly surfaced. There was no easy way to go about breaking the news to him. No matter what she said or how she said it, he would be furious at her deception. What if he was so angry, he decided not to go back to the lighthouse? She'd have no one to take care of Gramps or the lighthouse. She'd either have to leave Gramps alone or abandon Debbie in her moment of need.

Neither was a possibility.

She swallowed the words she knew she must say. She'd have to wait to tell him.

Nathaniel could hardly breathe. Didn't she realize what an enticing situation she'd put them in by sitting in bed? Even if he did pride himself on his patience and perseverance, he wasn't a saint.

"What did you want to talk about?" he asked, needing to somehow distract himself from this predicament.

"Nothing in particular," she responded.

He'd been sure she had something in mind, something related to his shame regarding Mrs. Pinkie's obviously poor opinion of him. The neighbor probably hated him as much as Debbie did. "Are you sure?"

She nodded, then smothered a half-yawn. "Tell me everything you've done over the past two days."

At the softness of her voice, he was all the more keenly aware of the softness of her body that spread out near him. But apparently she had no clue that she posed such a great temptation to him, to the promise he'd made that he wouldn't touch her again unless she asked. Because every muscle in his body tensed with the need to lay down next to her, wrap her in his arms, and crush her body to his.

"I did some crabbing both mornings," he whispered, slanting his gaze to her legs where her skirt had twisted higher, revealing her shapely calves and ankles. *Oh, God*, he silently prayed, closing his eyes against the sight. *Lead me not into temptation*.

"Did you have a good catch?" Her shoulder brushed

against his arm.

He clenched his jaw and forced himself not to lean into her. This was agonizing. Maybe it would have been better to leave rather than fight his wayward desire. He shouldn't have gotten onto the bed with her. Maybe if he sat on the floor. Maybe the hard wood would drive some sense into him.

Before he could move, she rested her head against his shoulder. Her loose hair tickled his chin, beckoning him to run his fingers through the strands flowing down about her the way he loved.

He held himself still for another long moment, but there was no way he would be able to sit next to her and talk. He could sit next to her and kiss her. He could sit next to her and caress her. He could sit next to her and hold her. But he could not sit next to her in a bed and talk.

"Abbie." His whisper was strained. "I think I should move."

She didn't respond.

When he glanced down, her eyes were closed. Her long lashes fanned out against the dark circles that had formed. Her breathing was slow and even.

She was asleep.

The tension eased from his muscles, and he relaxed. He waited a few moments, wanting to make sure she was indeed slumbering. Then he started to extricate himself.

He'd moved less than an inch, when her hand slid across his abdomen and seared his flesh. She nuzzled her face into his arm. "Don't leave," she whispered. Her eyes were still shut, and he wasn't sure if she was awake or not.

His body was pinned in place by her fingers against his stomach. As he stared at her hand, the pressure and heat was all he could think about.

With a growing sense of panic at his weakness, he looked at the door. He had to get away from her before he did something crazy.

He counted to five and then slowly tried to remove himself one more time. But as he moved, she slid her hand further around his waist. "Hold me, Nathaniel."

Hold me. The soft request pulsed through him, pumping harder until it was all he heard. He'd told her that if she wanted his touch, she'd have to ask him. And she had. Hadn't she?

He glanced down at her face, to the tired lines now smoothed in slumber. Had she really asked him, or was she only speaking in her sleep?

As though sensing his question, her lashes lifted, revealing her eyes, which were more green than brown. For just an instant, he caught sight of her desire and knew that she'd invited him into her arms, that this was no dream-induced request.

Without wasting another moment, he cast aside his reservations and scooted down to the pillow, pulling her with him and tugging her close. She offered no resistance, but instead curled there as eagerly as a purring kitten.

He wrapped his other arm around her so that she fit against his side, her hand still resting on his stomach, her head against his chest.

She closed her eyes again and exhaled.

After a moment, he closed his eyes and breathed out his contentment too. This was home. He felt it deep in his soul. He couldn't be sure of much else in his life. But this was where he belonged.

He'd missed her so much in the two days she'd been gone that he'd nearly gone crazy with the need to see her. The last hour on the island, he'd resorted to pacing back and forth in the sand near the dock, until finally he'd pushed aside the fears that had kept him from rowing into Newport. He'd been desperate enough to see her that he'd been willing to face the ghosts that lingered from the past.

When his feet had landed on the dock in Newport, he'd expected the longing for a strong drink to rise and beckon him to the nearest tavern, but he hadn't felt anything but an urgency to see her. Of course, he'd tipped his hat low and avoided the main thoroughfares.

He'd told himself he would keep his stay short, that he needed to find out for himself if she was doing okay. But what he'd really wanted was the reassurance that she still cared about him. That the last few days together on the island hadn't just been wishful thinking on his part.

He tightened his arms around her and basked in the sweet sensations coursing through his veins. This was better than he could have imagined. Yes, she'd been sleep deprived. And yes, she'd just gone through a difficult experience with almost losing her sister. But she'd asked him to hold her.

Her invitation was a bigger answer to prayer than he could have asked for.

He wasn't sure how long he laid with her, holding her and listening to her gentle breathing. But when the neighbor woman exited the house awhile later, Nathaniel realized it was his chance to sneak out undetected. As much as he wanted to stay with Abbie through the evening and hold her all night long, he couldn't shirk his responsibilities, especially since she was depending upon him to take care of Hosea and light the lantern.

Slowly, he slipped away from her. This time she was sleeping deeply enough that she didn't protest. Once standing, he couldn't make himself leave the side of her bed. He stared down at her, so delicate and beautiful but so strong. She'd survived a great deal in her life and had only grown stronger as a result.

After tearing himself away, he returned through town and slinked through the shadows, still not ready to face the awkwardness that was sure to ensue when old acquaintances realized that he didn't recognize them anymore. He didn't want to deal with that yet. Maybe never. Was there anything wrong with hibernating on Rose Island and living in obscurity? As long as he had Abbie, that's all that mattered.

Along the marina, he quickly found Abbie's skiff. The wharf was busy with fishermen beginning to come in with their daily catch, along with those who were returning from a day of pleasure sailing. He positioned himself at the oars, pulled his hat down, and was relieved to leave the bustling harbor behind.

Even so, he couldn't keep from studying several passing yachts. His pulse quickened at the sight, especially when he realized he understood everything about them and their magnificent sails. He had the distinct impression that he'd have no trouble sailing one, should he ever have the opportunity.

How did a simple lobsterman turned lighthouse keeper have such knowledge? Such luxurious sailboats belonged to the wealthy, who could afford to own and race them. Perhaps he'd been a part of the hired crew on a yacht at one time?

A wave rose, and the spray splashed him in the face. He plunged his oars deeper, and as he did, he saw himself standing in a yacht with the rain and waves battering him. Empty brandy bottles rolled around at his feet and clinked together as the thunder cracked overhead.

The memory was so vivid, Nathaniel could picture it almost as if he was sailing again.

He bumped up his hat and peered again at the vessels moored in the harbor. Suddenly, he knew he'd been on a yacht when he'd had his accident. He couldn't remember why or with whom, but he'd been in a storm, had been working to bring the yacht to safety, and had been hit in the head by the boom and knocked overboard.

Which of the enormous boats had he been on?

They were too far distant now to examine closely. Perhaps next time he was in Newport he'd walk along the docks and see if any vessels sparked his memory further. At the very least, he'd have to ask Abbie about the connection to the yachting. She'd surely be able to fill in everything he needed to know.

Chapter 13

Abbie had hoped that Nathaniel would row back over to see her the next afternoon, and when he didn't, she was disappointed—more so than she wanted to admit.

She spent most of her time taking care of Pollyanna, along with preparing meals and attending to Debbie and the baby's needs. She tried to do so cheerfully. But with each day she was gone from the island, she felt herself wither like a rose cut from its life source.

She told herself she just missed rowing in her boat and being outside with the warm sea breeze against her skin. But even during the couple of times that she'd walked down to the shore with Pollyanna, the sunshine and the water and the breeze hadn't brought her their usual comfort.

When she'd peered across Newport Bay to her distant island home, she'd realized she had to stop denying the truth. Yes, she missed being home. But she missed Nathaniel more.

Had she really asked him to hold her?

The brazen request made her flush every time she thought about it. She supposed she'd been too tired to think clearly. She didn't remember much of what had transpired, except that he'd stretched out next to her and gathered her in his arms. The last thing she recalled hearing was the steady thump of his heartbeat against her ear. When she'd lain in bed ever since, she'd had the overpowering desire to have him next to her again.

It was a strange feeling, one she'd never had with Nate. In fact, she'd always felt the opposite—an overwhelming sense of relief when he hadn't joined her in bed.

Whatever the case, she had to keep her distance when she next saw Nathaniel. After all, the three-week trial was coming to an end. Mr. Davis would visit the island soon. Hopefully, he'd arrive when Gramps was thinking clearly and living in the present. Maybe the superintendent would even conclude that Gramps' senility wasn't an issue and give them permission to stay. She wasn't sure how she'd explain to Mr. Davis who Nathaniel was. And after passing up her chance to tell Nathaniel the truth during his visit, she had no idea how or when to bring it up with him either.

But she still had a few days to figure something out.

In the meantime, the separation from Nathaniel was for the best, even though she couldn't stop wishing he'd come again.

On her fifth day in Newport, when a soft rap sounded on the door in the middle of the afternoon, she opened it, expecting to find another neighbor bringing a meal. But at the sight of Nathaniel standing on the stoop, his hat pulled low again, her stagnant pulse charged forward like a sail catching the wind.

She had the urge to fling herself into his arms, especially when he adjusted his hat so that she saw his eyes. They were bright green and alive and full of energy. Standing there, he was suddenly larger than life. With a scruffy layer of unshaven stubble covering his jaw, he looked less like a gentleman and more like a rugged light keeper—an incredibly good-looking light keeper.

He didn't say anything, but a slow smile curved his lips, almost as though he'd read her thoughts about his appearance. "Hi," he said simply, but the one word ricocheted through her, only amplifying how much she'd missed him.

"Hi."

He looked at her again, and the twinkle in his eyes told her he was remembering their last time together and how she'd wanted to be with him, even to the point of inviting him up to her bedroom and lying with him in her bed.

Was he expecting her to drag him upstairs and jump into bed again?

From his crooked smile, she guessed that the thought had crossed his mind. Did he think that after one encounter, she'd be like clay in his hands, that he'd be able to flash a smile and mold her any way he wanted?

She was stronger than that, wasn't she?

"I came by to see how Debbie is doing," he said.

"She's improving every day."

"And the baby?"

"They named him Henry after Menard's employer, Henry Cole. For helping to save the baby's life."

"Henry Cole." Nathaniel's brow furrowed. "That name sounds familiar."

Did Nathaniel have a connection with Henry Cole

somehow? "Everyone knows it," she said. "The Coles are the wealthiest family in Newport."

Nathaniel stared down the street into the distance. What did he remember?

Nervousness rippled around her stomach. What if his visits to Newport began to unearth his memories before she could gather the confidence to talk to him?

"So baby Henry is healthy?" he asked.

"Healthy but noisy. Now that he's more alert, we've discovered that he has a very good pair of lungs."

"I don't suppose that means he's keeping you from getting enough sleep?" Nathaniel's attention shifted back to her, and his eyes danced with mirth. "Maybe you could use a nap this afternoon."

The possibility of lying down and snuggling into the crook of his arm was more than a little appealing. She'd gotten up twice the previous night to rock Henry back to sleep, and she was tired after chasing Pollyanna around all morning.

But she only shook her head and tried to give him an innocent smile, pretending not to know what he was referring to. "No, I wasn't planning on any naps for myself this afternoon." Even though now would have been the perfect opportunity, since Pollyanna was once again sleeping.

"My arm makes a good headrest," he said, and this time something besides humor flashed in his eyes.

"I'll keep that in mind."

His smooth smile slid back into place, making her stomach do a crazy tumble. "Remember, all you have to do is ask again."

"I was exhausted last time you came," she explained, trying to cover her embarrassment. "I promise I won't throw myself at you this time."

"That's one promise I won't hold you to."

The longer their conversation continued, the more she realized she was entirely out of her league bantering with him. He was practiced at the art of flirtation in a way she never would be. To keep from making a fool of herself, she changed the subject. "How's Gramps doing?"

"He's asked about you and Debbie and the new baby several times."

"He has?" Delight coursed through her. Before Nathaniel had arrived, Gramps hardly recognized her or Debbie. And now he was inquiring after them both *and* the baby? All the more reason for making a case with Mr. Davis that Gramps' was well enough to retain the keeper position. It would be worth a chance. At the very least, she had nothing to lose.

"He's doing really well," Nathaniel said, confirming her thoughts.

"Because you're so good with him."

Nathaniel shrugged. "He's a joy to be with."

"Then it sounds like the two of you don't need me to return anytime soon." She leaned against the door frame with the casualness she'd seen him exhibit from time to time.

He swiped off his hat and stepped into the doorway next to her. There wasn't enough room for both of them to crowd together, but he stood there anyway, a mere inch away. He reached over her head, placed his palm against the door frame above her, and leaned in even more. His nostrils flared and something hot sparked in his eyes.

"Don't think for a minute I like being apart," he whispered thickly. "I'm going crazy without you."

Her knees buckled, and she had to hold onto the wooden

trim to keep from slipping down and turning into a puddle on the floor.

"You'd better be coming home soon." His sights drifted languidly around her face, leaving a trail, almost as if he'd caressed her with his fingers.

Her breath hitched.

"Are you?" he asked.

"Am I what?" She couldn't keep herself from staring at his mouth, even white teeth, firm lips, and strong chin.

"Coming home soon?" Those lips lifted into a lopsided smile as though, once again, he sensed the power he had over her.

She was almost tempted to fan her hot cheeks. Instead, she ducked under his arm and backed into the parlor, needing to put space between them. "I might be able to come home in a few days."

"That's too long." His voice was low.

They'd only been together a few minutes, and already the air between them was heated. She had to cool things down, and quickly.

"Menard's mother sent a telegram." She sat down on the sofa, making sure a pile of unfolded clothes provided a barrier next to her. "She'll be arriving this weekend."

Nathaniel lowered himself to the opposite side of the laundry, leaned back, and crossed his legs at the ankles. "I don't know how I'll last to the weekend without you, but I shall try."

How was it possible for him to stay so calm? She couldn't. Not when she was so keenly aware of his every word and every movement.

Thankfully, he refrained from any further flirting. Instead with his easygoing manner, he launched into sharing all the things he and Gramps had done during the past two days. He had a way of turning an ordinary event like collecting eggs from the hens into a story that had them both laughing.

"Last night when I went up to check on the light," he said, growing more serious, "I saw flickers of lanterns on the west side of the island."

"Was someone digging?"

"This morning I went over to investigate and found holes again. Covered, but barely."

"So, I was right before?"

He nodded. "It appears someone believes there is a hidden treasure on Rose Island. They must not want anyone else to suspect it, so they're coming out and digging at night."

"Or maybe someone has finally spotted Gramps treasure hunting and decided that it's worth investigating."

"Is it anything to worry about?" he asked. "Should I go out next time and confront the treasure hunters and tell them to stay off the island?"

"No." She didn't want Nathaniel meeting strangers in the dark, possibly armed men who wouldn't take kindly to being disturbed. "It could be dangerous."

"I'll be careful."

"Wait until I come home, and I'll go with you."

He gave a short laugh. "Absolutely not, darling. The last thing I want is to put you in danger."

Darling. The word rolled off his tongue now and then. It jarred her every time. She liked the endearment, but she suspected it was a word that men in Nathaniel's social circles tossed around with little thought.

"Abbie?" Debbie called sleepily from the bedroom. "Who's here?"

Abbie sat up. Debbie wouldn't be happy to have Nathaniel in the house. Her sister had been too preoccupied to mention anything about him or the deception over the past week, but now that Debbie was regaining her strength, she'd be furious if she discovered that Abbie was encouraging Nathaniel's affection.

Abbie stalled. Her gaze locked with Nathaniel's. She didn't want him to leave yet.

His expression was sad but resigned. Debbie didn't like him, but he accepted it, at least for now which served only to stir the guilt inside Abbie for making him bear a weight that wasn't his own.

"Abbie?" Debbie's voice was louder this time.

Abbie stood and crossed to the bedroom. She opened the door a crack and peeked in to see that her sister was sitting up against the headboard nursing Henry. "Nathaniel's here. He's come to help this afternoon. With watching the children."

At the pronouncement, Abbie glanced over her shoulder to see Nathaniel shake his head in protest.

"Abbie," Debbie's voice dripped with frustration, and her eyes filled with warning—the warning to be careful not to take things too far.

"He won't stay long." Before Debbie protested further, Abbie closed the door.

When she turned, Nathaniel was standing and twisting his hat in his hands. "I don't think I'm very good with children. In fact, I'm certain I was quite awful with them."

"You'll learn just as quickly as you have everything else," she reassured.

It wasn't long before Pollyanna awoke from her nap. At first, Nathaniel was somewhat stiff-mannered in his interactions with her. But soon, he was sitting on the parlor floor, building a castle out of her blocks, and telling her a fairy tale. She was enthralled and crawled onto Nathaniel's lap.

Nathaniel quirked a brow at Abbie in the rocking chair, where she bounced Henry, who'd been fussing since his feeding. She smiled and mouthed, "I told you so."

When Pollyanna announced that she needed to go potty, Abbie passed the baby to Nathaniel. "Sit in the rocker and pat his back," she instructed, as she led Pollyanna to the backdoor that led to the outhouse.

"What if I break him?" Nathaniel called after her. Panic filled his face, and he held the baby like he was a rattlesnake about to strike.

Abbie couldn't contain her laughter. "I'm sure Henry will survive for five minutes in your arms."

"How can you be certain?" Nathaniel stared in dismay at the baby.

"Just try to relax and rock him."

He sat back stiffly and swayed the chair with jerking motions. Abbie smothered another laugh before exiting with Pollyanna. When they stepped inside a few minutes later, Abbie stopped short. Nathaniel was gliding back and forth in the rocker. He dwarfed the wooden chair and would have looked comical in it, except that his expression upon Henry was tender and awe-filled.

"He's so tiny," Nathaniel whispered.

Henry peered up, wide-awake. He'd stopped his fussing, wasn't making a peep, and seemed entirely engrossed with Nathaniel's face.

"I think he likes me," Nathaniel said with a soft smile.

As Nathaniel continued to rock the baby, Abbie joined

Pollyanna on the floor next to the block castle. All the while she played with her niece, her attention kept straying to Nathaniel, her heart melting a little more each time she watched him with the baby.

After Nathaniel rocked Henry to sleep and entertained Pollyanna again, Abbie finally urged him to return to the island.

"I don't want Gramps to get worried," she said with her hand on the doorknob. "If he gets overly anxious, he might decide to take the spare boat out and search for you."

With Debbie awake again, Pollyanna had gone in the bedroom to tell her mom about the castle she'd built. Henry was still asleep in the bassinet next to the rocker, where Nathaniel had laid him earlier. Abbie was relieved to have a moment alone with Nathaniel before he left.

He leaned his shoulder against the door and gave her a grin that had a strange way of reducing her insides to a fluttering mess.

"Did we ever talk about having children?" he asked.

The question startled her, and for a second she struggled to find an honest response. Then his attention dropped to her mouth, and any notion of answering him fled, especially at the heat that flared to life in his eyes.

"You'd make a good mother."

"And you'd make a good father," she managed, trying to calm the swirling in her middle.

He hesitated before commenting. "Something tells me I've never considered it, that I was even against becoming a father."

"That's okay. I never gave much thought to being a mother." Truthfully, she'd never once contemplated having children. She'd always been too busy with all of her responsibilities. Even if she'd had time, she didn't have many happy memories of her mother and hadn't been eager to jump into that role for herself.

Nathaniel was silent for a moment, staring at her hand still resting on the doorknob. Finally, he lifted his eyes and met her gaze. The openness and the desire there took her breath away. "Maybe we can consider the possibility of having a baby," he said so softly that she almost couldn't hear him.

The implication of his words sent not only embarrassment charging through her nerves, but also heat. She had to look away before he saw too much.

"Not right away," he said hurriedly. "We still need time to fall in love with each other before we fall into bed."

At his too bold words, her cheeks burned. "Nathaniel," she rebuked, glancing around to make sure they were still alone. The conversation was unlike any she'd ever had before, and she knew she had to put a stop to it immediately.

"I mean," he rushed, "it's not like I haven't thought about—you know..." He cleared his throat. "You're a beautiful and desirable woman."

She squirmed with the desperate need to bring an end to this too-intimate discussion. What could she do to change the nature of the conversation, to make him be quiet?

"I clearly didn't show you enough tenderness before," he continued. "And I despise myself for pushing you away—"

She reached up and touched her fingers to his lips to cut off his rambling. But the moment her fingers came into contact with the firmness and warmth of his mouth, her stomach tumbled head over heels and landed at her feet.

From the flare that lightened the green in his eyes, she knew he'd had the same reaction. Before she realized what he was doing, he captured her hand, turned it over, and pressed a kiss into her palm. The kiss was hot and lingering. She gripped the doorknob harder to keep from swaying into him.

"I promise," he said between kisses, "you won't push me away again. I'll—"

She rose on her toes and did the first thing that came to mind to stop him from saying anything else. She pressed her lips against his.

Once her lips met his, she didn't know how to proceed. She'd never initiated a kiss with Nate, had never wanted to. She squeezed her eyes shut and let her lips rest against Nathaniel's. If nothing else, she'd accomplished what she set out to do—she'd silenced him.

For a long moment, he didn't move, and she held herself motionless, growing more mortified by the moment. She started to pull away, but before she could, his lips opened and gently covered hers, capturing and holding her captive in one soft but sweeping motion.

The pressure of his mouth was unlike anything she'd ever experienced, tender and yet demanding all at once. Although she'd been the one to start the kiss, he deftly took over, taking the kiss deeper, so that somehow it seemed to reach down inside and extricate a pleasure so sweet she couldn't keep from swaying against him.

The hardness of his chest brushed against her, in sharp contrast to the exquisite softness of his kiss. She didn't realize that her fingers were sliding up his abdomen until she had his shirt gripped in her fists. Her touch, she realized, was her invitation to him, that he'd kept his hands off her during the kiss. But now that she'd initiated the contact, he'd willingly responded by grazing his hands up her back.

His hands rose, until one hand tangled in her hair and the other splayed across her spine, pushing her against him with greater urgency. His lips moved harder and faster, stirring that deep sweet pleasure into a breathless need she didn't understand. All she knew was that she wanted—no, *needed*—him in a way that was entirely new.

Was this, then, what a passionate, loving marriage could be like? Was this what God had intended it to be? Was this what Nathaniel had been alluding to when he'd said he'd make sure she wouldn't push him away again?

The truth was, against the tide of his kiss pulling her deeper and with the solidness of his body against hers, she only wanted to be closer to him, to have him go on holding and kissing her forever.

As though sensing her rising desire, his fingers sank deeper into her hair. He gave a soft moan against her lips that ricocheted to every corner of her body, smoldering along every nerve until she didn't know if her legs could hold her weight. She clutched his shirt to keep herself upright.

Without breaking the kiss, he started to scoop her into his arms, but at that moment, the door jerked open against them, flooding them with outdoor light.

She broke away from him at the same moment he did from her. She spun, mortified to find Menard standing on the stoop, his eyes as round as silver dollars behind his spectacles. The distinct scent of horseflesh and hay preceded him after his long day in the Cole stables. His garments were sweaty and flecked with dust.

Nathaniel nodded at Menard. "Just saying good-bye to my wife."

Menard stared with an open mouth, and he stood as still as

a hitching post.

Mortified, Abbie could only do likewise, even though she wanted to turn around, run up to her bed, and dive under her covers.

Although she and Menard were embarrassed by the situation, Nathaniel apparently wasn't in the least bothered. Grinning, he grabbed his hat from the floor, where somehow it had fallen during their passionate kissing. He raked his fingers through his loose, sandy hair before donning his hat.

He leaned in to her, and she sucked in a breath in anticipation of him kissing her again, even if only a short good-bye kiss. But his lips passed by hers, grazed her cheek, and found her ear. Just the soft burst of his breath there was her undoing.

She closed her eyes at the sensations that charged through her again and fought the urge to clutch him and not let go.

"We can continue where we left off anytime." His gravelly whisper rumbled down to her belly. "All you have to do is ask, and I will happily oblige."

His lips connected then with the hollow part of her ear in a short, hard kiss. She was ready for him to swivel her around and kiss her lips the same way. But he stood back, tipped his hat low, and shouldered his way past Menard.

Menard jumped aside, giving Nathaniel plenty of space and bowed at him in respect. Nathaniel was already striding away and didn't notice, or if he did see the gesture, he didn't think anything was unusual about the deference.

She watched him stride off with his long, confident steps. Her heart swelled with something strange and wonderful. Was she falling in love with Nathaniel?

With breathless anticipation, she waited for him to look

back at her. She willed him to turn one last time. When he was halfway down the street, he glanced over his shoulder at her with a grin, as though he'd known she was following his every move. He winked and then continued on his way.

Undeniable love crashed over her like a wave on the edge of a storm, and she couldn't keep what she suspected was a big silly grin from spreading across her face.

Menard shook his head and stared after Nathaniel as well. "I can't believe it."

She couldn't believe it either. She wasn't sure how she'd fallen in love, but she couldn't explain her feelings any other way. She loved everything about Nathaniel—his willingness to help at the lighthouse, his kindness to Gramps in so many different ways, and even today with his gentleness to both Pollyanna and Henry. The memory of his tender expression when he'd been holding Henry made her heart ache.

He'd been so sweet and giving and thoughtful to her too. He anticipated her needs even before she did—like letting her sleep later, cooking breakfast, reading to her at night, helping her with even the most menial of tasks.

And what about her birthday? No one had ever made her birthday as special as he had.

She released a long sigh of satisfaction. Yes, she loved him.

"I can't believe it," Menard said again. "I just can't believe it."

"It's all right, Menard," she said. It had to be all right. Even if the future was uncertain. Even if she still needed to confess her dishonesty. It was clear that he cared about her, maybe even loved her in return. Love could overcome all obstacles, couldn't it? He seemed like a reasonable man. Surely he'd find it in his heart to forgive her.

"I never thought I'd live to see the day when that man stepped into my house." Menard's eyes were still wide and full of amazement.

"What do you mean by *that man*?" As the words slipped out, Abbie wasn't sure she wanted to hear Menard's answer.

Menard pushed his spectacles up to the bridge of his nose. "That man happens to be Nathaniel Winthrop III."

Chapter 14

Abbie's pulse slowed to a crawl, and she shook her head. "No, he can't be Nathaniel Winthrop III." Her mind flashed to his ring and the NRW inscribed there.

Everyone in Newport knew who the Winthrops were every bit as much as they knew about the Coles. Both families lived in Newport every summer, and the Winthrops were almost as rich as the Coles and just as prestigious, if not more so. Of course, Abbie had never seen either of the families, not with the isolated life she led on Rose Island, and apparently neither had Debbie.

Nevertheless, Menard loved sharing tales about his employer and the various families that came to visit the Coles' enormous beachfront home. If anyone would recognize Nathaniel Winthrop III, Menard would.

"It's not him," she stated, hating that her voice and hands shook. She reached behind her for the front door handle to hide the trembling.

Menard waved a hand absently as though brushing away her denial. "I suspected as much the day I rowed out to the island to fetch you for Debbie's birthing, but he was at a distance, and we were in a hurry."

"Maybe it's just someone who looks like him."

"It's him, all right," Menard insisted. "It's his face even if he's not wearing the right clothes."

Abbie swung open the door and stepped inside wishing she could step as easily away from Menard's news. "If he really is Nathaniel Winthrop III, then why hasn't his family sent out a search party? Why haven't they been looking for their long-lost son?"

Menard followed her into the house and closed the door. "They haven't searched for him because they believed he drowned in a boating accident a few weeks back. His friends all claimed he fell overboard and sank beneath the waves."

Abbie strode to the kitchen and grabbed a pan, not caring that she banged it as she placed it on the stove. Everything in her resisted the idea that *her* Nathaniel was *the* Nathaniel Winthrop III. He just couldn't be.

"In fact," Menard continued, "there was a huge funeral for him about two weeks ago. The Coles attended, along with almost half the population of Newport."

Dread settled in Abbie's stomach, chasing away every ounce of pleasure she'd experienced only moments ago. *No!* her mind shouted. *No!* Menard had to be mistaken. Even if he wasn't, she didn't care. If Nathaniel's family thought he was dead, then what harm would come from letting them continue to believe it? They didn't need or love him as much as she did.

As the protest and excuses rose, shame washed over her. She couldn't imagine the grief they'd experienced thinking

Nathaniel had drowned. They would be ecstatic to learn he was alive and well. They would surely fill his head again with all the memories he'd lost—this time the right memories.

Even though she wanted to hold onto her hope that love could overcome all obstacles, she realized now how flimsy that hope truly was. Nathaniel would return to his old life and forget about her, especially when he learned just how much she'd deceived him. He'd been nothing but trusting and honest with her during the past weeks. All she'd done was tell lies. And not just one lie. But lies piled upon lies so that at times she could no longer distinguish what was true.

Throughout the evening, Abbie couldn't think about anything else. When she answered a knock on the door after dinner, she was startled to find Mr. Davis, the local lighthouse superintendent, standing there with a wide smile on his face.

Suddenly nervous, she invited him in for a cup of coffee and some of the leftover cranberry bread that Mrs. Pinkie had baked for them. But the superintendent only shook his head and smiled wider.

"I stopped by to inform you that the Lighthouse Board reached a decision regarding your tenure at Rose Island Lighthouse."

Behind her, silence descended over the front room where everyone had been resting after dinner. Menard had helped Debbie out of bed for the first time, and she'd walked to the sofa before collapsing. Now she laid there with Pollyanna, while Menard rocked the baby.

Abbie had the urge to step outside and close the door behind her so that no one else could hear the superintendent. But before she could move Mr. Davis spoke again. "We're extending your position there for another six months, at the end of which, I'll evaluate the situation again."

For a moment she couldn't make sense of his words. The three-week trial was nearing a close. Had he already decided?

"Yes, I made my decision," he said as if he'd read her mind.

"Then you visited the island and saw how well Gramps is doing?" She wasn't sure whether to be excited about the prospect or dread it. For if Mr. Davis caught sight of Nathaniel, he'd recognize him as Nathaniel Winthrop III. She suspected most people would be able to identify him. Too bad she wasn't most people. She might have prevented herself from making a huge mistake—one she didn't know how to fix.

"I didn't need to visit," Mr. Davis replied. "I received reports that Nate has been behaving himself. What's more, he's been managing the lighthouse all week while you've been here in town. That speaks louder than words ever could."

Abbie couldn't summon the expected excitement. Mr. Davis was giving her what she'd begged for—more time at the lighthouse. But he wasn't giving it to her the way she'd planned.

At her lack of enthusiasm, his smile dimmed. "I hope he's treating you the way he should."

Abbie swallowed her confession—the words she should tell the superintendent, the truth about who Nate was—but somehow she couldn't. "Oh, it's nothing like that," she said, trying to muster enthusiasm. "I was just hoping you'd see how well Gramps has been doing lately..."

Mr. Davis's kind eyes regarded her. "I'm glad he's doing better, Abbie, but as long as Nate continues to do his job, then we don't need to worry about Hosea's condition, do we?"

She wanted to argue with him and demand that he sail over to the lighthouse and talk with Gramps. But she bit the words back and instead mustered a smile. "Thank you, Mr. Davis."

They made small talk for another minute before the superintendent took his leave. As she watched him walk away, the silence behind her made Abbie want to walk away too. Both Debbie and Menard's sharp gazes seemed to stab her in the back and rebuke her.

She closed the door slowly before turning to face them. "Well, go ahead and say it. Tell me what an idiot I've been."

Debbie sighed in exasperation and exchanged a frustrated look with Menard. Pollyanna was lying next to her on the sofa, sucking two fingers on one hand and intertwining her other hand into Debbie's hair.

Menard stopped rocking, his thin face crinkled with anxiety. "I'm most worried about what the Winthrops might do to you and Gramps once they discover that you've kept Nathaniel on the island without alerting anyone."

"I didn't know he was Nathaniel Winthrop."

"At the very least, you should have alerted the local authorities you found an injured man."

Abbie sank to the nearest chair. Menard was right. Although the front windows were wide open and a cool breeze blew in, the cluttered room, with its scattering of toys and baby items, closed in and stifled her.

Menard's expression remained grave. "The Winthrops won't let an incident like this go unpunished. They'll charge you with kidnapping and who knows what else. You might end up in prison. They could make sure you and Gramps are thrown off Rose Island and out of Newport forever. Maybe they'll even petition to have me fired from my job at the Coles."

Abbie shuddered. She'd only wanted to help Gramps. She'd only wanted to keep him in the place that brought him comfort and security. But in trying to protect Gramps, had she made matters irreparably worse?

"I won't say anything to Nathaniel," she said. "What he doesn't know won't hurt him—"

"Abigail!" Debbie's sharp tone made Pollyanna sit up and stop sucking her fingers.

"His family and friends already think he's dead," Abbie rushed, suddenly desperate.

"Someone is bound to see him eventually and recognize him," Menard interjected. "Like I did. And then what?"

"I'll keep him on the island. He doesn't have to come to Newport—"

Debbie snorted. "Oh, so you're planning to tie him up hand and foot next time he decides to visit Newport? Or lock him in the oil house?"

"That's a good idea," Abbie replied, although half sarcastically.

"And what if his memory returns?" Menard stood up with Henry, who'd begun to fuss. "I've heard stories of people who over time regain parts of their memory or even all of it. What would you do if that happens?"

"It's been nearly three weeks, and he doesn't remember anything. I almost get the feeling he doesn't want to remember."

"Regardless," Debbie said, brushing Pollyanna's cheek as the girl snuggled against her again, "you have to put an end to the deception. It's gone much too far. Menard told me what he saw you doing with Nathaniel when he arrived home."

Heat flooded Abbie's neck and cheeks.

"You promised you'd keep your distance from him," Debbie persisted.

"I have. I promise, that's the first time we've..." Her voice came out a strangled whisper. "It won't happen again."

"But if he thinks you're married, then it's only natural he'll expect—um—more." Debbie glanced down at Pollyanna, who was staring up at her with wide eyes as she sucked her fingers. "The bottom line is, you can't continue. You must stop this whole act immediately."

Abbie shook her head. "I don't know how to tell him the truth without hurting him."

Debbie was quiet, her perceptive gaze fixed on Abbie. "You love him, don't you?"

Abbie couldn't answer which spoke loudly enough.

Her sister laid her head back wearily and closed her eyes. For a moment, the only sounds were Henry's half cries and Menard's soft shushing.

"I want you to go home tomorrow," Debbie finally said.

"I'll wait until Menard's mother arrives."

"No," Debbie insisted in a tone that bade no arguments. "You need to go home tomorrow and tell Nathaniel everything." She opened her eyes and glared at Abbie. "Everything. Do you understand?"

Abbie felt as though she were five years old getting her hand slapped.

"If you don't tell him tomorrow, then I'll send Menard over to inform him for you."

"What if the Winthrops have me thrown in jail? Who will take care of Gramps then?" She didn't want Gramps to experience any problems on her account.

"We'll handle the consequences," Debbie said weakly.

"We always have."

Debbie was referring to all the other instances in their life when they'd faced challenges—especially when their mother had run off. Nevertheless, Abbie didn't know if she could deal with the consequences of telling Nathaniel the truth—namely the consequence of losing him and having him hate her, because surely that's the only way a man like Nathaniel Winthrop III would react.

"Tell him tomorrow," Debbie said again.

When Abbie dared to meet her sister's eyes, the plea mingled with a sadness and pity that embarrassed Abbie. Maybe her life hadn't turned out as idyllic as Debbie's, with two healthy children and a husband who loved her. Maybe she'd resorted to a fake husband with no memories as a way to finally find someone who cared about her. And maybe she was prone to making messes and unable to find ways to clean them up.

But she didn't want anyone's pity. If nothing else, she was a strong woman. She'd learned she didn't need others to survive. In fact, she was better on her own where no one could reject and hurt her.

She stood and started to walk to the stairs.

"Abbie?" Debbie's voice demanded an answer.

"Don't worry," she said. "I'll tell him."

Nathaniel closed the metal lid on the wick container. The word "Wicks" was stamped across the front, along with the words "U.S. Lighthouse Establishment." Then he examined the new wick he'd carefully and smoothly trimmed and positioned inside the lamp.

He should have noticed that the wick needed replacing in the morning when he'd extinguished the lantern, while it was bright rather than in the dusk when he was in a hurry to get the lantern lit.

As it was, he'd waited and had fumbled through the whole experience of pulling back the pinion, turning the outside tube, and tugging the blackened wick free. He'd inserted the new clean wick and attempted to replace all the parts in their original position.

Even now, he watched the low flame, praying he'd done everything right. He'd wait another thirty minutes before turning the wick up further. It had only taken him a couple of nights to realize that if he cranked up the flame too soon, it would smoke and fill the lantern with a ghostly black.

He ducked through the door onto the gallery and leaned against the railing. A blanket of clouds had moved in and blocked the setting sun. But his thoughts and sights weren't directed to the west tonight. Instead, he had eyes only on the east, on Newport and the beautiful woman he'd left there a few hours ago.

He had to admit, Abbie had surprised him when she'd risen on toes and silenced him with a touch of her lips. He guessed she hadn't planned to kiss him. In fact, once her lips touched his, she'd seemed as much surprised by the contact as he'd been.

After several long moments of waiting to see what she planned to do, it had become clear she had no idea how to kiss. When she'd started to pull away from him in embarrassment, he'd realized that she'd shown a great deal of courage and trust to initiate the intimacy. She'd opened the door a crack and had given him a subtle invitation. He hadn't been able to let her go without capitalizing on the opportunity, knowing that if he missed the chance, he might not get another. At least not soon.

Before she broke free, he'd kissed her back with all the passion of a real kiss. It scared him to think about how he knew so much about kissing and flirting. But he'd put his knowledge to good use with Abbie. He'd wanted to make the kiss as memorable and pleasurable for her as possible. Strangely, he'd turned the kiss into something that had seared him to his soul. In the process of drinking her in, she'd seeped into his blood, pumped through his body, and was now a part of every beat of his heart.

He hadn't wanted the kiss to end. He'd been ready to sweep her into his arms, carry her up to her bedroom, and deposit both of them onto her bed. It was probably a good thing Debbie's husband had interrupted them. It had kept him from doing something foolish. He'd meant what he'd told Abbie, that he wanted them to fall in love first before falling into bed. He didn't care that they'd shared intimacies in the past already. He was determined to do things right this time.

But would his determination be enough? The longer he was with her, the more he was drawn to her, so much so he couldn't keep from wondering why they hadn't experienced attraction to each other before. The sparks had been flying between them from the first moment he'd awoken after his accident. Why hadn't there been any sparks earlier in their marriage?

He frowned and stared out at the bay, at a lone boat sailing toward the harbor. What puzzled him even more was the fact that Abbie hadn't known how to kiss. Why hadn't she? Surely, he'd kissed her plenty of times when they were courting or in the early weeks of their marriage. He may not know himself well, but sensed that he was the kind of man who enjoyed kissing. At least, he'd enjoyed kissing Abbie this afternoon. Actually the word *enjoyed* didn't do justice to the experience.

One taste of her lips made him crave her more than a drunkard his next drink. He'd been able to think of little else while rowing home and fixing dinner for Hosea. If he felt that way now, he must have when they'd first been married. He couldn't imagine not wanting to kiss her thoroughly and completely every chance he had.

So why, then, was she so inexperienced? What had kept him from kissing her?

He couldn't wrap his mind around what their relationship may or may not have been like before the accident. The clues were too confusing. All he knew was that now that he'd kissed her, he would have trouble being around her more than before.

Had he fallen in love with his wife?

He'd told Abbie they needed more time to fall in love with each other. But he was fairly certain he didn't need any more time. He didn't want to mistake physical attraction for genuine love. But over the past few days of being without her, he'd realized how many things about her he appreciated, loved, and missed.

All the same, he would force himself to continue to take things slowly with her. After all, there was no rush, not when they had the rest of their lives together, the rest of their lives to kiss each other the way they had earlier. That prospect brought a smile to his lips.

After he was certain the lantern flame was high enough and the beam rotating in its usual pattern, he descended. First, he peeked in Hosea's room and made sure the older man was safe and resting comfortably before heading down to his bedroom.

He perched on the edge of his bed and fought the agonizing longing to be with Abbie again. Did he dare return to Newport tomorrow? What would she think if he came two days in a row? Would his enthusiasm scare her? Or would she welcome him?

He opened Hosea's Bible. Every night he'd gotten into the habit of bringing it with him into his room and reading before he snuffed out the light. He'd decided to branch out beyond the 2 Corinthians passage he read to Hosea every evening. As before, he suspected that to truly change his ways—whatever those had been—he wouldn't be able to do it in his own effort, at least not long-term. He needed strength that went beyond his, the supernatural strength that came from God, which would enable him to fight temptations and live with integrity.

The Bible fell open to the Gospels. Nathaniel had already read them over the past four nights. Tonight he flipped further into the New Testament, moving past Corinthians. He had the suspicion again, as before, that he'd never read the Bible for himself. He might have once been godly and gone to church, but he'd probably been too busy or preoccupied to read the Bible or pray.

But now, could he afford to be too busy to tap into the Source of real strength? Especially if he hoped to live a better life?

He stopped at the sight of a thin scrap of paper tucked between two pages. He might have glided past the sheet altogether if he hadn't been going slowly.

The paper was square-shaped and sheer, almost translucent. And it was yellowed and brittle and likely very old.

Nathaniel hesitated picking it up, half afraid it might crumble if he touched it.

Setting aside his reservations, he lifted it carefully. It almost appeared blank. But when he raised it closer to the lantern on his bedstead, he caught sight of faint traces of ink. He studied it for a moment, trying to make out what appeared to be a map. As he shifted it and tried to read it from a different angle, the thin paper slipped from his fingers and fluttered down, floating out of his reach, until it slid under the dresser.

He got down on his hands and knees, stuck his hand into the narrow space, and groped for the paper. His fingers brushed against wads of dust and crusty insects before coming into contact with a chain—like that belonging to a necklace. He attempted to pull it out, but when it wouldn't budge, he realized it was hanging out of the bottom drawer.

Withdrawing his hand and sitting up, he tugged at the drawer and found that he had to yank hard to open it since it was so full. Once he'd pried it loose, he frowned at the wad of sand-covered clothes that someone had apparently hastily stowed in the drawer. The stench of them told him they had likely been stuffed into the drawer dirty and wet.

Probably by Abbie.

He smiled. She was certainly not going to win any awards for her neatness.

As he unraveled the stiff, wadded clothing, his pulse stuttered. This was a man's clothing. And not just any man's clothing. From the edges finished by elegant stitching, the fixed cuffs with shaped tabs, and the delicate pleats at the front, he could tell the shirt was of good quality and tailored, unlike his own factory made shirts.

He unrolled the trousers and matching vest to discover more of the same high quality—a single-breasted waistcoat that matched the trousers, with narrow bands at the side seams.

For several moments, he stared at the garments, certain he'd seen them before. He wanted them to be his and not some other man that had visited Abbie during his absence over the winter. But why would they be his? Had he been wearing them the day he'd returned? And if so, why had Abbie stuffed them in the drawer?

The questions taunted him as he held them up one at a time and realized they were exactly his size. These were definitely his garments, but how had he, a poor drunken fisherman, happened upon such clothing?

He moved to the edge of the bed and stared at the crusty, sandy clothes now scattered on the floor. He'd made an effort earlier today when he'd rowed into Newport to scan the yachts that were moored, hoping that one of them would spark something in his memory. But nothing else had come back to him.

He'd forgotten to ask Abbie about yachting. Now it looked like he'd have even more questions when she returned over the weekend.

After how well things were going between them, he wasn't sure he wanted to stir up the past. What if he unlocked something that was better left in the dark? What if he discovered information that had the potential to ruin the tenuous but growing attraction between them?

He reached for the clothes, folded them up, and placed them back into the dresser. He struggled to push the drawer in. Once it closed, he decided that's how he'd keep his past, wadded up and closed away forever. All he wanted was the future and the chance to be a better man.

Chapter 15

With each dip of the oars bringing her closer to Rose Island, Abbie's strokes became weaker and slower. All morning, she'd delayed leaving Newport, and now she was delaying again.

She dreaded the task that awaited her. In fact, she dreaded seeing Nathaniel again knowing he was Nathaniel Winthrop III.

Last night after Pollyanna had gone to bed, Menard had told her everything he knew about Nathaniel Winthrop III, and very little of it had been flattering. Several years ago, Nathaniel had been engaged to marry Henry Cole's only daughter, Victoria. Apparently, the wealthy socialite had rejected Nathaniel not once—but twice. And had married her bodyguard instead.

Menard had felt sorry for Nathaniel at the time since the young man had always been so kind and loving to Victoria. After the failed wedding attempts, Nathaniel had fallen into a despondency and had unfortunately started drinking heavily. Then after his father had died, he'd gotten even worse, if that were possible.

Abbie wasn't surprised by Menard's revelation. She'd already suspected that Nathaniel had past pains that haunted him. Whatever the case, Debbie's admonition reverberated in Abbie's head: *If you don't tell him tomorrow, then I'll send Menard over to inform him for you.*

Abbie had no choice. She wanted Nathaniel to hear it from her first. Not from Menard. Not from someone he met in passing. Not from Zeke or Mr. Davis or anyone else. Since she'd been the one to let the misunderstanding pass unchecked, she had to be the one to make it right—*if* there was any way to make it right.

A gust of wind sent a wave against the bow. A glance to the western sky told her that a storm was building. The waves were running high. If the wind increased, the water would grow treacherous.

Without dawdling any further, she dug the oars deeper and crossed the rest of the distance with the power and speed she'd developed over the years. She caught sight of Gramps whitewashing the west side of the bastion, but Nathaniel was nowhere in sight.

She docked and unloaded the few goods she'd brought with her. As she started up the slope toward the house, her heart tapped with mounting anxiety. When her chickens came running out of the brush to meet her, she greeted them with as much enthusiasm as she could muster, but her attention strayed to the top of the hill, to the garden, to the house, to the distant shore.

Where was Nathaniel? Maybe he didn't have to know

she'd returned. Maybe she could avoid him for a little while—

"Looking for me?" he called.

When she climbed several feet more, she saw him in the grassy, level plain between the lighthouse and the old fort. He was leaning against a rake and watching her. Despite the distance separating them, his eyes were bright with happiness and his grin welcoming.

"I didn't think you were coming home until tomorrow." He took off his hat, wiped his brow with his arm, and replaced his hat. His face was scruffy, telling her he hadn't shaved again. But it made him all the more rugged and appealing, especially because he'd discarded his shirt and was wearing only his thin undershirt, which hugged the muscles in his chest.

He didn't look like a wealthy gentleman who had a horde of servants to wait on him and had every luxury he ever wanted and then some. Was this really Nathaniel Winthrop III? What if Menard was wrong?

"I guess you missed me so much that you couldn't stay away another day?" Nathaniel's voice teased her.

She was glad he hadn't moved from his spot. She didn't know how she'd resist him if he came too close. "Debbie said she'd get along fine without me today."

"Just admit it, darling. You missed me."

Darling. That word again. The word a fancy rich man would use. She wanted to bang herself over the head with his rake for her stupidity, for ignoring all the clues that would have revealed his identity to her sooner—if she'd paid attention.

"Looks like you're hard at work," she said, needing to keep the topic safe. "What are you doing?" He'd cleared an area of about twelve feet by twelve feet, cutting back weeds, grass, and the overgrowth of brush, which he'd stacked into a mound nearby. It appeared that he was now in the process of leveling the ground.

He'd followed her gaze, his shoulders puffing in admiration of his work. "I'm building a shed."

"Do we need a shed?" *We?* There was no *we* in their relationship anymore. Not that there ever had been.

"Perhaps we don't need a shed." His grin inched higher, making him achingly handsome. "But our new cow will."

Her pulse gave a hop and then doubled its pace. "What do you mean *our new cow*?"

"Yesterday in Newport, I ran into some dockhands bringing several milking cows down the gangplank of a newly arrived steamer. I talked with the captain about purchasing one."

Abbie had dreamed about owning a cow, but even before Gramps' pain medication had consumed their income, they'd never earned enough for something like that. She supposed a man like Nathaniel was accustomed to purchasing anything he wanted without thought to the cost. Perhaps he'd worked out a trade or payment plan. Whatever the case, the cost of the cow wasn't worth worrying over, not when she had much bigger things to concern herself with—namely telling him who he really was.

"When I mentioned to Hosea my idea to surprise you with a cow, he said you've always wanted one," he continued more hesitantly, as though sensing her mood.

Nathaniel had wanted to surprise her with the cow? Her heart melted a little. He was so sweet and considerate and generous. How could she disappoint him now, not when he was watching her clearly hoping to please her? She could wait to tell him about his identity. Maybe tonight after the lantern was lit after he finished reading to her.

His brow furrowed. "If you'd rather not—"

"A cow is perfect."

"You're sure?"

"I couldn't ask for anything better." And she meant it. Part of her was thrilled that he knew her well enough to understand the kind of gift that would make her happy.

He smiled, her answer apparently satisfying him. "I decided seven chickens and six cats weren't enough. You needed another pet to talk to."

Abbie couldn't contain her smile, and Nathaniel chuckled in return. She loved the rumble of it and the way his face relaxed.

"And how will you build a shed?" she asked, deciding to ignore her conscience altogether for a little bit longer. "Should we use one of the rooms in the fort instead?"

"Maybe temporarily," he said. "But I'd like something closer to the house by winter." He went on to enthusiastically explain his intention of tearing out the rafters in the old fort for wood and had already drawn a plan, with Gramps' help.

When Nathaniel finished describing the shed, the wind was whipping against them with stinging velocity, and the waves were slamming hard into the bastion. A few drops of rain splattered against Abbie's head, signaling the storm that would soon unleash upon them.

"I'd hoped to have more done by the time you returned," he called as he jogged toward her with a glance at the darkening clouds overhead. "But since you clearly wanted to see me again..."

When he winked at her, any last barriers she'd tried to

erect since last night came crumbling down. He stopped in front of her, and the rain splashed against them more earnestly. Abbie couldn't make herself move away as she should. His nearness, the solidness of his chest, the brawny strength in his upper arms all reminded her that she'd been wrapped in those arms and against that chest yesterday. And that she'd liked it. A lot.

As he smiled down at her, the tenderness in his eyes mingled with a blaze of desire that told her he was remembering their exchange yesterday too. That he'd liked it as much as she had. He didn't make a move to touch her, but that didn't stop every nerve in her body from wishing he would.

He was the most amazing man she'd ever met. It didn't matter he was Nathaniel Winthrop III and had once had a wild reputation. He was good now. And that's all that mattered.

A shout near the lighthouse drew their attention. Gramps waved at them with an urgency that sent them both scurrying up the bastion.

"A boat capsized!" Gramps yelled, pointing to the bay. "Don't know how much longer those fellows can hang on."

Abbie didn't wait for Gramps to finish. When the words *capsized* left his mouth, she started sprinting down the sandy path, back to the beach and her skiff.

She was shoving it out into the water and hopping inside when she felt a tug of resistance against the stern. A glance over her shoulder revealed Nathaniel knee-deep in the waves holding on. "Let me go after them," he shouted above the roar of the waves. "It's too dangerous for you."

She gave him her answer by reaching for the oars and slicing them into the water. He helped her shove off and then surprised her by hopping in. "I won't let you go out in this alone," he called, reaching for the extra oars stowed under the benches. He held her gaze for only a few seconds, but it was long enough for him to communicate that they would weather this storm together.

She nodded before plunging her oars deeper.

In the distance, through the rain and waves, she caught sight of the capsized boat and several men clinging to it even as the waves threatened to wrench them away. As she navigated in the direction of the trouble and strained against the waves, she was grateful for Nathaniel's additional strength.

She wasn't sure how or when he'd gained his aquatic and navigational skills. Actually, she wasn't sure about anything anymore. She'd come out to the island with one purpose—to tell Nathaniel who he was and what she'd done in deceiving him. But now, after being with him again, she didn't know how she'd have the strength to get the words out.

The truth was, she loved him. Desperately. No matter her plans to stay strong and be fine on her own, she didn't want to lose him. Not now. Not ever.

Nathaniel heaved the oars with all his might. The rain was beating against his slumped back. With the crack of thunder, the spray of the waves, the dampness of his clothes, he was transported to the yacht on the day of the accident. He heard himself shouting instructions to his companions, instructing someone—Samuel—to get the flotation devices for the women.

Who was Samuel? The face of a young man floated before him. His cousin. Another face flashed into his mind. Charles.

His friend. He'd been telling Charles to be careful, to go slowly.

"Bring the stern to the men." Abbie's call interrupted the vividness of the memory. "If they come over the gunwales, their weight will capsize us."

Nathaniel didn't ask any questions. He simply did as she instructed, trusting her expertise. Even with her help to maneuver the skiff, the waves tossed the little boat like a bobbing apple in a bucket.

"Climb over the stern," she shouted to the men, who, from the looks of their uniforms, were soldiers from nearby Fort Adams. As he helped drag the first soldier into the stern, one whiff of the man's breath said it all. The soldier was drunk. Or at least had been drunk. The storm and near-drowning seemed to sober him up. With wide eyes, he crawled past Nathaniel and huddled in the hull, shivering and spluttering.

Abbie was fighting the pressure of the sea to keep the backside of the boat toward the other men, shouting commands to them above the whistling of the wind and ravaging of the waves. She was half-standing, and from the way blood vessels in her neck protruded, Nathaniel could tell she was using every last ounce of her strength to keep their own boat from flipping over.

"Grab his arm," she shouted, this time at Nathaniel.

Nathaniel grasped the coat of the second man. Amidst the jostling and tilting of the skiff, somehow he hauled the soldier over the stern, dumping him ungraciously into the middle, next to his friend.

The last man clinging to the overturned boat was too far away. They would have to row around to the other side to reach him. But it was also plain the soldier was losing strength.

He could barely keep his head clear of the water.

Before Nathaniel knew what Abbie was doing, she stood and tossed a rope over the boat so it practically landed in the man's hands. He grabbed onto it first with one hand and then the other.

"Be careful!" Nathaniel shouted to Abbie. The waves were tempestuous and seemed to crave destruction. Part of him wished she'd sit down and let him do the hazardous work. Another part of him watched her in admiration. Her agility and quick thinking was saving these men.

For several long moments, they maneuvered the skiff until the rear of the boat was closer to the last soldier.

"Let's pull him," Abbie called.

Nathaniel clutched the rope and yelled to the man. For a moment, the soldier refused to let go of his tenuous hold on his boat. But as an enormous wave crashed over him, he released his grip. Together, Nathaniel and Abbie towed the man toward the stern. Coughing and choking, the soldier surfaced below Nathaniel.

"I've got you!" Nathaniel shouted, as he strained on the rope and lifted the man out of the water. The wind and rain lashed against them and threatened to toss them both into the depths of the sea.

Fear radiated in the soldier's eyes. Thankfully, he was sober enough to hitch his leg over the edge and help pull himself up. Nathaniel hunkered lower to gain leverage to hoist the man the rest of the way. At the same time, the man swung his other leg into the boat. Before Nathaniel could move out of the way, the soldier's heavy boot crashed into Nathaniel's temple.

Pain ripped through him, and he fought against a wave of

blackness that shoved him to the brink of oblivion. His head seemed to swell, and the pressure in his temple was explosive.

"Nathaniel?" Abbie's voice penetrated through the thick haze. "Are you all right?"

"I'll be fine," he replied, even as he closed his eyes and fought the dizziness and nausea that swept over him. He breathed deeply, trying to expel the overwhelming pressure before he was sick.

Another crack of thunder reverberated through him. He needed to help Abbie bring the boat to safety, but he could do nothing but breathe—in, then out, hoping to still the racing of his heart.

Strange images whizzed into his conscience, images of an elegant older woman—the one dressed in the mink coat. His mother. Then images of a younger version of himself. His kid brother Nicholas. He pictured his enormous home in New York City and the beachfront home in Newport. *The Arbor*. He saw his seventy-seven-ton yacht moored at the New York City Yacht Club. And he vividly pictured his smaller yacht, the one he kept in Newport. He wasn't one of the crew. He was the master.

His mind spun with all the information pouring into it—the trips to Europe, the operas, the extravagant parties, and the balls. His senses reeled with visions of glittering diamonds, brilliant jewels, and the brightness of a dozen chandeliers. The sounds of laughter, clinking of crystal, rustle of silk. The scents of cigars, perfume, and the richest of sauces.

He shook his head to clear it, needing to make sense of what he was experiencing. But the impressions only magnified, until he wanted to yell out his frustration. For long minutes, memories crowded his mind from his childhood, his tutors, his days at the elite private boarding school, and then his study abroad at Oxford.

When the skiff bumped against something, he clutched his head and tried to sit up, surprised to see that Abbie had managed to row them to a dock in Newport. Several fishermen hovered above the boat, apparently having witnessed the rescue and now eager to lend a hand.

Nathaniel couldn't move. The pounding in his skull nailed him to the bench as more memories resurfaced and played through his mind.

He was startled when the rough, weatherworn hands of one of the fishermen gripped him and assisted him out of the skiff onto the dock. As he found solid footing, he mumbled his thanks.

He realized he was the last one out of the boat, that the three soldiers were shivering on the shore. Abbie stood near them, dripping wet, answering the fishermen's questions and giving instructions on transporting the soldiers back to the fort.

In a daze, Nathaniel glanced around the marina through the rain, everything as familiar as if he'd been there a thousand times. His gaze slid to a stop on a sleek yacht moored not more than a hundred feet away with the slanted cursive lettering—*The Tempest*—painted in blue on the hull. His yacht. He stared at it for a long moment.

And he knew. Knew with certainty. He was Nathaniel Winthrop III. His family had been important in New York City for generations, not only prominent and influential, but also very wealthy.

He swallowed hard, pivoted, and peered across the white-capped waves to the distant island he'd been living on for the past few weeks. If he was Nathaniel Winthrop, what in the world had he been doing on Rose Island working as a light keeper? How had that happened?

And why had he believed he was Abbie's husband? Was there a period of his memory that still hadn't come back to him? A period during which he'd gotten married to her?

No, that wasn't possible. According to Abbie, they'd wed last November. But he'd been in Florida with his mother and brother in November. His heart thudded faster at the memory. He'd definitely been in Florida in November and December. He'd been there for a private funeral and to make arrangements to have their Florida house sold…

After his father had committed suicide.

Nathaniel turned glossy eyes to Newport to the direction of Ocean Drive, where *The Arbor* was located. His thudding heart slowed to a crawl as the despondency of his father's death came back to him. They'd gotten the news of the death from Father's physician. A servant had discovered Father's lifeless body in bed, along with several empty laudanum bottles.

Of course, Mother had told the newspaper reporters that Father died of a heart attack. She hadn't wanted anyone to learn the true cause of his death, just as she'd never wanted anyone to know the true cause of the ailments that had driven her to have him locked away in their Florida home.

When Nathaniel had returned to New York City in January, he'd tried to drown out his memories of his father. He'd worked at forgetting everything as furiously as he could. He'd filled his life with drinking and revelry so that his days and nights had revolved around one party after another. When he'd arrived in Newport for the summer season, he'd continued the pattern.

Nathaniel stared at the town that spread out before him. Nausea churned in his gut like the stormy wind that was churning the waves, but this time the nausea wasn't from the hit to the head. No, the memories of the man he'd once been sickened him to the core. He loathed that man. He hated everything he represented and everything he'd done.

He bent over and gave way to the queasiness, retching into heaving waves and emptying his stomach. When he straightened and wiped his mouth with his sleeve, he caught Abbie's gaze.

She was still speaking with the fishermen. But her forehead furrowed with anxiety as she took him in.

Why did Abbie think he was her husband? He had no recollection of getting married to her. None. He wasn't Nate, the lobsterman. And he wasn't an acting light keeper. The reason he hadn't known anything about the lighthouse was because he'd never been in one. He may have been a scoundrel and a drunkard, but he wasn't the scoundrel and drunkard who had abandoned Abbie just two months after their wedding.

Surely, she couldn't believe he was her husband? Surely, she wasn't so confused as to mistake him for Nate, especially if she'd rescued him in the tailored garments he'd found last night in the drawer.

He shook his head in a futile attempt to make sense of everything, but only one thought remained. She'd lied to him. From the very beginning, she'd known he wasn't Nate. But she'd allowed him to believe he was.

The nausea in his stomach rolled again. It surged swiftly, and he crouched and was sick once more. When he ceased heaving, he felt her hand on his back.

"Nathaniel, what's wrong?" The concern in her voice only

ignited his frustration and anger. How dare she ask him what was wrong? Not when he'd just discovered that everything he'd believed for the past three weeks was a lie.

Everything.

"Did you swallow too much sea water?" she asked.

He jerked away from her touch and straightened. The rain slashed against him with punishing force. Without his hat, which he'd somehow lost, droplets ran unchecked down his face. "You lied to me, Abbie," he gasped out harshly.

She flinched but didn't deny his accusation or question him to find out what he was referring to. He saw by the darkening brown-green of her eyes that she already knew. She was guilty, and she wasn't hiding it.

For an endless moment, they stood on the dock, the waves spraying against them and the wind whipping with fury. The gusts of anger picked up speed inside him. All this time he'd trusted her. He'd believed everything she said. He'd even cared about her.

And she'd let him. She'd known all along, and yet she'd allowed him to make a fool of himself by throwing himself at her, begging her, and wooing her, when he had no place in her life. How she must have laughed each night in bed.

"I was going to tell you today," she said above the roaring wind and waves. "That's why I came back early."

"You should have told me right away," he said, not caring that his tone was ruthless.

"I know." She held out her hands to him as though she could make things right. "I'm sorry."

He took a step away. He didn't want her to touch him. "You're despicable."

The light in her eyes went out. Instead, bleakness settled

into her expression. And resignation.

No, he wasn't accepting her apology. What kind of person would lie to an injured man who'd lost his memory? He'd been vulnerable and helpless, and she'd taken advantage of him.

His mother was probably frantic with worry and wondering what had become of him. The thought of all she'd gone through over the past few weeks made him sick to his stomach again. He had to return to her immediately.

He started down the dock toward the shore.

"Nathaniel." The wind carried Abbie's plea away. But the shame and desperation in it were clear enough. He sensed that she wanted the chance to explain to him why she'd deceived him. Only he didn't want to hear any excuses.

She'd made him fall in love with her. How could she have trifled with his emotions so heartlessly? How could she have let him hand her his heart so openly and willingly? Only to brutally crush it with her deception?

"Please..." she shouted.

He halted and spun around. She stood where he'd left her, shoulders slumped, every line in her face dejected.

She could say nothing that would diminish the pain of her betrayal. It would be better for both of them if they cut things off immediately.

"You had your chance to tell me the truth," he shouted back. "And now it's too late to try to make things better."

Rain drenched her, and a wave crashed up behind her, splashing her. Deep sorrow radiated from her face and spanned the distance between them to wrench at his heart—or of what remained of his heart. A small part of him wanted to feel sorry for her. If she hadn't been lying about her real husband—and he suspected that she hadn't been—then she probably had been going through a hard time.

But that still was no excuse for deceiving him so thoroughly and for so long. No, he could never forgive her. It was best if he put her out of his life and forget that the past three weeks had ever happened.

"I'm leaving," he called. "And I don't want to see you ever again." With that, he turned and started walking in the direction he knew would take him home.

Chapter 16

You're despicable. I don't want to see you ever again. Nathaniel's words crashed through Abbie over and over.

She stood unmoving on the dock long after Nathaniel walked away and stared at the rain slapping against the planks. She was numb. Weak. And utterly lost.

She had no excuses, no explanations, and certainly no pity for herself. Everything he'd said had been correct. She was despicable and didn't deserve to see him again. Instead, she deserved his wrath and hatred.

Even so, her chest ached with the pressure of the sobs that were swelling deep inside. She'd lost Nathaniel. She'd had no right to have him in the first place, but for the short while they'd been together, she'd had a taste of the beauty of a real marriage. It had been a piece of heaven on earth.

Now that sweet taste was gone, and bitterness replaced it.

She'd never meant for him to hate her so fiercely. But what could she expect after hurting him?

From the instant he'd stepped onto the dock and raised his head to look at her, something had been different. When his confused and angry gaze had connected with hers, she'd realized his memories had returned.

If only she'd taken the time to explain everything to him earlier when she'd arrived back on the island. She wasn't sure if anything could have made a difference, though. She would have hurt him regardless. But at least in admitting the truth, she would have kept a tiny piece of what remained of her integrity. As it was now, she had nothing left. She truly was loathsome.

At distant shouts behind her in the bay, Abbie lifted her head. She didn't want to do anything at the moment but cry. She had the urge to jump in her boat, row back to the island, and throw herself onto the beach into the sand and bawl as loudly and long as she wanted.

But when she turned and saw that another boat was in trouble—this one a fisherman in his cutter—she sprang into action. She unwound the dock line, jumped into her skiff, and grabbed the oars.

It didn't matter that the waves had grown even more precarious. It didn't matter she was putting her life in jeopardy. In fact, if she died today saving a life, so be it. After all that she'd done to hurt Nathaniel, she'd accept whatever punishment came her way. Even death itself.

Nathaniel's feet squished in his boots with each step he took up the stone path to the front door of the Italianate-style villa. Manicured gardens and flowerbeds and fountains surrounded the three-story granite home. It sat on a small rise that overlooked the ocean, positioned so that almost every rear window gave a picturesque view of the beautiful coastline.

He'd garnered a few curious glances as he'd started down the street lined with other such magnificent homes—maybe not as grand as the Winthrop cottage—but impressive, nonetheless. He half-expected one of the other New York families to send a servant chasing after him, mistaking him for a poor immigrant, and demanding that he leave the area.

But he'd plodded up the front walkway of *The Arbor* without any confrontation. Although the rain had tapered, the long walk from the marina to his family residence had given him time to think about all that had happened.

His anger toward Abbie was still raging. He doubted it would ever diminish. But he realized his love for her wouldn't diminish easily either. He supposed that's why her betrayal pierced him so deeply.

He paused in front of the dark walnut door with its multi-leaded panes and elaborate carvings of grapes and vines. Was he ready to enter his old life again? After the time away and all he'd experienced on Rose Island, could he go back to his previous lifestyle?

He reached a hand for the cut-glass doorknob but hesitated. Already, he felt despair reaching out for him, intertwining him within its grasp and dragging him down.

For a few blissful weeks without his memories, he'd been able to live without the heavy burdens that had plagued him for so long. He'd given up his vices. He'd lost the craving for alcohol. He'd even been able to forget about his father and the undeniable fact that he was bound to turn out the same way. He'd been able to believe that he could be different.

Was that still possible? Even though he now remembered

who he really was, could he continue to seek after God and his strength? Maybe some good could come from his experience on Rose Island after all. He didn't have to be on the island to read his Bible and live with integrity.

He twisted the doorknob and swung the door open to reveal the spacious front hallway with its stylishly carved cornices, the elaborate pediments over the doors, and the frescoed ceiling with its glittering chandelier. The marble fireplace was polished to a gleam, and the gold-framed mirror above it shone brilliantly too.

Nathaniel waited for a sense of homecoming to wash over him, to be relieved at stepping into the house he'd lived in every summer. But he felt as out of place there as he surely looked.

As vigilant as always, Carver, their butler was already approaching him. The long, lean man had served their family for decades. He was the same now as Nathaniel remembered from his childhood—tall, distinguished, perfectly groomed, with only a smattering of gray in his otherwise black hair. He spoke with an English accent and was always very proper. More than that, he was loyal to their family to a fault.

"Sir, I must ask that you step outside. No one is allowed into this residence without an invitation."

Nathaniel glanced down at his scuffed boots and plain brown trousers. The linen shirt he'd hastily donned before joining Abbie in her rescue attempt was also plain, patched at the elbows and threadbare at the cuffs.

He wasn't dripping wet anymore. But his clothes were still damp enough that they stuck to him, making him look gangly and gaunt. With the beginning of a beard and his overlong hair, he understood why Carver didn't recognize him.

Nathaniel waited for Carver to get closer, for him to study his face, and for a welcome smile to replace the irritation.

But Carver passed him without a second glance, opened the front door, and waved his hand outside. "Please depart at once."

For a moment, the abruptness of his manservant rendered him speechless. Was Carver so quick to judge by outward appearance that he wouldn't look a man in the eyes and judge his worth there instead?

Nathaniel sucked in a guilty breath. Who was he to condemn Carver? Not when he would have laughed such a man out the door in the past. Or worse.

"I must insist," Carver said his voice rising in irritation. "We are not a charity house—"

"Carver," Nathaniel interrupted. "It is I, Nathaniel."

Carver's gaze snapped to Nathaniel's face, and his eyes widened. His face turned pale, and he stumbled back a step. "Mr. Winthrop, sir. I didn't know... I beg your pardon... I wasn't expecting anyone."

"I understand," Nathaniel said. "My homecoming is rather sudden."

Carver took another step away, and his eyes filled with fear, almost as if he thought he was seeing a ghost.

"Would you be so kind as to let Mother know I'm home and that I'll be in the sitting room?" Without waiting for Carver to respond, he crossed the hall and entered the front room that served as a receiving parlor for guests. Although he wasn't a guest, he felt as out of place in the sitting room as he'd felt in the front hallway.

He avoided walking on the large carpet at the center of the room and made his way to the carved walnut settee with its unique oval medallion back. His mother had recently purchased it, along with a matching chair, and had them upholstered in a dark pink velvet she called *cranberry*.

As he took in the glossy fabric, he decided against sitting on Mother's beautiful furniture with his bedraggled clothing. Instead, he wound through the room, attempting not to bump into the treasures of hand painted vases, lovely globe lanterns, and delicate dishes. He halted at one of the long windows and peered past the silk taffeta draperies. Even those, he dared not touch for fear of somehow leaving a damp fingerprint.

At the hurried tap of footsteps and rustling of skirts, he pivoted away from the window in time to see his mother enter the room, followed by Nicholas. They both stopped short at the sight of him.

His mother cried out, covered her mouth, and would have collapsed had Nicholas not caught her.

"Mother," Nathaniel said, starting toward her.

Nicholas guided her to the nearest chair and gently lowered her to the plush cushion. Her blonde hair was arranged in a high pompadour style set in place with a diamond pin, with a few curls dangling over her forehead. She was attired in a day dress of black Chantilly lace over rose-colored satin and was as lovely as always.

She couldn't take her eyes off Nathaniel's face. When he knelt in front of her, she lifted a fluttering hand to his chin, then his cheek. "Is it really my Nathaniel?" she asked in her breathy voice.

"Yes, Mother." He lifted her hand to his lips and pressed a kiss there. His fingers brushed against her diamond bracelet as well as the jewel-encrusted rings she wore.

Tears glossed her eyes and several spilled over.

Nicholas was quick to press a handkerchief into her hand, which she used to dab the corners of her eyes. His brother, as always, was impeccably dressed and groomed. They shared the same light hair and green eyes, but Nicholas was shorter and thinner compared to Nathaniel's athletic build.

"We thought you'd drowned. That you were dead." Her voice trembled as much as her hand. "How can this be that you're here and alive?"

He shook his head, wondering how he could give details about his absence over the past weeks without bringing up Abbie or Hosea. For a reason he couldn't explain, he didn't want his family to know about them. At least not yet.

"What happened?" Nicholas asked. "Where have you been all this time?"

Nathaniel fumbled to find the right words. "Well…the blow to my head took away my memories. So for the past few weeks, I didn't know who I was. I couldn't remember anything about my past. I had no recollection of my name, my family, or where I lived."

His mother's eyes filled with horror, and she cupped a hand over his cheek again. "Oh, my poor darling boy!"

Nicholas stared at Nathaniel's clothing with disgust. "So you've been wandering around this whole time not knowing who you were or where you were from?"

"Something like that," Nathaniel said. "But today—a short while ago—my memories returned. And I came right here."

"Oh, my darling." His mother wiped at more tears. "I can't bear to think of how difficult your life has been these past weeks. It breaks my heart."

Had his life been difficult? No, actually it had been pleasant and peaceful. Sure, he'd worked hard in a way that he'd never had to before. But he could honestly say he'd enjoyed learning all that he had—taking care of the lighthouse, crabbing and clamming, even the cooking and the cleaning. But how could he explain that to Mother and Nicholas? They'd never understand.

"I'm fine, Mother," he assured her. "And I'm home now. That's all that matters." He rose and tried to push aside the discontentment that rose just as swiftly.

Nicholas sized him up again and then finally nodded, as though he'd convinced himself that he was seeing Nathaniel and not an apparition. Two years younger, Nicholas had always been more serious and studious. In recent years, with his father's problems growing worse, Nicholas had buried himself in his books and schooling every bit as much as Nathaniel had buried himself in alcohol and women.

Women.

Nathaniel's pulse pattered to a dying stop, leaving a slow, awful burn in its place as one final memory returned. The day of the accident, Mother had asked him to visit Kitty Martin and propose to her. Nathaniel almost groaned aloud. He certainly didn't love Kitty. In fact, he hardly knew her. He was ashamed to admit that she was only just one of the women he'd spent time with during the spring.

On that last fateful day, he hadn't wanted to visit her. But he'd known he needed to propose to her, though everything within him had resisted.

Because Kitty Martin was pregnant. With his child.

Nathaniel swallowed the bile that formed in the back of his throat. He'd already emptied his stomach and had nothing left. Even so, he felt nauseous again. He swayed and the room grew blurry. Only Nicholas's steadying hand kept him from toppling.

"Carver," his mother called in alarm, "send for the physician. Right away."

Dizzy and weak, Nathaniel leaned against his brother.

"We must get Nathaniel to his room," she continued. "He's clearly very ill."

Nathaniel agreed. He was ill. But not in the way his mother thought. Now that he knew exactly what kind of man he'd been, the despicable life he'd lived, the selfish and immoral way he'd treated women, he couldn't bear to go on.

No wonder he'd been content to live without his memories. No wonder he'd been in no hurry to return to his present life. Because now that he was here again, the longing for oblivion swept over him. He had an intense urge to lose himself in darkness, where he wouldn't have to remember or face anything ever again.

Chapter 17

After turning on the lantern, Abbie plodded down the tower steps, praying that this time Gramps would be asleep. But a peek into his bedroom door revealed his empty bed.

Her head dropped with discouragement, and she continued down the stairs. At the bottom, she caught sight of him in the parlor, pacing back and forth as he'd been doing for hours. His forehead wrinkled with worry, and he was wringing his hands together.

Abbie paused in the door and watched him with growing helplessness. He'd been agitated since yesterday, when she'd returned to the island without Nathaniel. Although Gramps had finally fallen into a restless sleep on the sofa last night, he'd awoken this morning and begun pacing again. He'd been at it all day, only stopping to eat a few bites.

Every time she attempted to talk to him, he asked her the same questions. Where was Steele? Why hadn't he come home? Was he hurt?

Nathaniel's absence had pushed Gramps back into the past, and he hadn't returned. With each passing hour, he'd only grown more confused.

The rain pelting against the windows filled the silence of the room and covered over Gramps' halting but slapping footsteps.

Abbie fingered the family Bible on the oak end table. Next to it lay *The Tale of Two Cities,* with a long piece of dried seagrass marking the spot, where Nathaniel had last read to Gramps.

"I can read to you," she offered. She picked up the Bible and flipped it open to the place Nathaniel had marked—2 Corinthians. "Please, Hosea. Sit for a little while and let me read your favorite Bible passage."

"Steele will read when he returns," Gramps retorted without breaking his stride.

"I'm sure he won't be able to make it back tonight," Abbie said. "Not with the way it's raining."

Gramps kept pacing.

Abbie watched wearily. She'd already tried to convince him at least a dozen times since nightfall. But he wouldn't be dissuaded from his vigil. He was determined to stay awake until Nathaniel returned.

Abbie didn't have the heart to tell him he'd be waiting forever. That Nathaniel wasn't ever coming back. That she'd ruined everything.

"Please, Hosea," she pleaded. "You have to get some sleep."

"I can't sleep until I know Steele is safe."

"I'm sure he's staying in Newport for the night and waiting

until morning before attempting to return home."

"As long as the light is on, he'll come back. He always does."

If only just one person in her life was truly that reliable. A scream of frustration lodged in her throat. With forced calmness, she closed the Bible and returned it to the end table.

You're despicable. I don't want to see you ever again. Nathaniel's words haunted her every move. She shouldn't be surprised that he'd left her. Her lies had been completely unacceptable. She should have been honest with him from the moment they'd met that first morning.

Even so, after spending so much time together, after many tender moments, after believing love was possible, he'd wrenched her heart out when he'd left. She supposed she'd wanted his affection for her to be strong enough to withstand the mess she'd made of things. She'd harbored a tiny grain of hope that he'd understand why she'd lied and would forgive her. And she'd longed for him to see her as valuable enough to hold on to, in spite of her mistakes.

But he'd shoved her aside and walked away. Just like everyone else in her life had.

The hole in her chest where her heart had once been now throbbed with pain—and at times it was excruciating enough to bring her to tears. She'd decided she wouldn't cry. But the unshed tears burned in her throat and eyes, nonetheless.

When Nate had left last winter, she'd been hurt too. Disappointed. Frustrated. But the pain paled compared to this.

She sucked in a sharp breath. She could do nothing to ease Gramps' agitation any more than she could ease her own. In fact, once word reached Mr. Davis that Nathaniel was gone, he'd pay her a visit. This time she wouldn't fight leaving the island. This time she wouldn't use deception to attempt to stay. She'd admit the truth to the superintendent—that she and Gramps were alone.

She watched Gramps one last time. He plodded across the room six steps, pivoted, and tramped back the way he'd come, his shoulders slumped, his head hanging, his tired eyes rimmed with dark circles.

The sinking feeling inside told her his agitation now would pale in comparison with what was to come when she attempted to row him off Rose Island for the last time. It would be a nightmare. But it was a nightmare she could no longer avoid.

The next morning, Abbie awoke with a start. The light coming in through the gap in the curtains indicated that morning was well under way and that she'd overslept. It was a common problem for her. After having to get up throughout the night to check on the lantern, she'd always had a difficult time rousing and crawling from bed.

She'd been grateful when Nathaniel had eventually taken over turning off the lantern for her in the mornings. It was one of the many things he'd done that she'd appreciated. Now that he was gone, she realized all the more what a caring and considerate man he was.

As she stepped out of bed, her gaze snagged on the cross Nathaniel had given her for her birthday, the one he'd shaped out of driftwood. It was propped on the dresser against the attached mirror. Hope had radiated from him when he'd handed it to her. She'd almost allowed herself to hope that maybe someone could finally love her enough to stay.

Her heart throbbed with fresh pain as his words clanged through her once again. *You're despicable. I don't want to see you ever again.*

So much for allowing hope to fill her. It was gone now. She was alone again. And she was better alone. Wasn't she?

She stopped and listened. The house was too quiet. A glance out the window revealed that the rain of the past two days had stopped, which would account for some of the stillness after the constant pelting. The house was also devoid of clattering pans and the sizzling breakfast Nathaniel had prepared each morning.

Even so, she couldn't prevent unease from winding through her as she dressed. A peek into Gramps' room told her he'd never made it up to his bed. She could only pray he'd grown so weary at some point during the night that he'd fallen asleep on the sofa again.

Doing her best to avoid each squeaky floorboard, she tiptoed downstairs and poked her head into the parlor, expecting to see Gramps covered in one of Gran's afghans and snoring in deep slumber. But he wasn't there. Or anywhere else in the house.

Maybe he'd finally put Nathaniel's absence behind him and returned to his usual routine of whitewashing. She hoped that was the case. His agitation was difficult to handle, and she wasn't sure she'd have the patience for another day of his pacing.

"Hosea!" she called as she stepped outside. Her stomach rumbled, the sign that she needed to cook breakfast. But first she wanted to assure herself that Gramps was doing better and that they could go back to living as they had before Nathaniel had washed up on the shore and given them both hope.

The fog was heavy around the bay, enough that she decided to keep the lantern going until the clouds lifted. A steady mist had settled in as well, making the gray day more dismal. Although the thorough watering was beneficial for her garden, she was ready for the rain and storms to move on.

She said good morning to the cats and chickens, checked on the new growth of beans that would need to be picked just as soon as the rain stopped, and made sure the cistern was collecting the rainwater.

"Hosea!" she shouted as she rounded the bastion and searched for him at its base. Since he wasn't working on the tower or oil house, she assumed he'd gone down to the bastion for the morning.

She stopped at the far rounded edge and rested her hands on her hips, puzzled that he wasn't in any of his usual spots. Was he still in the house? Had he by chance fallen asleep in Nathaniel's room?

With her heartbeat tapping an ominous rhythm, Abbie raced up to the house. She banged through the door, not caring anymore how much noise she made. Uneasiness slithered through her, even though she told herself she had nothing to worry about, that she'd find Gramps.

One look into Nathaniel's deserted room only fanned her worry. She scoured the house all the way from the tower to the small cellar, finding no sign of Gramps. She retraced her steps to every place he normally whitewashed and, as before, found no evidence he'd been there at all that morning.

Growing more frantic by the minute, Abbie sprinted to the old remains of the fort, passing by the area that Nathaniel had been clearing, the place he'd promised to build her a shed for her new cow. But now the shed would never be completed for a cow they'd never have. It would be one more ruin on the island. One more reminder of how easy it was to fail.

As she neared the dock, she was relieved to see that both boats were secured. Surely, that meant Gramps was still there, that he'd only wandered off, perhaps to do his treasure hunting earlier in the day.

"Gramps!" she shouted as she jogged along the beach. She called for him above the roar of waves until her voice was hoarse, and she scoured the island until hunger and fatigue drove her back to the keeper's house.

Upon her return, she prayed she'd find him in the house and was frustrated to discover that he was still nowhere in sight. Another thorough check of the house and tower gave her no clues to his whereabouts—not even the tiniest hint.

Once she'd eaten, she spent the rest of the day searching the island. She covered every inch of the interior, retraced her path around the coast, and rowed the circumference, praying as she went that she wouldn't find him floating in the tide.

When darkness settled, she called off her search. As much as she wanted to continue looking for him throughout the night, she could think of nowhere else he might be.

Wet and sick with worry, she climbed the hill back to the house. The darkness of the coming night pressed down on her. The lantern, which she'd accidentally left running all day, was dark now. It had probably run out of oil or wick or both, and she would be late in getting it started.

The heavy responsibility of her duty only added to the roiling in her stomach. She had to focus on the light, even if she didn't want to. It was what Gramps would have wanted if he'd been in his right mind. He would have told her they had a sacred duty to make sure the beacon was shining every night, that lives depended upon it.

She swung open the backdoor and stepped into the dark kitchen. Strange silence met her. Even before she was able to locate the lantern, she could tell something was wrong. As she struck the match and touched it to the wick, she gasped at the sight that met her. Someone had ransacked the kitchen, emptied drawers, upended crates, knocked over chairs, and dumped food canisters. It looked like a cyclone had ripped its way through the room.

She stepped over items, made her way to the parlor, and lifted the lantern to find that it had been ravaged as well. The intruder had dumped books from the shelves, pulled papers from the desk, and knocked knickknacks to the floor.

Her heart slammed hard against her ribs. Maybe the intruder was still there.

She silenced her racing thoughts and listened for several long minutes. Although she didn't hear anything except the wind rattling the tower and vents, she crept as quietly as possible through the house, searching for the trespasser. All she found was more of the same destruction in each room.

When she finally reached Gramps' room and assured herself that the perpetrator was nowhere in sight, she dropped to the edge of Gramps' bed and released a shaky breath. As far as she could tell, the intruders hadn't taken any of their possessions. If a thief had hoped to find something of value, then he'd been sorely disappointed. They had nothing. What little Gramps had saved, he kept buried in a jar in the backyard.

Abbie stared around Gramps' room, a mirror image of hers across the hall, except that he usually kept his neat. Now every drawer was opened and emptied on the floor. The contents of the chest in the corner were likewise dumped and in disarray.

Who had done this? And why?

She guessed that someone must have come ashore while she'd been out searching the interior of the island. She'd been gone for hours during the afternoon and hadn't been paying attention to the boats passing by.

Although the thought that someone had rifled through every personal item they owned repelled her, the realization that Gramps was still missing disturbed her more. It was almost as if the rainy mist had swallowed him up.

"Oh, Gramps," she whispered through trembling lips. "Where have you gone?"

In his confusion and anxiety over Nathaniel's leaving, had he decided to search for him? If so, had he gotten lost? Even though Gramps knew Narragansett Bay inside and out, perhaps he'd wandered off and forgotten where he was.

All she knew was that she'd do anything to find him.

Chapter 18

Nathaniel didn't want to get out of bed ever again. He'd slept fitfully for the past two days with the help of the laudanum the physician had given him. Yesterday both Mother and Nicholas had come to his room and attempted to persuade him to join them for dinner. But he'd sent them away.

He'd told himself last night, when he'd taken another dose of laudanum, that it would be his final time. After all, he'd seen the effects of the drug on his father—the way it consumed and controlled a person.

Something in Nathaniel's conscience told him to fight against the need for the opium-based medicine the same way he was fighting against the need for a drink. After weeks of being free from alcohol, he had to stay that way. If he started drinking again, he'd spiral downward, just like he had before.

He'd lived with integrity over the past month. And he'd liked that new man.

The problem was, that new man hadn't been real. He

hadn't been Abbie's husband or Hosea's son-in-law or an acting light keeper. All it had taken was one step back into his old life for him to realize how awful he truly was.

He was lazy, self-indulgent, calloused, spineless, and immoral. Maybe he could handle those qualities about himself when he was unattached. So what if he ended up like his father as a single man with no one to hurt except himself? But he couldn't bear the thought of having a wife and child who would bear the brunt of the shame and pain he would perpetually bring them.

He opened an eye and glanced at the bottle of laudanum on the bedside table. The liquid beckoned to him. It begged him to dull the nightmare of the life that faced him, the life that would always be filled with regret.

Was that what had happened to his father? Had he known how much pain he'd caused everyone in his family? Had that knowledge pushed him to hide even further behind his bottles of rum and laudanum?

Nathaniel groped for the bottle and realized his fingers were shaking. He could hardly stretch his arm and only managed to bump against a piece of wood. As the object fell off the table and onto the mattress, he blinked hard.

He grazed it, realizing it was the cross of hope that Victoria Cole had given him over four years ago, when she'd said good-bye to him on the dock in Provincetown, when she'd told him with stinging finality she could never marry him.

Victoria's father had originally made the cross after he'd been shipwrecked. He'd given the cross to Victoria's mother, who'd written a letter to go with the memento, sharing her struggle to put her faith in the true Beacon of hope rather than in her circumstances or a man, both of which would change.

Over the years, the cross of hope had passed through numerous hands until miraculously it ended up with Victoria. Nathaniel had thought for sure Victoria would keep the cross forever, especially since it had once belonged to her mother. But when Victoria had said good-bye to him, she'd handed it to him.

Had she known that someday he'd be all out of hope, all out of a reason to live, all out of strength to go on?

He fingered the grains of wood and remembered the cross he'd made for Abbie that was a replica of this one. Somehow, when he'd lost his memories, he hadn't forgotten what the cross stood for. Had God been trying to point him to the true Source of hope even then? What about now?

He shook his head. He was too lost, too unworthy, too undeserving to be able to make his way back. Holding up his hand, he stared at the gold signet ring on his finger. His father's ring. The one Mother had given him after Father's funeral.

With disgust, he tugged it off and slapped it down next to the cross. He'd never wanted to wear it, had wanted to toss it deep into the ocean. But Mother had been so insistent he put it on that he'd finally compromised and worn it on a chain. Even that had felt like a burden.

At a knocking on the door, Nathaniel burrowed under his cover and buried his head into his pillow. He wasn't ready to face anyone yet.

"Mr. Winthrop, sir?" Carver opened the door a crack.

Nathaniel didn't answer.

"Someone is here and insists on seeing you."

Nathaniel groaned. "Tell the visitor I'm not feeling well and cannot be disturbed."

"I've told her numerous times you're ill, but she says

it's urgent."

Was it Kitty Martin? Had she heard of his return and already arrived to start the wedding plans?

"She said to tell you it's about Hosea."

"Hosea?" Nathaniel sat straight up, and the covers fell away. The grogginess from his drug-induced slumber dissipated. Darkness shrouded the room, the heavy silk tapestries blocking out daylight and trapping in stale air. His head pounded and his tongue stuck to the roof of his mouth like dry toast. But he was awake and more alert than he'd been since arriving home.

Abbie was here.

For an instant, the longing for her was so sharp he couldn't drag a breath into his lungs. He needed to see her, to be with her, to touch her, more than he needed anything else.

He swung his legs over the side of the enormous four-poster bed and tried to stand. But his knees gave way, and he sank to the edge.

"Shall I inform her you will be down shortly, sir?" Carver asked through the crack in the door.

"Yes," he croaked. But as soon as the word was out, he cradled his head in his hands. What was he thinking? Abbie had lied to him. Had led him on for weeks. Had hurt him. Had taken his heart and stomped all over it.

"No!" he shouted as Carver began to close the door. The anger he'd felt since he'd walked away from her at the dock flooded his soul. "Tell her I don't want to see her. That I meant what I said."

"Very well, sir."

The door clicked shut, leaving Nathaniel in the stifling darkness.

How dare she come here and try to see him by throwing around Hosea's name? After the way they'd parted, after the harsh words he'd spoken, he certainly hadn't expected her to seek him out. Abbie was a strong woman, and she had too much pride to contact him after he'd told her he never wanted to see her again.

So why had she come? Was she so riddled with guilt she couldn't function without attempting to apologize to him again? Was she needing to assuage her conscience in some way?

For a moment, he considered the fact that he'd been too hard on her when he'd left her on the dock. That he should have taken the time to listen to her explanation. That maybe she'd had a perfectly logical reason for deceiving him.

He stood again, and this time forced his bare feet across the room. Before he could stop himself, he was out the door and shuffling down the hallway toward the main spiraling stairway. He didn't have to speak with her long. Actually, he didn't need to speak with her at all. Talking to her again would be much too painful and dredge up hope he didn't want to allow himself to feel again.

No. Instead, he'd stand at the top of the landing out of sight and take a small peek at her. To make sure she was all right.

"Mr. Winthrop is currently unavailable." Carver's voice rose up the stairway.

"But he's home?"

"He said that he doesn't want to see you. And that he meant what he said."

Nathaniel glanced down the stairway in time to see Abbie's face blanch. She took a step back, as though Carver's words had struck her. As much as Nathaniel wanted to view her with revulsion, the longing for her swelled up again. Or at least the longing for the woman he'd once believed her to be—kind, caring, hardworking, and tenderhearted.

He didn't know what was true about her anymore. If she'd lied to him about who he was, then what was to stop her from lying about herself?

"Did you tell him I need his help with Hosea?" Her voice was tight, as though she was on the verge of crying.

"Yes." Carver steered her toward the door.

"You told him I can't find Hosea?"

She couldn't find Hosea? Nathaniel's normal body functions ceased, leaving him in a state of utter stillness. What had happened to the sweet old man? Had he wandered off?

Nathaniel's heart and lungs started working again at double the speed. The rift between him and Abbie wasn't Hosea's fault. Hosea had been confused about Nathaniel's identity all along. It wasn't as if Hosea had purposefully tricked him the way Abbie had.

"I'm sorry, miss," Carver was saying as he ushered Abbie out. "But there's nothing more we can do for you."

Nathaniel's mind flashed with a picture of gentle Hosea. Had Nathaniel's absence worried him? Perhaps Hosea left the island to search for him? Perhaps he hoped that by finding Nathaniel he could spare Abbie more heartache. After all, Hosea had already witnessed Abbie's husband leaving her once, and he wouldn't want her to go through it again. He likely wanted to spare his granddaughter another loss.

No wonder Abbie had been willing to seek him out. She was the kind of woman who'd do anything for her gramps, including humiliating herself in front of him and begging for help.

Including lying. And deceiving.

Nathaniel stiffened. Had she lied these past weeks to protect Hosea?

Before he could sort through his thoughts, Carver escorted Abbie through the door and closed it behind her, against her protests. When he turned and sighed, Nathaniel realized that the old butler hadn't taken any delight in his task. His mouth tightened into a frown, and his eyes filled with sadness.

Nathaniel started down the stairway. He supposed that's what people did for those they loved. They made themselves carry through with tasks they wouldn't otherwise consider. Was that what Abbie had done for Hosea?

At the sound of Nathaniel's footsteps, Carver straightened and the lines in his face smoothed into a mask of gentility. "Mr. Winthrop, sir. May I help you?" He rushed up the stairs to meet Nathaniel.

"I think I will speak with Abbie," Nathaniel replied.

Carver hovered near, as though expecting him to falter or sink to his knees. Nathaniel still felt weak, but with each step he took, he seemed to gain strength. When he reached the bottom and started toward the door, Carver cleared his throat. "Would you like me to fetch your trousers first, sir?"

Nathaniel glanced down to see that he was wearing his drawers and undershirt. He'd neither combed his hair nor shaven since his arrival. He guessed he looked as bad as he felt. Not that he particularly cared what Abbie thought about him. In fact, he didn't care at all. He only wanted to talk to her because he was concerned about Hosea.

Even so, he couldn't chase after her down Ocean Drive without getting dressed first. He'd already brought enough shame to his family. He could avoid more, couldn't he?

"You're a wise man, Carver," Nathaniel said, giving the servant a half smile. "It probably is best if I put my pants on before going out. And my shirt too?"

Carver smiled in return. "Shall I send the footman after your visitor, sir? And request that she wait?"

Nathaniel gripped the polished banister and shook his head. "No. Let her go for now. I know where to find her. As soon as I'm cleaned up, I'll pay her a visit instead."

At the idea of returning to Rose Island, energy surged through him. For the first time since arriving home, the weight of his despair lifted just a little, and he felt like doing something besides lying in bed. He wasn't sure what had happened with Hosea. But he was suddenly determined to find out.

Abbie cried out in frustration as the wind whipped the foamy waves into a fury. She stared across the bay and realized that any attempt at crossing back to Newport would be perilous. In fact, with the heaps of dark clouds pushing in from the west, she guessed they were in for another summer storm and that she'd need to turn on the lantern.

But all she wanted to do was return to town and see if Menard had formed a search party. Debbie had promised she'd rally their friends and neighbors to search along the Newport coast.

Abbie had already spent the morning in Newport, banging on doors and asking everyone about Gramps. She'd even gone to the Winthrop's to garner Nathaniel's help. But after his refusal to see her, she'd finally rowed back to the island in case Gramps had returned home.

When he hadn't been anywhere in or near the house, she'd scoured the island again, praying she'd come across him digging in a solitary spot she'd missed yesterday. But her afternoon of searching had amounted to nothing. And now she was stuck on the island for the night, or at least until the storm blew over.

As she trudged up the bastion, the rain began to fall in heavy, pounding rivulets. She released another cry of both exhaustion and anger. "Where are you, Gramps? Where did you run off to?"

She hastened her steps, but stopped abruptly as a red beam pierced the air. The beam came from the tower room and swept out over the east before rotating around to the south and then west.

Someone had turned on the light.

Her heartbeat picked up its pace, and hope sprang to life in her chest. Had Gramps returned? She hadn't noticed any other boats at the dock. But someone could have rowed him over while she was out searching. Maybe Menard had brought him and then rushed to return to Newport before the storm hit.

She ran as fast as her waterlogged skirt would allow. She shoved open the kitchen door and burst inside, halting at the sight of Nathaniel leaning casually against the door frame that separated the kitchen and parlor. He was staring straight at her, as if he'd been waiting for her to enter.

He'd apparently lit the lantern that hung above the kitchen table because it illuminated the disaster of the room that she hadn't yet picked up. It also highlighted every magnificent line in his cleanly shaven face, along with his clenched jaw, flaring nostrils, and glowering eyes.

He was attired in fashionable navy blue trousers and

matching waistcoat over a starched white linen shirt. He'd tossed his suit coat onto the kitchen table, along with a silk necktie. The dark color of his suit contrasted with his light sandy hair and tanned skin.

After visiting his family's mansion this morning, the display of wealth had overwhelmed her. Both the outside and inside of his home had been opulent beyond anything she'd ever seen before. She'd understood in a way she hadn't before the chasm that existed between them. They were vastly different, from opposite social classes, with clashing lifestyles and values and goals.

Seeing him cleaned up and dressed in the tailored clothing that shouted his wealth, she realized once more the unbridgeable gulf that separated them. She'd been a fool to believe for an instant that anything could exist between her and Nathaniel.

Slowly, she pushed the door closed behind her, so that she stood inside, bedraggled and dripping wet. Her hair hung in tangles, her blouse and skirt stuck to her body, and her bare feet were coated in sand. She looked as much of a mess as he looked neatly put together. They couldn't have been more opposite in every way.

"What happened here?" His voice was cold, and his angry gaze swept over the room, touching on the overturned chairs, spilled canisters, and drawers hanging from their hinges.

"I don't know," she answered, viewing the house and her belongings through his eyes. What must he think of her now? "It was like this last night when I returned from searching for Gramps."

"Then you weren't hurt?" For a second, his eyes alighted on her with concern.

"No." But she supposed she very well could have been. Whoever had barged through their home with so little regard could have been dangerous to her too.

"It's not safe for you out here alone," Nathaniel said, as if he'd been thinking the same thing she had. His eyes glinted with anger again, and his mouth twisted into a tight line. He walked to the recipe box that had belonged to Gran, now upturned, with the small slips of paper scattered on the floor. He bent and retrieved several recipes and slid them into the box.

He picked up a few more and shuffled them so they were all facing the same direction. "I want you to stay with Debbie until we discover who caused all this damage."

At the arrogance in his tone, she stiffened. "I'm not going anywhere."

He straightened and pinned her with a glare. "You can't remain here alone."

"I can and I will." Her tone was equally steely.

"I won't let you."

"You won't be able to stop me." Her ire quickly rose. Did he think that because he was Nathaniel Winthrop III he could walk into her home and order her around like a king would his vassal? She narrowed her eyes and glowered at him.

Something in the way he tilted his head told her he had enough power and money to stop her if that's what he wanted. But instead of persisting, he gave an exasperated sigh and scooped up another handful of recipe cards.

"Did they take anything?" he asked after a moment of silence.

"They?"

He shot her another look, as if to say she was naïve. "The

people who did this. Did they steal anything?"

"I don't think so. There's nothing to steal."

He finished picking up the last of the cards and added them one by one into the recipe box. "If they weren't here to steal from you, then what were they searching for?"

"Who says they were searching for anything?"

He paused in his efforts and narrowed his eyes on her. "If they didn't get what they wanted, they'll be back."

She shivered.

He must have noticed because he nodded toward the doorway that led upstairs. "Go get changed, and then you can tell me everything you know about Hosea. Let's hope it helps us figure out what happened here."

She crossed her arms and hugged them to her chest. She wasn't sure what was making her more chilled—her wet clothes or Nathaniel's anger. When she'd gone to visit him this morning, she'd hoped he wouldn't be as furious with her anymore. She'd prayed that the mention of Hosea's name would draw on his sympathy. After all, he had no reason to be mad at Hosea. But all hope had vanished when he'd sent her away.

Now, with him standing in the house, she couldn't keep from wondering if she'd made a mistake going to him. He was clearly still very upset with her. Although she wanted his help in finding Gramps, she wasn't sure how she could bear to be around him and face his bitterness—especially knowing she was the cause.

"Look, Nathaniel," she started but then didn't know what to say. Should she use this as an opportunity to apologize again and attempt to explain why she'd used him? Maybe on some level that's the reason she'd sought after his help in the first place, because she'd wanted the chance to talk to him again.

He finished putting the last of the recipe cards into the box and closed the lid. He set the container on the top of the sideboard. But instead of releasing it, his large hand enveloped it, and he lowered his head. With his back facing her, his slumped posture shouted his dejection.

"I'm sorry for hurting you." The words spilled out before she could stop them. "What I did was—well, it was vile."

The muscles in his shoulders tensed, but he didn't say anything.

She had a sudden longing to cross to him and comfort him somehow. But she was sure he'd bolt if she did anything of the sort. "I didn't start off attempting to deceive you. It just sort of happened. Then once you thought you were Nate, I didn't correct you."

His grip on the box tightened. The agony radiating from his body was palpable. She hated that he was hurting and that she could do nothing to ease his misery.

"I hate myself for what I've done, for the pain I've caused you. And I don't expect you to ever forgive me—"

"Let's focus on finding Hosea." He released the recipe card box and crammed his fingers into his hair.

She nodded. "Okay."

For a minute, he stared straight ahead at the sampler on the wall that Gran had stitched. "Go change, Abbie," he said. "Please."

This time she ducked her head and crossed the room. Sadness swelled in her chest and up into her throat. She'd ruined everything. She should have known better than to think that he'd ever be able to look at or speak with her again.

He was here to help Hosea. That was it. And she couldn't

expect anything more.

A sudden crash against the front window made Abbie jump. She spun to see water running down the glass pane. For long seconds, she stared and tried to make sense of what had happened.

Nathaniel strode across the room, his frown deepening. As he opened the door, the wind jerked the door and slammed it inward with such force that it shook the walls. At the same instant, another forceful slap hit the window, and this time she realized it was a wave.

A new storm was upon them, and apparently this one was descending with a vengeance. Abbie could only remember one other storm that produced waves high enough to reach the house. The storm of 1876, a year after Gran had died. Waves had crashed so high that they'd drenched the first floor of the keeper's dwelling with a foot of water. The storm had torn the boats from the dock and swept them out to sea. It had flooded and ruined the garden. It had even caught Gran's pet goose in its grasp and drowned it.

Pets. Her chickens. And the cats. What if they were caught in one of those powerful waves?

Abbie picked up her skirt and ran. She had to save them. After losing so many people she loved, she couldn't lose her animals too.

She darted past Nathaniel, who was attempting to wrestle the door shut. When he shouted a warning after her, she didn't stop. The fury of the waves and the screaming of the wind ripped away the sound of his voice. The wind attempted to beat her back and push her down, but she fought against it until she was at the oil house.

She didn't waste any time but dropped to her knees where

the mother cat and kittens lived. She bent low against the already saturated ground, pressed her cheek to the grass, and peered into the small space.

Amidst the spider webs and debris, frightened glowing eyes peered back at her.

She squirmed into the space, heedless of the dirt, and her hands made contact with fur. But of course, the frightened kittens only scrambled to get away from her, unable to comprehend that she wasn't the cause of the noise or waves, that instead she was there to rescue them.

"Come on, sweet ones," she crooned. She lunged and managed to grasp one of the fur bundles and then a second. Although they fought against her, clawing her hands and wrists, she scooted out and bumped into Nathaniel. He was kneeling next to her, the wind whipping his hair and clothes. Wordlessly, he took the two kittens from her.

For a moment, his anxious gaze met hers, pleading with her to return to the house. But she only sucked in a breath and slithered into the dank tight space. She glanced back in time to see him stand and dash off.

Relieved that he'd decided to help her, she forced herself to crawl under the oil house in spite of the filth. She performed the feat two more times before she'd captured all the kittens and their mama, Martha. The tomcats were nowhere to be found, and she hoped they'd find refuge further inland.

When Nathaniel sprinted across the yard with Martha, he yelled something over his shoulder at her, likely instructions to follow him inside.

Another enormous wave crashed against the bastion, sending a spray of water across her garden. She realized she was running out of time. However, she ran the opposite direction toward the beach and the ruins of Fort Hamilton, where her chickens normally took refuge. The tide was already as high as the fort by the time she sloshed toward the low brick building.

Frantically, she searched for the creatures, calling out to them, although she knew they wouldn't be able to hear her above the angry roaring and surging waves. As she rounded the fort, she caught sight of several of the chickens perched on a boulder.

She'd almost reached them, when a hand grabbed her from behind and halted her. "It's too dangerous to be out." Nathaniel shouted at her above the noise.

She twisted to free herself but he didn't release her. "I have to save the chickens!"

He shook his head and bent toward her ear. "They're not worth the risk."

"They are to me." She lurched forward, planning to drag Nathaniel with her if need be. Thankfully, he didn't try to stop her but hunkered his shoulders and strode forward with her.

The hens didn't resist as she and Nathaniel swooped them up. She found a fourth taking refuge behind the boulder, but couldn't locate the other two or the rooster.

With the chickens in arm, they dashed across the low, open space that led to the bastion. Before they reached the higher ground, a surge of water, like that of a tidal wave, rose above them.

"Run! Run! Run!" Nathaniel shouted, glancing behind him with fear etched into every tight line of his face. He seized her arm and forced her to run faster, practically lifting her off the ground with his effort.

They were only halfway up the hill when the wave

crashed. The spray hit their backs, and water rose above their knees. The force of the tide threatened to drag them out to sea. But Nathaniel strained to hold them in place.

When they were finally free of the clawing fingers of the sea, he scrambled forward, dragging her through the wet sand and weeds. By the time they reached the house and fell inside, Abbie was gasping for each breath.

Nathaniel released the chickens to a flurry of irate squawking and beating wings, forced the door closed behind them, and bolted it.

"I have to rescue the others," she managed through her wheezing lungs.

"You're not going out unless it's over my dead body." He planted himself in front of the door and crossed his arms. His wet hair hung over his forehead, above his furrowed brows and eyes that fairly spit fire at her.

She scratched the back of the closest chicken, which was standing in the middle of the kitchen table. "You have no right to tell me what to do."

He shrugged but didn't move, except to deepen his scowl.

She wanted to fight against him, but she couldn't muster the will. He'd helped her save her cats and chickens. He'd likely saved her life by keeping her from being dragged out to sea by the tide.

One hen cackled and pecked at a pile of oats on the floor. "Two of my chickens are still out there," she said.

"I'll buy you a dozen more after the storm passes." His wet garments clung to him and were covered in sand and seaweed. "But you've already put yourself in danger being here on the island by yourself, and I won't allow you to put yourself in any more."

Even though his eyes still glittered with anger, she could see something else in his expression—concern. She couldn't be upset at him because he didn't want her going out again, not when it might mean he still cared.

A wave slammed against the window and propelled her into action. Right now, they didn't have time to stand around arguing. She didn't know how much longer the glass pane would hold out before cracking into pieces and allowing the waves and rain to flood the first floor of the house.

She didn't want to think about the stories she'd heard of storms that raged so furiously that they'd torn apart island lighthouse dwellings like hers and swept them into the sea. As she tried to block out visions of her home sinking to the bottom of the sea, another wave hit the window. Glass splintered and crashed to the floor. And seawater poured inside.

Chapter 19

Nathaniel wedged the damp blanket into the crack along the window. The board he'd nailed there earlier in the night had held against the wind and waves. But the cracks around the edges had allowed water to seep into the house.

Together, he and Abbie had boarded up all the first-floor windows with planks that had been stored in the cellar—probably for an occasion like this storm. The pressure of wind and water had knocked out two of the kitchen windows and one in the parlor. At least the boards were keeping out the worst of the seawater.

Gingerly, he stepped through the inch or so of water that covered the floor. The chickens had perched on the kitchen table to avoid getting wet, and Abbie had long since moved the kittens and their mother upstairs to her bedroom, where they would be safer.

He'd picked up most of the belongings to keep them from being ruined. In the process, he'd found the thin map that had fallen from Hosea's Bible. It had still been under the dresser where he'd left it.

He'd tucked it into Hosea's Bible in the parlor but had been almost sick to his stomach at the sight of the ripped and battered pages. Whoever ransacked the house had made a point of denigrating the Bible, clearly having no reverence for it.

His blood turned cold at the thought of what might have happened to Abbie if she'd been home by herself when the intruder attacked, and he was relieved again that he'd decided to come. At the sight of the storm clouds, he'd almost ruled against the trip. Thankfully, he'd left early enough that the crew of his yacht hadn't been in too much danger. He'd encouraged them to return to the marina immediately and wait to retrieve him until after the storm passed.

When he'd walked into the keeper's house and saw the destruction, shock had rippled through him. Every step he'd taken in his search for Abbie had been torture. He'd expected to find her hurt. Or worse.

After being unable to locate her anywhere, he'd dropped to the sofa and expelled a shaky breath of relief. Then anger had pushed through him with such force it had left him breathless. Anger at the intruders for putting Abbie in danger. Anger at her for being so vulnerable. Anger at himself for not being there for her.

Even after hours of battling the storm, he was still livid. Every time he looked at the destruction. Every time he looked at her. Every time he thought about what could have happened, he wanted to punch something.

Deep down he wished he hadn't walked away from her that day his memories had returned. He half-wished he'd pretended to be ignorant. He could have continued to live on Rose Island with Hosea and Abbie, and none of this would have occurred. Or at least he would have been here to ensure the two were safe.

He was here now, he consoled himself. He shuddered to think how she would have managed this storm alone. Another gust of wind rattled the roof, and the battering of a wave shook the house on its foundation. He was afraid that one of these times a blast would hit the lighthouse so hard that it would rip it from the bastion altogether. Or knock the tower off the house.

With a fresh spurt of anxiety, he started up the steps toward the lantern. He didn't want Abbie up there. But she'd insisted on watching over the light—making sure it was still burning brightly, although he couldn't imagine what ships would venture out on a night like this. If any seafaring vessels were foolish enough to be in the storm, then they deserved to be thrashed.

As he mounted the last flight of steps and poked his head through the hatch, Abbie was standing on a stool, using a rag to sop up rainwater leaking through the windows. Even with her attempts and even though they'd patched the leaky tower windows as best they could, never-ending streams poured in and ran down the walls, pooling on the floor.

She didn't pause in her efforts to acknowledge his presence behind her. From the stiffening of her back, she knew he was there, but she remained silent. Over the past hours, they'd been too frantic, too busy, too consumed with protecting the lighthouse and keeping it running to have time to engage in conversation. Other than hurried instructions to one another and concerns over Hosea's whereabouts, they'd spoken very little since her apology when she'd first walked in the door.

He watched her for a long minute. She'd changed out of her dripping garments some time ago, at his insistence. But her skirt was wet again and her blouse damp as well. With the entire house leaking, he supposed trying to stay dry was futile. Even so, he didn't like knowing she was damp and could catch a chill.

Outside, the night was as black as the bottom of the ocean. The lighthouse beam hardly penetrated the thick darkness of the storm clouds. From the rushing whine of the wind, the heavy patter of rain, and the pounding of waves, he had the feeling the storm wasn't about to let up its fury any time soon. "I want you to go change again," he said.

She finished wringing the water out of her rag into a pail on the floor before she responded. "Since you know full well we're not married and that you're not my husband, perhaps you can stop acting like you are."

"What?" He wasn't acting like her husband. He started to protest, but she cut him off.

"You've been bossing me around all night."

"I don't believe in husbands bossing around their wives."

"Well, then, maybe you're bossing me around because you're rich and arrogant and used to getting your way."

Was he used to getting his way? His newfound memories reminded him of all the times when he had indeed used his charm, money, or power to get something he wanted. He supposed it was one more fault to add to the growing list of his sins.

The self-loathing rose to choke him and only spurred his frustration. "Maybe I'm bossing you around because in spite of everything I still care about you." Once the words were out, he wanted to reel them in, especially when she froze. He could admit he was worried about her and Hosea, but he didn't want to care about her anymore. He wanted—needed—to put her from his mind. After what she'd done, he didn't want her to have a place in his life. Did he?

She pivoted slowly until she was facing him. The lantern beam flashed above her head and illuminated her eyes, which were wide and filled with hope. She searched his face, and he couldn't help doing the same with hers. Even with a smudge of dirt across her forehead and her hair hanging in a tangled mass, she was beautiful. Her features were well defined and delicate, like those of a porcelain doll. But her sun-browned coloring and the smattering of freckles on her nose proved that she had no wish to be placed upon a shelf and admired.

She watched him, uncertainty returning to shadow her face.

"Why?" he asked. Part of him didn't care anymore, but the other part of him needed to know why she'd lied to him.

She lowered herself until she was sitting on the stool. Her shoulders slumped, and she fixed her gaze on her hands in her lap. "I did it for Gramps."

Nathaniel had suspected as much, but he needed to hear it from her.

"Before you came, he'd stopped remembering who I was." Anguish laced her voice. "But the first night you were here, he recognized me."

A burst of wind rattled the vent and the windows so vehemently that for a second Nathaniel was afraid the tower would fall in on itself. But the whistling gust passed, leaving a gentler pressure in its wake.

"I wanted to tell you the truth," she continued, "and I kept promising myself that I would. But every day, Gramps kept getting better. And I knew it was because of you."

"Why me?" When she flinched, he realized his tone was harsher than he intended.

"I don't know," she said, lifting honest eyes to meet his. "But he likes you. And trusts you."

He shrugged.

"And you're good with him," she added almost shyly. "You always seem to know just what to say and do to calm him down. You're kind and patient and genuinely caring…" Her voice trailed off in embarrassment.

He'd recognized a change in Hosea too. Over the days of being together, Hosea had called him Steele less often and addressed him as Nate more. But Nathaniel had a difficult time believing that his presence had caused that difference in Hosea. "I don't think it was me."

"Even Debbie saw it when she came to visit," Abbie said. "Gramps hadn't recognized Debbie or Pollyanna for months. And that day on the island, he did. He called her by name and went over and talked with Pollyanna."

From the earnestness of Abbie's expression, he realized she truly believed he'd made a difference with Hosea. "You decided that helping restore Hosea's memory was more important than helping restore mine?"

Her head dropped again in a posture of defeat. "I realized that moving would disorient Gramps and make him worse. So when I saw that your presence was healing him, I hoped it would make him fit enough in the superintendent's eyes not to need Nate anymore. I hoped the superintendent would see that Gramps was well enough for us to run the lighthouse alone, like we have these past years, and to let us stay indefinitely."

"Then what? After the three weeks, were you planning to throw me out?"

At the accusation in his tone, her head shot up. "No, not like that. I knew I couldn't keep deceiving you, that I had to tell you."

His gut churned as it had the first day he'd learned she'd lied to him. He wasn't upset she'd used him to help Hosea. He understood why she'd done it. She loved her grandfather and only wanted to prevent him from being evicted off the island.

No, he liked her all the more for loving her grandfather so much that she was willing to go to such great lengths to protect him. Abbie was sacrificial and giving and loyal.

But…he didn't like that in the process of making him believe she was his wife, she'd allowed him to feel so deeply for her. Now what hurt most of all was the realization that their relationship had been just a sham.

He stuffed his hands into his trousers and swallowed the bitterness. "I thought our feelings for each other meant something. I thought what we had was real. And it's hard to face you knowing you were just pretending—"

"I wasn't pretending anything. I vow to you, everything that happened between us was real. Very real." Her lashes swept down, hiding her eyes. Even so, her face radiated with embarrassment.

He wanted to allow himself a measure of satisfaction at her confession. But he couldn't, not when one glaring fact stood between them. "You're still married to Nate, aren't you? Nothing can be real, not when your husband could return any day."

She twisted her damp skirt into a tight fist, unwound it,

then twisted it again. "He won't be returning. Not now. Not ever."

"How can you be so sure?"

"He's dead." The finality of her tone and the starkness in her eyes confirmed her words. Quietly, almost ashamedly, she told him about the body local fishermen had found after the spring thaw and her realization that it was Nate even though no one else suspected it.

"By not telling Mr. Davis about Nate's death, I'd hoped Gramps and I could continue to live on Rose Island," she admitted. "But I should have been honest from the start. Once I started lying it was all too easy to keep going."

"But if Nate's absence was working to your advantage, then why didn't you correct the superintendent when he thought I was your husband?"

"Because Zeke had pressured Mr. Davis into kicking us off the island anyway. That's why he came out the day you arrived, to tell us we had to leave."

"So you pretended Nate had returned?"

"I didn't mean to," she said. "Especially at first. But as time went on, I realized your presence could help buy me more time to come up with an alternative for Gramps."

He nodded in understanding. For a long moment, neither of them spoke as he digested all that she'd revealed.

"I'm sorry, Nathaniel," she finally said. "I was wrong and selfish and should have told you the truth right away. I wanted to tell you many times, but the more I cared about you, the harder it got . . ."

"So you really did care?"

She didn't meet his gaze. "Yes. Really." Her voice was almost breathless. It did strange things to his gut and made him want to reach for her. "You should know I tried very hard not to feel anything for you. I didn't want to complicate things."

He nodded. "You did try to stay away. I give you credit for that. But of course, since I believed myself to be Nate and thought I'd been a horrible husband, I was working hard to be better."

"And you were wonderful. You were the best husband any woman could ask for."

His battered, sin-laden soul soaked in her praise. "Nate must have been a terrible husband for you to think I was the best by comparison." He'd attempted a jest, but his words only brought a shadow to her face.

She stared out the rain-splattered window, although there was nothing to see but darkness.

"I'm sorry," he started. "Now that I understand what a scum I really am, I doubt I would have been much better than Nate." He would have been lousy. Just like his father.

"That's not true." She shifted her sights to him again. "You showed me the truth about what God intended for marriage to be like."

"Only because I didn't realize what a complete lout I am." All the frustration of the past two days came back to pelt him with as much stinging velocity as the rain.

"You're not a lout, Nathaniel. You're sweet, kind-hearted, generous, tend—"

"No, I'm not. Apparently, you don't know much about me or the kind of life I've lived."

She was quiet a moment, but her eyes still shone with kindness and admiration. "You're right. I don't know much."

"I've earned the nickname Bad Boy of Newport." He wasn't sure why he felt the need to tell her everything, but suddenly he had to come clean. The admiration would fade from her eyes, but that was for the best anyway, wasn't it? It would be much easier to be around her if she despised him.

"While you're out here working hard and taking care of Hosea, do you know how I spend my days?" His tone had turned so biting that she recoiled. But he didn't care. She would be better keeping her distance from him. "I spend my mornings sleeping off a drunken stupor so that by afternoon I can get up and get drunk all over again."

She didn't seem shocked by his revelation.

"I can't remember having one sober day in the past six months."

"You didn't have a single drink while you lived here," she replied quietly.

He shook his head and raked his fingers into his hair. "I lived recklessly, foolishly, and dangerously. I never passed up a dare and did awful things in the name of fun." He was too ashamed to admit some of the pranks he'd pulled with his friends.

"I've never met a man who is more careful and wise and conscientious."

"I haven't worked hard a day in my life. I'm lazy, undisciplined, and spoiled."

"You helped me and Gramps with our chores. In fact, you always did more than you had to."

"Abbie," he pleaded, wishing she'd stop making him appear better than he was. He didn't want to tell her the worst, but he knew exactly what would silence her litany of compliments. He took a deep breath and released the words that were sure to hurt her. "I spent time with a lot of different women."

Her eyes met his. And, sure enough, hurt flashed there. He wished with all his heart he could say he'd never been intimate with anyone else. But the truth was, he'd been immoral and lived for his own pleasure.

When she didn't respond this time, he realized his words had accomplished what he'd set out to do. He'd helped her to see the reality of who he was. In case she wasn't convinced, he'd make sure. "Before my accident, I learned that I'm to become a father."

The color drained from her face. "A father?"

He nodded and stuffed his hands deeper in his trouser pockets.

Emotions played across her face—confusion, hurt, anger, and finally understanding. She leaned against the window, heedless of the leaking water she was soaking up.

"Even worse," he said in a hoarse voice, "I don't want to take responsibility. I hate the thought of having a child. So you see, I'm the worst of sinners."

She didn't contradict him. She didn't look him in the eyes. And he doubted she would be able to ever again.

He bowed his head. The weight of the defeat that had plagued him over the past few days settled fully upon him. Silently, he lowered himself into the hatch. She didn't stop him. He didn't expect her to. Even so, his heart ached with a new pain. The pain of having loved someone and lost her.

Yes, he loved Abbie. Loved her with all his heart. It didn't matter anymore that she'd deceived him. She'd assured him that what had happened between them had been real, even if everything else had been a lie.

Whatever the case, he wasn't good enough for her. He never had been and never would be. Now she knew it too.

As dawn turned the darkness of night into a dismal gray, Abbie lowered the binoculars and rubbed her tired eyes. The waves that had swelled to twenty and thirty feet high had diminished. Though the sea was still foaming and gnashing its teeth, its hunger had waned.

They'd survived the worst of the destruction. The tower and house were battered, windows blown out, shutters hanging loose, and shingles ripped away. But they were still standing, although all around, the grounds were flooded. Her garden was ruined, the oil house washed away, and the skiffs gone.

She'd weathered the storm—both physically and emotionally. Nathaniel's revelations about his past—particularly the fact that he'd been with other women—had rocked her to the core. But she'd had plenty of time to think about his confession and had concluded that his sins were no worse than hers. They both had done things they weren't proud of. If she wanted him to forgive *her*, then she had to forgive *him* for his sins too, didn't she?

He hadn't come up again during the long night. She'd heard him hammering more boards and knew he was trying to keep the water out of the house, the same way she was attempting to protect the lantern.

One thought kept returning: no matter how he'd lived in his past, he'd been a new man when he'd lived here on Rose Island. He'd been every bit the good, honest, hardworking man she'd claimed he was. Even without his memories, he'd been conscious of his mistakes to some degree. But instead of letting those mistakes defeat him, he'd risen above them and had become a better man.

If he could do that once, couldn't he do it now that all of his memories had returned?

She rolled her shoulders to stretch out the tension and started down the steps. A peek into her bedroom showed the kittens curled up asleep with their mama on the unmade bed. Martha raised her head and looked at Abbie, as if to thank her before snuggling against her babies contentedly.

If only life were so easy, Abbie mused. If only she could as easily put the hardships behind her and find contentment.

When she entered the kitchen, she stopped short at the sight of Nathaniel on his hands and knees, mopping up water. The chickens were still on the kitchen table, and from the scattering of oatmeal and corn there, she guessed that he'd fed them. As they squawked for her attention, she made the rounds, scratching each one in turn.

Nathaniel stopped to watch her with a wry grin. "They clearly like you more than me."

"That's because they know I'm not thinking of turning them into chicken soup."

"More like golden-battered chicken legs."

She smiled and gave Daisy an affectionate scratch on her back.

Nathaniel stood up and stretched. His trousers were wet at the knees and filthy. His white linen shirt was untucked and streaked with dirt. He'd rolled up his sleeves, revealing his strong tanned arms. Even in his disheveled state, he was still a dashing man. She had no doubt women had been attracted to him in droves, not only for his looks, but also for his charm and money.

As if sensing the direction of her thoughts, his smile fell away. He dropped his rag to the floor. She was surprised that only a thin film remained, which meant he'd likely been hard at work soaking up the water for hours. She could also see he'd begun putting the house in order. He'd pushed in drawers, righted chairs, and returned canisters to the shelf. The pots and pans hung on the wall above the stove. The cups and plates were stacked neatly in the sideboard.

He'd done more in one night than she could have accomplished in a week.

"I made a pot of coffee," he said, heading to the stove.

She breathed in the freshly brewed aroma and watched as he poured first one mug and then another. When he handed her one, she took it gratefully, wishing he'd look her in the eyes so he could see her admiration.

Instead, he hid behind his mug.

"Let's rest for a few minutes," she suggested, crossing toward the parlor. As she stepped into the front room, she was again startled at the progress he'd made in cleaning up the destruction. He'd returned books to the shelves. He'd organized logbooks and put the desk in order. He'd stacked papers, folded afghans, and placed the Bible on the side table next to Gramps' chair.

The chairs and sofa were stacked with items that still needed to be put away. Thanks to Nathaniel's quick thinking in getting things off the floor, he'd likely saved their possessions from being ruined by the flooding.

She cleared a spot on the sofa big enough for both of them and sat down with her mug, holding in a tired groan. Nathaniel didn't follow her into the room. Instead, he leaned against the door frame.

"Thank you for everything." She waved a hand around the parlor. "I don't know what I would have done without your help."

He nodded and took a sip of coffee. With the boarded windows, the room was dark, except for the light that squeezed through the cracks. In spite of the dimness, the discouragement in his face and posture was difficult to miss.

"Please," she said, patting the cushion next to her. "Sit down and rest with me."

He hesitated.

"You deserve a break more than I do."

He came slowly and lowered himself to the sofa, as far from her as he could get. For a moment, they sat silently drinking their coffee and listening to the waves slap against the bastion.

"We both made mistakes," she finally said.

"Mine are worse."

She quirked an eyebrow at him. "Worse than lying to you about your identity?"

"Yes. Ten times worse."

"In God's eyes, sin is sin. He detests lying as much as he detests drunkenness."

Nathaniel sighed, as though he had no desire to have this discussion with her. When he made a move to get up, she stopped him with a touch to his arm.

"No matter what we've done, He offers his forgiveness freely. You've read the verse from Second Corinthians dozens of times this summer to Gramps, the one about God not counting men's sins against them."

Nathaniel looked down at her fingers on his arm. "My sins are too numerous for His forgiveness."

"They're not too numerous for me to forgive," she said.

His gaze shot to hers, and his eyes widened in surprise.

"I guess if I'm able to forgive you, the powerful and almighty God can too."

"Why would He?" Self-loathing laced his voice.

She didn't know how to answer his question. She couldn't claim to have much spiritual wisdom for herself. After all, she'd hadn't exactly been on God's good side, had disappointed Him and pushed Him away, just as she had the people in her life. Regardless, the words from Corinthians resounded within her. "Therefore, if any man *be* in Christ, *he is* a new creature; old things are passed away; behold, all things are become new."

Nathaniel joined her in saying the verse. When they were done, they sat quietly with the sacred words echoing around them.

"It's all in your past, Nathaniel," she said. "Whatever you once were, you don't have to be that man anymore."

His brows rose above skeptical eyes, and he started to protest.

"You don't," she silenced him. "Before your memories returned, you lived like a new man. You can continue living like that. You don't have to go back to the old."

For a moment, he regarded her as though he might actually believe her. Then his expression fell and filled with despondency. "I never wanted to become like my father, but once I started down the same path he traveled, I realized that I'm destined to become like him."

"That's the silliest thing I've ever heard."

"I've proven myself to be too much like him."

Her coffee grew tepid as she listened to Nathaniel share about his father. How, from a young age, his father had battled melancholy. For days on end, he'd lie in bed and refuse to get up. Nathaniel's mother had done everything she could to make him happy. She'd planned parties, pleaded, and tried to live a perfect life so that, perhaps, she could draw him out of his dark cave. Every once in a while, he had emerged, and life was happy for a while. Until his mood gradually darkened and he retreated once again.

"Nicholas and I lived for those happy times," Nathaniel said, "when we could be a normal family, when we could all be together, when we felt our father's love."

Abbie reached over and squeezed Nathaniel's hand. When she began to retract, he intertwined his fingers with hers.

"Then after one Christmas, when I was about ten, Father had one of his spells. He went into his dark cave and never came out again. He tried really hard. I think that's why he started drinking, because he hoped the drink would loosen him up and help him forget about the darkness in his head. And although the alcohol may have helped at first, in the long run, it only added to his melancholy."

Nathaniel's fingers tightened around hers. She shouldn't like the feel of his hand in hers, but she did. She loved the way his fingers fit against hers, the strength in his grip, the warmth of his touch.

"His mood became so dark that Mother had to move him to our house in Florida. She didn't want anyone to know how morose he was, and so she swore Nicholas and me to secrecy."

Nathaniel drained his cup of coffee and placed the empty mug on the side table. He glanced down at their intertwined hands. "Father never protested the move. I think he probably wanted to be away, didn't want to see us and add to his guilt. After years of drowning himself in drink and laudanum, he committed suicide over the winter."

Abbie set her mug aside and grasped his other hand so that she was holding both. She couldn't say anything that would take away his pain, but she also couldn't sit by and let him think he would turn out the same as his father.

"My mother left when I was only six," she said. "I didn't know she was going away. I didn't realize she was thinking about it. But one day, when Debbie and I came home from school, she was gone. She packed her bag and left without a good-bye. Not a single word. Not a hug. Not even a clue why she was going or when she'd be back."

"I'm sorry," he murmured, and it was his turn to squeeze her hands in comfort.

"I waited for her return for weeks, months, and years." Abbie's throat thickened as she thought about the little girl who'd gone up into the tower every morning and evening to check the sea for any sign of her beautiful mother rowing to the island. "But she never came back. Never wrote. Never sent the tiniest message."

The rejection still stung deeply. She'd always wondered what she'd done to drive her mother away. She'd tried to figure out how she could have been a better daughter, good enough to make her mother love her. Maybe if she'd worn her shoes more often or said her prayers better or picked up her room. After all these years, she still didn't understand what she'd done wrong. Only that she'd failed somehow to earn her mother's love. For, surely, a woman who loved her daughters wouldn't be able to leave them behind and never visit them again.

Abbie shook off the painful memories and straightened her shoulders. "My mother made her choice, but that will never be the one I make." She couldn't keep her voice from shaking with emotion. "We are separate from our parents, and we're not destined to make their mistakes. We have the power, with God's help, to choose to walk a new path."

The passion of her words reverberated through her soul, speaking to her, regardless of whether or not they touched Nathaniel. If she ever became a mother, she wouldn't desert her family. Not unless death took her first.

"Come here," Nathaniel whispered, tugging her against him.

She didn't resist as his arms enveloped her. Instead, she rested her head against his shoulder and wrapped her arms around him too. She didn't realize that tears had slipped onto her cheeks until he lifted his thumb and gently brushed them away.

He cradled her in the crook of his arm, pressing a kiss against her head. The pressure in her chest welled up and tightened her throat. For a moment, she wanted to sob for the pain they'd both experienced in their lives, the heartache, the losses, the disappointments.

"It's okay," he murmured in her hair.

She closed her eyes against the tears.

"We'll be okay." The words were certain and filled with strength. And somehow she knew he was right. That in God's strength, they would be okay. Maybe the pain and heartache wouldn't disappear, but they could walk a different path than any they'd known before.

She let herself relax against him in his embrace. With the steady thud of his heartbeat in her ear, she fell into an exhausted slumber.

Chapter 20

Nathaniel awoke with a start and listened for the noise. He'd heard something—a bang or shout. But when only the silence and stillness of the parlor met him, he relaxed against the sofa.

The light coming in from the cracks around the window told him that it was still daylight. Even so, the room was shrouded in shadows.

A soft sigh and movement against his chest reminded him of where he was and what had happened. He glanced down to find that Abbie was sleeping in his arms. The weary lines on her face attested to the stress of the past few days. She'd had to deal with a lot in her search for Hosea and then battling the storm.

He still had no idea where Hosea may have gone. After how thoroughly Abbie had searched the island, he had to believe, like she did, that Hosea wasn't there. At least he prayed so. He doubted the man would have survived the ferocity of last night's storm if he'd been out in it.

The longer Hosea was gone, the more Nathaniel feared the worst had happened, that somehow Hosea had drowned. What else could keep him away from home? Even so, the moment the storm abated, Nathaniel planned to go out and start the search all over again. He could do nothing less.

Even if Hosea was by some chance still alive, Nathaniel doubted the superintendent would allow Abbie and Hosea to stay on Rose Island, not after he discovered Nate had never returned and was in fact dead.

Where would Abbie and Hosea live? With Debbie?

He couldn't imagine what Hosea would do living with Debbie. What would he whitewash? Where would he dig? He would be entirely lost and confused. And the same with Abbie. He knew her well enough by now to realize that she wouldn't flourish with her sister in the confines of a tiny home in town. She needed the freedom of the island—the sea spray against her hands, the sand between her toes, and the sun kissing her face.

Her beautiful face. Nathaniel allowed himself the pleasure of feasting on her features as he'd done earlier, when she'd fallen asleep. If she'd known he was staring at her so openly, she would have pulled away in embarrassment.

As it was, he'd watched her to his heart's content and savored the knowledge that even after everything he'd shared about his past, she hadn't condemned him, hadn't pushed him away, hadn't been sickened or repelled.

Instead, she'd offered her forgiveness and accepted him for who he was, glaring flaws and all. She was a rare woman to be able to sit with him and hold his hand and encourage him to carve a new path for his life.

With the warmth of her body wrapped against his and with her breath steadily rising and falling, he could almost believe that it was possible for him to move forward and be that new creation in Christ. He could almost believe that he wasn't destined to become like his father, that he could be different, be the man of his own choosing.

She released a soft sleepy sigh and burrowed deeper against him, nuzzling her nose into his chest.

He tightened his arm around her waist, not ready to relinquish this moment alone with her just yet.

"Hmm," she murmured.

I love you. He wanted to bend in and whisper the words in her ear. But he held himself back, knowing he had no right to say them to her.

"Nathaniel?" she said almost inaudibly, her eyes still closed.

He pressed his lips against her head to force his declaration back and to reassure her he was still there.

At the slight kiss, she moved her arm from where it had been casually draped at his waist to his chest. Her fingers splayed across his heart. The friction of her hand through his shirt made him suddenly conscious of the full length of her—so soft, so pliable, so exquisite.

All he had to do was scoot down just a little more and he'd be laying on his back. He'd pull her down next to him. Then he'd feast on much more than her face. The thought sent a jolt of heat into his blood. Her hand across his heart was warm and surely the sign that she wouldn't reject him.

No! The battle warred within him. The man he used to be might have taken advantage of the situation without a second thought and without remorse. But he didn't want to be that man anymore. He swallowed hard and held himself rigid as he fought against his selfish desire for her.

Her lashes lifted, showing her to be growing in her wakefulness. Once she was fully awake, she'd surely realize the nature of their situation on the sofa. She'd sit up and put distance between them.

But instead of pushing away from him in mortification, she gave him a small smile that was much more alluring than she likely realized, one that almost made him groan with the need to swoop down and claim her mouth.

She lifted her fingers to his cheek and caressed the stubble that had formed. "Nathaniel," she whispered, her attention shifting to his mouth.

He sensed that her whisper was a beckon to kiss her. Hadn't he told her that all she needed to do was ask and he'd oblige? He knew her well enough to realize she didn't offer invitations lightly, that if he spurned it, he may not ever get another chance.

Before he could think of a hundred reasons why he shouldn't, he bent in and touched his lips to hers. She expelled a sigh of contentment that bathed him, soaked into his body, and set him ablaze.

Her lashes dropped, but not before he caught sight of the matching desire in her eyes. It was the signature and stamp on her invitation that he hadn't realized he was waiting for. With one hand at the base of her neck and one on the small of her back, he lifted her and angled himself to receive her, capturing her mouth against his with a force that contained all the passion that had been developing since the day he'd met her.

She wasn't tentative as she'd been the first time they'd kissed. She was ready for him, eager and hungry all at once. Her fingers tangled in his hair at the same moment that her lips tangled with his, meeting him with the same fervor that he met her.

The pleasure of kissing her was unlike anything he'd experienced before. Sure, he'd given way to the carnal desires of his flesh many times in the past, but this wasn't anything like that. This was pure and beautiful and passionate, straining his nerves to an almost painful breaking point.

He realized suddenly that he'd never known love like this. Whatever he'd experienced before had been only a faint shadow in comparison.

Maybe it was because he'd always been inebriated and the effect of the alcohol had dulled his senses. Now he was keenly aware of every move, every breath, every touch.

Or maybe the experience had never meant as much because he'd never truly been in love. Oh sure, he'd once believed he loved Victoria Cole, the woman he'd almost married. But what he'd felt for her paled in contrast to his feelings for Abbie. Maybe the depth of his love for Abbie made the moment all the richer and more fulfilling.

Whatever the case, he was completely and totally caught up into the kisses and transported to a place where they were together, truly together, without anyone or anything threatening to pull them apart.

But even as he allowed himself to be swept away with her, a small voice resounded in his head, warning him to be careful, that he was a new man and that he needed to live with integrity. If he truly wanted to chart a different course for his future, then he had to start now.

"Abbie," he murmured against her lips. He stilled his hands and tried to bring his pounding heart under control. He couldn't dishonor her, and that's what he'd do if he let their passion continue unchecked. It had been one thing to kiss her when he'd thought they were married. But now...he had no business sharing intimacies with her.

She tugged away, mortification coloring her cheeks.

He tucked his fingers under her chin and forced her to look at him. "Darling, if I go on kissing you, I won't be able to stop."

Her cheeks flushed even further, which only served to make her all the more appealing.

"You're beautiful and amazing, and I don't want to hurt you in any way."

"You won't hurt me." She smiled. "You should know by now, I'm much sturdier than I appear." She started to dip in, focusing on his mouth, clearly intending to continue the kiss.

He couldn't move except to smile. "Have mercy on me, darling."

"No mercy," she whispered, even as her lips landed against his and demanded another kiss.

He nearly groaned at the pleasure he derived from her initiation, from the fact that she longed for him as much as he did her. As her lips plied his, he didn't want any mercy. He wanted to let her have her way with him.

But again, as before, he had to remain honorable. He kissed her thoroughly and relished every taste, but then before he deepened the kiss, he broke away and jumped up from the sofa.

"I want you, Abbie," he said hoarsely, combing his fingers into his hair and stalking across the room. "But I won't use you."

She remained on the couch, quiet and unmoving, and he was afraid that his declaration may have offended her. When he chanced a glance, she was watching him with an almost humorous glimmer in her eyes.

He stopped pacing and smiled. "So you take delight in being the cause of my agony?"

"Perhaps. A little." She brushed her skirt down.

He gave a breathless laugh.

At the clatter of dishes in the kitchen, followed by a muttering that was distinctly human, he froze. She bolted from the couch, fear rippling across her face.

He put a finger to his lips cautioning her to remain quiet. She nodded but glanced around, as though looking for a weapon that she might wield against the intruder.

The house was silent for a long moment. The crashing of the waves told him that the sea was still tumultuous—perhaps not as dangerous as during the storm, but enough to make a crossing to the island treacherous. Who would have chanced being out on the sea today?

Nathaniel reached for the long-handled shovel in the ashbin next to the stove. He cautioned Abbie back as he edged toward the kitchen door. He peeked around the corner to see a short, nearly bald man with age spots on his head retrieve a tin plate from the floor.

Nathaniel lowered the shovel and stared at the old light keeper, having to blink twice to make sure he wasn't seeing a ghost. "Hosea?"

At the sound of his name, Hosea dropped the plate again, along with the piece of toast that had been resting on it.

Abbie was at Nathaniel's side in the doorway in an instant. "Gramps?" Her mouth hung open in disbelief.

Hosea picked up his dish and straightened with a grimace, his joints clearly bothering him. The tufts of silvery hair above his ears were sticking out, and his clothing was disheveled and wet, but otherwise, he didn't look different than he did any other day.

Abbie sagged in relief, and Nathaniel caught her to his side, slipping his arm around her middle and supporting her. "Where have you been?" she asked in a wobbly voice.

Hosea sat down at the table in a spot that already contained a bowl, spoon, and cup. The chickens were nowhere in sight. Nathaniel could only assume that Hosea had shooed them outside when he'd come into the kitchen and discovered them there. "I've been trying to eat my dinner in here quietly so I wouldn't disturb your sleep. You both looked exhausted."

Nathaniel guided Abbie to the place across from Hosea so that she could sit before she collapsed.

"Where have you been the past few days?" Abbie asked again, as Nathaniel helped her slide into the chair.

Hosea glanced at her as though she'd asked him why the sea is wet. "I've been taking care of the light, like I always do," he retorted sourly.

"No, you've been gone—" she started but then stopped when Nathaniel squeezed her arm. He hoped she saw his warning in his eyes not to press Hosea too far. He likely hadn't had his pain medicine during the past few days, and that made him more aggressive.

Hosea rose from his chair, his brow furrowing angrily. "Are you accusing me of not doing my duty?"

Abbie shook her head. "It's just that there was a storm, and we were worried about you—"

"So you don't think I can take care of myself?" Hosea slammed the table, rattling his dishes and making Abbie jump. "Well, I'll have you know, I'm perfectly capable of managing this lighthouse all by myself. If you don't think so, then go ahead and leave."

Abbie frowned in clear frustration. She'd only wanted to discover where Hosea had been for the past couple of days, and he'd turned the conversation back on her, like she'd been the one to do something wrong.

Nathaniel rounded the table and put a steadying hand upon Hosea's shoulders. "All is well, Hosea. All is well." Hosea met his gaze, confusion and agitation there making his irises dark. After several seconds, Hosea nodded and sat down, his expression softening, the confrontation apparently forgotten.

What if Abbie had been right when she'd claimed that he had a calming effect upon Hosea? For whatever reason, Hosea liked and trusted him. Nathaniel doubted that Hosea would ever heal completely from his senility. Such a condition wasn't like a broken leg. But could he make enough of a difference that Hosea would be well enough to stay on Rose Island as the keeper? Isn't that what Abbie had hoped for in the first place?

After seeing Hosea's reaction to Abbie, Nathaniel understood more fully why she'd lied to him. Not only did Hosea have a short temper, but he was a danger to himself. Abbie's concern about moving her gramps was legitimate. If he had to leave Rose Island permanently, would he ever be able to adjust?

Nathaniel patted Hosea's shoulder one last time and then moved to the stove to start another pot of coffee. As he opened the oven and stirred the smoldering remnants of coals, his thoughts tumbled over one another.

He guessed he had a day, maybe two, before his crew attempted to sail over and retrieve him. He'd only come to lend a hand to Abbie in finding Hosea. Now that the older man was home safe, Nathaniel had no excuse for lingering.

Unless...

He closed the stove door and clicked the handle into place. What if he stayed for a short while? Or at the very least, what if he rowed over every day to help?

Certainly, Mother might have a thing or two to say about him spending his time out on the island as opposed to reentering society life. But how could she object to him helping with such a good cause? Especially because it was wholesome and would keep him from the drinking and partying and scandals?

She'd surely agree that whatever kept him from returning to his debauched ways was a valuable pursuit—at least in the short run, until he could make sure he was strong enough to face his friends and his old life.

The name Kitty Martin came to the front of his mind as swiftly as a summer gale and threatened to capsize him and drag him under with a melancholy that was heavy and suffocating. Kitty Martin and the baby. His baby.

He swallowed the bitterness and the sudden thirst for something strong and numbing. He didn't want to face reality and the consequences of the mistakes he'd made. At least not yet.

Maybe if he remained on the island for a few weeks to help Hosea and Abbie, he'd gain perspective and the strength he needed to embrace Kitty Martin and the new life waiting for him as a father. He couldn't avoid it forever. But he wanted to put it off for as long as possible.

Chapter 21

Gramps had returned to the island in a dilapidated skiff that was rusted and leaky and should have been turned into scrap metal. As Abbie inspected the boat for any sign of ownership, her pulse ticked an ominous warning—Gramps was becoming too difficult for her to take care of on her own.

The waves slapped the hard-packed sand with punishing strength before rushing further up the beach to claw at her feet. She glanced from the skiff to the distant Newport shore and swallowed the fear that bubbled up every time she thought about Gramps rowing over and battling the high, foaming waves.

She couldn't believe he'd made it. The trip would have been a daring feat for a seasoned rower like herself even now that the sea was calmer, much less earlier in the day when Gramps had made the crossing. Of course, she'd learned everything she knew about rowing from Gramps. He'd once been just as skilled as she was. Even so, the thought that he'd put himself in such grave danger made her realize she had to come up with a new plan to keep him safe.

She still had no idea where he'd been or what had happened to him. Any further attempt to discuss it had resulted in more accusations and agitation. She could only speculate that he'd gone out to search for Nathaniel and hadn't been able to return until the storm subsided.

Later, after his pain medication took effect and after he had the chance to sleep, she'd try talking with him again. Maybe he'd be more reasonable and clearheaded then.

With a sigh, Abbie patted the dilapidated skiff before heading back to the lighthouse. The wind had stopped its roaring but was rough. The storm may have dealt its fury and moved away to punish someone else, but the aftermath would likely loiter for another day or so.

She'd spent the past hour walking the beach and checking for any flotsam or jetsam. Aside from the normal boards and broken crates and debris, she hadn't found anything that needed immediate attention.

Nathaniel and Gramps had been caulking the tower windows when she'd left. As usual, Nathaniel's easygoing demeanor and gentleness with Gramps had worked its magic. Gramps had been smiling and laughing and enjoying himself as the two worked together.

Although she'd been relieved, she realized Gramps' pleasant mood wouldn't last forever. Once Nathaniel left, Gramps would return to his usual cantankerous self.

Nathaniel hadn't mentioned leaving, but she'd noticed him peering east at Newport, as though he expected a vessel to arrive at any time. She had no doubt that after the long night fighting the storm he was ready to go home to his mansion, change his clothing, and fall into bed. She didn't blame him. He'd worked hard all night.

She drew a deep breath of salt and sea air and lifted her face to the western wind, letting it pour over her, plastering her hair and clothing to her body. The pressure against her skin only made her long for Nathaniel again, as she had a dozen times since they'd kissed on the sofa after their nap.

Her heart was full with all that Nathaniel had shared about his past, his father, and his fears. No matter his mistakes, no matter the guilt, no matter the distance he'd fallen, he wasn't too far away that God couldn't reach him with grace. Maybe over time, Nathaniel would come to accept that too.

Meanwhile, she would encourage him and thank God for the chance to start over with Nathaniel, this time being honest and open, not hiding anything.

She smiled as she neared the house, not letting the sight of the flattened garden or missing oil house diminish her gladness, which she realized had everything to do with the handsome young man inside who she was anxious to see again after being apart for the past couple of hours.

Was this how it felt to be in love? Her heartbeat pinged against her chest with her growing anticipation.

She pushed open the door and stepped inside to the aroma of boiled potatoes and oven-roasted chicken—one of the poor hens that had drowned in the storm. Since the windows were still boarded, the lantern at the center of the table was lit, revealing plates and silverware already placed for dinner.

Nathaniel was spooning green beans from a pot, having apparently salvaged what remained in the garden. At the sight of her, he grinned and dumped the beans hastily into a serving bowl. "I was hoping you'd show up soon."

"I'm sorry if I've kept you waiting." She couldn't take her eyes off him to give the meal the appreciation it was due. She wanted to rush to him and wrap her arms around him. After all, she'd told herself that she'd be brave, as she was earlier.

But now that she was near him again, now that he was there so real and so devastatingly handsome, she couldn't get her feet to move. She could only stare like the sappy, lovesick girl that she was.

He all but tossed the bowl of beans on the table and rounded the table toward her. "As a matter of fact," he said as he reached her, "you have kept me waiting."

She started to apologize again, but he cut her off by snaking his arms around her and dragging her against his torso. His sights fixed upon her mouth, which sent delicious shivers skittering over her skin.

"You've kept me waiting for *this*," he murmured as he decisively captured her mouth in a kiss, a kiss that immediately drew her in so she felt as though she were falling head over heels into a long dizzying tumble. She grabbed on to him to keep from sinking breathless to the floor.

When he broke the kiss, his lips curved into a grin against hers, as if he'd garnered exactly the reaction he'd wanted. She loved the nearness of his sandpapery stubble, the brush of his nose on hers, the warmth of his breath against her mouth. She couldn't get enough of his arms surrounding her, the pressure of his hands against her lower back, and the rise and fall of his chest matching hers.

She wanted more of him in a way she'd never wanted any other man. Without thinking this time, she lifted onto her toes and gave him the same kind of kiss he'd just given her. He met her with a fervor that made her forget about the hot dinner on the table with its mouth-watering aromas filling the air. Her only hunger was for him. From the way he responded, she sensed he felt the same way.

"My, this meal smells and looks delicious." A chair scraped across the floor, making Abbie jump. Seemingly oblivious to the two of them kissing like their lives depended upon it, Gramps lowered himself to his spot at the kitchen table and rubbed his hands together in anticipation.

Nathaniel released her the same time she stepped away from him. She wanted to cringe in mortification that Gramps had caught them kissing. Before she could slink away, Nathaniel reached for her hand and stopped her. His grin rose higher, and his gaze darted to her lips. The gleam in his eyes told her he wouldn't let her get away with scurrying off in embarrassment, that he meant to kiss her again in full view of Gramps.

When he tugged her toward him, his crooked grin was too difficult to resist. She fell against him and lifted her mouth to meet his. The kiss this time was hard and short, but nonetheless passionate. He released her and then pulled out her chair with a flourish. She couldn't keep from smiling, but she didn't dare look at Gramps.

"You newlyweds are so fun to be around," Gramps said as he plucked a crispy golden leg of chicken from the platter.

Newlyweds? Was this what it was like to be a real newlywed? Her thoughts turned to her first few days with Nate in the house after their wedding, how awkward and stiff and distant they'd been with each other. Of course, it hadn't helped that he'd been hungover half the time. Even so, what she'd experienced with Nate hadn't been remotely close to the desire that Nathaniel had awoken within her. At the time she hadn't cared, had in fact been repelled by Nate's advances.

She focused on scooping potatoes onto her plate, trying not to think about the fact that she most definitely wouldn't be repelled by Nathaniel's advances. She might welcome them, welcome him. She'd never understood why some women seemed to willingly, even happily, accept the marriage bed.

Until now…

The possibility startled her and sent guilt coursing through her. She didn't dare meet Nathaniel's gaze, lest he read her brazen thoughts.

Somehow over the past weeks of acting like a husband and wife, their inhibitions had slipped away, and now it was too easy to fall into the roles they'd been operating in all along. But she couldn't forget that they'd never been wed, that they were from two different worlds, and that Nathaniel wasn't at Rose Island to stay.

During supper, Nathaniel sensed Abbie's confusion because it matched his. When Hosea had called them newlyweds, the word had jarred him as much as it obviously had her. He'd had the urge to whack himself in the head numerous times over the course of the meal for the way he'd carried on with Abbie after she'd returned to the lighthouse.

It didn't matter that he hadn't been able to stop thinking about her from the moment she'd left to search the shoreline. It didn't matter that he couldn't keep from reliving the kisses they'd shared earlier. He shouldn't have kissed her again when she came back, at least not so many times. Maybe one short, chaste peck would have sufficed.

Deep inside he had the feeling nothing would satisfy him

except for making her wholly and completely his. Even then, he suspected that he'd need his entire lifetime and then some before he'd ever stop wanting her.

The problem was, he wasn't free. More than anything, he wanted to ignore his other life in Newport and continue his existence on Rose Island as he had before, but he couldn't. Both Abbie and God may have forgiven him for the loose and immoral lifestyle he'd lived. However, that didn't erase the consequences of what he'd done. As difficult as it was to face the fact that he was having a baby with Kitty Martin, he couldn't run away from the pain and heartache.

His father had run from his problems. He'd hidden and cowered and closeted himself away because he hadn't wanted to confront reality. If Nathaniel had any hope of traversing a different road than the one his father had taken, then he couldn't start the journey by running and hiding. No, he needed to return to Newport and do what was right—go to Kitty Martin and marry her.

He was glad Hosea talked steadily most of the meal, giving him the opportunity to formulate the words he must say. He had to tell her the truth about his plans to marry Kitty. And he had to leave as soon as possible. The longer he was with Abbie, the harder it was getting to deny himself the pleasure of being with her.

He wanted to be a man of integrity and honor, but he was fallen. After the life he'd already lived, he had limited strength to resist temptation. If he stayed, he'd only be placing himself into a situation that would be nigh impossible for his weak flesh to handle.

He had to leave Rose Island. Yes, he wanted to help Abbie and Gramps. But he'd end up hurting them if he didn't go when his crew came for him.

As if the thought of his crew had materialized them, a knock sounded on the door.

He jumped up before Hosea or Abbie could. "Probably my men coming back for me."

Abbie stopped chewing and stared down at her plate as though she'd already figured out what his eagerness for his crew meant.

He swung open the door and was surprised to find a giant of a man standing on the stoop. He held a long rifle, and behind him were two boys, both shouldering guns as well. The man must have been equally surprised by the sight of Nathaniel because he whipped off his hat and glared. His eyes were small compared to the size of his dark bushy eyebrows. A long black beard and mustache filled the rest of his sun-roughened face.

"Who are you?" he barked, examining Nathaniel's once clean and pressed suit, along with his leather shoes that had been polished to a shine but were now ruined and dull from exposure to the water.

Before Nathaniel could think of an appropriate answer, Gramps shoved away from the table and was on his feet yelling. "You're not taking me again, Zeke! I told you. I don't know where it is."

In no time, Abbie was at Hosea's side, attempting to hold him back.

Nathaniel studied Zeke more closely. So this was Zeke Crawford? The last time the man rowed past the island, he'd been too far away for Nathaniel to see him clearly. But now every scar, pockmark, and sunspot was there. None of it made him look any nicer from this distance than he'd looked from his dory.

"Who the blazes are you?" Zeke asked again studying Nathaniel as if he recognized him but couldn't quite place him.

Hosea answered before Nathaniel could. "This is Nate, Abbie's new husband."

Zeke guffawed. "You really are crazy if you think this here is Nate..." Zeke's voice trailed off, and he glanced to Abbie, who lifted her chin defiantly. His small eyes widened as he looked from Abbie to Hosea to Nathaniel and back. Then he broke into obnoxious laughter and slapped his thigh.

"Well, I'll be trussed up and tossed into the sea," Zeke said, his mirth finally tapering off. "You're one smart girl, ain't you? Sure had me fooled. And sure as rain had the superintendent fooled."

"I don't know what you're talking about," Abbie replied.

"Looks like you and your crazy grandpa will be leaving the island after all." Zeke's smile was much too gleeful. "After fooling Mr. Davis, I doubt he'll ever let you near another lighthouse as long as you live."

Nathaniel didn't have to be a wizard to realize Zeke had discovered that Abbie had lied about her husband being back. Zeke had obviously met the real Nate at one point or another and knew Nathaniel didn't belong.

"The superintendent told me earlier in the week that the job is ours," Abbie persisted. "And there's nothing you can do about it now."

"Oh, I can do something, all right," Zeke said with another spiteful smile. "It's my duty as a servant of the lighthouse service to inform my superiors of any and all wrongdoing—"

Hosea snorted. "If anyone's been doing wrong, then it's you, coming in here and forcing me to show you where the treasure is."

"You're talkin' nonsense, you crazy old man," Zeke said, all humor leaving his voice and his face, replaced instead with dark shadows.

Nathaniel's mind spun as he pieced together the clues he'd picked up during the past few weeks. What was Zeke really up to? There was clearly more to the man than he was letting on.

"That's where Gramps was the past couple of days, wasn't it?" Abbie pushed her way forward so that she was almost nose-to-nose with Zeke. "You took him. He got away, and now you've come back to kidnap him again."

Zeke's brows furrowed, making his face all the gruffer. "You're about as crazy as your grandpa. And I intend to make sure Mr. Davis knows it."

Abbie scowled and bunched her fists.

Afraid that she'd take a swing at Zeke, Nathaniel laid a steadying hand upon her arm. She stopped and glanced at him.

Let him go, he silently urged. She had to realize that with Hosea's memory loss, there would be no way to prove that Zeke had kidnapped Hosea. Hosea might be able to relay some information about what had occurred, but it wouldn't be enough for the authorities to do anything to Zeke. Besides, with Hosea's senility, who would believe him even if he was telling the truth, especially when pitted against Zeke, who had proven to be cunning?

No, if they wanted to fight Zeke, they'd have to do it another way.

After another round of insults and threats, Zeke and his boys left. Nathaniel stood at the open door and watched them retreat down the hill toward the shore. He tried to formulate a plan—any plan—that would allow Hosea and Abbie to stay on the island and remain safe from Zeke and others like him.

More than anything, Nathaniel wanted to continue helping just as he had before. But something whispered deep inside that to be a man of integrity, he had to walk the first steps down the new path laid out before him, a path that didn't involve Abbie or her gramps.

The new path wouldn't be easy. In fact, following it would likely be one of the hardest things he'd ever done. But it would be right.

In the meantime, he'd find a way to protect Hosea and Abbie. It would be his parting gift to them.

Chapter 22

At the sight of the yacht at the dock, Abbie's heart began to tear apart. She knew what it meant. Nathaniel was leaving. And this time he wouldn't come back.

He hadn't said those words, but the distance he'd kept from her had spoken loudly enough. Last night he hadn't come to read to her after he'd finished with Gramps. He hadn't ascended to the tower at all. And in the morning, other than greeting her, he'd hardly spoken a word to her. It was almost as if he'd already sailed to the mainland and left her behind.

Of course, after Zeke's visit, her mind had been spinning with thoughts about what would happen to her and Gramps next? Where would they go? How would she be able to keep him safe? She could no longer put off getting work of some kind in Newport. She had to find a job. Right away.

"Abbie," Nathaniel called from near the dock, where he'd been speaking with the crew of his yacht. He waved a hand at her.

She lowered the bucket of clams and her rake but didn't make an effort to walk toward him. Her feet were stuck as surely as if someone had buried them in the sand and packed it down.

Rays of morning sunlight slipped through the clouds and slanted down, seeming to shine directly upon the yacht, spotlighting it in all its glory. It was a magnificent sailing vessel. But there was no need for the glaring reminder that she was losing Nathaniel. Her heart already knew that well enough.

He called something to one of the men before starting down the beach toward her at a slow jog.

She still didn't budge.

When he reached her, he stopped a few feet away, almost as if he was afraid to get too close. He didn't speak, and the rushing slap of the waves filled the space between them. The sea was softer and gentler now that the stormy weather had moved on. But the storm still raged inside her chest, swirling her insides and threatening to drown her.

"Abbie," he finally said, looking up from where he'd been digging the tip of his shoe in the sand.

She couldn't meet his gaze. She didn't want to see the pity in his eyes. The last thing she wanted to remember about him was the desire she'd seen there the previous evening when he'd greeted her at the door and kissed her.

"I have to go back to Newport and marry the young woman who's carrying my child."

Although she'd been expecting him to say as much, the words stung nevertheless. She managed to nod.

"I wish there was some other way," he said in a hoarse whisper. "But I can see no other."

She fought down the lump in her throat. "I understand."

"Thank you."

No matter how drawn they were to each other, there could be no future between them. Even if Nathaniel had been free to consider her, there were too many barriers standing in the way of ever being together.

Nathaniel twisted his shoe in the sand again, his face lined with the same misery that was surely etched into hers.

"We each have our own very different lives." She sucked in a breath to fortify herself for what she knew she must say. "And it would be for the best if we don't see each other again."

He was silent for another long moment. "Abbie," he whispered, this time pleading with her. The plea was so heart-rending that she couldn't resist lifting her eyes to his. The green was as dark as the dense eelgrass beds had been this morning after the storm. "I want you to know that I love you as I have no other woman—"

"Don't say it," she interrupted as both regret and pain swelled in her chest and finished ripping her heart in half.

"I'll never love anyone else again the way I have you," he said in a voice laced with agony.

A sob rose into her throat, and she had to swallow hard to keep it from breaking loose.

"Good-bye, Abbie." He spun and jogged to his waiting yacht, his shoulders slumped and his pace slower than before.

Tears stung in her eyes. She wanted to call him back, wanted to keep him from leaving, wanted to shout that she loved him too. But if she encouraged him, she'd only make the parting more difficult for them both.

She had to let him go. It was the only way.

Nathaniel stood in front of the keeper's house on Goat Island and pounded the door again. In the late afternoon sunshine, the tower windows were the filthiest he'd ever seen on a lighthouse. They were streaked with black smoke, bird droppings, sea spray, and all manner of dirt and dust blown about by the wind and rain.

Although he'd sailed past the short, squat, octagonal tower many times in his past, he'd never paid close attention to it. But now, after running a lighthouse and understanding the importance of maintaining the equipment, he scowled.

From the shabbiness of the attached keeper's dwelling, Nathaniel could only surmise that Zeke Crawford was too busy with other activities to give the lighthouse and dwelling the attention they needed. Nathaniel had a hunch what those *activities* entailed.

Just as Nathaniel raised his fist to knock again, the door opened a crack, revealing one of Zeke's boys, who was blinking sleepily.

"Go get your father," Nathaniel ordered in his haughtiest voice.

The boy took in Nathaniel's fashionable attire, from his new hat down to his crisp pinstriped trousers and patent leather oxfords. Nathaniel had dressed the part of a wealthy New York man and had used his showiest gray stepper, with his new brougham waiting over on the shore. He was freshly shaven, his hair neatly trimmed, and had even made sure to don his fanciest gold pocket watch, with triple chains hanging down in decoration.

Nathaniel leveled a glare at the boy that would surely send him away to do his bidding. "Tell him Nathaniel Winthrop III is here to see him."

The boy scampered off, letting the door close behind him. Nathaniel tapped his toe as he waited. Since he'd disembarked from the yacht into Newport this morning, he'd done nothing but plot and scheme.

Now the moment of reckoning was upon him, the moment he'd discover if all his suspicions were correct. He prayed he wasn't wrong, because if he was, he didn't know what else to do.

He took a step back and peered beyond the lighthouse and keeper's cottage out into Narragansett Bay in the direction of Rose Island, slightly to the north and west from Goat Island. His chest hadn't stopped aching from when he'd said good-bye to Abbie this morning.

All the way back to Newport, he'd felt like he was falling into a deep, dark hole, like the one he'd been in after he'd regained his memories. All he'd wanted to do was return to *The Arbor*, find his bed, and burrow under the covers.

But when the yacht had bumped against the dock in the marina, it was as if God had rattled him and reminded him he wasn't going back to the old way of living. He was pressing on and forging a new trail.

When he'd returned home, his mother had been visibly relieved to see him, likely having worried that he'd decided to drown himself—this time for real. She'd begged him to have tea, but he'd kissed her cheek and told her he had important business to take care of first.

Even now, as he waited at the keeper's door and tapped his foot, he couldn't keep from seeing the anxiety in his mother's eyes and knowing she was frightened that she'd lose him to the same melancholy that had taken Father.

He'd reassure her later, he told himself. First, he had to

make sure Abbie and Hosea stayed safe. After working the greater part of the day to put his plans into motion, Nathaniel had to play his part well, or Zeke wouldn't take the bait.

"This better be important," came a loud voice, "or I'm not gonna be happy." The door swung open all the way, and Zeke's hulking frame filled it. His dark hair stood on end. He'd neglected to put on a shirt and stood only in his drawers. He and his boys had obviously been sleeping the day away.

Zeke let loose a long yawn before his sights registered Nathaniel's familiarity. "You again." Zeke eyed Nathaniel. "What are you doing here?"

"I have the map."

"What map?"

"The map you were looking for when you tore apart Hosea's house."

Every last trace of weariness dissolved from Zeke's countenance. He straightened and peered around, as though making certain no one else was listening.

The taut muscles in Nathaniel's spine relaxed. He'd guessed correctly. Now he had to maintain his poker face and play his cards just right.

"How do you know about the map?" Zeke scratched his hairy belly and scrutinized Nathaniel more carefully. "Who are you anyway?"

"I'm Nathaniel Winthrop—"

"Ain't you supposed to be dead? Thought I heard tell of a funeral and all the newspapers making a big deal out of a drowning or something."

"Do I look dead?"

"'Course not. So, if you ain't dead, you've been living at Rose Island Lighthouse pretending to be Abbie's husband so she could live there?"

"Do I look like the kind of man who would do such a thing?" Nathaniel used his snobbiest tone, one he'd perfected over the past couple of years.

Zeke narrowed his eyes. "Then what were you doing out at the lighthouse?"

"I'm a family friend. That's all."

Doubt and suspicion shrouded Zeke's face. Nathaniel just smiled, a smile he hoped conveyed the truth—that the people of Newport would believe him and not Zeke, much the same way it worked with Hosea.

Nathaniel crossed his arms and waited as Zeke cursed under his breath for a full thirty seconds. When Zeke finally scowled at him sullenly, Nathaniel pretended to pick a hair off his suit coat. "I found the map in Hosea's Bible."

"It weren't there when we look—"

"That's because I'd already removed it for safekeeping."

Zeke rubbed a hand over his protruding belly again.

Nathaniel wanted to remark that it should be a crime for men as big and hairy as him to go without a shirt, but he bit back his comment and instead focused on the task at hand. "I know why you requested to work the lighthouse here on Goat Island."

"'Cuz it's a job."

"Because you're a treasure hunter."

"I'm a light keeper."

"I hired an investigator today to track down your files from the Office of the Lighthouse Board." Nathaniel pulled a folded sheet from his pocket. "I have here a list of every lighthouse you've worked at over the past ten years."

Zeke started to protest, but Nathaniel flapped open the

sheet and began to read. "Hog Island, Prudence Island, Pomham Rocks, Sandy Point, and Goat Island."

"So what?" Zeke said defiantly. "That don't mean nothin'."

Nathaniel retrieved a second sheet of paper from his coat pocket. "I also hired another investigator today to research the history of hidden treasure in Rhode Island. I learned that various legends include—" he snapped open the sheet and scanned it "—Hog Island, Prudence Island, Pomham Rocks, Sandy Point, Goat Island. And of course, last but certainly not least, Rose Island."

Zeke shook his head as if he couldn't believe Nathaniel had gone to such lengths.

"I was already familiar with many of the tales regarding the pirating here in Rhode Island. The stories of Captain William Kidd and the buried treasure. But I'd always assumed, like most people, that they were just myths."

Zeke's eyes sparked. "They ain't myths, that's for sure."

"Hosea doesn't seem to think the treasure is a myth either." Nathaniel waited for Zeke's reaction.

Zeke smiled knowingly. "Not after he found that map hidden in old Fort Hamilton. Said it had been tucked away in the fort since it were built and had probably been on the island even longer."

"With his memory issues, you believed him anyway?"

"He slipped up and told me a year or so before his memory got real bad."

"And you've been biding your time to move over there ever since so you could find the treasure without anyone knowing you were searching for it?"

Zeke guffawed. "That about sums it up. Me and my boys haven't found anything here on Goat Island. Figured it was about time to move on."

Nathaniel didn't have to ask the rest. Zeke was the one he'd seen at night from the tower, digging up the coast of the island, coming over under the cover of darkness to start treasure hunting on an island he soon hoped would be his new home.

Then, after the news that the superintendent was allowing Hosea, Abbie, and "Nate" to remain on the island, Zeke had needed a new plan. So he'd come after Hosea, with the hope the older man would lead them to the treasure or, at the very least, the map. When that hadn't worked, Zeke had returned and ransacked the house himself, looking for the map or any other clues regarding the pirate loot.

Nathaniel suspected a man like Zeke wouldn't stop until he found the treasure or was satisfied it didn't exist. Nathaniel shuddered to think about the next time Zeke went to Rose Island treasure hunting, if Abbie was there by herself. There was no telling what he was capable of doing next. Unless Nathaniel gave him what he wanted…

With exaggerated meticulousness, Nathaniel folded each of the sheets of paper and returned them to his pocket before meeting Zeke's gaze, which was eager, almost zealous, in his anticipation.

"As I said, I have the map." Again, with feigned nonchalance, he picked a hair off his coat sleeve.

"And what will you be doing with the map?"

"Let's put it this way. I'm not the sort of man who goes looking for buried treasure. Why would I bother when I don't need it?"

Zeke looked across the span of water to the shiny new brougham and the sleek horse waiting on shore. He visibly swallowed his eagerness. "That mean you'll sell me the map?"

"I don't need your money." Nathaniel dropped the decibel of his voice until it resembled granite.

This time when Zeke looked at him, his bushy brows rose in confusion. "I don't suppose you're planning to hand it over to me simple and nice-like. Not when you could have given it to Hosea."

Nathaniel didn't respond, not even to smile.

Zeke shuffled, glanced around the disheveled room behind him searching for something—anything he could give Nathaniel in exchange for the map. "Name your price," he finally said. "And I'll find a way to pay you."

"I don't want a payment," Nathaniel said evenly. "I want you to send a telegram to Mr. Davis and tell him you're ready to be transferred to a new position."

Zeke laughed at the suggestion.

Nathaniel schooled his face into his most serious expression. "A position that's far enough from Rose Island that you won't go back after you find the treasure."

Zeke's mouth stalled around his response. Nathaniel used the silence to pull a third slip of paper from his pocket. He handed it to Zeke. "I've taken the liberty of finding an open position. It's in Maine."

Zeke shook his head. "No sir. I'm not moving to Maine. Not on your life."

"Very well." Nathaniel spun on his heels and began to cross to his footman waiting in a rowboat. "I'm sure I'll easily be able to find someone else interested in the treasure map." He took three more steps before Zeke called out.

"Wait."

Nathaniel stopped, suppressed a self-satisfied smile, and

glanced at Zeke in the doorway.

With his scraggly hair, long black beard, and hardened demeanor, Zeke could have passed for a pirate. "Heard tell there's buried pirate treasure in Maine too."

Nathaniel shrugged. He didn't care what Zeke Crawford did in Maine so long as he was gone and unable to threaten Abbie and Hosea anymore. "Send a telegram to Mr. Davis telling him you want the transfer. Once that's done, you can come see me about the map."

His footman held out a hand to help him into the boat. Nathaniel paused before stepping down. "Oh, and if you mention anything to the superintendent about Nate's comings and goings on the island, the deal's off."

"Nate," Zeke spat Abbie's husband's name. "Shoulda known that lazy drunkard hadn't changed his ways."

The words sank into Nathaniel's soul like a fishhook threatening to drag him down. But he pushed them away, out of his mind, at least for the moment. Instead, he steeled himself and glared at Zeke. "If you cause any more problems for Abbie and Hosea, I'll track you down and accuse you of stealing from me."

Zeke didn't respond, except to clamp his mouth shut.

Nathaniel didn't wait for Zeke to think of a comeback. With his poker face still in place, he stepped down into the boat and took a seat. He held himself stiffly and severely until the footman rowed well away from the pier. Then he let out a long breath of relief.

Zeke had swallowed the bait. Now it was only a matter of reeling him in slowly, one inch at a time. By tonight, if all went as planned, Zeke would have his treasure, and he'd leave Abbie and Hosea alone. They'd be able to stay on Rose Island as long as they wanted, especially after Nathaniel made a point of talking with Mr. Davis about paying for an assistant to help them.

After several more errands, Nathaniel's carriage rolled to a stop along the wharf in the marina. He spotted Menard near a small skiff and hurried toward Abbie's brother-in-law.

"Do you have everything?" Nathaniel asked, nodding at the grain sack already tucked under a bench in the boat.

"Yes, sir." Menard's eyes were especially large behind his spectacles and regarded Nathaniel with a kind of awe he found slightly disconcerting. Thankfully, Menard had agreed to help him when he was finished with his work for the Coles for the day. Menard was the logical choice for this endeavor since he knew the island better than most.

"When you're done, I want you to extract a promise from Abbie that if she sees lights on the island during the next few nights, she won't go out to investigate."

"How long will it take him to find the treasure?"

"Hopefully, he'll locate it tonight. But just in case he doesn't, I don't want Abbie to go out and confront him."

Menard nodded in agreement.

Nathaniel had already spoken about the plans in-depth earlier in the day when he'd ridden to the Coles and tracked Menard down in the stable. Now there was nothing more to say.

Nathaniel reached to shake Menard's hand. "I appreciate your help."

Menard returned the shake before shifting his feet and stepping back as though embarrassed. "I know you don't have to do this," he said haltingly. "But it means a lot to Debbie and me that you're helping Hosea and Abbie."

"I just wish there was more I could do." Namely, stay on the island himself and take care of them both. But it wasn't possible, and there was no sense in even contemplating it. Doing so would only stir up discontentment for what he needed to do. With Kitty Martin.

"You're a good man, Mr. Winthrop," Menard said, his face wreathed in seriousness. "Real good."

The praise was unexpected, certainly not the usual compliment he received. He couldn't remember the last time anyone had thought him anything other than *bad*. He pushed down the rebuttal and the litany of his mistakes. For now, he allowed himself to believe that maybe, just maybe, he could truly change his ways.

Chapter 23

The day dragged slowly by. Abbie finished cleaning up the debris strewn about the lighthouse yard. She compiled a list of all the supplies to replace what they'd lost in the storm and to repair the house and tower.

The damage wasn't as bad as what they'd experienced in '76, when the wind had reached near hurricane force and moved the tower one and a half inches, so that it broke the plaster inside the house and the glass chimney in the lantern.

Even so, the water damage was extensive. It would have been worse if Nathaniel hadn't been there to help. She was determined to do all she could for the lighthouse before Mr. Davis arrived and asked her and Gramps to leave.

After dinner, Abbie scraped the remnants of clam from the bottom of the cast-iron skillet and tried to ignore the pain that squeezed her chest every time Nathaniel came to mind. She didn't want to think about him anymore. She wished she could cut him loose from her life as easily as she could cut loose a snagged fishing line.

But no matter how busy she'd kept herself all day, he was in her thoughts.

At the squeak of the backdoor opening, her pulse leapt with anticipation. As she spun, she tried to mask her disappointment at the sight of Menard stepping inside. Sand and dirt covered his boots and trousers, and he looked like he'd been wrestling a seal on the beach.

"Abbie," he said in his soft-spoken voice.

"Debbie? The baby?" Her heart jumped into her throat at the thought that something had happened to them. What other reason did Menard have for coming to the island?

"They're fine." He closed the door behind him.

"Are you sure?"

Menard smiled, the corners of his eyes crinkling. "Yes, my mom is still visiting and taking good care of them all."

Abbie heaved a relieved breath. "Then why are you here?"

"Mr. Winthrop sent me."

For a moment, Abbie couldn't register who Menard was referring to, then it dawned on her, and her stomach did a crazy backward flip. "Nathaniel sent you?" She hoped she didn't look as eager as she sounded.

"I'm helping him get rid of Zeke Crawford."

"And how are you doing that?"

"I can't give you the details tonight," Menard said, glancing down at his sand-caked boots. "But Nathaniel instructed me to make you promise that if you saw any strange lights on the beach this week you'd stay away."

Abbie planted her hands on her hips and frowned at Menard. "So Nathaniel thinks Zeke's been the one coming out to the island and digging for treasure?"

"Probably."

Abbie mulled over the news, not entirely surprised. Zeke had mentioned a treasure a time or two.

"If all goes as planned," Menard continued, "you and Gramps won't need to worry about Zeke Crawford bothering you any further."

Abbie didn't know what difference that would make now. She and Gramps wouldn't be able to stay on the island much longer, whether Zeke pestered them or not. She had to do the right thing and tell Mr. Davis the truth, that Nate wasn't with them, that he was dead.

She'd expected Mr. Davis to come today. Surely tomorrow. She should probably ask Menard if he'd help her begin to move some of their possessions, but she couldn't force the words out.

Menard put a hand to the door. "So, you'll give me and Mr. Winthrop your word you won't go out exploring if you see any lights along the coast?"

"I promise." If Zeke wanted to hunt for treasure, so long as he didn't bother Gramps, she saw no reason to stop him.

Menard nodded his approval and started to leave. He paused halfway through the door. "I like Mr. Winthrop. He's not anything like the rumors made him out to be."

Abbie longed to add her praise for Nathaniel. Every moment of his time on the island had been special. *He* was special. And she'd never forget him. Ever.

She couldn't speak past the tightness in her throat to answer Menard. As if sensing the sadness of her loss, Menard said good-bye and let himself out.

After washing the supper dishes, she hauled two kitchen chairs outside as Gramps and Nathaniel had gotten in the habit of doing each evening, when the weather cooperated.

Although Gramps complained that Steele wasn't there to challenge him in backgammon, eventually he agreed to play Abbie. She might not be his first choice as an opponent, but she was determined to keep some sense of routine, at least for their final days on the island.

They played several games before Gramps grew irritable. She decided his mood matched hers. Except that she had to hold her emotions inside and pretend everything was fine, while he no longer had any inhibitions preventing him from acting however he felt.

"That must be Steele," Gramps said, pushing aside the backgammon board and standing. He lifted a hand to shield his eyes and peered toward Newport.

Abbie followed his sights to a boat rowing steadily toward Rose Island with a lone figure at the oars. She couldn't prevent a small thrill from whispering through her. What if Nathaniel had changed his mind about marrying the other woman? What if he'd decided that nothing else mattered except for being with her?

She didn't want to appear overly eager to see him again, so she took her time putting the kitchen chairs and game away. She even made a stop in her bedroom to check on the kittens that were still living inside the house. While she was there, she just happened to brush her hair and leave it hanging in loose waves over her shoulders. And she just happened to change her blouse into something fresh and clean.

Of course, she wasn't grooming herself for Nathaniel. Not in the least. He'd seen her at her worst plenty of times, so there was no need to make herself more presentable. Even so, before leaving, she stopped at the bureau mirror and pinched her cheeks to redden them.

Her gaze snagged on the cross he'd given her for her birthday. A tiny alarm flared in her head, one that said he'd already left her twice, that he'd already squelched her hope, and that she shouldn't allow herself to harbor any further hope he might stay.

But she couldn't keep the expectation from budding again anyway, in spite of the warning that she might get hurt all over again.

Finally, when she was certain she'd given Nathaniel enough time to make it to the dock and secure his boat, she exited the house. She forced her steps into a slow amble down the bastion, even though the butterflies in her stomach were flying as fast as a blue heron heading south for the winter.

When she rounded the bend that led to the dock, she stopped short.

There, coming slowly up the beach with bent head and slumped shoulders, was a man. As though sensing her presence, he halted. With his hands stuffed into his trouser pockets, he lifted his head and met her gaze.

The fluttering in her heart came to an abrupt halt, and she sucked in a startled breath.

It couldn't be.

She blinked to make sure she wasn't seeing things. The vision didn't disappear.

It was none other than Nate, her husband.

"Wait, Nathaniel!" His mother's voice echoed from the upstairs hallway.

Nathaniel paused with one hand on the front door. The footman was waiting with the carriage in the circular driveway. Although Nathaniel craved an excuse not to go out again for the evening, he had to leave. He had to visit Kitty Martin. Tonight. Now. Before he lost his will to do what was right and ended up back in bed, under the covers, guzzling laudanum.

His mother hurried down the spiral staircase, the train of her purple silk evening gown trailing behind her. At her throat she wore a lilac ribbon with an oval amethyst in the center that matched her amethyst bracelet.

He approached the stairs and smiled up at her. "You look lovely this evening, Mother."

She descended the last few steps gracefully, but she didn't return his smile. Instead, worry lines wrinkled her forehead. "Please stay home tonight, Nathaniel." There was a sadness and anxiety in her eyes that told Nathaniel she was trying to save him from himself. She assumed he was going out to party with friends, as was his custom. Now that she had him home again, she only desired to keep him from making the same mistakes he had before.

"I've had the cook prepare a lovely meal of canvasback duck with currant jelly. Your favorite." She cradled her hand in the crook of his arm, even though he hadn't offered it to her, and she guided him to the dining room.

"Mother," he said gently.

"Nicholas and I both want to hear all about your adventures while you were away from us." She rushed to speak before he denied her dinner request. "We've hardly had the chance to see you or speak with you since you've been home."

"I know. And I'm sincerely sorry for that." He stopped, forcing her to as well. When he extricated his arm from her hold and took a step to the door, her delicate shoulders deflated.

"Please, Nathaniel," she said, reaching a jeweled hand toward him. Her fingers shook, and suddenly he understood in a way he never had just how much his wild living had affected his mother, how much she'd worried about him, and how much she tried to protect him from becoming like his father.

"I promise I'm not doing anything that will get me into trouble this evening." He bent and placed a kiss upon her brow.

"Then stay," she insisted.

He was weakening. He wanted more than anything to give in to her. But he couldn't. If he didn't leave tonight, now, he might never. He sighed. "I'm going over to propose to Kitty Martin like I should have the day I went yachting and almost drowned."

His mother stared at him with a blank expression, as if she didn't understand what he was talking about. Then she waved her hand like she was brushing away a pesky mosquito. "Don't worry about her, darling. Once she learned of your drowning, she admitted she wasn't pregnant, that she'd made it up because she loved you and wanted you to marry her."

Nathaniel's body drained of all sound, and a stillness so completely filled him that he heard every rapid beat of his pulse. For a long moment, all he could do was stare at his mother and attempt to absorb her revelation.

"I think perhaps her parents put her up to the lie to force your hand. After all, the Martins have been trying for years to make Mrs. Astor's list and simply haven't been able to do it."

Mother was referring to Mrs. Jacob Astor's special list that contained the most prominent and wealthy families in New

York society, which she used in sending out invitations to her annual ball. Nathaniel wasn't so sure why such a list mattered and why people aspired to be on it. But the Winthrops, with their money and connections, had always been close to the top of the list. He supposed his mother could have invented her own exclusive list if she'd set her mind to it.

Nathaniel tried to form a sentence, but his breath stuck in his chest. His head swirled with a relief so intense he almost bent over and wept. He wasn't having a baby. He wasn't going to be a father.

"As a matter of fact, the Martin's left Newport a couple of weeks ago. Kitty is, of course, completely ruined now, and it serves her right."

Guilt reached inside and wrenched him. "Even if she's not carrying my child, I'm still to blame for her ruination. I should be a man of honor and marry her anyway."

Mother shook her head, and the sad, weary lines reappeared in her forehead. "Nathaniel, unfortunately there are other young women who offered themselves to you, hoping you would do the right thing by marrying them. But you can't possibly marry each woman, can you?"

His mother's blunt words should have made him squirm in discomfort, but his guilt weighed him down.

"You can't change the past," Mother said softly. "But you can change the future."

He couldn't move, not even to lift his head. The shame of all he'd done came back in wave after heavy wave. He could honestly say, like the apostle Paul, that he was the worst of sinners. But could he also say, like the apostle, that God had shown him mercy so that, in Him, Christ might display His unlimited patience?

He wanted to say it. But he wasn't sure he was strong enough yet.

His mother's fingers brushed his cheek, her rings clinking together. "Stay home tonight. It's not too late to start over."

For a moment, he wasn't sure if he agreed with her. But finally, he lifted his arm. "Dinner smells delicious."

The brightness of her smile rivaled the glittering crystal of the chandelier dangling overhead. She slipped her hand around his arm, tiptoed, and kissed his cheek. "I love you, Nathaniel Richard Winthrop."

"Hi, Abbie," Nate said. He didn't move to cross the distance between them.

Neither did she. In fact, she couldn't make her voice work to answer. She could only stare. His physical appearance hadn't changed much over the months he'd been gone. He was still the same broad-shouldered, muscular-armed, well-built man. His beard was thicker and his hair in need of a cut. But he wore one of his familiar flannel shirts with a pair of worn trousers, which she could tell had been recently patched in the knees.

Although he looked the same, there was something different in his expression, in his eyes. Was it sadness? Remorse? Regret?

She couldn't put her finger on it, except that he seemed somehow older and tired.

"I bet you weren't expecting to see me," he said.

A gull circled nearby, followed by several more swirling in wide circles. Thin clouds streaked the sky, turning it violet as the sun began its descent.

She tried to respond but felt as though she'd swallowed a

mouthful of sand. Was she conversing with a ghost? Or was she so tired that she was seeing things?

"How are you?" he asked almost timidly.

"You're supposed to be dead."

"I am?"

"Yes, your body was found by Brenton Point in the spring."

He glanced down at himself and then back at her. "Guess it was someone else. 'Cause as far as I can tell, my body's right here."

Her heart thudded with strange confusion as she tried to make sense of what she was seeing. "The fishermen found your pocket watch with the dead body. It said *To Crabby* on the back."

Nate patted the pocket on his trouser where he normally carried his watch. "Before I left, I sold my watch to pay for train fare."

She could only gape at Nate with a thousand thoughts running through her head. *Nate's not dead* began to clang the loudest. *Nate's not dead. Nate's not dead.*

How could she have been so mistaken?

"Guess that dead man has to be someone else," Nate said.

"If you're not dead," she said, her voice wavering with all the uncertainty inside, "then where have you been all this time? I don't understand how you could walk away, be gone for months, and never once tell me where you were."

He flinched as though she'd smacked him across the cheeks. "How's Gramps?"

"Do you care how Gramps is doing?"

He lowered his gaze to his boots. Chagrin lined his face.

She wanted to lash out at him and tell him to go away. She

didn't want him to be there, didn't want him walking back into her life. The only man she desired was Nathaniel—sweet, sensitive, caring, and amazing Nathaniel.

The longing for Nathaniel rose so swiftly that she swayed and thought she might be sick from the pressure of it.

Although she'd known Nathaniel had left to marry the mother of his unborn baby, she'd been praying for a miracle or at the very least hoping that he'd change his mind and come back to her. But now…there was no going back to what they'd had. No chance of having him. No slim possibility of being with him, even if he decided that's what he wanted. Not with her husband alive and well.

After all this time, Nate was supposed to be dead. Gone. Out of her life. Now he was standing before her. She should be happy he was alive and safe. Happy that he'd come back. But her chest rumbled with a hollow anger.

"Where have you been?" she demanded again.

"In Providence," he admitted hesitantly. "With my brother's family." Even as he spoke the words, despair rolled in to cloud the air around him. He clearly hadn't resolved his brother's death and was still hurting.

Even though she felt nothing toward this man who was more of a stranger than a husband, she was bound to him. For better or worse. For richer or poorer. Until death parted them.

The ache in her heart throbbed. The pain was intensely raw. She had to press her hand against her chest to keep from crying out.

As much as she wanted to run away and pretend he wasn't there, it wouldn't do any good. As much as she wanted to wake herself up from a bad dream, this was reality. The reality was that Nate was alive. He was here. And he was her husband. She couldn't change any of that. The only thing she could change was herself.

The fire of her anger flickered out, and she hung her head. She'd been insensitive to his pain once before and had pushed him away. Could she learn from her mistakes and do better this time?

"How is your brother's family doing?" She managed to get the words out and look at him.

Nate stared at the sand as though he might weep. With his hands still stuffed in his pockets, he appeared lost.

For long moments, the crash of the waves and the cry of the circling gulls were the only sounds. Finally, Nate seemed to gather the inner strength to meet her gaze again with his sad one. "I'm sorry for leaving you, Abbie. I shouldn't have done it, and I promise not to do it again."

Chapter 24

Nathaniel tipped the oar and helped Menard direct the skiff toward the northern end of the island. He hadn't planned on returning to Rose Island. The last time he'd left, he'd told himself he would never come back, that it would be much too difficult to face Abbie, knowing he couldn't have her.

He'd spent the past three days with his mother and Nicholas. At his insistence, they'd had no guests but had, instead, taken time to grieve and heal together—finally being able to speak about Father and all that had happened over the years.

During that time, Nathaniel had waited somewhat impatiently as his investigators brought him news, first of Zeke uncovering the treasure, then of Zeke packing up his belongings. Just a few hours ago, he'd received the news that Zeke had vacated Goat Island Lighthouse and left on a steamer bound for Maine. Zeke's leaving provided Nathaniel with the chance to visit Rose Island again. In fact, the more he'd thought about going back, the more he realized he could do nothing less.

He needed to see Abbie more than he needed to breathe or eat or sleep. He hadn't been doing any of those things well over the past few days since he was consumed with wishing he was with her. Although his guilt and shame over his past affairs with women haunted him and told him he wasn't worthy of her, he wanted to believe that maybe she could eventually learn to love him anyway.

She'd certainly been attracted to him. There was no denying the passion that had sparked whenever they touched.

But could she ever love him? Enough to marry him?

Yes, he wanted to marry her and be with her and love her. He wanted to live with her and Hosea on Rose Island, and he wanted to go back to the comfortable and simple life they'd led together before his memories had returned. Even though he loved his mother and Nicholas, he didn't want to reenter society life. He didn't want to visit with old friends. And he didn't want to return to New York City in a few weeks for the next social season.

Ahead in the skiff, Menard directed the boat through the thick eelgrass beds. Menard had been more than willing to accompany him to the island to see for himself what had become of the buried treasure. Now that they were here, Nathaniel didn't think he'd have too much trouble convincing Menard to row around to visit Abbie and Hosea once they were done.

"Over there," Menard said, pointing to a clump of brush that sat back from the shore. "That's the start of the trail."

They worked together to drag the skiff to shore. Then

Menard set out, leading the way. When they arrived, it was clear that Zeke had been there. He'd dug deep and hadn't bothered to fill in the hole. His footprints, along with those of his boys, littered the ground.

Nathaniel poked around at the hole. "Looks like Zeke wanted to make sure that Abbie and Hosea were well aware that he'd found the treasure."

Menard stared down into the hole alongside Nathaniel. He pushed his spectacles up on his nose and wiped the perspiration from his forehead. The August day was thick with humidity and the promise of more rain.

"It was a brilliant plan, Mr. Winthrop," Menard said again, as he had already a hundred times. "There's no way we can ever repay you for what you did, but I want you to know that you can always count on me for anything."

"And you know that you can do likewise," Nathaniel replied. "If you ever need anything—anything at all—I'm here for you."

They made quick work of filling in the hole before hiking back to the skiff. They rowed around the island toward the dock. At the shore, Nathaniel stopped short at the sight of Abbie walking down the beach in their direction. Nathaniel had to restrain himself from jumping out of the boat, running to her, sweeping her into his arms, and kissing her soundly.

After their difficult good-bye earlier in the week, he'd only confuse her if he didn't show some restraint—at least until he made clear he was free and wanted to marry her. For the time being, he'd have to remain collected.

He smiled and lifted a hand in greeting.

She halted, but didn't smile and didn't lift her hand even an inch. In fact, she didn't appear the least bit happy to see him. If anything, she appeared skittish, as if she'd like to turn around and flee to the house. Her beautiful eyes were wide and her face pale.

"We came to make sure that Zeke collected the buried treasure," he called. Apparently, he had his work cut out for him in winning her heart again. But he'd done it once, and he'd do it again. He was, after all, a master at patience and persistence. With Abbie, he'd learned that equal parts of flirting and nonchalance seemed to draw her to him. He'd enjoy wooing her again and building the romantic tension between them until it was taut enough to tow her in. His grin widened at the thought.

As he and Menard clambered ashore, Abbie came no closer. She clutched her hands to her sides and remained stiffly in one spot.

"Mr. Winthrop sure did fool Zeke." Menard beamed with pride. "I don't think Zeke ever once suspected it was a fake map or fake treasure."

Abbie finally spoke. "What do you mean by fake?"

"Mr. Winthrop hired a mapmaker to develop an entirely new treasure map that was a replica of the one he found in the house. When I saw them side by side, I couldn't tell the difference, except, of course, the trail to the treasure."

Abbie's eyes widened upon Nathaniel, but before she could comment, Menard continued his explanation. "He also put together a chest of artifacts that I buried out on the island. Some real nice jewels and coins he fixed up to look old."

Nathaniel hadn't planned to inform Abbie the lengths he'd gone to, but he supposed she deserved to know that the genuine map was safe. He doubted it would lead to a treasure, but Hosea could continue to search to his heart's content.

"You gave Zeke a treasure?" Abbie asked, her voice rising in disbelief.

"It wasn't much," Nathaniel started.

"I would have been plenty pleased to find it myself," Menard admitted. "I'm sure Zeke Crawford thinks the world of himself now."

Abbie only shook her head, her eyes rounding in wonder.

Nathaniel had to force himself not to grin like a proud peacock. But inwardly he gave himself a huge pat on the back. Maybe with this move, Abbie would warm up to him sooner rather than later. "Since he believes he found the treasure here," Nathaniel explained, "he'll have no need to come back. In fact, he took a light keeper position in Maine."

"A position that Mr. Winthrop orchestrated," Menard added.

Abbie glanced between them until her gaze landed upon Nathaniel. And he saw in her eyes what he'd been hoping for—admiration. And longing. Pure, unhindered longing.

Heat wrapped a tight coil around his gut. He barely held himself back from crossing the distance toward her.

"I'm not going to be a father," he blurted.

At his announcement, she sucked in a breath, and he knew she understood what he meant. Even so, he rushed to explain himself. "She was never pregnant. She made it up to force my hand in marriage. When she thought I'd drowned, she had no choice but to admit her ploy."

For long seconds, none of them said anything. Menard stood as still as a marble sculpture, as if by doing so he could make himself blend into the setting.

As the emotions rippled across Abbie's face, Nathaniel couldn't hold himself back any longer. He spanned the distance in several long strides. Before he reached her, she held out her hand to stop him.

"No, Nathaniel," she choked out the words, her face etched with anguish.

"I'm free," he whispered. "And I want to marry you."

Tears welled in her eyes, but before she could respond, a figure rounded the bend and started down the sandy path toward them. At first Nathaniel thought it must be Hosea, but the man was much younger. He was stocky, with thickly built arms and legs, and had a tanned and weathered face similar to those of the local fishermen. He would have been ruggedly handsome if not for the beard.

Nathaniel's pulse quieted to a low thud as he took in the man's clothing…the same brown trousers and red-checkered shirt that Nathaniel had worn when he'd lived on Rose Island.

The man walked with a comfortable step, one that said he knew his way around the island, that it was home. And when he stopped next to Abbie, he was self-assured, as though he belonged by her side every bit as much as he belonged on the island.

Nathaniel's pulse ceased beating completely. A cold, eerie silence settled into his veins. He wrenched his gaze from the man and almost frantically sought Abbie. When their eyes collided, the tears, the sorrow, and the regret there told him everything.

This was Nate.

The man nodded at Menard. "How's Debbie?"

Menard's eyes were enormous and his spectacles magnified his shock. He was clearly as taken aback by Nate's sudden appearance as Nathaniel was. "She's doing well," he stuttered. "Just had a baby."

Nate's expression was polite, but he didn't press for more information before he shifted to study Nathaniel, starting with his black hat down to his new shoes.

"I'm Nathaniel Winthrop."

"I know who you are." Nate regarded him coolly. "I've seen you in Newport before."

Nathaniel looked to Abbie for any sign she'd told Nate about them. Her eyes were the brown-green color of churning seawater during a dark storm. They pleaded with him not to say anything. The tight muscles in her features revealed the torture of this moment. The agony mirrored his own, and he realized he'd only make things worse for her by saying anything about all that had transpired.

He swallowed the burning in his throat. "We just stopped by so I could…." He stumbled over his words. So he could tell Abbie he loved her? So he could propose marriage? So he could kiss her?

Nate glanced between him and Abbie several times before focusing on him again. This time his eyes were wary, as if he sensed the unfolding turmoil.

Nathaniel patted his coat pocket, reached inside, and pulled out an envelope. "We stopped by to give this to Hosea." He handed the envelope to Abbie.

She took it with trembling fingers.

"It's the original map I found in his Bible, with a few clarifications from my mapmaker friend." Nathaniel clasped his hands behind his back so that Nate wouldn't see that his were trembling too. "It's his, and he deserves to have it."

Just like Abbie was Nate's.

"Thank you," she whispered. When she met his gaze for a final time, he knew she was thanking him for everything—for helping her on the island, for protecting them from further threats from Zeke. And for not saying anything about their relationship to Nate.

Nathaniel held her gaze for a long last moment, needing to have one final look at the beautiful woman he'd loved—but ultimately lost.

Abbie couldn't make herself move from her spot on the beach, even after the boat was well away from the shore.

Nate shifted his feet but didn't leave either. He stared after the boat almost wistfully.

The past few days since Nate's return had been uneventful. Thankfully, Gramps had accepted Nate's presence as easily as he'd accepted Nathaniel's. Of course, Nate wasn't interested in spending time with Gramps any more now than he had been when they'd first been married. He tolerated Gramps, was even patient with him, but made no effort to engage him. She supposed Gramps sensed Nate's disinterest because he didn't seek him out the same way he had Nathaniel.

Nate hadn't made any efforts with her either. He mostly avoided her and had been sleeping in the bedroom off the kitchen. She supposed, eventually, he'd want to share her bed again. But for now, she needed time. Time to forget about Nathaniel. Time to heal her broken heart. And time to reconcile to the fact she would never be with the man she loved with all her heart.

Nate released a bitter laugh. "Looks like we make a fine pair." He'd stuffed his hands in his trousers, and his shoulders slumped in the dejection that had been his companion since his return.

Her throat ached too much to talk to him. So she just shrugged and continued to watch the skiff grow more distant.

"We're married but both in love with someone else."

His quiet statement shot through her with the noise of a gun blast. "In love with someone else?" She stumbled over the guilt that was suddenly strewn everywhere.

He nodded, his eyes fixed on the skiff. "I may not be the most intelligent guy to walk the earth, but it don't take any brains to see that Nathaniel Winthrop is crazy in love with you."

She shook her head, wanting to protect Nathaniel. But before she could form words of denial, Nate shifted and met her gaze directly. "And you're in love with him too."

Her mind whirled with a dozen stories, and she tried to figure out how to explain everything. "I thought you were dead."

He shrugged. "I don't blame you."

She watched him and attempted to gauge what he was thinking and feeling. "Even so, I shouldn't have—"

"I love my brother's wife." This time when their gazes connected, she could see the truth, the heartache, and the agony.

"I've always loved Gloria," he admitted, his voice cracking. "But in the end, she chose Ross over me."

Abbie's body tensed. She wasn't sure she wanted to hear Nate's tale, suspected it would only hurt her. But she also needed to finally know the truth.

"When I moved here, I tried to start over, tried to forget about her," he continued. "And when I met you, I hoped maybe I could love you instead."

Abbie's heart pricked.

As though sensing the pain his revelation was causing her, his expression turned apologetic. "You were—are beautiful and caring and full of spirit. And I loved being with you..."

"Until Ross died," she finished for him as she began to understand what had happened.

Nate nodded, bowing his head in shame. "After Ross died, I couldn't stop thinking about Gloria and how she was alone with her baby. I wanted to go be with her and take care of her. But I didn't want to leave you either."

So he'd drowned his confusion and heartache with alcohol. She didn't say the words. The shame that cloaked him said it well enough.

"When she sent me a telegram to say she had no place to live anymore, I left. I went to Providence to help her. The money from the pocket watch not only helped me get there, but also helped me put a down payment on a room for her."

Abbie nodded. Strangely, she understood what he'd gone through, and she wasn't angry with him. If anything, she was relieved to discover he hadn't left because of something she'd done wrong.

"I didn't know how to explain the situation to you. So I took the coward's way and didn't say anything. But the longer I stayed with Gloria, the more I realized that I couldn't live a double life. It wasn't fair to her or you."

"So you didn't tell her about me?" Abbie asked.

"I told her last week."

"And she kicked you out?"

"No. I decided to come back. And she agreed with me that returning to you was for the best."

"But you still love her?"

He stared at the retreating boat again. "Yep."

"Does she love you?"

Nate's jaw worked up and down before he answered. "She's still in love with Ross. And I don't think she'll ever get over him."

Abbie shifted to peer at the fading skiff too. The heaviness of Nate's pain mingled with hers. They'd both loved and lost. And now they were hurting terribly. But they were here. Together. And they were still married.

They could push each other away and be miserable. Or they could walk the first steps forward toward healing. Maybe they'd never forget their first loves. Maybe they'd never completely heal. Maybe they'd never fall in love with each other.

But by coming back to her, Nate had made an effort to repair their marriage. She could give him credit for that, couldn't she? As much as her traitorous heart resisted, she knew she had to make an effort too. If Nate was trying to forget about Gloria, then she had to try to forget about Nathaniel.

Eventually, with enough time and work, maybe they would be able to put the past behind them and forge a new life. Together.

She reached for Nate's arm, hoping to hold his hand. She wanted to assure him she forgave him and hope to feel his forgiveness for her in return. His muscles beneath her fingers stiffened. She slid her hand down, hoping he'd remove his from his pocket. But he only jammed his hand deeper.

She waited for several heartbeats for him to connect with her. But when he didn't move, she dropped her hand. His jaw clenched and unclenched. He didn't say anything more before spinning and walking away.

Chapter 25

NEWPORT, RHODE ISLAND

MAY 1881, NINE MONTHS LATER

Nathaniel Winthrop III wrapped the dock line around the cleat, basking in the cool May breeze coming off Newport Bay. All the while he and his crew sailed *The Tempest* into Narragansett Bay, he'd refused to look in the direction of Rose Island.

He hadn't wanted to return to Newport. After he'd left nine months ago, he'd told himself he'd never return. But Mother had pleaded with him to accompany her to help ready the cottage for the summer. Nicholas had just left for a tour of Europe, and Nathaniel hadn't wanted to leave all the responsibility for the Newport home on Mother's shoulders.

Truthfully, part of him wanted to spend the few short weeks he was in Newport convincing Mother to sell the home. Then he'd be able to cut his ties with Newport once and for all.

The other part of him knew that he had to confront his hurts and pains in Newport head-on before he could truly heal. He'd learned that last fall when he'd returned to New York City. He'd longed to find another secluded place to hide, like Rose Island, where he'd be away from the activities and friends that would tempt him to return to his old lifestyle.

For a few days after being back in New York City, he'd cowered away, not going anywhere, making himself a prisoner in his own home. At the time, he'd also been dealing with the pain of losing Abbie. More than that, he'd been living in fear. Fear of sinning. Fear of failing. Fear of falling back into the same pit he'd been in before.

He'd hidden, until his mother had said the same thing to him that Abbie had: *It's all in your past. Whatever you once were, you don't have to be that person anymore.* After the reminder, he'd realized that if he wanted to change, he couldn't hide from every temptation. If he sheltered himself from danger, he'd never have the chance to grow stronger. Strength came from facing the temptation, looking it in the face, and then walking away from it.

He'd done that repeatedly all winter and spring. He'd proven to himself, to his family, and, most of all, to God that he was serious about being a new man. At first his friends eyed him strangely when he'd turned down their invitations, drinks, and women. But he'd stopped caring what they thought of him. Of course, he had too much money and prestige for them to reject him completely. Nevertheless, he'd been able to shed his old reputation and start a new one—where people knew him as reliable, considerate, and giving.

Nathaniel took a deep breath of the sea-tinged air and hefted himself out of the yacht and onto the dock. The wooden planks swayed against the gentle swell of the waves in the marina as he walked toward the wharf, where hopefully a carriage would be waiting for him.

As hard as it had been to leave Abbie and Rose Island, he realized now if he'd stayed, he never would have had the opportunity to grow—at least not the same way he had by going out and blazing a new course for the new man he'd become. There were times when living with integrity had stretched him beyond his limits. There were times he'd fallen into bed at night feeling like a failure. There were times he'd wanted to dull his aching heart with a glass of rum or bottle of laudanum—especially when he'd pictured Abbie together with Nate. Such images were torturous—even still.

Just the thought of her again beckoned him to turn around and stare at the Rose Island Lighthouse to see if he could spot her. One glimpse of her wouldn't hurt, would it?

He put his head down and lengthened his stride. Yes, one glimpse would do neither of them any good. It would only stir up thoughts and feelings that needed to remain buried. She was a temptation he doubted he would ever be strong enough to withstand, and in this case, he was better off staying as far from her as possible. Which was one reason he'd wanted to remain in New York City for the summer season.

But facing Newport, the memories here, and all that had happened was still an important part of his healing process. As much as he'd wanted to avoid the pain, he had to push forward as the man of God he was becoming.

As he reached the wharf and realized the carriage wasn't there yet, he checked his pocket watch, only to note he'd arrived early. He could stay and wait, or he could walk to the house.

"Mr. Winthrop?" a surprised voice came from behind him.

Nathaniel spun to see a thin, gangly man wearing spectacles rowing his skiff to a nearby dock. Behind him in the boat sat a little girl and a young woman holding a baby.

His pulse gave an unexpected extra thump. "Menard? Debbie?" It was after all, Sunday, a day of rest. Menard would have the day off to spend with his family.

Menard grinned and lifted a hand in greeting. "Mr. Winthrop, I thought that was you."

A warning bell went off in Nathaniel's head, telling him to say a quick hello and move along. If he lingered, he might not be able to keep himself from asking about Abbie. The less he knew the better, because if he discovered that Nate hadn't been treating her right, he was liable to get back into his yacht, sail over to the island, and teach Nate a lesson or two.

"We're just now returning from visiting Gramps and Abbie," Menard said as he steered the skiff alongside the dock. "We spent the afternoon with them."

Abbie. At the mention of her name, Nathaniel's heartbeat tripled its speed. *Don't ask about her. Don't ask about her. Don't ask about her.*

"How are they doing?" The words popped out, and he was embarrassed to realize how eager he sounded. To hide his emotions, he reached down to help Menard secure the dock line.

Menard glanced behind him to Debbie, who shook her head curtly, a warning not to say anything. Menard offered Nathaniel an apologetic smile. "They're doing just fine."

Fine? That told Nathaniel absolutely nothing.

Likely, Debbie had seen Nathaniel tying up his yacht and had already warned Menard not to speak about Abbie. He didn't blame Abbie's sister for wanting to stay silent. That was wise. She had only Abbie's best interest in mind and didn't want her to get hurt. If Nathaniel showed up again, it could cause strife, especially if Abbie and Nate had reconciled and were happy together. And if they weren't happy...

Nathaniel's muscles tightened at the thought, and he had the urge to hit something. Yes, it was best if he didn't know how Abbie was doing.

"How is the baby doing?" he asked, looking pointedly at Henry, who was sitting contently on Debbie's lap and chewing on the strings of her bonnet.

For a few minutes, he chatted with them about Henry and Pollyanna and Menard's job with the Coles. They even talked about the weather before Nathaniel said his good-bye and started to walk away.

"I don't understand why we can't tell him." The wind carried Menard's exasperated whisper to Debbie.

"I already told you," she whispered. "It would never work between them. They're from two different worlds."

"Yes, but—"

"Besides, you know his reputation."

"I've heard he's changed."

"He'd use her and break her heart all over again."

Nathaniel wanted to spin around and tell them he could hear everything they were saying, but at that moment, a brougham came rolling to a stop in front of him. One of the footmen that the Winthrops employed stepped down and greeted him.

As Nathaniel entered the carriage, he glanced over his shoulder at Menard, who was now standing on the dock staring after him. Something in Menard's eyes encouraged him, even urged him to visit Abbie.

The look was all it took to set Nathaniel's blood on fire with the need to go to her. Whether right or wrong, he had to face her one last time. He wouldn't be able to rest until he did. Then he could walk away from her and be a stronger man as a result.

The next morning, the sunshine was too bright as Nathaniel made his way up the sandy embankment toward the lighthouse. He pulled the brim of his hat low over his tired eyes. He'd hardly slept at all last night, his thoughts too full of Abbie and Rose Island.

When he'd dragged himself out of bed, he'd had an overwhelming urge to crawl back under the covers and disappear there for the next three weeks until he left for New York City. His head throbbed, his body ached, and most of all his heart twisted with pain.

No matter how much he'd tried to deny it and forget about Abbie over the past months, he still loved her. And being this close to her but not being able to have her was killing him.

It was that thought that had prodded him to get dressed. He'd realized his disappointment, pain, and heartache would only fester if he didn't bring some kind of finality to his love for her.

He'd believed coming to Newport would be enough, that he'd be able to face the pain of losing her and begin to move on. But at Menard's silent urging, he realized he'd never be satisfied or have true closure if he didn't visit her one final time.

The breeze coming off the bay was cold for the May

morning, and his fingers were frigid beneath his leather gloves from rowing across in the borrowed skiff. His ears and cheeks stung from the chilled air, and he wondered again that he hadn't waited until later in the day when it was warmer.

He flexed his fingers, trying to bring warmth back, and noticed the lump in the glove where he wore his signet ring. The ring that had once belonged to his father. What had once been a heavy weight of guilt around his neck, God had redeemed. Now he wore it where he could see it all the time, as a reminder that the old things had passed away.

He was a new creation, he reminded himself as he climbed the sloping hill. He could handle whatever came his way today, not in his own strength, but in God's.

His footsteps slowed as he passed old Fort Hamilton and the spot he'd once so enthusiastically begun to clear in anticipation of building a shed for a cow he'd purchased. The spot was now overgrown.

He forced his feet to climb the last rise and took in the house, the tower, the oil house, outhouse, and garden all at once. The roof of the keeper's cottage had been repaired with new shingles, and an oil house had been built in the same spot as the one that the storm had swept away. But everything else was the same.

His sights snagged on the woman kneeling in the garden pulling weeds. His heart constricted, even as his pulse sped with undeniable desire.

Her long hair hung in a loose braid, with wispy tendrils curling around her neck and ears. Her bare heels poked out from her skirt, already dirty and sandy in the early morning.

A bittersweet smile tugged at his lips. She'd probably already been clamming or crabbing this morning, walking barefoot along the beach, as she always did.

Her skirt was pulled taut along her backside, outlining her womanly figure all too clearly, and he jerked his gaze away. Where was Nate? Perhaps he was out lobstering. Or sleeping after tending to the lighthouse during the night.

Memories flooded Nathaniel's mind of all the mornings he'd cooked her breakfast. He'd always been eager to get his first glimpse of her after she'd awoken. He'd loved the way her eyes had shone with appreciation when he'd pour her a cup of coffee. And he'd loved how she'd eaten each bite of breakfast with relish, her eyes dancing with delight.

No, he told himself sharply. *Stay focused. Do what you came to do. Then leave.*

Almost as if he'd spoken aloud, Abbie glanced over her shoulder in his direction. At the sight of him, her eyes widened and stayed on him.

For an interminable moment, everything else ceased to exist except the two of them. She didn't smile, but a light of joy brightened the green in her eyes and sent his pulse skittering.

She still cared about him. He didn't know if the emotion on her face was love. But it came very close. Although she worked to hide her reaction to him by ducking her head, satisfaction spilled through him. No matter what had happened over this past year between her and Nate, she hadn't forgotten about him. He could take comfort in that.

When she glanced at him again over her shoulder, he was struck by how beautiful she was in the sunshine. The brightness that had only moments ago been torture was now shining down on her, illuminating every lovely curve of her face, her cheek, her jaw, her lips. Although she was still petite and delicate, she was less angular, her features fuller in a way that was entirely too alluring, a way that sent heat pumping into his bloodstream.

Stop. The silent command pounded through his head. He couldn't lust over another man's wife.

"I just returned to Newport yesterday," he said. "And wouldn't you know it, I ran into Menard when I was docking?"

Her back, still facing him, heaved up then down as she expelled a deep breath. For several seconds, she didn't move. Then, somewhat clumsily, she pushed herself up from the ground. As she turned and placed a hand on her stomach, Nathaniel took an involuntary step back at the same time a sickening swell of nausea rose.

Her hand rested gently, almost reverently on her rounded abdomen. Her very rounded abdomen.

"You're having a baby," he said before he could stop himself, wishing his tone wasn't so defeated and sad.

She nodded solemnly. Clouds rolled in to replace the joy that had been there only moments ago.

Suddenly, all he could think about was the fact that she'd been intimate with Nate and that now they were having a baby together. As always, the picture of her in any other man's arms drove him mad. He loathed thinking of her with anyone but him.

Now, here she was, with the evidence right there. Undeniable.

He glanced down at his shoes and wished he hadn't come. He supposed he'd secretly hoped that Nate had run off again and that Abbie would ask him to stay. But it was clear Nate had been very much involved in Abbie's life. Too involved.

Nathaniel swallowed the nausea and met her gaze again.

This time her eyes contained hurt.

He mentally slapped himself. *Pull it together. You can do this. You're a new man living in God's strength and not your own.* "Are you happy, Abbie?" he asked, and he was glad that his tone was soft this time.

She caressed her protruding stomach before looking at him. "I didn't think I'd ever want to have a child. After what happened with my mom, I was afraid to become a mother."

He nodded, remembering the stormy day when they'd bared their souls to each other. He'd never been able to talk with anyone else as openly as he had her, and he doubted he'd find anyone like her ever again.

"But then I told myself the same thing I told you—that we're not destined to make the same mistakes as our parents. We're separate from them and can choose to be different."

He'd thought of her admonition often during the past year. It had held him in good stead during many dark days when memories of his father had dragged him down.

She lifted her chin in that strong almost defiant way she had. "I won't leave my child. Ever."

He couldn't keep from smiling. "You're a strong woman, Abbie. You'll do whatever you set your mind to."

At his encouragement, her lips curved into a slight smile, and a bit of the light returned to her eyes. He was struck again by how beautiful she was. The pregnancy suited her. She was still thin but contained a roundness that filled her out and made her even more desirable.

He shifted and looked at the house to hide his longing. Completely inappropriate longing. She was married and had a life with Nate. As long as she was happy, he could move on. "So you're happy?" he asked again.

"Yes. I am." Her answer was quiet but contained an

assurance that satisfied him. That's all he needed to know. His heart would always ache at the thought of her. He'd never be able to walk around Newport without thinking of this beautiful woman. And he'd never stop loving her. But he could leave now in peace.

He nodded. "I'm glad you're happy."

She studied her toes in the damp soil and looked as if she wanted to say something more.

He waited, giving her the chance to tell him anything. But when she pressed her lips together and didn't speak, he felt himself deflate. He had no reason to stay any longer on Rose Island. He'd discovered what he needed, and he'd resisted his desire for her. It was time to go.

"Do you mind if I say hi to Hosea?" he asked. Even if Hosea didn't remember him or thought he was someone else, he wanted to satisfy himself that the older man was healthy and happy too. "When I was rowing over, I saw him whitewashing the bastion."

"Yes, he's down the path."

Nathaniel studied her one last time and started forward.

"Are you happy?" she called after him.

Her question stopped him. Was he happy? No. He wasn't happy to discover that Abbie had been with another man, not when he'd wanted her for his own. No. He wasn't happy that he'd have to leave her again. But she'd moved on with her life. She was having a baby with Nate. And she was getting along just fine without him—even if he still very much needed and wanted her.

Besides his heartache over her, he was pleased with the direction his life was going. "I'm forging a new trail. It hasn't been easy. But I'll never go back to where I was before."

At his answer, she smiled. "I knew you could do it."

The genuine confidence in her voice washed over him and seeped into his soul. She'd always believed in him, even when she'd known the worst about him. She'd never despised him for the man he once was. She only saw the godly man he was capable of becoming. And he loved her for it.

When their gazes collided, the light was back in her eyes, and this time he had no question about what he saw there. Not just affection or care. She loved him. The pureness of it radiated and reached out to him, almost pleaded with him to love her in return.

He dropped his attention to the ground so she wouldn't see his reaction—the overwhelming love he had for her. It wouldn't be fair if he expressed that love and encouraged her affection away from Nate. It was better to keep his feelings safely hidden from her.

With his head down, Nathaniel rounded the house and descended the path that led to the bottom of the rounded wall that supported the lighthouse. Sure enough, at the base of the gravelly trail, Hosea was dipping his roller in a bucket of whitewash.

"Hello, Hosea." Nathaniel stopped a few feet away, even as the waves splashed up against the rocky ledge that jutted out and provided a narrow strip to stand upon.

Hosea jumped in surprise and jerked the long-handled roller out of the bucket, sending whitewash flying into the air. Several drops splattered against Nathaniel's pants.

Hosea didn't move and stared at Nathaniel wordlessly.

"I'm sorry if I startled you," Nathaniel said. "How are you doing?"

Hosea lowered the roller into the bucket, never once

taking his eyes from Nathaniel. "I thought you were dead."

"Dead?" Who did Hosea think he was today? Steele or Nate or someone else? Maybe seeing Hosea hadn't been a good idea. The visit would confuse him more than he already was.

Hosea wiped his hand across his eyes as though trying to clear his vision.

"You look like you're doing well, Hosea." Nathaniel retreated a step toward the path, deciding that Hosea would fare better if he simply left. "But I can see you're very busy. So I won't disturb you any further."

"What are you doing here? You got pneumonia and died."

"Pneumonia? When did I get that?" Was that how Steele had died? Was Hosea now convinced Steele was dead?

Hosea shook his head as though trying to clear the confusion. "Then you didn't get pneumonia and die?"

Nathaniel wasn't sure who Hosea was referring to. From experience, he realized it was best to agree with the older man or he'd only grow more confused and agitated. "I guess I've forgotten what happened, Hosea. But I'm here now. And that's all that counts, right?"

Hosea took off his hat, rubbed the balding spot on his head, and broke into a grin. "You're right. You're here now. And that's all that counts."

Nathaniel relaxed and smiled back. Before he could say anything more, Hosea grabbed his arm and propelled him up the bastion path. "This is amazing. Truly amazing," he muttered as he hustled as fast as his stiff legs would take him.

"Abbie!" Hosea called when he reached the grassy yard near the house. "Abbie!" Hosea didn't slow his pace. If anything, he was running and dragging Nathaniel along behind him.

At the sound of her name, Abbie turned to greet Hosea. But not before Nathaniel witnessed her wiping tears off her cheeks. The smile she gave her grandfather was forced, and Nathaniel saw right past it to the pain that etched her face.

Had he caused that pain? Had she started crying after he left?

He knew the answers to both questions already. The real question was why? Why was she upset?

"Abbie!" Hosea shouted again. "Look who came back to us! It's Nate."

Did Hosea think he was Abbie's Nate? A strange quiet descended over the swirling in Nathaniel's head.

"Nate's not dead after all!" Hosea said. "We had that blasted funeral for no reason."

Nathaniel didn't resist as Hosea lifted his arm in the air as if to prove he was living and breathing.

"It's a miracle." Hosea beamed up at him. "Isn't it, Abbie?"

She hesitated, then nodded at her grandfather, before giving Nathaniel an apologetic look. When she did, the truth hit him.

Nate was dead.

Chapter 26

Abbie tried to smile brightly for Gramps, but she couldn't muster the enthusiasm. All she could think about was Nathaniel's face when she'd stood and showed her condition. His face had gone pale, and he'd taken a step away, as though he'd seen a shark. More than that, his eyes had filled with revulsion.

She'd known he didn't want to be a father. He'd been tortured with thoughts of failure last year when he'd believed he was to become a parent. When she'd turned to see him standing there on Rose Island, alive and well, she'd allowed herself to harbor hope that maybe he could accept her the way she was, child and all.

But she'd been wrong to assume he would have changed his mind about wanting children. After his experience with his father, he'd likely always be plagued by fears of becoming a father. Even though God was clearly at work in his life, old insecurities didn't magically disappear.

She should know. There were still times when she doubted that she would be a good mom. Maybe she wouldn't abandon her child, but she would make her own mistakes. She wouldn't be perfect. No one was.

Even so, the moment she'd seen Nathaniel, she hadn't been able to keep herself from loving him all over again. It came out as if it had a will and strength of its own. She'd done her best to suppress her feelings for Nathaniel over the past year, especially when Nate first returned. She'd thought Nate was attempting to do the same—trying to forget about Gloria. She'd thought they were moving forward and forging a new life together.

But as the summer had moved into the fall, Nate continued to be distant with her. He'd kept to himself in the downstairs bedroom, hardly speaking with her or Gramps. He'd resumed his lobstering and, for a while, kept busy with that. She'd tried to take more initiative, talk to him, spend time with him, and draw him out. But he'd clearly been missing Gloria. She could admit she'd missed Nathaniel too, but she'd wanted to forget about him, wanted to move on, wanted to be a better wife to Nate than she had the first time.

Finally, in December, on the eve of their one-year wedding anniversary, she'd resolved that since they were inevitably linked together, they had to work on their marriage. They had to do all they could to give themselves a chance to be happy together.

So, she'd planned a special dinner for Nate that evening. When he'd come home from lobstering, he'd been surprised at her efforts. And afraid. When he came to the table after changing into clean clothes, his breath smelled of rum. She tried not to think about it, did everything she could to connect with him—even hinting at sharing intimacies.

He seemed disinterested, and so she was surprised when later in the night he came to her room and crawled into bed with her, drunk. It hadn't taken long to realize the only way he could face sleeping with her was when he was inebriated. The experience of being with him had been as unpleasant, if not more so, than when they'd first been married. His visits had been few and infrequent, apparently as unpleasant for him as for her.

Even so, she'd suspected she was with child shortly after the new year. She'd wanted to wait to tell him until she was sure. But she never had the chance.

"I was so certain that Steele wasn't coming back," Gramps said, smiling broadly at Nathaniel. "But here he is. And that sure does make my day."

"Seeing you makes my day too," Nathaniel said, switching from Nate to Steele like he always had.

"I'll challenge you to backgammon tonight," Hosea said.

"Only if you want to get beat," Nathaniel said good-naturedly.

Hosea laughed, a sound that was all too rare recently. At the happiness on Gramps' face, tears stung Abbie's eyes. Nathaniel was so good with Gramps. If only Nathaniel would be here tonight to play the game with Gramps.

Abbie released a long breath to ease the ache in her throat. She was embarrassed to admit that she cried all too easily lately, a condition that Debbie assured her was due to the baby.

Across the distance, Nathaniel caught her gaze again, but this time there was something sharp in his gaze that hadn't been there before.

"I can see you're happy to see your wife." Hosea slapped Nathaniel on the back like they were old chums. "Go on over and kiss her. I know you want to."

Again, Nathaniel was able to go along with Gramps with an ease that would have put any playactor to shame. He gave Gramps an affectionate thump on his back in return and smiled at him broadly. "Of course, I'd like to kiss my bride. But I'd rather do it in private—just in case I get a little carried away."

Gramps hooted, socked Nathaniel in the arm, and started toward the bastion path. "I can take a hint. I'm going. I'll let you two have your reunion in private." With his chuckles ringing in the air, Gramps disappeared down the hill.

Once they were alone again, Abbie knew there was only one thing left to say to Nathaniel. "Good-bye."

His green eyes narrowed upon her and turned almost black. "I'm not leaving yet, Abbie. Not until I find out what's going on."

Something about his glare made her skin prickle with hope. *No*, she told herself quickly. *No, no, no. Don't hope he's changing his mind.* Yesterday, when Menard had been visiting, he'd mentioned rumors that the Winthrops would be returning to Newport soon.

Debbie had squelched Abbie's hopes. "What? Do you think a rich man like Nathaniel Winthrop III would ever give up his servants and his big home to come live here with you?"

"He did once," Abbie started.

"Only when he didn't realize who he was or the wealth he had," Debbie interrupted. "He wouldn't willingly subject himself to living on Rose Island."

Debbie's words rang through Abbie's head, growing louder by the second. Even if her pregnancy hadn't repelled

Nathaniel, the truth was, she couldn't leave Rose Island now any more than she could a year ago. So as long as she continued to work out the details that would allow Gramps to stay, she was bound to give him the secure home he needed.

Debbie had been right when she'd finished the conversation by telling Abbie to forget about Nathaniel Winthrop, that she'd only cause herself more heartache if she harbored any expectation that something could happen between them.

"So…" Nathaniel said. "Why were you planning to let me leave without telling me that Nate is dead?"

"You didn't know?" Surprise shot through her, stiffening her aching back.

"How would I?" His voice was laced with frustration. "I've been gone—"

"But you said you saw Menard yesterday. I assumed he said something and that's why you came."

"No." Nathaniel's eyes flashed. "I'm guessing Debbie thought it best if I stayed away."

Abbie nodded.

"And you?" Nathaniel said in a low voice. "Did you think it best if I stayed away too?"

"No, I wanted to see you again," she admitted. "But I knew you wouldn't want to stay once you saw me like this." She rubbed her hand over her abdomen and felt the tiny bump where an elbow or knee or foot was pushing out.

"I was leaving because I believed you were married." His tone was anguished. "I'd reassured myself that you were happy. And I had to leave before I did anything to ruin that happiness."

He was rooted to his spot. She wanted to plead with him

not to leave, to stay with her forever. But as much as she longed to cross to him, she only shifted her feet in the cold, damp soil of her garden.

She'd had time over the past months to think about all the people who'd left her at one time or another in her life. Whether the people left her intentionally or not, the abandonment hurt and likely always would. But the one thing she'd begun to realize now that she was having a baby was that maybe she'd been wrong about God abandoning her too.

What if God felt about her the same way she felt about her baby? After all, God was her Father, and the Bible promised that He'd never leave or forsake her, much the same way she'd promised never to leave or forsake her child. If she was determined to follow through on her promise to her child, how much more capable was God of doing the same for her?

"What happened?" he asked.

She knew he was referring to Nate. Although nearly five months had passed since his death, a chill still crept over her every time she remembered it. "He went to Providence to check on his brother's wife, Gloria," she said.

"To *check*? Or to stay with her?" Nathaniel's voice rang with accusation. He'd apparently made it his business to find out why Nate had left her the first time.

She didn't want to talk about all that had transpired, still felt she was partly to blame, but she couldn't hold back from Nathaniel. He deserved the truth about every sordid detail.

She sighed. "I don't really know. He told me he'd be back, that he just needed to make sure Gloria and her baby were making it, especially since she hadn't written to him as she'd promised she would."

"But he didn't return?"

"He was gone the rest of the winter. I figured that he couldn't make himself leave. Until I got the letter from Gloria last month. He died of pneumonia shortly after he arrived in Provincetown."

No matter their problems, no matter the coldness between them, no matter that Nate had never been able to let go of Gloria, Abbie hadn't wanted him to die, especially with their child growing inside her.

Nathaniel didn't speak. He stood waiting for her to finish.

"Maybe if I'd told him I was pregnant, he would have stopped drinking. Maybe if I'd loved him better, he wouldn't have gone back to her. Maybe if I'd been a better wife, he would have been able to love me in return."

She fell silent, the weight of all that had happened settling over her.

"I'm sorry, Abbie," he said gently. "Who knows what might have happened if he hadn't caught pneumonia. He might have returned to you."

"I'm not sure if he would have had the strength to do it. He just couldn't change, even though I think he wanted to."

"Most of the time we can't change on our own. We need God's help."

With a start, she realized Nathaniel could have turned out the same way. He could have left Newport, wallowed in his sorrows, and returned to his drinking. But by the power of God, he'd torn himself away from his past and had gone someplace different.

She was proud of him. He'd grown into a strong man.

"Why did you tell me you were happy?" He was studying her, as though trying to understand how she was really doing.

"Because I am happy. I may have regrets about Nate. But

I'm learning to be content with the life I have."

"Content?" His brow quirked, and he sauntered toward her. With each step that he drew closer, her heartbeat slammed against her ribcage harder, especially because there was something dangerously alluring about the way he was regarding her.

"Yes. Aren't you?"

"I'd like to say I'm content," he said in his all-too-low tone that did funny things to her pulse. "But I can admit that I'm not content in the least."

As he closed the distance between them and his sights landed on her mouth, her pulse sped. When he stopped in front of her, she caught the whiff of his aftershave.

He didn't touch her, but his gaze lingered over her face, caressing every inch of her skin and lighting her on fire so that a low flame burned in her belly. When his nostrils flared just slightly and his eyes glowed, she knew he was feeling the same attraction.

"Is there anything I can do to help you be content?" she asked, her voice coming out more breathless than she'd intended.

"There's really only one thing that will make me content," he replied.

She leaned toward him, her body keenly ready for him.

"Marry me," he said. His attention lifted, and his eyes filled with so much anticipation and anxiety all at once that she couldn't speak. "Please, Abbie. Marry me. It's the only thing that will make me truly happy."

She'd thought his contentment hinged upon a kiss and was entirely taken aback by his suggestion. Was he asking her because he felt sorry for her? Because he felt obligated?

Because he didn't know what else to do to help her?

"We'll be fine," she reassured him. "Last fall, Menard and Nate used the map to help Gramps find the real buried treasure. It wasn't easy to locate, but thanks to your efforts to make the map more readable, they eventually found the treasure. It was actually a sizeable amount. Nate took some of it to help Gloria. And now after Nate's death, I've been using the remainder to hire an assistant. Mr. Davis is willing to let Gramps stay here on the island, as long as we have the arrangement."

Nathaniel grinned at the news. "If you marry me, then you won't need your assistant anymore. You can use the treasure proceeds for something else."

Even though she had the overwhelming urge to fling herself against him and merge her life with his just as she'd wanted to for so long, there was still something between them. Literally.

She glanced to her belly, to the baby. He hadn't wanted to be a father of his own child. How much less would he want to be a father to someone else's?

As though sensing the direction of her thoughts, he hesitantly lowered his hand to her stomach. As his fingers spread across her full abdomen, she sucked in a breath at the heated contact. His eyes rose to hers for only a second, but it was enough to see that the touch stoked his blood too.

"I want to have this baby with you," he whispered. "I want to be here to help you and support you and take care of you."

A thrill whispered through her heart. Even so, she hesitated.

"Besides," he continued, "maybe this baby is one more opportunity for me to grow stronger, to walk the new path, to be the father I never had."

She placed her hand over his. "Are you sure?"

"I know I'll still face many fears in the days and weeks to come. But I can't wait to watch her running along the beach barefooted, just like her mother."

"Then does that mean you want to stay on the island?" She'd go wherever he went. She knew that now. But she loved Gramps, too, and couldn't imagine trying to move him. It was the same problem that had thrown her into a relationship with Nathaniel in the first place.

Nathaniel brought his other hand up to her stomach, and the heat of his touch once again filtered through her body, filling her with need for this man she loved.

"I can't think of anyplace else I'd rather be," he whispered, "than right here on this island. With you."

"And that would make you content?" she whispered back.

He nodded. "Very." Then he tilted his head, and his sights dropped to her mouth. "There is one more thing that would make me even more content."

She smiled. She didn't need to ask, but she did anyway. "And what is that?"

"This." He bent down and in one swift movement took possession of her lips, laying claim to them with a power and finality that made her forget about everything but him. His arms surrounded her, pulling her against him as much as the fullness of her stomach would allow. His hands slid up her back, and his lips made a trail down her chin to her neck to her collarbone.

Her fingers dug into his arms, and she couldn't hold in the words she'd wanted to say to him for so long. "I love you, Nathaniel."

His lips stalled against the pounding pulse in her neck. His warmth flowed against her. With a shaky breath that contained the depth of his emotion, he pressed his lips against her ear. "I've loved you from the first moment we met. I've never stopped. And I never will."

Chapter 27

ROSE ISLAND LIGHTHOUSE, RHODE ISLAND

SEPTEMBER 1881, FOUR MONTHS LATER

Nathaniel placed the steaming cup of coffee on the wooden tray next to the plate of bacon and eggs. He straightened the red rose on the side and picked up the tray.

"I'm running this up to my wife," he said to Hosea, who'd already returned from the outhouse and taken his spot at the table, as he did each morning, with bacon and two fried eggs. "You start without me. I'll be down in a few minutes."

Hosea's fork stopped halfway to his mouth, and he released a grin and snort at the same time. "A few minutes. I'll believe that when I see it." Hosea took a bite of eggs and waggled his eyebrows at Nathaniel. "My mind might not work like it used to, but I know for a fact that last time you said you'd be down in a few minutes, it was more like a few hours."

"Now, Hosea," Nathaniel scolded playfully. "My wife's a

slow eater. I can't help that, can I?"

Hosea guffawed.

Nathaniel put his finger to his lips. He hoped to retain the current state of silence in the house, at least until he had the chance to finish his breakfast. And his breakfast didn't involve eggs or bacon.

He grinned at Hosea over his shoulder and climbed the stairs to the bedroom. As he inched the door open, his pulse spurted at the sight that met him. Abbie was sprawled out in bed, her hair spread around her and her long lashes resting on her cheeks. She was as beautiful in slumber as she was awake.

For a moment, he retreated and waited. But before he made up his mind whether to wake her or let her sleep longer, her lashes lifted. At the sight of him, she smiled.

He smiled back, quietly closed the door, and tiptoed across the room. She stretched and yawned before sitting up against the headboard, her feet tangled in the covers. Her hair tumbled over both shoulders and hung in waves down the lacy nightdress he'd bought for her.

"Good morning, beautiful," he whispered as he placed the tray in her lap.

She brought the rose to her nose and smiled. "You're spoiling me, you know."

"It's my number one job." He leaned down, and she rewarded him with a tender kiss.

She scooted over and made room for him on the bed next to her. He sat, relishing the length of her body against his.

"Did you already eat with Gramps?" she asked innocently.

"I haven't eaten," he replied. "Yet."

A flush moved into her cheeks as she took a bite of bacon. "Help yourself."

"With that kind of invitation, how can I resist?" He bent in and nibbled at her earlobe.

She gave a sigh of satisfaction that only made him hungrier. "You know you don't need invitations anymore to steal kisses from me, don't you?"

He leaned back so he could see her brown-green eyes. "I like knowing you want me."

"I think you like to feed your pride," she whispered, giving him a playful nudge with her shoulder.

"Just for that, I'm going to make you beg for the next kiss."

She laughed softly. "I never have to beg too hard or for too long."

He dipped in and let his lips linger above hers without touching, letting their breaths mingle. He loved these playful moments as much as the tender ones. That wasn't to say the first months of their marriage had been all bliss.

No, they'd had to deal with his mother's frustration with not only a secret wedding a day after his arrival in Newport, but then also with his choice to move to Rose Island. Although his mother was gradually adjusting to the fact that he wanted to live as a light keeper, she still hadn't stopped visiting every few days and bringing them gifts. He'd had to send back the servants she'd wanted to hire for him, but he tried to be gracious with most of the other gifts, within reason.

And of course, several times a week, he rowed over to spend time with her while he attended to family business. He'd assured her that no matter where he lived, he could continue to manage the family's fortune and affairs.

Overall he could tell that his mother was pleased he was no longer following in his father's footsteps and that she wouldn't complain too much about where he lived, so long as he was happy.

Debbie had been harder to satisfy, however. No amount of reassurances had convinced her he was no longer the Bad Boy of Newport, that he wasn't planning to run off and leave Abbie for the first new woman who came along.

Even though he was a changed man, he realized it would take time for others to believe in him. That lack of trust was one of the consequences of his sinful living. God had forgiven him, but not everyone else could do so as easily.

In spite of the obstacles, he loved living on Rose Island with Abbie—this time without pretense, fully and truly as husband and wife. He appreciated the simplicity of life on the island just as he had when he'd lived there last summer, although he could admit he liked having an endless supply of money that he could use to spoil Abbie. He'd already finished the shed and had brought over a cow, along with a few more chickens.

He loved helping run the lighthouse. He loved helping keep their house organized. He loved spending time with Hosea. And most of all, he loved being with her.

"Nathaniel," she whispered against his lips, as she set the breakfast tray aside. "Kiss me."

"Gladly." He let himself languidly graze her lips, tasting the saltiness of bacon there.

A soft gurgle interrupted them. The gurgle was followed by a coo.

"I thought she was asleep," he whispered, glancing at the bassinet next to the bed. He'd rocked the baby to sleep before going down to make breakfast, wanting to give Abbie a chance to rest longer. He enjoyed holding their daughter every chance he got. At two weeks old, she was the most beautiful creature he'd ever seen—next to her mother, of course.

He pushed himself up, but Abbie latched on to his arm. "She's making happy noises."

He hesitated.

"Do you know why?" Abbie asked.

He quirked a brow.

"Because she has the best daddy a girl could ever ask for." Abbie's eyes shone with love and pride. "You're a good father, Nathaniel. Thank you."

His gaze snagged on the two driftwood crosses sitting side by side on their dresser. The one that had been given to him, and the one he'd made for Abbie. They were nearly identical. God had indeed blessed them with more hope than he could have imagined.

He swallowed the sudden lump in his throat. He'd never wanted to be a father. But now he couldn't imagine life without their little girl, Hope.

Hope cooed again.

Abbie pulled him down further so he was lying beside her. "She'll be fine. But I won't be. If you don't finish kissing me."

He grinned. "I'll never be finished kissing you. And that's a promise."

"Good." She wrapped her arms around his neck, drawing him closer. "That's a promise I'll never let you forget."

Author's Note

Dear Reader, thank you for reading the fifth and final book in the Beacons of Hope series. I was delighted to be able to write this last story and follow the cross of hope on one more journey, this time with Abbie and Nathaniel.

In this final book in the series, I once again chose an East Coast lighthouse as the setting. After much research, I finally decided upon Rose Island Lighthouse for a couple of reasons. First, I wanted the lighthouse to be close to Newport. Ida Lewis was a famous female light keeper who lived on Lime Island, which is in the same vicinity as the Rose Island and Goat Island lighthouses in Newport Bay. Ida is famous for her many rescues and was honored by her community, national media, and even the President of the United States. One of her rescues involved four young men of prominent Newport families who were sailing and capsized their boat. At one time, she also rescued three drunken soldiers from nearby Fort Adams.

Another reason I chose Rose Island Lighthouse was because of all the pirate lore that surrounds Rhode Island. In particular, the Newport area is a trove of pirate history. During the 1660s through the mid-1700s, many pirates made Rhode Island their home and buried treasure all around the bay. People still hunt for lost pirate treasure there today.

A final fascinating aspect of Rose Island is the extreme weather. In 1876, the wind reached near-hurricane speeds and shook the tower violently. Two years later, another storm moved the tower one and a half inches so that it broke the plaster inside the house and the glass chimney of the lantern. Several months later, a different storm actually took the tower's chimney down and flooded the lighthouse.

With the rich Newport crowd, along with the possibility of buried pirate treasure, as well as the extreme weather, I couldn't resist making Rose Island the home for my story. Today people can stay for an extended visit in the Rose Island Lighthouse and experience what it was like to be a light keeper.

Another inspiration for my story is a woman by the name of Abbie Burgess who served with her father at Matinicus Rock Lighthouse in Maine. One time while her father was away, she not only saved her family from a dangerous storm that smashed into the keeper's cottage, but she also saved her pet chickens. Although her mother advised against going out into the storm, Abbie couldn't bear to think of losing her chickens and was able to save all but one. During that whole time, she kept her family safe and the two lighthouses on the island running.

Thank you again for joining me in my journey with the Beacons of Hope. I hope the books have inspired you to visit a lighthouse or two. More than that, I pray you've been both encouraged and inspired to trust in the Giver of Hope. Maybe, like Nathaniel, you've let yourself be haunted by your parents' mistakes. Perhaps you've even started down the same destructive path. I pray God will help you break free of your chains and help you walk in His freedom down a new path. If you're like Abbie, having been hurt or abandoned by the people you thought loved you, I pray that you will recognize that God will never abandon you. He is always there offering you His hope, love, and forgiveness. Please, *never forget* all that He offers.

Jody Hedlund is the bestselling author of multiple novels, including *Love Unexpected*, *Captured by Love*, *Rebellious Heart*, and *The Preacher's Bride*. She holds a bachelor's degree from Taylor University and a master's degree from the University of Wisconsin, both in social work. Jody lives in Michigan with her husband and five children. Learn more at JodyHedlund.com.

Beacons of Hope Series

Shipwrecked and stranded, Emma Chambers is in need of a home. Could the widowed local lighthouse keeper and his young son be an answer to her prayer?

Love Unexpected
BEACONS OF HOPE #1

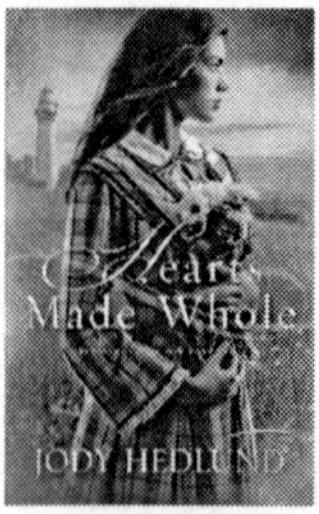

Caroline has tended the lighthouse since her father's death. But where will she go when a wounded Civil War veteran arrives to take her place?

Hearts Made Whole
BEACONS OF HOPE #2

Vowing not to have anything to do with lighthouses, Tessa Taylor is the new teacher to the children of miners. Can the light keeper's assistant break through her fears and win her heart?

Hope Undaunted
BEACONS OF HOPE #3

Heiress to a vast fortune, Victoria Cole has everything she wants, including the perfect fiancé. Having left two other men at the altar, Victoria is sure that now she's found her true love and will finally live happily ever after.

Forever Safe
BEACONS OF HOPE #4

More From Jody Hedlund

A complete list of my novels can be found at jodyhedlund.com.

Would you like to know when my next book is available? You can sign up for my newsletter, become my friend on Goodreads, like me on Facebook, or follow me on Twitter.

Newsletter: jodyhedlund.com
Goodreads: goodreads.com/author/show/3358829.Jody_Hedlund
Facebook: facebook.com/AuthorJodyHedlund
Twitter: @JodyHedlund

The more reviews a book has, the more likely other readers are to find it. If you have a minute, please leave a rating or review. I appreciate all reviews, whether positive or negative.

CPSIA information can be obtained
at www.ICGtesting.com
Printed in the USA
FSOW02n2349140417
33126FS

9 780692 770870